W9-CHF-770

THE NEMESIS MISSION

DEAN ING

TOR

A TOM DOHERTY ASSOCIATES BOOK
NEW YORK

This is a work of fiction. All the characters and events portrayed in this book are fictitious, and any resemblance to real people or events is purely coincidental.

THE NEMESIS MISSION

Copyright © 1991 by Dean Ing

Cover art by Joe DeVito

A Tor Book
Published by Tom Doherty Associates, Inc.
175 Fifth Avenue
New York, N.Y. 10010

Tor® is a registered trademark of Tom Doherty Associates, Inc.

ISBN: 0-812-51173-5
Library of Congress Catalog Card Number: 91-21445

First edition: October 1991
First mass market printing: September 1992

Printed in the United States of America

0 9 8 7 6 5 4 3 2 1

For Bill and Ole,
who, each in his own special way, made it fly.

ACKNOWLEDGMENTS

Anyone who designs solar-powered aircraft stands on the shoulders of pioneering giants. Bob Boucher and Paul MacCready led the way, and we all owe them. I also shamelessly borrowed visions from members of the Experimental Aircraft Association, who fly where major corporations fear to tread.

I could not have faithfully described the antics of a T-33 after all these years. Thanks to Ted Voulgaris and Ole Christiansen for letting me take notes as they reminisced together and zoomed their hands through the air.

Mark Knowles gave me firsthand experience in the kinds of aerial maneuvers I don't even want to think about on the ground. Jim Curran lent me wings, too—so of course I had someone steal his Piper in the book. Hey, what are friends for?

As for the Nemesis design, it may or may not perform as advertised. But thanks to master modeler Bill Fletcher, we know that a big subscale Nemesis will soar—polymers, carbon filament, and all.

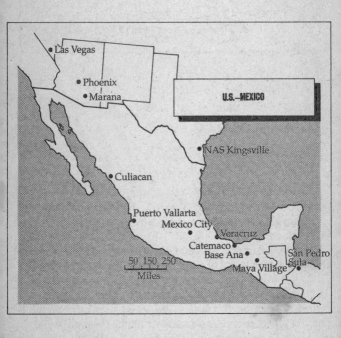

Las Vegas

Phoenix
Marana

U.S.—MEXICO

NAS Kingsville

Culiacan

Puerto Vallarta
Mexico City
Veracruz
Catemaco
Base Ana
San Pedro
Sula
Maya Village

50 150 250
Miles

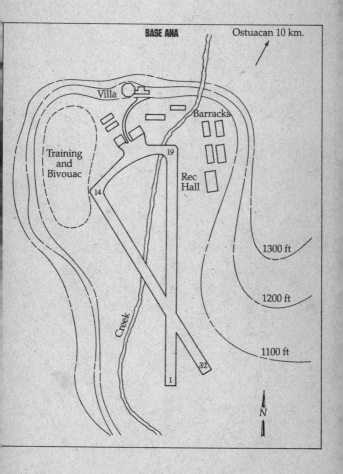

BASE ANA   Ostuacan 10 km.

Villa

Training
and
Bivouac

Barracks

19

14

Rec
Hall

1300 ft

1200 ft

Creek

1100 ft

1

32

N

THE NEMESIS MISSION

ONE

Monday, April 10

MEXICAN OFFICIALS HAD never been overly polite to Harry's kind of archaeologist, so on his latest expedition into the mountain wilderness of Southern Mexico, Harry Rex Brown simply changed his title. It was only a small fib, surely almost no deception at all in the eyes of God Almighty, for Harry to bill himself as an anthropologist in the field. Anthropologists only take notes; archaeologists dig, and take samples.

Harry knew very well that samples imply relics; and a conviction for the illegal export of Mexico's ancient Maya relics is among the surest ways for a scholar to become an expert on the kinks of homosexual predators in some Mexican prison.

So Harry applied to no one, certainly not to Mexico's director of antiquities, for any sanction because it made things simpler, and Harry liked to do things the simple way. Which was not to say that Harry was a simple man. A Mormon with a graduate degree from BYU, good Spanish, and a decent command of Maya—still the first tongue

of many Indios in Southern Mexico—Harry knew how to
charm a village godfather. He could hire all the help he
needed without the folderol of government documents.
That is why it took Harry almost three months to get himself found, shot at, and chased all the way to Guatemala.

The chase moved slowly, both parties being afoot. No
human could move very fast beyond the trails of the high
rain forests of Chiapas, where a vine could grow six inches
thick with thorns the length of a man's hand, and still fail
to strangle the tree it climbed. Harry's porters avoided
casualties because they were in better shape than their pursuers for climbing limestone ravines in a moist green hell.
Harry's guide, Yaxpoc, thought perhaps the airplane that
buzzed his little group was an arm of the Mexican Air
Force.

"Then it should have the triangle insignia," Harry replied, catching a good glimpse of what looked like an old
Lockheed jet trainer as it swept away toward the sun.

"It has none at all, Señor Harry," murmured Yaxpoc,
pointing with his chin in the old way. The Maya ways
made a lot of sense when a man needed both hands to grip
a limestone outcrop that looked like a head of gray broc-
coli and crumbled rather more easily. Harry nodded and
kept on climbing, his sweat-soaked old snapbrim hat
askew.

Although this was not the first time Harry had seen
muzzle flashes winking in his direction, Mexican troops
were rarely this tenacious. Harry had learned early in life
to take setbacks cheerfully in his pursuit of the Lord's
work; but now his cheer became strained by suspicion.

Only a genius of jungle travel or a certified damned fool
will plunge through such a maze after dark. Harry said as
much to Yaxpoc after they made camp, noting that the
smudge of their pursuers' campfires was almost a mile
behind them. "After several expeditions with you," he
added, "I think you may be the genius I need now."

Yaxpoc, taciturn as always, inclined his head. "What
is your wish," he asked softly.

"Could we get near enough to these federales to learn why they seem so determined? Near enough to hear them, I mean."

Though he often paused to give a question time for consideration, Yaxpoc answered this one instantly. "We could not, Señor Harry, of a certainty. But alone, I think I could."

Harry thought that over. Yaxpoc was of average height for a Maya, a full head shorter than Harry's six-foot-two; and his coppery skin blended better into the shadows of the bosque, the high Chiapas rain forest. Better still, Yaxpoc's squarish little feet made no more noise than the shadows did. Best of all, he seemed willing, though it meant at least an hour each way in darkness that soon would be relieved only by patches of moonlight.

Harry and the porters, none of them bloody-minded men, fingered their machetes and spoke little until Yaxpoc returned at moonset, and the little fellow scared them witless as he padded into camp bearing a strange tale. The troops were well armed, yet none wore uniforms; and their fires were not the careless fires of troops. Their accents, Yaxpoc thought, were not Mexican. He thought them perhaps taller than his own Maya people, with barrel chests. Imagining that they were alone, they used smatterings of a language Yaxpoc had never heard. Their word for themselves was senderistas, men of the path—though Yaxpoc thought the word particularly odd; these men had proven themselves as willing as anyone to abandon a beaten path.

Yaxpoc knew why Harry was curious about the impatience of those pursuers. Mexico's narrow waist, the Isthmus of Tehuantepec, spans a portion of several states: Tabasco, Veracruz, Chiapas. The people of this region all share the kind of patience that borders on the catatonic. Yet here were a dozen armed men chafing among themselves, anxious to be done with chasing after a yanqui with wings on his feet, and they wished aloud that they were back on the slopes of the mighty Sierra.

Growing coca.

It was at this point that Harry spoke with the porters, for the first time, of the recent plantings they had seen where corn would be expected. By tradition, only corn and coffee were grown on the steepest sides of volcanic slopes, sometimes so steep that it seemed the stuff must have been seeded with a howitzer to be harvested by monkeys. In his previous expeditions Harry had never observed coca bushes and would not have recognized them anyhow. Disturbed, fearing the answer, Harry asked: "Is this the coca that men chew with ash to lend them energy?"

"I do not know," Yaxpoc said. "It has never been our way."

"I have heard that it is such stuff," said Ocosil, a younger man whose admission might have carried a twinge of guilt in it.

"It is still not our way," Yaxpoc repeated, his meaning clear. Ocosil did not respond.

"I think," said Harry, "that these men are not federales at all. I think they were tending the seedlings we have seen, and they do not wish us to speak of it. They may not stop at the border of Guatemala."

"It is common talk in our parajes," said Yaxpoc, using the local jargon for "villages." "Now and again such men buy food from us. They say it is not yet time to become our friends."

Harry arranged his bug net for sleep, a signal that the parley was at an end. "If they are who I think," he warned, "we must be underway by dawn."

That was all Harry needed to say. When the first of the morning toucans clacked his foolish greeting to the dawn, Harry's little group was a half-hour closer to Guatemala.

In passing the seedlings a few days before, Harry had given them little thought, noting only that underbrush had been cleared for shrubby young plants. He had been intent as ever on the overgrown mounds that sometimes proved to be ancient platforms and, in a few cases, temples of crudely dressed limestone. If a man could discover a hidden passageway into a temple, it was just barely possible that he might find the kind of ceremonial place that had made Ruz Lhullier famous, midway through the century.

Even this, for Harry, was less important than finding a crypt that contained proof, *proof*, that the people who built it had been Nephites, men of the lost ten tribes of Israel. Nephites, many Mormons believed, had settled Central America many centuries ago. Harry Rex Brown was already convinced this was factual, but hard evidence would be a wonderful thing. If that evidence had to be *improved* somehow, well, Harry knew God pretty well, and felt that God would not allow him to do a thing unless God bloody well wanted him to.

On a previous expedition, Harry had found not only a temple north of Tzimol but a mighty pyramid under its age-old blanket of trees and vines. Not as high as Palenque, maybe, but high enough for Harry. He had found the passageway he sought, or at least Yaxpoc had, but the steep stairwell had been found centuries before by someone who left the tip of a Toledo steel blade between blocks of cut stone while forcing entry. Harry had taken the artifact, reasoning that it was not truly a relic.

Harry might have taken more artifacts on that trip, using whatever reasoning he could dream up, except that someone had beaten him to it. The only things of value left inside were the classic Maya carvings and wall murals, which Harry copied with rubbings and Polaroids after studying the carvings for a week in vain. The evidence of Nephite presence that Harry was looking for was a Star of David.

Copies of the Polaroids, rubbings, and even that Spanish swordtip, had brought enough money in the States to finance Harry's next expedition after he refreshed his wife's bank account in Orem, Utah. Private collectors cared about such details and they were as secretive as they were barmy, but they paid huge sums for a museum piece.

The money was not Harry's bottom line, of course. He felt certain that even if his methods were subject to sharp criticism in certain stodgy corners—which included virtually the entire field of archaeology—the name Harry Rex Brown would echo down the corridors of history, or at least the corridors of Brigham Young University, once he found proof of the Nephites in Chiapas.

Of all the embattled notions of Mormonism, the most romantic is the idea that ancient Israelites of the Nephite persuasion settled Central America. No proof of this idea had ever been found—for the excellent reason, said some, that the idea was terminally weird.

In his sacred quest, Harry felt that it was a confounded nuisance to be rousted by terrorists a thousand miles from their killing fields, but this was obviously what was happening. For Harry, who kept up with current events as well as anyone, quickly realized why his pursuers seemed so unusual by Mexican standards.

They were not Mexicans at all. They were leftist guerrillas of the Sendero Luminoso, the Shining Path. They came from the highlands of Peru and called themselves Maoist Communists, though Mao himself had repudiated them as bizarre savages. And the only known friends of the senderistas were Colombians, the drug lords of Cali and Medellin.

Harry did not know how these crazies got to Mexico, and he cared less. But if prior behavior was any guide, and if Harry's group didn't stir their stumps at double-time, none of Harry's people would live to puzzle it out. Senderistas liked to torture people, and they were determined as only zealots can be.

At Yaxpoc's heels, Harry trotted toward the Guatemalan village of Quingua with fresh motivation. If he paid his team well, and managed to reach Guatemala City without getting waylaid by the local brand of thugs, he could climb aboard a Boeing before the senderistas knew it.

Harry's luck held. Two days later, settling into an airliner seat for takeoff, he allowed himself to relax and to hope he would never encounter senderistas again. In this, he was destined to be disappointed.

TWO

Tuesday, April 11

CESAR MACHADO STOOD at the lake's edge, frowning at the mounded horizon of green against blue, its inverted images shimmering in the waters that stretched before him. Kneeling beside him to study the smear of footprints, Teniente Gonzalo was still almost as tall as Machado. Teniente was by far the biggest of the armed group, hairy shins protruding from short baggy trousers, the assault rifle properly slung over a beefy shoulder. "I make it recent, perhaps within the hour," Machado growled. He knew that Teniente would not reply unless asked. "Your views, Teniente." A command, but offered gently.

"An hour." Teniente sighed and stood up, fetching a dog-eared map from inside the long poncho, an excellent compass in one hand. Moments later, the words Machado did not want to hear: "We are now in Guatemala, Cesar."

"Isn't this part of the Montebello lake chain?"

"Yes, but it does not respect political boundaries," Teniente replied, refolding the map.

In the far distance, a faint roll of thunder echoed across

the water, signaling a presence Machado sometimes valued but also disliked. As if to endorse that presence, a brief message crackled from the two-way radio Teniente had laid against a rotting log. "Condor to Bushmaster: Come in."

Machado's face said that he was in no mood to take orders from an elitist flying a mile overhead. He caught Teniente's glance and jerked his head toward the bulky set, the sort of equipment you expected from Cubans: heavy as a brick but just as dependable. "We are turning back," he said, and trudged away.

Teniente understood, and flicked the handset on after three strides. "Bushmaster Two here."

"Your quarry is out of bounds, Bushmaster. We have no accommodations with people there."

Knowing that Machado could hear both ends of the conversation, knowing too that Machado disliked taking this man's orders even when backed by the senderista commander, Teniente replied, "Our position already noted. Bushmaster One leading us back to the plantation."

"My compliments to Bushmaster One. This was a good little exercise for us," was the reply. "On your next return to Ana, the party will be mine."

"Understood; Bushmaster Two out," Teniente said, carefully noncommittal as always with the same husky tenor.

The others stood aside as Teniente passed them to take up the traditional position behind Machado, then fell in line. Peruvians all, they would talk little on the trail, a built-in wisdom for men raised at three-mile altitudes. They could certainly chatter like parrots during rests, however; and this time they surely would.

In truth, thought Teniente, the man who gloried in the code name Condor had given little cause for Machado's surliness this morning. In person, however, the Condor's elitist manner was enough to make any senderista spit. The men had met and partied before at Base Ana, the heart of their new struggle for Mexico, but only an idiot could fail to spot Cesar Machado's dislike for El Condor. The rich Colombian pilot, anything but a fool in Teniente's view, never seemed to take offense and never showed less than a Hidalgo's manners. All the same, it was easy enough to sit in a silver yanqui bird and speak lightly of a three-day trek through Mexican rain forest as a little exercise. Machado's group exercised every muscle in their bodies while the Colombian exercised only his backside, and his ego. In an hour the Condor would be lounging about the airbase that cocaine profits had bought, or flying over the gulf coast if it pleased him. Meanwhile Machado's team would still be three days from their young coca, forced to avoid roads because the Mexican army sometimes mounted checkpoints in the border region. You never knew when you might run afoul of some Mexican captain who was ignorant or allergic to bribes.

Three days before, a peasant wearing the blue of a Chamulan had told Machado that the group blundering through tender coca plants was led by a yanqui. Perhaps, Teniente thought, the yanqui was as anxious as anyone to avoid Mexican roads and Mexican officials. In any case, the Maya were not likely to talk to outsiders about the coca crop. A yanqui might; but not with a bullet in him.

Machado and Teniente had originally been brought together by their beloved Professor Guzman back in Peru's University of Ayacucho. The fiery professor had chosen Cesar Machado to lead a cadre of true believers in the workers' armed struggle, and Teniente to be part of that cadre.

The skin across Teniente's high cheekbones stretched in a smile. Changes had come fast in those days, beginning with code names. Guzman, fountainhead of the movement, had become Colonel Gonzalo. Machado, orphaned in his teens by the hated Peruvian army, chose to keep his own name, a "catch me if you dare" message to his own government.

Teniente's name had been Huanca, abandoned instantly when Machado joked that Huanca was a philosophical child of Colonel Gonzalo; and from that day forward, Teniente Gonzalo wore that name with pride.

Now, skirting the next lake, Machado delayed their lunch break until they were well inside Mexico again. During the previous night Teniente had not been able to shake off the sensation of being watched. Machado might be the forebrain of his group, but in Teniente lived the instincts of its Quechuan Indian soul. No amount of university training could have quenched that.

Most of the men were changing socks, knowing that a guerrilla army marches first on its feet and afterward, if at all, on its stomach. Corncakes were produced, dried goatmeat chewed endlessly before swallowing, water consumed. No one chewed coca; these altitudes were not high enough to require the stuff. Today, refined extracts of the coca leaf created cartels so rich they could challenge entire governments—while sapping the energies of the capitalist yanquis. The cartel lords were capitalists too, but their money had bought a fresh start for the Maoist struggle and in return the senderistas farmed coca.

Teniente lay back, eyes closed, only half listening to the idle talk, surrendering the map when Machado asked for it. The tiny clicks meant that Machado was opening the spectacles he used for reading; the soft rubbing of flesh on flesh signaled Machado's rubbing fingers across eyes that tended to cross when he was weary. Machado had once been touchy about that; it had made him the butt of jokes as a child, until he had learned to fight. After that he had learned to steal, and only then had he bought the glasses that let him become a reader.

Machado's vision problem had caused Professor Guzman to make one of his most peculiar demands, even before their movement became a force to be feared. Exactly why he had commanded that Cesar Machado learn the ancient Maya language was still dim in Teniente's mind; something about the expansion of the movement. Machado had learned the glottals and half-swallowed consonants well enough, and a decade later, as if Guzman had dreamed the future in detail, it had become necessary for the guerrillas to emigrate or be killed. Their secret voyage to Mexico's isthmus, in wallowing old steamers provided by El Condor and his friends, had left them squarely in the center of the only region on earth where Maya was the language of the farmers and villagers, a population in which the senderistas must hide as they gained strength in Mexico.

Machado's band, of course, was only one of many in the isthmus region. It was merely the luck of the draw that had led the yanqui's group past Machado, and rotten luck that the yanqui kept up a pace so quick that only twice had they been within range of a rifle bullet.

The failure of this mission was not so important, thought Teniente. Even the crop, so crucial to cartel lords, was secondary to their senderista allies. But when enough seasons had passed and enough coca transformed into money, bribes could become mountainous. At that point, the cartel people had promised, billions could be channeled into political campaigns friendly to the senderistas. The shining path was long and stony, and in Peru it had led to an impasse. According to the cartel leaders, Mexico would prove more amenable to a revolutionary party with its own cash crop.

THREE

BECAUSE VERACRUZ IS a port city on the Gulf of Mexico, the United States Consulate on Avenida Juarez is not all that far from the docks, and State Department employees know the areas to avoid. That is why Miguel "Mike" Contreras viewed his work for the evening ahead with something less than joy. "My God, that's switchblade country," he muttered to himself when he had read the files. "Why couldn't this guy Fray Roberto run his drops from the zocalo?"

The zocalo, in almost every Mexican city, was the town's exact center of nighttime activity, complete with bandstand, the standard meeting place for lovers, vendors, and just plain loafers. To commit an act of violence in the zocalo is a violation of the social contract on a par with hurling a turd through a church window. That made every zocalo a park suitable for children, though that park might be awash in tidal waves of trash and many of those children might be barefoot and threadbare. But the file on this Fray Roberto, whoever he really was, said he knew his tradecraft. He probably reasoned that every kid in Veracruz hung out at the zocalo, with both eyes open. You'd never get mugged, but if you ever dropped a Chiclet it would never hit the ground. No place for grown men to exchange love notes.

But Fray Roberto's choice was a known bordello. Contreras made a spider of his fingers and passed them through his hair, scratching vigorously as he did. The brief telephone call from Fray Roberto had not hinted at love, but had implied the passing of a note. Fray Roberto had passed only one previous note, in July of '89 to Mike's predecessor, an old CIA hand now retired.

That single note had justified priority flags a month after the man passed it. Fray Roberto had warned that presidential candidates Luis Galan would be assassinated in a certain way, by a certain group, during a certain period. In August, Galan was hit in the manner predicted and by the mobsters specified. One of the most startling points was that Galan was not Mexican, but a candidate for president of Colombia. Why had the informant gone to the Americans instead of the Colombians? The smart guess was that he trusted Americans to inform the right people. A smarter guess was that Fray Roberto might also be storing up Brownie points with the U. S. government.

Clearly, Fray Roberto was privy to the innermost secrets of Colombia's drug lords; yet here he was on Mexico's gulf coast. The warning in '89 had been the first whisper of a hint that people near the top of the cartels were spending time in Mexico, far from their old Colombian havens. More rumors had followed from other sources. When the man did not resurface, analysts thought he might be dead. Only now, in the past hour, had he called in again.

Of course the switchboard woman had known the old spook was medically retired, and had let Mike explain the retirement. "Then send another Yankee. The same signals," the man had said before ringing off.

As if we carry little placards hung around our necks,

Contreras thought. *God; maybe we do.* Though Contreras had grown up in Tampa, he bore the coloring of a Latino and his Mexican heritage was detectable in his accents, English and Spanish and Maya. The CIA's other man in the consulate was blond as Heidi, had learned Spanish in Pennsylvania, and might never manage to be taken for anything but a yanqui. Mike knew damned well which of them would have to take this message drop, and promised himself a dinner at La Bamba first.

Mike checked the time. It would not be dark for hours, and until 3:00 P.M. the consulate was still open for business. In season and when the cut-rate tour ships visited Veracruz, cheap tequila was the river that washed a flood of U. S. citizens down Avenida Juarez and into the consulate. Today, the scent of bougainvillea was the most active thing in the air—not counting Mike's perspiration and the occasional whiff of yuchh from the dockside area. The truth, Mike admitted to himself, was that he preferred open countryside to narrow streets.

Mike slapped the file folder against his leg as he headed for the file room, wishing this were the next day and that whatever was going to happen tonight had already happened and he was in the hospital or downstairs basking in congratulations. Cloak and dagger work made him nervous; basically Mike was a backpack and grenade man.

Precisely *a las ocho en punto*, eight on the dot, Mike sidled the last few steps in streetlamp shadows to the opening in a high wall where, in the traditional way, big double doors swung inward for patrons of whatever was on sale. From the reek of Three Flowers pomade that nearly flattened him, Mike figured no one could mistake the nature of the goods; he was tempted to whistle "Love for Sale," if he could have whistled at that moment. Instead, he found a smile for the shopworn matron who showed him to one of the tiny scattered tables in the courtyard. He ordered coffee as if this were any ordinary cafe, and tried to be subtle as he studied his surroundings while lighting up that big black cigar. The file workup on this contact had been very clear: the place, the time, the bow tie, the big black cigar, and the refusal to smoke it, once lit. Well, no hay problema there, after one sniff Mike Contreras could no more have taken a heavy hit from that cigar than he could have swallowed a live owl.

Mike had to admit it: The place catered to one of his frequent fantasies. A fellow sits down innocently enough around some public place, a park or a bus stop, and if he's not very careful he will soon be noticing the attractive women pass, assessing them; all right then, *grading* them. Women might not like that, but hey, he told himself, they probably did it too.

And when you grade a person, you're grading her for something particular. *What you're doing is thinking how much fun she'd be in the sack*, he admitted silently, *getting yourself turned on in the fifteen seconds it takes for a total stranger to approach and then disappear, completely innocent herself though you become guilty as hell, if desire is any sin.* It had never occurred to Mike that a whorehouse might be arranged in such a way as to provide exactly that park bench fantasy he had enjoyed so many times. Whenever a really scorchy number sashayed by, all you had to do was whistle. It now dawned on Mike that maybe a lot of men, maybe most, shared that weakness for public sex fantasy. He wondered again if women shared the same weakness, and concluded that no woman he had ever met would tell him if she did. He sighed and turned his attention to the accommodations.

Each of the tables was for two. Several other men were sitting among the potted plants like furtive nocturnal creatures, glancing this way and that as if undecided whether they were predator or prey. Some sat with young women and some were alone, spaced well apart, although as he watched one of the couples left their table and set off at almost a lope for a doorway he had not noticed before, the woman leading. She was not Mike's type. He knew better than to combine his kind of business with this kind of pleasure, and remembered to avoid looking with any interest whatever at the other men who, like Mike, made no secret of their gazes as a lovely black girl swayed past en route from nowhere to nowhere, hoping for a sale in the middle. She was evidently someone's type, provoking a muttered summons, lowering herself sleekly into a seat.

Mike might have missed the man emerging from that distant doorway alone if the man had not brushed past him on the way to a table where two glasses of amber liquid sat unattended. The man did not sit down, but only paused to finish his drink. He tried a sip of the second drink, laughed abruptly, and put it down as if satisfied that he had penetrated some small deception, looking idly around, and then not so idly at the flagstones near Mike's feet. Mike ignored him. The man drained his cup and looked straight into Mike's face, then at the flagstones again, shrugged, and dropped a banknote on the table before he headed for the street. He had gone before Mike got the message.

A zaftig brunette in spike heels and fifty yards of black lace swiveled between the tables, taking her good time, her pace slow enough that a man might detain her with a word, and the glance she turned on Mike Contreras would have rewarmed his coffee. Mike dropped his gaze. On a flagstone near his right foot lay a cardboard pack of cerillos, those classy little Mexican matches with their own sliding tray. The matches had not been there when he sat down. It was too late to get a good look at Fray Roberto now, but as Mike had guessed, the man had not worn clerical garb and looked nothing like a priest should look. Mike brought up his cloth napkin and coughed to cover his next move, dropped the napkin, and picked up the cerillos pack, which did not rattle. Whatever might be inside, it wasn't matches. And when he straightened up again, the plumpish brunette was sitting down, doing her best to give him a beaver shot while he was still bent over. Mike realized then that she had misconstrued his cough.

Mike was not a rude man, and while thrusting that match pack in his pocket he decided against simply bolting for the street. In the next ten minutes he reflected that, when a woman is truly explicit about getting laid, she can offer a man more tawdry amusements than Coney Island. He pretended to consider them all before taking his leave, hat carried strategically before his fly. The tip he left her was perhaps not the tip she had in mind, but it was a hundred-thousand-peso banknote, roughly thirty dollars American. If he left her disappointed, she certainly managed to hide it.

A quick look satisfied Mike that the cerillos pack had been stuffed with a page of notes, hand-printed. While hurrying back to the consulate he almost forgot about his contact and lost most of the little he recalled about Fray Roberto, because he was mulling over that ten-minute education from the lacy brunette.

FOUR

Friday, April 21

On a delicious April morning near North Bend, Oregon, Ben Ullmer soaked his old bones in sunlight outside his firm's engine test cell and enjoyed a cigar in the only way left to him since his doctor's ultimatum. The man beside him, small and lean and older than he looked, swigged at his Sharp's and squinted at Ullmer as he observed, "Doc Freud would have a time with you, Ben. Why do you only chew and suck on that thing instead of lighting up?"

"Same reason you drink near beer on your morning break, Hardin; we're survivors. Sawbones says if I smoke, it'll kill me." He squinted back at Wes Hardin in mock ferocity. "And I'd skin you if you tried to bring alcohol on the premises." That squint, full of bogus challenge, was a thing they had developed without ever speaking of it, their substitute for a grin. Old Georgia cracker and younger Texan, they played hard to match their own stereotypes, but only against each other, and they worked hard not to grin. If you showed your teeth, you lost.

"No fear of that," Hardin snorted, draining the can. "I don't import good Texas Shiner Bock all the way to Oregon so you can get your horny ol' paws on it."

Ben knew his top man's peculiar tastes, and had no real objections even to Hardin's storing near beer in the office cooler. He sighed and stretched, and wondered. Could he have made a going concern out of Aerosystems Unlimited without this tough little Texan from Abilene? Maybe, but also maybe not. From the first, Ben had known he needed a second engineer capable of checking design work, and it didn't hurt if that man was a former naval test pilot. One good look at the guy with the ideal resume, a guy who even flew a tiny Christen Eagle stunt plane to the interview, and Ben had found himself sold. Wesley Hardin was, in addition to everything else, the right size for the job: under five feet seven and weighing, he claimed, one-forty soppin' wet.

Ullmer hired Hardin on the spot, knowing that in this little hellion he had a better man than himself for dealing with military brass. He needed such a man because he needed the U. S. military money. As a new player in high-tech games, Ben realized his customer had better be a U. S. military arm that makes a profit, and can afford some risks. The only military service in U. S. history that has ever shown black ink is the United States Coast Guard, which had confiscated and sold enough doper hardware by the end of the 1980s to equip a small navy. Most of that hardware was in the form of vehicles: speedboats, aircraft, pickup trucks and big diesel rigs found at coastal rendezvous sites, and the occasional cargo ship unlucky enough to be caught in the act.

The vast majority of these vehicles had been used to bring drugs onto U. S. soil. The resale of all these uncommon carriers—Chris-Crafts, BMW's, Cessnas, and Peterbilts—hardly dents the profit margin of the drug lords, but it yields enough money to let the Coast Guard play by new rules. The Coasties invented a new rule in 1989, but told almost nobody about it, when aircraft designer Ben Ullmer left the National Security Agency: They gave him a contract to produce the damnedest drug interdiction aircraft that ever flew. It was Ben who'd dubbed it the Nemesis.

Now, though only two of the craft were flying in Coastie hands, Ben was satisfied that they were already proving themselves. Two more were nearly complete in the Aerosystems assembly plant that loomed behind the men, a structure that might have been a pair of aircraft hangars joined end-to-end in this rural valley near the Oregon coast. The Aerosystems runway, less than a half-mile in length, was obviously not suited to anything but light aircraft. This in itself was misleading.

With so many years of aircraft experience, Ben was ex a lot of things: ex-Georgia Tech; ex-Air Corps, when pilots sometimes helped overhaul their own P-40 Warhawks; ex-Lockheed skunk works, which had built the blindingly fast SR-71; and finally ex-NSA, where Ben had developed Black Stealth One. The theft of that invisible ghost, after a monumental foul-up at the very top of U. S. intelligence, had enraged Ben Ullmer past all forgiveness. He had left the NSA determined to be his own boss, because aircraft development flowed in his veins.

The needs of the Coast Guard aero engineering staff might have been best served by one of two men. Burt Rutan was not available, but suddenly in '89 this legendary Georgia cracker had surfaced as a private contractor. Ben was determined not to be an ex-engineer until they planted him in the ground, and no one can forcibly retire a sixty-seven-year-old who owns the company. His contract for a stunning new spy plane might have been expected, he realized; but finding Wes Hardin so soon was the capper. And Ben had known for many years that if you wanted to keep the best people, you allowed their near beer.

Hardin, who always seemed to have eyes along his backbone, crumpled the empty can into his pocket and grabbed ear protectors that hung like a yoke around his neck. "Uh-oh," he said in a parody of haste, "she's caught us screwing off. Damn, I knew this would happen," he added, adjusting the protectors over his ears as he disappeared into the test cell.

Ben realized then that his assistant, Marie Duchaine, had been standing quietly behind them. Her glance at the departing Hardin was amused, but Marie's amusement had its limits.

Ben saw that Marie was waiting with a pill in one hand and a cupful of water in the other, then glanced at his wrist. "How long you been here," he grouched, knocking the pill back with the water.

"Not very. How long would you have forgotten your pill?" Marie had left the NSA with Ben and could not have been intimidated by a regimental combat team. Accepting his shrug as her answer, she went on: "I just took a call on the scrambler line. A certain pair of nabobs want to see the Nemesis assembly line, and of course they want the big boss to show them around."

"My wife is busy," he growled, responding with his own brand of humor to something in her tone. "And so am I, and they'd have to be cleared by the Coasties before—" he realized that Marie was waiting to drop some small bomb of information. "Dammit, Marie," he said, with a curmudgeon's glare. "What is it?"

"I wouldn't worry about their clearances; it's Sheppard and Aldrich. Might be fun," she added quickly to derail real anger. After so many years with Ben Ullmer, she knew his problem with blood pressure. Ben was a man whose fuses were sometimes long, sometimes short, but always lit. "You can afford to smile at Mal Aldrich now."

"That'll be the day," he said, but something faintly suggestive of a grin did twitch at the side of his mouth. Dr. William Sheppard, among the NSA's top wizards, had always valued Ben. Mal Aldrich, who had stood between Ullmer and Sheppard, was another matter; unimaginative, wary of technical risks, Aldrich had never shown much confidence in the sort of men who sported southern-fried accents, refused to wear ties, and enjoyed working in an engine test cell. Aldrich had once called Ben a hick; Aldrich did *not* know that Ullmer's title for him was "the bean-counter." It was typical of Ben that, while he knew it was essential to tally figures, he undervalued anyone who actually felt happy doing it. Ben Ullmer was an administrator's nightmare.

"I don't suppose they told you what it's about," he said.

"You suppose right, but they're flying in Monday," Marie said, and turned away. She might have added, "Maybe they want to steal another airplane," but then he would have needed another pill.

Ben watched her stride away with innocent appreciation, noting the movement of those fine hips as he would note any other well-designed chassis. On a deeper level, he was thinking about another kind of structure: political structure. Aldrich was no more important than a small scar that a man could carry forever, but Bill Sheppard sometimes faced the President in Security Council meetings. Sheppard did not waste his time playing the casual rubberneck; if he showed up in person, you knew the Nemesis birds were getting close scrutiny in the highest places.

At best, it could mean one of the other services wanted to order a few of these birds. Not CIA; they would have sent their own people. Not army or marines either, in light of the very special nature of the Nemesis project. Navy or air force? Just possibly; and a delayed order for a few could put Aerosystems on a financial footing as sound as bedrock. The problem was that, if they wanted several airplanes in a hurry, Aerosystems might be forced to subcontract some of the work; and then the quality of Nemesis aircraft would go to hell in a hurry.

Ben Ullmer would not go for that no matter what they promised, no matter how they threatened. A Nemesis bird did not work like military hardware, taking mudbaths and bullet holes and working just as well for a twelve-thumbed yahoo as it did for more careful folks. When a Nemesis craft cleared the Aerosystems runway in the middle of the night for its acceptance hop to the nearby Coastie base, it was a tender machine, temperamental as a Lotus formula car, intended to be touched throughout its service life only by trained perfectionists, flown out by Ullmer people and turned over to pilots who had trained with Ullmer people, not an almost perfect airchine but absolutely by-God dead solid perfect, and it was going to stay that way as long as Ben Ullmer had a milligram of fight left in him.

At worst, somebody had already dreamed up some hairy-ass scheme for one of the two spookships he'd delivered to the Coast Guard, like lining the pressurized cabin with a ton of armor plate so it would hardly fly at all, and fitting it with—who knew? Rockets, medevac stuff, a cruise missile, any of the million missions a Nemesis was *not* designed for.

Ben stopped grasping at ever worse scenarios and decided to let each day bring its own cargo to him, stuffing the unlit cigar into a shirt pocket as he opened the door to the test cell. He liked Bill Sheppard, but loathed the idea of seeing him on Oregon turf, his own turf now, because Sheppard had shown up before to study projects that didn't seem to be NSA's business. It always turned out to be monkey business.

And every time, it meant trouble for somebody.

FIVE

Monday, April 24

Bɪʟʟ Sʜᴇᴘᴘᴀʀᴅ ʜᴀᴅ no trouble getting clearance to land at the Coast Guard's base in Oregon because, as a ranking scientist with the NSA, he got very cordial treatment—including transportation from Fort Meade, Maryland to Oregon in one of the few executive jets the Coasties owned. Sheppard was small, erect, neatly academic; people tended to address him as Dr. Sheppard. Mal Aldrich reported directly to Dr. Sheppard and, when the two men were alone, unfailingly called him that. When anyone else was present, Aldrich called him Bill as often as he could. Bill Sheppard understood perfectly, and forgave Aldrich without a second thought. When pushing the limits of technology you needed people of tremendous vision, and other people who could not see the horizon with the Hubble telescope. If Mal Aldrich was one of the latter, well, you didn't need a telescope to count beans and the NSA had a lot of beans to be counted.

And sooner than accept a weekend of fishing with Aldrich, Bill Sheppard would have splintered his own ancient bamboo flyrod over his knee.

Aldrich had been selected to work with State Department and CIA as long as it took to reach some decisions on the Nemesis, and they'd told him to share with Sheppard those details, and *only* those, necessary to conduct NSA's end of the business. But it was Sheppard who must decide whether a Nemesis could perform long-range surveillance better than any spy satellite. The recent Veracruz contact had mentioned, among other things, a guerrilla airbase in Mexico.

In the chain of command, Aldrich's position was what Ben Ullmer would call a pure organizational fuckup, but Sheppard understood and did not complain. For one thing, Uncle's intelligence agencies had become more wary after Black Stealth One had been lost. For another thing, the NSA director was trying Aldrich in the top tier of need-to-know decisions; giving him a taste of power. That's what you did to season a man struggling for a position of influence, you let him ease his foot onto a political accelerator pedal and you watched to see whether he crept along like a Hong Kong dowager or tried to spin his wheels.

Aldrich deplaned from the HU-25A jet Falcon first, struggling with a two-suiter that must have weighed thirty pounds, because Mal Aldrich never went anywhere without plenty of clothes. Sheppard followed with his rumpled bag, the few necessities of a man who had nothing to prove. On this trip, Ben Ullmer would do the proving.

"This must be the limo, Bill," said Aldrich to the back of his head, the Coastie crew scurrying around them on postflight chores, and Sheppard turned to see that it was not exactly a State Department limo but at least it had four doors. The Coast Guard had never been the service of luxury, which must have weighed heavily in their decision to go with Ullmer. Ben Ullmer could magic up a small production line in a one-car garage.

A young man in civvies popped from the car as it stopped beside them. Slender and inches shorter than Aldrich, he moved swiftly with perfect assurance that he was wasting no motions. "Gentlemen, I'm Jared Cutter. They said you didn't want VIP treatment, so I get to drive you to Aerosystems Unlimited—and may I get the IDs over with?"

They produced them, Cutter seeming perfunctory as he handed them back, but *I'll bet this young buck memorized my fingerprint whorls*, Sheppard thought. As it turned out, Cutter had more important things to remember. Sitting up front with the Coastie driver, amicably twisting to face the visitors, Cutter said he was an engineer and onetime marine aviator, now a production team leader with Aerosystems. "I'll have my type rating to pilot a spookship shortly," he added.

"I didn't know Ullmer was building anything but Nemesis," Aldrich said.

"That's its nickname, sir," Cutter said, too openly pleased with his work to be abashed by these men. Theirs, his manner seemed to say, was simply another world; he was more than satisfied to be part of this one, in which sharp young men and women competed to become birds of passage.

As Cutter turned his head to glance out, the coastal light fell upon his face just—so, and Sheppard realized that his wife, a rather good amateur painter, would kill for light like this; dispelling shadows, leaving every detail strongly lit, the light made Cutter the very graven image of an aircrew member. You didn't say "airman" so readily anymore, because of the women. And that fact, combined with Cutter's slender good looks, made Sheppard ask a question more bluntly than he would have if he'd thought about it for a moment.

"Mr. Cutter, how do you like the mixed crew arrangement?"

An instant's pause, then a flashy smile: "Takes a little getting used to, sir. It's not as confining in a Nemesis as you might think, and we cope. If you can't cope with it, you don't stay in the program long,'' he added with an easy shrug.

Aldrich, who had been briefed in some depth, said, ''I gather the submariner ideal profiles didn't match a Nemesis mission.''

''Very few submarines fly, sir,'' Cutter replied, deadpan. ''I've only had my wings three years—interservice transfer from the navy—but we had female flight officers there too. You get used to it.'' Pause. ''It helps when they're as good as ours.''

''But you haven't actually been on a long Nemesis patrol yet,'' Aldrich persisted.

''There aren't any old-timers in spookships yet, sir,'' said Cutter, his gaze suggesting that he would enjoy a change of subject. ''Except for Mr. Hardin, of course. And Morrison; they're the ones you want to ask about that.''

Sheppard cut in smoothly as they crossed a bridge spanning a broad reach of what seemed to be salt water. ''How does a Nemesis handle, as compared to the other stuff you've flown?''

''Christ! No comparison,'' Cutter's grin flashed again, powered by the energy of a young aviator's enthusiasm. ''It'll demand all your concentration during takeoff and landing, like flying a Cessna in choppy crosswinds, 'til you get up above it all. Up where she belongs, a spookship is a feather with manual controls. Of course she won't climb with a Tomcat, but she'll push mach one in a dive. And maneuver? Sweet,'' he added, with a graceful forward thrust of one hand that began palm down and ended palm up. ''Her flight envelope is very special though. You never forget you're in an ultralight. Mr. Hardin says you don't want to punch out of a spookship because you'll fall for more miles than you'll have to walk.

''Actually, you don't punch out. No ejection seat; you roll over and fall out, or pop the canopy and damn' well climb out. Of course nobody's ever done it except him.''

Sheppard: ''Who?''

"Wes Hardin," Cutter said, in a tone that implied, "who else?" Aviators had their heroes too, and Cutter left little doubt how he viewed Hardin.

"Ullmer never even hinted he'd lost one of these in testing," said Aldrich. If Mal Aldrich had had a tail, Sheppard thought, he'd be wagging it.

"Oh, the copilot brought it home; Morrison, I believe. It wasn't an emergency, it was just to see if you could get out with your chutes and life-support pack. Aeronautical history is full of cases where people kept on *not* getting out, and nobody knew why. Then somebody's wingman would watch him try, and they'd finally understand the guy couldn't possibly get out, for some reason nobody had considered. That does wonders for a man's confidence, I can tell you.

"Anyway, getting clear is no problem in a spookship. The problem is, you could use up all your oxy and pass out if you deployed your chute too soon. Mr. Hardin fell nine miles before he opened that chute, and had plenty of air under him when it deployed. He called it peripheral testing. You don't want to hear what Mr. Ullmer called it," Cutter added and then went on quickly, "that's just scuttlebutt; happened before I hired on."

They had passed beyond sight of water now, the blacktop taking them between low hillocks with forested heights in the near distance rising perhaps a thousand feet. An ancient and fondly recalled odor made Sheppard inhale, a mixture of cut grass and cow manure that always said Wisconsin to him, even though this was rougher, wilder country, with cliffs that had not been smeared into submission by glaciers. The view of fenced grassy pastures with dairy herds and well-weathered clapboard farmhouses made an outright denial of anything more high tech than an egg candler, and Sheppard smiled. Ben Ullmer had found himself a wonderful hideyhole in Oregon, pushing aerodynamic horizons back in a place where, whenever you needed to clear your head for thirty seconds, you could lean your eyes on the view and think about forever. *Train-*

ing will tell, he told himself. The NSA facility where Ullmer had worked near Elmira, New York had seemed almost as innocent, as relaxing. Too bad old Ben didn't know how to relax.

One of these days, Ullmer's consuming passion was going to kill him. But before it did, what little Sheppard knew of the Nemesis craft told him that the old man and his hand-picked design team had created another anomaly; an airplane that flew in ways no other aircraft ever had, not even Black Stealth One, NSA's hellbug. By the time the sedan nosed off the highway onto a graveled road, Bill Sheppard had begun to feel an old excitement.

No guard kiosk stood near the big ramshackle gate of weathered timbers flanked by eight-foot chain-link fencing, and as the driver scrunched through gravel with a key for the padlock, Aldrich frowned toward his superior.

Cutter caught it. "Worried me, too, at first. But there's nothing to see unless you get inside the main facility. That fence isn't as simple as it looks and neither is the gate. Believe me, they know we're here." Aldrich looked impressed. This was the kind of security the NSA loved.

SIX

Monday, April 24

YOU REALLY STRETCHED a point, Wes Hardin reflected, when you called Nemesis assembly a production line. Ullmer was right to do it his way, using only three teams, each team building a Nemesis craft from the first vacuum-bagged part to installing the final canopy decals. It was exactly the reverse of, say, a Ford assembly line, because every man and woman on each team became truly expert in every phase of the work. It allowed Ullmer to get by with only a few major fixtures, doubling up on inexpensive hand tools so that he could build a small fleet of implausibly advanced aircraft on a Coastie budget. It took a little longer—over a month to build an aircraft—but no way had yet been found to do it any better and the only way to build or fly a spookship was the very best way.

Sure played hell with the schedule, though, when a team leader had to spend the day with visiting VIPs. Lacking Wes Hardin, the Spook 3 team would be only eleven strong, and that made a difference. Well, Morrison would just have to double up for a few hours, moving from the half-assembled Spook 4 to the delicate bird Hardin's own team was finishing.

"Mr. Hardin, Mr. Hardin: to the office, please." The blare of loudspeakers was an old-fashioned touch, but Duchaine's soft voice made it bearable. Ullmer would probably have turned up the volume and growled, "Hardin, get your tail in here."

Hardin stripped off his latex gloves, then shrugged out of his white coverall and ducked beneath Spook 3's starboard wing, checking his sportshirt for wrinkles as he strode toward the windowed officed that occupied one end of the building. The navy had taught him that neatness counted.

In a big corporation he would have waited to be ushered into the president's sanctum. Knowing how Ben Ullmer hated that kind of wasted motion, Hardin hung a right at Duchaine's work station with its bank of computer screens and snagged a jelly doughnut before passing through to Ullmer's office.

". . . was carrier-rated in an S3A Viking until 1980," Ullmer was saying to the seated men, so he knew the old boy was introducing him before he even got there. Not a wasted minute; that was Ben Ullmer. "Master's in aero engineering but—come on in, Hardin, and take that fat pill outa your face—but blew an eardrum during the service, which took him off flight status."

Cutter, of course, he knew; and the younger man was staying sensibly silent. To keep from feeling like an idiot but unwilling to interrupt the man who signed his checks, Hardin shook hands with the strangers, one sharp-faced with an aggressive smile and one smaller, almost Hardin-sized, wearing a bow tie.

"Got his ear fixed," Ullmer went on, "left the navy and worked for Gates uprating Learjets, flew on an aerobatic team of Christen Eagles, and damn' near offed himself in a Bede 5 that came unglued in midair. After that, he threw in with us. I gotta admit, by now he knows almost as much about a Nemesis as I do." When the old man stood up, the others did too. Nodding toward the smaller of the strangers, he went on: "This is Dr. William Sheppard, a deputy director at NSA. You can tell him anything you know. Ditto for Malcolm Aldrich, who's liaising between NSA and we-have-to-guess," he added. "Get 'em outa my hair, will you?" Aldrich's broad smile almost flickered off for an instant, but then regained its full wattage.

Around a bite of doughnut, Hardin began with a lie, "Glad to oblige," because that was what you said when growing up in small-town Texas even when strangers showed up while you were busiest. "We're not bonding any assemblies today so you don't have to use respirators. But you'll have to wear gloves, and please don't touch anything without asking first. At this stage of Spook 4's assembly, even the natural oils on your fingers could ruin a panel bond. Okay?"

The men nodded and filed from the office, Ullmer sitting down again with a sigh that plainly said good riddance to them all, and when Hardin glanced toward the NSA deputy in the hall he saw that Sheppard was trying to hide a grin.

"That's just Ben's way," Hardin said quietly.

"We've known him for years," Sheppard replied, letting the grin come, with a movement of his head that included Aldrich. "I'd take him back in a microsecond."

They entered the assembly area, pausing to don flimsy gloves from a dispenser. "There's hardly any metal in these birds, so it's not as loud in here as you might expect," said Hardin, leading them between white-painted lines on the concrete floor. A few of the assembly team for Spook 4 glanced around in mild curiosity, all wearing coveralls and gloves. Their bird existed only as big shells of polymer and filament waiting to be assembled, yet it was obvious that those pieces could be carried around by hand, many times lighter than shells of aluminum and steel. Hardin nodded and kept walking until they reached the sliding doors, broad as a tennis court, which dominated one end of the building.

Nothing dominated the craft that faced those doors: on first impression, an enormous manta ray carrying a missile in its teeth. Hardin watched their faces as the NSA men gaped, and felt a familiar thrill, partly pride, mostly awe. He had helped build it, but might never become blasé about it.

The nose of Nemesis 3 was a huge canopied bullet broadening to a delta halfway back, her horizontal tail surfaces in front of her wing in a layout known as canards. Twin rudders, canted toward each other, protruded from the rear on tubular booms. She squatted so low on her nose gear, as if kneeling, that they could see where the dull grayish blue of her underside became the metallic midnight blue of her upper surfaces, the slender missile shape of her nose extending far ahead of her wings. A glistening canopy followed the lines of that bullet, the canards protruding from just beneath the canopy like small, graceful wings. The long bullet extended back beyond a second canopy to become a flattened delta, as if some giant had squashed the rear of a forty-foot missile. And from that subtly widened delta section emerged a wing of another sort, its tips scimitared like talons. It seemed to stretch forever toward those taloned tips.

"Dear Lord," Sheppard muttered, turning his head sharply to take it all in, then bringing his gaze back to the fuselage. "What is the span of this thing?"

"About ninety feet to the tip fences," Hardin said. "It's very slender, as you see; that's why it looks so long."

Aldrich found his voice at last. "I could never understand the advantage in putting the horizontal tail up front."

"For one thing, she'll never stall with that canard layout," Hardin replied. "Canards add a lot of lift, too, and the whole trick in the Nemesis is getting bags of lift with low drag. Robs you of some direct vision downward, but with her cockpit display you won't care."

"Once you get used to it," said Cutter, who had flown

in Spook 2 before her delivery. At Hardin's glance he added, a bit defensively, "It _does_ take some getting used to."

"Sure, but Rule Number One: Trust your instruments. Or get out and walk," Hardin said, motioning for the others to follow. He ducked beneath that huge cantilevered wing that seemed to reach its talons out far beyond any possible need, and pointed to the twin rudder booms. "The rudders don't have to be big and heavy if you stick 'em way out behind on those tubular booms. Remember, this bird weighs less than a compact car, and to keep it that way we don't have many power assists."

Sheppard: "Exactly how much mass?"

"About twenty-three hundred pounds."

Aldrich: "Plus crew and fuel, of course."

Hardin, a bit smugly: "_Including_ crew and fuel. She's designed for very small crew members; I weigh one-forty, and I'm the fattest cat flying these things."

Sheppard stopped, frowning, with flat disbelief in his face. "How? The Rutan Voyager wasn't much bigger than this, and when it started around the world it weighed six or eight tons."

"But that was years ago," Hardin reminded him, "and besides, they had to carry fuel for ten days. We carry enough to get us up on-station with some reserve, and solar panels do the rest. The whole top half of a Nemesis is covered with solar cells, forty thousand watts of power. When Ben showed me the set of induction coils in Spook 1's propeller shroud so the blades could act as an electrical rotor, I just about shit me a brick. I mean, now that's _smart_; instead of an electric motor driving a prop, the propeller _is_ part of the motor. Come around here, you can see the shroud better."

As Sheppard hid his amusement with Hardin's Southwest twang and the use he made of it, they followed at the little Texan's beckoning, bent almost double to avoid that endless wing. From the rear they could see the circular shroud, almost a man's height, that swept up from the fuselage centerline to enclose a multiblade propeller. In effect the shroud itself was a small circular wing, guiding airflow for high efficiency.

"I'm doing a few thumbnail calculations, Hardin," said Aldrich with some satisfaction. "No way you can get forty kilowatts from a surface this size."

"Not at sea level," Hardin agreed easily. "That's why she needs a turbo-charged rotary engine to climb. But when you're twelve miles high, there's not much to impede the sunlight; you can uncouple the engine from the propeller, shut it down, and run on plain ol' sunlight because solar panels are about five times more efficient when you're grazing the top of the stratosphere."

"He's got you there," Sheppard smiled to his companion. "So how long can you really stay on-station, Mr. Hardin? I'm not sure I can believe what I heard."

"How long would you like? She comes down when we need a crew change, or more microwaved meals. But for the Nemesis herself? Essentially forever." He saw that look again and gave them a self-deprecating grin. "Aw, I know she needs maintenance now and then, and even an electric propulsion system needs work sooner or later. Point is, gentlemen, she's happy up there a lot longer than we are. She's got a mission-adaptive wing."

Sheppard, nodding: "Doesn't look like it has variable sweep."

"Nope. Something a lot more advanced; a first, Ullmer tells me. You need a thin wing to get up near mach one, but that'll fall right out of the air when you get down to a hundred knots. If you could thicken the wing—make it swell up—on command and with precision, you could land at, oh," he waved a hand lazily in the air, smiling gently, "maybe twenty knots. A fat wing is no good for high speed, but it's great for loiter and landings."

"Incredible. Rubber wings?"

"Plastic skin under the solar cells, stuff kinda like Kynar. It's piezoelectric, almost like muscles, and when you apply a little voltage to it, the stuff will change shape.

Wish Spook 3 was all hooked up, you could see the critter flex and shimmy like my sister Kate. Anyhow, trust me: they do it.''

Aldrich seemed determined to find some inconsistency in all this, which amounted to a quantum leap beyond any known aircraft. ''You're telling me this thing will do mach one, or loiter twelve miles high at twenty miles an hour?''

''No sir, she's limited at mach oh-point-niner-two, which gets a little slower as you get higher, but it's not quite mach one. And while her sea-level landing speed isn't much above twenty—a man can run faster—the air's mighty thin up at her loiter altitude. She loiters at around two hundred knots on-station. She can go lots faster but any slower and,'' he finished by lowering his hand gradually.

Aldrich: ''Stalls, you mean.''

''Mushes, sir,'' Cutter put in, glad to be part of the process. ''Not as dangerous as a stall, thanks to those canards up front.''

''I'd very much like to see one fly,'' Sheppard said, his tone wistful.

''Spook 1 and 2 are already operational over the Gulf of Mexico out of Kingsville, Texas,'' Cutter said. ''I've flown in one of those. But they take off and land in the dark. You'll need infrared glasses.''

''Cutter, we developed that IR technology,'' said Aldrich.

''Then I'd like to have a bitch session with you,'' Hardin replied, ''over the quality of the IR telephoto stuff in our spookships.'' Aldrich opened his mouth; closed it again. ''It's supposed to let you read a headline at night from fifty thousand feet. It doesn't, you're lucky to tell a cow from a horse.''

Aldrich only blinked, coloring slightly. Sheppard rescued him with, ''That's not his department, Mr. Hardin, but I'll pass it on. Thanks for the firsthand assessment.''

Malcolm Aldrich made no reply, but his expression did not give thanks. Instead, he held up an arresting forefinger. "Hold on. No matter how high you fly, the sun goes down every night. Where's your power then?"

"Thought you'd never ask. Accumulator cells store extra wattage during the day, and we use it all night long, like storage batteries. Actually a spookship does lose a little altitude during the night, even though it's soaring like a sailplane; but at dawn, up she goes again. We've had to restart an engine once or twice to get back up when there's a really hellacious haze. There's not a lot of extra *anything* in a Nemesis. That's why it does one thing perfectly, instead of a hundred things half-assed, like most military aircraft."

Aldrich took on a pensive look, but failed to find any objections. By unspoken agreement, they retraced their path between those white lines, Sheppard glancing back more than once as if assuring himself that yes, by God, there *was* an airplane that would fly nearly at the speed of sound, circle the earth a dozen times without refueling— and land at twenty knots. This special ability might not remain so special when ROTHR, Relocatable Over-the-Horizon Radar, became readily available to monitor the movements of smugglers. But exactly one of those was now in use, not far from Langley, Virginia—and it would not reach southern Mexico from there. The Nemesis could bring her radar in very, very close.

Spy satellites failed the Nemesis test on another point. They could look down on a given spot for only a few moments while passing overhead. A Nemesis could literally fly tight circles over that same spot, maintaining its ghostly surveillance for weeks, unseen, unheard. *Spookship indeed*, Sheppard decided. Nearing the offices, he roused himself from his private thoughts, which centered on the other ways in which this new technology might be used. "Hardin, you said a Nemesis is happy on-station a lot longer than you are. Lord knows, I'm not surprised. I'd think a man would get bedsores, sitting for weeks, ah, on end, so to speak. Or a woman," he amended quickly.

"You would if you couldn't get out and stretch your legs," Hardin replied. At this, the NSA men exchanged glances of confusion so poignant that Cutter turned away, his torso shaking with silent mirth. Hardin realized he had conveyed a wrong impression and hurried to correct it. "Here, I'll show you. Better yet, wait a sec; I'll let Morrison show you." With that, he strode off past a single mold in which all rudder booms were formed, stopping to exchange a few words with a woman who was carefully peeling a substance like cellophane from the mold.

They soon lost sight of him among the welter of molds, ugly devices on the outside, mirror-smooth inside. "I take it this Morrison fellow is the one you mentioned," said Sheppard to the young aviator.

"Yessir, but not exactly," said Cutter. "You want to bear in mind that things are more, um, unisex around here than most places."

Sheppard turned to ask for a clearer answer but turned back when he heard Hardin call his name. "Dr. Sheppard, you're in luck. Morrison's installing the pilot lounge hardware now. Come take a look."

With a start, Sheppard took the gloved hand, realizing now what Cutter had meant. Morrison, one of Ullmer's premier pilots, was an inch or so shy of five feet tall; and whatever else Morrison might be, she was obviously not unisex.

SEVEN

Monday, April 24

THE CHIEF THING Sheppard noticed about Colleen Morrison, once he thought beyond the mature figure and the short tangle of honey-tinted hair framing a pixie's face, was that she seemed all business. She made her own introductions in a husky, crisp contralto, her tempo upbeat with eye contact that, in a man, might have been considered macho. Had Sheppard been forced to describe those eyes he might have replied, "wolf yellow." Though innocent of makeup, they certainly got a man's attention.

"I suppose this is the best time to show you the pressurized section," she said, leading them in a roundabout path that avoided the work crew. "Even though we're a little rushed today," she added, with a glance at Hardin that was not overly warm.

She stopped them near a massive fixture twenty feet long, which proved to be a mold of the bulletlike forward fuselage, locked into a rig of circular tubes. As they watched, a burly worker unpinned the tubes and carefully turned the entire rig, repinning it securely, revealing that a piece of the mold had been removed. Inside lay part of the fuselage shell, already bristling with attachments for equipment. With the shell spun onto its side to ease its assembly, they could see into the cavity through the hole that would later be covered with that odd rear canopy. "We lay up prepreg carbon filament—that means it's already wet with resin—in the mold before it's pressure-bagged and heat-cured," Morrison said, "and then we put interface crap in place with fiberglass rivets. It's not really glass anymore, but that's the name of the technique. Basically you anchor things in the fuselage by bonding it, but adhesive bonds are tricky and you never know for certain if they're perfect."

"Hardin said these things *were* perfect," Aldrich said.

"He's been known to be right," she said, sliding a glance in her colleague's direction. "Fiberglass rivets are injected through the shell and the bonded piece. They cure that way. They're in tension, which is the best use of 'em, so they won't pull apart. And if they won't pull out, even a poor bond stays perfect. That's how you make it perfect: structural redundancy."

"Ah; so Mr. Hardin didn't tell us everything," Sheppard smiled.

"Hardin doesn't *know* everything. The pressurized part of the fuselage is a cavity separated into two sections," she went on, pointing out features as if this casual dig at Hardin were their version of backslaps.

Perhaps it's good-natured banter, certainly Hardin didn't react, but I wonder, Sheppard thought. *She could be one of those man-hating radical types.*

". . . two seats, naturally," she was saying, "but usually only one pilot's on duty. I suppose you know about the decision to use mixed crews; same-sex pairs tend to get on each other's nerves more after a week or so aloft. If you want my view, I think we get just as irritable, but we hide it better this way. Social conditioning, probably. Doesn't matter so long as it works, and it seems to. Anyway, every four hours you rotate duty. Literally; you pull your legs in and rotate the seat and, voila," she said with a gay, surprisingly girlish lilt, "you're facing the pilot's lounge. You have to duck a little, but you can stand erect under the rear canopy, and that's where you live; we say you're in the pipe, and you can see why. Less than six feet high, maybe six in diameter, ten long. Enough for a toilet, a bed you can adjust into a chair or couch, and this contraption over here." Stepping forward, she placed her hand on a spidery arrangement of tubes, straps, springs, and pedals, the whole thing approximating the size of a small adult. "Energy is at such a premium up there, the exercycle runs the TV accumulator. An hour of biking equals an hour of *General Hospital*, or whatever."

"We call it the glass jock," Cutter added for her. "You wouldn't think you could do everything on a glass jock that you can on a Nautilus machine, but you can."

"And do it while the duty pilot banks you toward a new heading, but be damn' sure your harness is snug," Morrison went on, grinning with a certain impudence at Cutter. "This'd be a great setup for bondage games, wouldn't it? Whatta you think, Cutter?"

Cutter met her frank gaze for perhaps one beat, then rubbed his jaw as he looked away, spots of color appearing under the tan on his cheeks. "Test it with Coastie pilots first," he muttered.

"You'll live to be an old pilot," she said as if it were a compliment.

Bill Sheppard knew better: Colleen Morrison had implied that handsome young Jared Cutter could be bolder. *So much for the radical feminist theory*, Sheppard chided himself.

"You could get a great suntan under the rear canopy. In fact you could be medium rare in an hour up there," Morrison went on, "so it's polarized and has coatings as well. Point is, you can pursue a lot of hobbies when you're off duty. Study chess or correspondence courses, read, listen to tapes, bike a lot. Pole vaulting is out, the hammer throw is out, training your attack dog is out. You could get pretty

ripe after a week without a shower, but we use prepack-
aged damp towels. Still, it's nice to flush cabin air now
and then.''

Sheppard, intrigued by the niceties in such a confined
space for what must be weeks at a time, asked, ''What's
your favorite hobby on-station?''

''She rides a little bitty broom,'' said Hardin, who may
have been waiting for just this moment. ''A whisk
broom.''

''And that's about all there is,'' the diminutive blonde
said briskly, ignoring Hardin, yet choosing this moment
to cut the session short. She made a ''this way'' gesture,
oblivious of the fact that these visitors were VIPs.

In most of the big aerospace companies, such behavior
would be grounds for instant dismissal. It was one measure of Ben Ullmer's genius that he drew such people
around him, and drew the best from them, even if some
of them got along like two werewolves in the same closet.
My lord, those two must go at it hammer and tongs, Sheppard thought. *They may fly mixed crews, but this is one
pair that won't mix.* It had been like that when Ben Ullmer
worked for Aldrich. Sheppard asked, ''Really: what do
you do to pass the time?''

''Write short stories,'' she said, almost whispering it.
''At least I try. Not very good at it, I'm afraid. You could
paper over the canopy with my rejections.''

''Ah.'' Sheppard could think of nothing else to say.
Given her gamine good looks and obvious brains, this little overachiever would get very few rejections of any kind,
he decided. *If it weren't for all that aggression.* ''It's been
very instructive,'' he said as they neared the offices. He
shook Morrison's hand again, impressed with her grip,
and followed Hardin into the offices.

Once he had delivered them, Hardin excused himself
and hurried back to the assembly area. Ullmer pushed his
granny glasses onto his forehead, leaned back and said,
''Well, doc, you gonna have to operate?''

Only then did Sheppard remember the gloves, stripping

them off, tossing them into a wastebasket while Aldrich and Cutter followed suit. "Actually, Ben, we did have a surveillance operation in mind, and I don't even have the need to know exactly what it is." *So why did the director send me with Mal Aldrich? Doubtless because he knows Aldrich and Ullmer didn't get along. Ben Ullmer writes his own tickets now, and he's perfectly capable of telling Mal where to put his secrets. And when NSA gives the kid-glove treatment to a civilian contractor, that contractor must have something unique and vital to national security. I'll bet my eyeteeth that Ullmer's birds will be following a tremendous shipment of contraband; drugs or arms.*

Ullmer vented one of his rare squeaky laughs. "If you don't know what it is, how can you know what you're looking for?"

"Good question." Sheppard glanced at Aldrich. "Mal knows, however, and I've always been a pretty fair guesser. I'll put this on record later, Mal: I'm satisfied that Nemesis aircraft will fill gaps in our coastal defense zones that nothing else can do as well. Not the aerostat blimps, not Blackhawk choppers, not even a team of those little jet Falcons like the one that brought us out here. And you can't loiter a KH satellite over one location for days; these Nemesis birds do have a unique advantage. From what I've seen, with so little metal in them I imagine they're stealthy as mice. And at only a fraction of the cost," he added, with another look at Aldrich. "Will that be good enough?"

Aldrich nodded. "There are a couple of other things, Bill. We'll have to report on its glide distance from operating altitude."

Sheppard, frowning: "Is that crucial?"

Aldrich: "They say it might be."

But Ben Ullmer was already drawing an antique from his desk drawer, a log-log decitrig slide rule he had used to design aircraft before he'd ever heard of a pocket calculator. After a single manipulation he said, "Simple enough: We can stretch a glide four hundred miles, give or take ten percent. Damn' if I know why that would ever be crucial, but if you jettison her remaining fuel a Nemesis will soar like a frigate bird. Even the Aurora wouldn't do that.''

Aldrich, startled: ''The what?'' Then, with a nervous glance toward Cutter, ''Cancel that. I don't want an answer.''

''Christ on Kaopectate, Aldrich,'' said the old man in exasperation, ''Everybody reads *Aviation Leak!* Cutter, me—well, almost everybody,'' he amended with a look that clerly excluded Aldrich himself. ''You want a special surveillance craft. This isn't the only kind. I don't give a muskrat's ass whether mine's the best kind for your purposes, but I'm humoring you people. Why? I guess because in spite of everything, I've still got a smidgen of patriotism left.''

''I'll pass that on,'' said Aldrich drily. ''And one last item: I saw no provision for weapons of any kind.''

Cutter, who had stood silent, jerked at this. ''But it's a pure surveillance—''

''That'll do, Cutter,'' Aldrich said smoothly, as though speaking to a child. ''It's all part of the equation.''

Ullmer sighed, then leaned back in his chair, hands interlaced behind his head, and spoke as if Cutter were the only man in the room with him. ''They're pure surveillance, all right,'' he said, ''and that pisses me off, but the Coasties made me optimize the design without even a Gatling gun. I didn't ever wanta build another airchine that can't take care of itself, but that's just what I've done.''

''We don't need weapons installed,'' Aldrich said. ''But that needn't concern you, Ben.''

Bill Sheppard had time to burn, but temperaments in the room were smoldering too, and tension lay thick as smoke in the air. He checked his watch. He saw Ullmer do the same, wearing that same old windup Breitling chronograph of his that must have been older than the slide rule. ''Well,'' both men said simultaneously, and shared a smile before starting their good-byes.

Ten minutes later, Cutter and the two NSA men swapped

observations as their driver took them back to that inno- cent little two-lane blacktop.

Eventually Sheppard asked, "Mr. Cutter, why did I get the impression that Morrison and Hardin are not the best of friends?"

"Because you have eyes and ears, sir," Cutter grinned at him. "No sweat; it's just one of those inside jokes in the plant, the way they cut each other up. 'Course, Hardin was military, and he picks his shots. Morrison's your basic shotgunner. She was too small to be a military pilot, and there's—ah—a certain envy there. Tell you this, though," he said earnestly; "if I ever get half as good in a Nemesis as she is, I'll be one happy aviator."

"Treat her right, and maybe she'll teach you," Aldrich smirked.

"She's my instructor already, sir," Cutter said, his tones cool. "When Spook 4 is delivered to the Coasties I'll make the delivery."

"I think you know what I meant," Aldrich said archly. "The lady seems to like you."

"And I like her, sir, and I have no intention of kissing my flight instructor as long as that factor exists, and with respect, sir, you're out of line."

Bill Sheppard squinted toward the distant line of bluffs, trying very hard to seem interested in the horizon; trying even harder not to show his satisfaction with young Jared Cutter.

EIGHT

Tuesday, April 25

A FEW DAYS after his return to Base Ana, Simon Torres found himself asked to defend its layout. "You know," said Elath, gazing down on Base Ana from the commanding view of the geodesic dome lodge, "as a military base this place was not laid out very efficiently." He spoke the slangy Spanish of a native Mexican Jew born and raised in the capital city, though he had emigrated to Israel while still a youth.

Coming from another man, this would have made Simon Torres smile, the deliberately disarming smile he used to hide irritation. From his ordnance expert and friend David Elath, it provoked only a shrug. "That was Escobar's doing," Torres replied, naming the man who had organized the Medellin cartel. He arose from a leather sofa with brandy snifter in hand to stand at Elath's shoulder. Elegant in gray slacks and sport shirt open to the navel, Torres stood a hand's breadth shorter than the burly Elath. "Be careful not to repeat that around Escobar's people, my friend."

The big man swigged at his Heineken and took his eyes from the scene that lay below, wooden barracks and mess hall aligned east of Base Ana's intersecting runways, hangars and guarded warehouse spread between the scissor-ends of those runways. The nearest part of this base, both a training and drug-processing center, lay no more than 300 yards away from the air-conditioned luxury of the cartel lodge, with its servants and its excellent wines; but to the hundreds of senderistas who lived in sweltering barracks when not tending far-flung coca plots, and who trained near the edge of the ever-encroaching jungle, this show of riches on the hill must loom like a reproach to their Maoist warrior's dream. "And what would they do, Simon; retire me?"

Another shrug. "Retirement" was merely a synonym for death. Colombian drug lords have many synonyms for death, just as Eskimos have many words for snow, having such close acquaintance with its many varieties. Elath had come to them after disgrace and forced discharge from the Israeli defense forces, bearing the scarred face and torso of a man who had not always been an expert with munitions. His mistake, he'd admitted to Torres, was in getting caught leaking technical data to the South African government. Not doing it, but getting caught at it; that distinction was important to Torres. It tagged Elath as a kindred spirit, a pragmatist who could understand and admit his errors. Though Elath was wonderfully useful training senderistas in demolition and booby traps, he also knew how to maintain American combat arms, including the brace of old air-cooled Browning fifties he had installed in the T-33 jet.

Even if Torres had not liked his armorer, he would have pretended to. And no man, he felt, could have a better companion at his back. Elath was one of those men who seemed always to know which nearby implement would best serve as a weapon in the fewest possible milliseconds of delay. Unlike most of the other cartel leaders from Cali, Torres enjoyed traveling light and fast without a dozen armed escorts. As long as the red-complexioned Elath strode at his side, Simon Torres would enter any cantina or dark alley in Latin America.

The most forcible reminder of Elath's specialty was that

broad shrapnel scar on his forehead that parted his curls of
sandy hair like an affectation. In his standard garb of tan whipcords tucked into jump boots, matching shirt with ironed
creases, epaulets at the big sloping shoulders, and sleeves rolled
to show the muscular forearms and the Rolex, David Elath
never failed to seem exactly what he was: a mercenary officer.

"They would not retire you," Torres said. "But like the
yanqui Mafia, they would demand more respect. And that
could create a problem for me, personally. I would rather
groom you to rise in the cartel than have to keep explaining
why I cannot discipline the man who loads my guns."

At this, Elath barked that barrel-chested laugh of his, swinging an arm up to clap Torres's opposite shoulder, an abbrevi-
ated bear hug by a man who considered himself an equal.

Torres did not mind. He needed Elath's complete loyalty more than he needed a toady.

When a faint concussión slapped the window, both men
turned to stare westward, toward the training area where
senderista teams sweated through humidity a man could
swim in. A score of tiny antlike creatures, dressed in every
sort of clothing from military fatigues to the off-white
cotton of peons, converged on something that sprawled,
a broken doll, on turf savaged by many a training exercise. "A grenade," Torres guessed, taking a sip of brandy.

Elath shook his head. "Too much brisance," he judged.
The shattering effect—brisance—of French plastic explosive was well-known, and some men fancied they could
spot it by the ear-splitting high pitch of its detonation wave.
The stuff provided by the cartel to its Peruvian crazies was
actually Czech, a bright orange plastique called Semtex;
but it had the same brisance, and would blow men to pieces
with the same chemical enthusiasm. Evidently it had done
exactly that a moment before.

David Elath was moving before he spoke. "I have to
take a look," he said over his shoulder.

"No, it's almost time to leave for the meeting at Catemaco," Torres objected. The villas of Torres and his peers
sprawled at the edges of Catemaco, a town near the gulf

and a three-hour drive to the northwest. Torres had been known to shave that time by almost an hour.

"*Debo que*, I must," Elath shot back, nearing the door. "They did something wrong, and the crazy bastards will keep on doing it wrong until half of them are in pieces and the other half ready to shoot me for teaching them. You know how they are," the words floating back as Elath trotted into the sunlight.

"I know how they are," Torres agreed to no one in particular. *Too bad,* he thought, watching Elath run down the hill like a fullback in yanqui futbol. The way David Elath sweated, he would be wringing wet when he got back. And though the Mangusta had an excellent air conditioner, Elath's sweat would soak the car's leather seat.

Bowing to the inevitable, Torres called sharply for a refill of his snifter. He would spend this half-hour delay in the most pleasant way possible, and then he would insist that Elath change his shirt before folding himself into the Mangusta for the ride to Catemaco. They might not be late if Torres really concentrated on speed, and that was one thing the Mangusta supplied better than a Corvette. Torres idly yearned now and then for a new Lamborghini like that of young Gaitan Palacios, at age thirty the spoiled brat of the Cali group; but price was not the problem. He knew the damned thing had the road clearance of a centipede and needed maintenance that was not available within hundreds of kilometers. The Mangusta's whopping Ford engine could be repaired anywhere and its chassis would clear most of the highway debris that one always depended on in Mexico.

Such factors were important to a man like Torres, who demanded as much of his machines as he did of his associates. But if one chose both very carefully, he could surround himself with the best of them. Elath, the Mangusta, and the T-33: each a bit old for such hard work, yet all fine choices. Life could be sweet if you chose your risks carefully, Torres reflected, watching the big man in tan whipcords kneel near the biggest piece of something that had so recently been a man.

AN HOUR LATER, Torres flung the Mangusta through a riverside bend and stabbed its big disk brakes hard enough to force its rear end to slide. He saw Elath's knuckles whiten as they gripped handholds and called, over the bellowing V-8 at their backs, "Detouring left of Cardenas. A delay we do not need." Elath nodded but did not take his eyes from the onrush of road. Torres had decided that his friend was in all ways consistent, the same kind of passenger as he was a warrior: smart enough to be scared, controlled enough to quell panic. Some brave men had been known to panic while sitting in the passenger seat of the black Mangusta. Torres was not a driver who always slowed for intersections, gravel, or animals of less than fifty pounds.

The police of Cardenas, a township almost large enough to claim a city's status, had become as tractable as other isthmus cities during the past year. This was most true at the top, as such accommodations began when city fathers discovered how generous the cartel could be, and were warned how vulnerable their economies might be to highways and railway bridges modified by Semtex. But some patrolmen still did not know enough to let the black Mangusta, or any other of the exotic machines driven by the cartel lords, go snarling on like a maddened cheetah. Though no patrol car could hope to match a Mangusta's blistering pace, radio waves could outrun it, and on Torres's last little jaunt through Cardenas he and Elath had been met with a roadblock and shotguns. It had taken twenty minutes for several anguished policemen to understand, via radio to their headquarters, that the fine, dashing, upstanding gentlemen in Darth Vader's automobile must be allowed his fun.

Not that this kind of reluctant welcome surprised Torres. Had he not been late for a strategy meeting in the villa of Maximilian Vega, he would have enjoyed the old whore, risk, and her handmaid, thrill; the deadly gleam of intent in the eyes of patrolmen as it glazed into new aware-

Paula

ness of new rules; and he would even have enjoyed pressing a few large bills into their hands just to see the glaze become satisfaction. Born in a Barranquilla slum in 1944, the youngest of five street-smart children, Simon Torres had watched an older brother develop as a soldier for coke-runners and saw how many police, themselves savagely underpaid, learned how to be civil to a brave lad with money to share. It had been cocaine money from his brothers that bought Torres a decent education, which he parlayed into the Colombian Air Force cadet program.

In those days, the Colombian equivalent of astronauts were a bright and fearless few who were posted to the United States for training, there to be type-rated for the Cessna A-37, a small twin-jet sold to Colombia for counterinsurgency missions. But while among the yanquis, Simon Torres fell in love with a Buick Roadmaster of a plane, Lockheed's T-33. It could mount more guns than the Cessna and flew almost 600 miles an hour, though it lacked the bombing capacity of the A-37. To Simon Torres the cadet, godhood consisted of unlimited freedom to fly a T-33 and to drive a De Tomaso Mangusta. To Torres the colonel, it also meant power to bomb the liver and lights out of drug-processing operations that competed against those of his brothers. To Torres the ex-colonel, who quit his country's service one jump ahead of an indictment, godhood included all of those other things plus the ability to put his tactical genius into play on the grand scale, not only national but international in scope.

When the lords of Medellin found common cause with the lords of Cali, they found Torres the equal of any of them in intelligence. Older members—Perez Palacios from Cali and Maximilian Vega from Medellin, to name the most powerful—felt that Simon Torres could use more caution. It was caution now that prompted him to avoid Cardenas; not with respect to police, but to Vega, Palacios, and the others. A sit-down on tactical matters was not to be avoided, and if you were late, you showed disrespect.

Discounting an unfortunate dog, the balance of the trip

was uneventful, avoiding towns as they sped northwest to pick up Federal Highway 180 near the gulf coast. The final twenty kilometers or so, Torres slowed because his Piaget said he would be on time, and the approach to Catemaco was always a feast for the eyes.

Even David Elath managed to relax, luxuriating in the air-conditioned rush of the Mangusta, the highway swooping up from the Coastal plain, circling the jewel of Catemaco as though seeking entrance past its great stone sentinels. This jewel is largely a secret well kept from tourism, ringed by volcanic peaks that soar almost a mile above gulf beaches, some eighty miles down the coast from Veracruz. Inside that cloister of old volcanoes lies a freshwater lake with its own beaches and islets, and on the interior slopes lies Catemaco. The ancient Olmecs knew a good thing when they found it, and left many a carved jade figure around the little town. The Colombian drug lords saw the same good thing, and in the past year had bought up much of its real estate. For men determined to own the entire isthmus region, with its drowningly humid gulf lowlands, Catemaco was as near as they would ever get to heaven.

Torres shot up one last tightening bend, snicked the Mangusta's gear lever down through third to second, and let the dust-powdered coupe burble gently into town. One never knew, in Catemaco, when a Bentley or the Lambo of young Palacios might come squirting out of a side street with arrogance equal to one's own.

"On time, as always," Torres mumbled to his friend, guiding the Mangusta up a winding drive, giving a lazy salute to Vega's gate guards as he passed.

"And I'm amazed, as always," said Elath with more resignation than spleen, "that we get here at all. I keep wondering what you expect to prove in this thing."

"Why, that life is sweet," said Torres, genuinely surprised; and his smile was as gentle as Elath had ever seen it.

NINE

WHOEVER HAD OWNED this estate before Vega got it, Torres decided, certainly had a taste for melodrama. Three stories of buff stone scaled by passion flower and surrounded by citrus fragrant with blossoms, its great width still made it seem low and Moorish. The stone steps to the front portico, broad as an avenue, had been scuffed by many a grandee's boots, once upon a time.

No matter how often he ambled up those steps, Torres the man had to remind Torres the impoverished boy not to duck his head in deference to that display. In one expensive gesture, Maximilian Vega had bought himself centuries of tradition. Vega himself was old Medellin money, but even had he been one of the new cocaine rich, he could have done that. When Torres grew tired of his speedy toys, he knew he could do exactly the same—and that was the whole point, was it not? Of course, the paltry hundred million dollars or so that Torres had squirreled away left him far in arrears of old Vega but, with courage and patience, Simon Torres intended to remedy that.

Elath walked a half-step behind, his combat boots creaking while Torres's $300 Italian loafers only whispered, and because both men knew their roles, Elath peeled off without a word into the small manicured jungle of the inner courtyard, candlelit and open to the evening sky. There he would stay with any other ranked hirelings who might be there, unless he was called for, snacking from the buffet and smoking, soaking up tradition if he liked or watching television with earphones, or playing imported video games, all of it set among hothouse greenery that included small papaya trees loaded with fruit. Electronic toys did not last long in this humid outdoor setting. Nobody cared; their replacement was, for drug lords, too cheap to be of concern.

No liquor was served in the courtyard, however, because the same willingness for direct action that made a man a good bodyguard also made him more likely to skirmish at inappropriate times, especially when he was drinking. Besides, there was always a chance that David Elath's expertise might be needed by the men setting policy and arguing tactics in the great hall on the second floor of the villa. A man's senses must not be dulled at such times. The men of Cali and Medellin had deadly rules against any of their number, or their cronies, showing the effects of liquor, marijuana, or any of the other substances that altered the mind.

Billy Borges of Medellin had brought that rule from the sons of Sicilians in Nevada, and Colombians knew better than to ignore rules that worked so well for the Mafia. So close were those Mafia connections that Billy Borges, whose real name was Guillermo, had taken the yanqui sobriquet as if he had been born with it. Torres thought Borges faintly ridiculous for that; it was the yanquis, after all, who paid billions of dollars to their enemies every year for the privilege of poisoning themselves. Billy's own addiction was gambling, often at the tables in Las Vegas, but that was different. When coca rots a man's septum through, he cannot grow another, Billy would say; but money could always be replaced. Billy had his hundred million and then some, and of all the cartel lords he roamed most easily among the yanquis, his English almost without accent. It was Billy who supervised cocaine shipments on the American side, always from a safe distance, a largely invisible presence to the harried agents of the Drug Enforcement Administration and other agencies.

Torres climbed the inner stairway and silently handed over his little armpit Walther automatic to one of the two blocky men who stood near the balustrade outside the great room. They were not supposed to have to ask; one of the ground rules laid down years before by Vega and old Palacios had been the checking of arms, because arrogance sometimes made men rash, and Colombians were a passionate lot. Torres had once seen Vega's crony, Solano, in such a rage that the man darted a hand toward a pocket weapon that, luckily for them all, he had left outside. Solano's lapse had brought smiles; no harm done, no apology needed. But Miguel Solano had not been treated the same since then.

The guards waited for Torres's nod and got it, and opened the double doors, and Torres stepped into a room fifty feet long, twenty feet to the hand-hewn ceiling beams. The windows in that room might stay open for years without removing all of the mustiness that tickled Torres's nostrils. He noted the five members already present and returned their greetings with politeness. Medellin's Max Vega and Cali's Perez Palacios were both present, and those elder statesmen of cocaine were the ones who really counted most.

Servants with strong backs had removed the huge wooden table that sometimes dominated the room, and on this evening Torres counted six heavy chairs, virtually thrones, in a semicircle around the cold fireplace. Gaitan, the son of old Palacios, sat near his father, almost effeminate with his frilled silk shirt and the slender arms poking from it. Borges, equally silly in a pinstriped suit that must have been hotter than a coca lab, sat near the straw-blond Vega, whose Castilian good looks had not yet faded with his years. The fifth man was Alvaro Bermudez, the high-ranking senderista whose Indio features and peasant ways masked an excellent education. He might pick his nose, but Bermudez could pick men as well, particularly men of action. So long as Bermudez was present, the cartel lords knew better than to imply that the senderistas were considered mere armed workers.

Torres took a chair near Palacios, settled back, and asked the obvious question: "And where is Escobar, brother Maximilian?"

"Valle de Bravo," said Vega, naming a lakeside spa where diplomats and cinema stars gathered to escape the killing smog of Mexico City. "He is dickering with officials over changes to la ruta coca, the cocaine route."

"I am more concerned about the dollar route," Torres replied.

"That is on the agenda," the elder Palacios said. "That, and the harvest our allies have promised. Solano is running a shipment from Veracruz and we expect no one else tonight, so brother Bermudez, we can begin."

Bermudez, never pleased with the limelight, mopped sweat from the folds at his neck. "This will be our first coca harvest of any size in Mexico, most of it from the best altitudes for growth, around a thousand meters. The bushes are not fully mature, especially those at higher elevations, and our men cannot work while they are chasing yanquis."

Torres did not respond; that fruitless chase had been a cartel decision. Vega said smoothly, "But a talkative yanqui may be worse than the loss of a few kilos of coca, brother."

"If he *was* a yanqui, and if he noticed anything," Borges drawled.

"We consider the issue closed," said Perez Palacios. "Now: As we all know, hard cash is becoming more difficult to get for operating expenses. Our laundering operations in Europe and the British West Indies have been hit very hard by the damned yanquis. That is why it is becoming necessary to smuggle yanqui dollars back here."

Young Gaitan Palacios rarely added anything new to the strategy of a meeting, but could be expected to second his father. He proved it with, "There is nothing as acceptable to a Mexican diplomat as American cash, brother Bermudez. Without a million a week, we cannot even meet those overhead expenses.''

''Yes; well, this harvest will not help much,'' Bermudez sighed.

Vega: ''We understand; do not concern yourself. *How much?*''

Bermudez, as if the low figure were his own fault: ''This year we may harvest an area of some five hundred caballerias.''

''A local measure. I have no idea what that is,'' muttered old Palacios.

''Momentito,'' said his son, producing a calculator. At this sort of trivia, Gaitan excelled. After letting his fingers twinkle among the keys, he said, ''Roughly twenty-two thousand hectares, two hundred and twenty-five square kilometers.'' Then he realized what he had said, and raised his brows, punching keys again. ''Only about fifty metric tons,'' he added, frowning. ''My God, even if we process the stuff ourselves and ship pure cocaine instead of paste, we will be lucky to clear a billion dollars for the entire year.''

Torres, watching the frowns and nods, knew as well as the others that this was a fraction of the profit they had grown used to. But now and again, he would hear such phrases with the ears of a slum child and would be struck, as now, by the absurdity of the numbers. *A billion here, a billion there. It all adds up*, smiling. *I am not greedy; for me, one billion is the magic number.*

Billy Borges let a faint, yanqui-style whistle escape his lips. ''These will be hard times,'' he said.

Vega slapped the arm of his chair with finality. ''We have all agreed on that, brothers. The tunnels into Arizona and New Mexico are lost to us since the yanquis began using seismic devices, but the Nevada cash reserve is just over one billion dollars. It must be brought through for payoffs, and soon,'' said the old man. ''We have reason to believe that none of our tunnels will remain secure. Brother Gaitan, how much did you say the Nevada load weighed?''

''Assuming it is all fifties and hundreds,'' Gaitan said, ''it should weigh around fifteen tons.'' Borges, who had stored the money, nodded. Gaitan added, "That much cash takes up a lot of room, too. I still wonder whether flying it out is practical."

"Of course it is," Torres put in, defending the scenario he had promoted among his intimates weeks before. "I could name a dozen kinds of old aircraft, most of them propeller-driven, that will do the job—and fly scores of passengers to Base Ana at the same time." He paused for effect. "Those passengers are the best possible insurance against our being stopped, once the aircraft is in the air."

"And fifty stupid middle-aged yanquis," Vega said dreamily, "can be kept blindfolded at Base Ana for a day or so before we release them. This will give us new respect."

"I thought they were to be ransomed," said Bermudez.

"That is what the yanquis will fear," the elder Palacios said, waving a lazy hand. "But borrowing a tactic from a gentleman named Arafat, we will claim that a revolutionary splinter group took those hostages. Of course, we have a certain influence with such groups so we become the brokers. After brief negotiations with the American government, we take the hostages from Base Ana by night, release them far away, and gain great credibility as men to be treated with diplomacy in future matters. The yanqui negotiators preen themselves, we gain legitimacy—and Brother Torres will have used those hostages for safe passage. Of course, it may be necessary to kill a hostage or so, at the outset."

Obviously, Torres thought, this pair of old men had been talking the scenario over, and had become even more firm in their resolve. *So much the better. I wonder if it has occurred to them that I might simply land the plane somewhere else than Base Ana and disappear with one billion yanqui dollars. Perhaps keep a few hostages for insurance. I will need extra hands, but Elath is my man. And if the sight of those bales of money makes my man difficult, that is what small-caliber Walthers are for.* To Borges he said, "Have your people located any suitable aircraft for us? I will need to check it out myself, and of course you must hire an entire crew with impeccable records. Pilot, copilot, flight engineer—"

"But," young Gaitan burst out, "I thought you intended to fly it yourself!"

The father placed a hand on the son's arm. "Patience, and guile," he cautioned. "The Americans do not allow just anyone to fly passengers out of their country, even innocent jaunts for real estate development in Mexico. The trick is to hire crew members who do not know one another, and to substitute our people during the flight. As for the real crew, well," he spread his hands eloquently, then made a dramatic thumbs-down gesture.

"In fact, we do not even need a very experienced copilot," Torres said, "so long as the man is one of ours. The flight stewards should be no problem; male attendants are quite common. As it happens, a young lady of my acquaintance was a flight attendant. She tells me she will be happy to tutor a few of our people, given the right inducement. She lives through her nose, these days."

"Not too dear a friend, I trust," said Vega.

"Not that dear," Torres agreed. It went without saying that the young woman would not outlive her usefulness. Among these Colombians, temporary employees were like matches to be lit for some brief use and then tossed aside. When the stakes were high, they were simply snuffed out, particularly if they had the sort of frantic cocaine addiction known to these men as "living through one's nose."

"I have a reputable firm," said Billy Borges, "searching for a suitable aircraft."

"Where are they based?" Vega injected.

"Los Angeles. Does it matter?"

Vega smiled. "No, so long as it is not Nevada. Our friends who run that state have far too much curiosity about our business. Our money is in Las Vegas, so the flight will begin there, but it must not leave any traces back to us."

Borges shrugged and replied, "My cover in Los Angeles is Mexican, and I have leased some cheap land between Puerto Vallarta and La Gloria just in case anyone thinks to check. I have even hired a Mexican contractor to scrape a few foundation sites and build a cabaña. The Los Angeles firm is preparing brochures and advertising. I will bring the drafts for cartel approval, naturally. But this,'' he added, pulling a folded sheet of paper from his coat, ''they have provided already.'' He handed the sheet to Torres.

The paper was expensive, with no capital letters in the embossed letterhead of ''management internationale'' but with a list of branch offices stretching across the top, intended to impress. Torres skimmed the first few lines to focus on the brief list of aircraft suitable for flying fifty passengers nonstop from Vancouver in Canada to Puerto Vallarta. He glanced up at Borges. ''From Canada?''

''There are many rich Chinese in Vancouver now, so the idea is plausible. But that was merely to make certain it has the range,'' Borges replied smugly. ''The flight begins in Las Vegas, but it will end a thousand miles beyond Puerto Vallarta.''

''Excellent,'' said Torres, inwardly burning with shame because he, a pilot, had missed such an obvious point. ''After we lease the aircraft, you can advise the firm of the change in plan.''

''Exactly. The reason I have no brochure draft now is that there is no point in showing you what management internationale has dreamed up for Chinese immigrants in Vancouver,'' said Borges. ''But we must buy the airliner, not lease it. There are fewer paper hurdles in the outright purchase of these airplanes than in leasing them.''

''Yes. My compliments, brother Borges,'' said Torres, his primary attention now on the list. ''Curtiss C-46? The consultant is an idiot,'' he said with a sudden headshake, and drew a slender gold pencil from his shirt. It was not declassé to carry anything clipped to a pocket if that thing was twenty-two-karat gold.

''Favor us, brother Torres,'' said Palacios gently.

Scribbling as he went, Torres said, ''The Curtiss has fair range but is dead slow and fifty years old. Most of those still flying have been used to transport cheap cargoes from time to time. It probably smells of batshit or Alaska salmon. No junketeering yanqui would willingly climb into such a thing today, even for a free flight to Mexico.''

He fell silent, then gave another headshake. ''The Boeing is nice and fast, and also has range, but the damned thing would sink right through our runway surface at Base Ana; it weighs well over a hundred metric tons. A-a-agh, and this Convair does not have half the range we need.''

''Our consultants probably imagine that we would not mind refueling en route,'' Borges murmured. ''I can hardly tell them otherwise.''

''No problem; I see a couple that might serve. The Bristol Britannia is not too heavy for the runways of Base Ana, with good range and decent speed. The same is true for the Douglas DC-7.'' Torres made deft ellipses around the two listings and passed the sheet back to Borges. ''Either of those would do. I have some familiarity with the Douglas cockpit layout, so naturally I favor it,'' he said. ''The other aircraft is British; I understand it was one of the last big liners before the jets. Still—I recommend the Douglas. The prices are modest, I notice, and they should be for aircraft this old. The noise inside will be tiresome after a time, but our passengers will be in no position to complain.''

Vega and the elder Palacios traded glances. Palacios essayed a tentative throat-clearing. ''One thing, brother Torres: You are, ah, confident that you could fly these things?''

Because of the flash of anger he felt, Torres donated a smile. ''In Colombian service I flew many an ancient bucket, some with four reciprocating engines, some with two. Some with three masquerading as four,'' he added, broadening the smile for effect.

Borges beamed with self-satisfaction and patted the pocket containing that folded sheet. ''I will see to the purchase. God knows I have enough cash on hand in the States, and I can do that as soon as I follow the Nogales shipment next week. Our first load went through without a problem, but the reprocessing in Tucson is expensive.''

''I am having a second reprocessing station built in Bakersfield, California, nearer to our major wholesalers,''

Vega remarked. "But sooner or later, my experts tell me, the damned drug enforcers will stumble on our latest ploys. We are considering certain Mexican foodstuffs as—"

The cry was filtered through distance and heavy walls, but all of them heard it, sharp and male and full of fury. Bermudez, for all his girth, was first to rise.

"Let trouble come to you, brother," said Vega, fingering the heavy amulet that hung from its golden chain on his neck. The double doors opened instantly. *The old devil has a radio beeper in that thing*, Torres realized.

One of Vega's guards stood in the doorway, a machine pistol drawn but pointing toward his feet. "Patron: at your orders," he pronounced the old Spanish ritual. Torres could see past the man where his fellow stared over the balustrade into the courtyard. The second guard was shouting, gesturing with his own machine pistol, his echoes and those of returning shouts a cacophony in which Torres could understand only one thing: One of those voices belonged to David Elath. *He knows better than to start a fight in this place*, Torres thought furiously, keeping his face full of polite interest.

Without raising his voice, Vega said, "Are we in danger?"

One of the guards at the door: "No, patron. A scuffle between two fools below."

Vega held up a hand, gently, almost lazily. "Tell them that the next one who moves or speaks without permission, you will silence him permanently." Then, as the guard relayed his command, he turned to the others and stood. "This probably concerns more than one of us, brothers. Let us see to our people."

Torres filed out last, already feeling a fool because, whatever Elath had done, he was Torres's responsibility. Lining the balustrade, the cartel lords gazed down to where two men stood, hands aloft, under threat of the guard's weapon.

Yes, Elath is one of them, he realized, feeling like a street urchin caught with stolen candy. *But what is that on his sleeve?* He knew instantly, of course; David Elath's raised left arm dripped crimson onto the flagstones from the bend at his elbow. Bloodied on his forearm but casual about it to the point of indifference, Elath looked up at them as a gladiator might have looked up at Caligula.

Elath's opponent, tall and gaunt, showed his teeth and glared at Elath, his chest heaving. Torres had seen him at the side of Bermudez but did not recall his name; a man of the country, however. A Peruvian, well liked by the senderistas.

Beside him, Max Vega said softly, "Your Jew, I believe."

"Yes. He would never," Torres began.

"His name?"

"Elath." At moments such as this, Simon Torres knew better than to insist on full equality; certainly not on Vega's own turf.

"The other I know," Vega said, then called down: "Madero, explain yourself."

"This whoreson, this foreign bastard, he thinks he can give me orders, I do not take orders from—" and Madero lapsed into a masterful string of Peruvian gutter argot, the fingers of his raised hands clutching as though Elath's throat were between them. Whatever he had used on Elath, his hands were empty now.

When Vega held up a restraining hand and Madero did not instantly fall silent, the old man nodded at the guard, who took deliberate aim. Madero's vituperation stopped as suddenly as if someone had cut his head off. Vega's hand restrained that of the guard as he called, "Elath. Explain yourself."

David Elath gazed upward. "The gentleman told me I had used my dirty foreign fingers on the buffet cold cuts. I apologized, and suggested to the gentleman that he might want to drink a few cups of coffee, and he drew his knife."

"You lying piece of pigshit, you gave me a filthy order," Madero screamed, the words running together.

"A suggestion."

"And why would you suggest that, Señor Elath?"

"Because," said Elath, smiling, "the gentleman is drunk."

At this, something in the Peruvian snapped. Bermudez

swore as he saw his man's hand swoop past his trousers, magically becoming a hand full of switchblade. "Stop, Madero," Bermudez cried.

The gaunt Madero did restrain himself, quivering with the effort, Elath still two paces away and still with upraised arms. "I really prefer not to discipline your man, brother Bermudez," Vega remarked softly. "But discipline is needed."

Young Gaitan Palacios snickered. "Let them discipline one another," he said.

Bermudez, perhaps because his man had already drawn first blood, shrugged. "I am amenable."

Torres hesitated for only a beat. Elath seemed the innocent party, certainly the injured one, but that was not important. The important thing was that Torres himself must not show weakness; and Elath was representing him. There was another consideration too: If Elath could not handle this drunken Madero, he was not the man Torres wanted. In a voice firm with command, the ex-colonel called, "David, you may take him."

Before Vega could order his guards to put away their guns, Elath was in motion, a backward shoulder roll that left a long smear of his blood on flagstones. Bermudez urged his man Madero to the attack, young Palacios jostling his elders as he edged closer to the balustrade to watch, mouth agape with fascination. _Little shit has probably never seen a knife fight,_ Torres thought. _Perez Palacios has raised a palo blanco of a son._

Madero advanced in a half-crouch, both arms bent and below his own eye level, left hand making slow circles, open for grasping, while the right hand waved that gleaming blade gently back and forth. A man unfamiliar with the tactic might not know what to focus on, and Madero would know by the darting of his opponent's eyes.

Elath did not seem his usual confident self and, slapping that open hand of Madero's aside, very nearly took a second slash on his own glistening left arm. Backing toward one of the small tables set among the flagstones, not taking his eyes from Madero, Elath kept that bloody left arm out, a defective shield for his softer parts, and groped behind him with his right. When Madero feinted, then lunged, Elath's backward leap brought him to the table where he whisked the fine linen tablecloth away, wrapping the cloth quickly around his injured forearm. *Finally did something right. What's wrong with him tonight?* The classic defensive move was to wrap one's jacket around the shield forearm. A blade might penetrate, but not always deeply, and by a quick flick of that arm while the blade was in the cloth, many a stiletto had snapped at the hilt.

But Elath's cloth bundle was a loose one. Madero knew that it was a poor shield, and sliced a tatter from it as Elath parried, still giving ground across those flagstones. The next moves flashed into play so fast that Torres almost missed them.

Madero moved a half-pace forward but jerked back as Elath's right arm swept up past his own hip pocket, emerging as a fist, and then Madero was fighting to regain his balance with a rocking motion on the flagstones, as if he had lost his equilibrium. Elath flung the roll of tattered linen into the Peruvian's face as Madero stumbled again. A harmless missile in itself, the tablecloth blinded Madero while Elath flung himself forward, feet first, left instep snugged behind Madero's right achilles tendon as the heel of his right boot crashed just below the knee of Madero's leg. The impact was almost silent but the sickening crunch of a ruined knee joint, locked and forced past locking, was audible to the balcony.

Madero managed to strangle most of his own scream, spinning away on his good leg, Elath rolling away and up aided by the pistoning of his arms. Torres knew that a well-balanced fighting knife need not be thrown by its tip if the combatants are close enough, and Madero was already falling as he hurled the switchblade, but Elath had already snaked his good arm out to snatch a heavy armchair knocked askew by the fight. Someone gasped, perhaps at the ease with which the burly Elath could lift and swing a fifty-pound carved oak chair.

The switchblade did not stick, but clattered off across flagstones as Elath swung the chair up, Madero sobbing in pain and rage as he covered his head, face on a flagstone, and then the chair came down, gently, without touching the fallen Peruvian. Elath placed his right boot exactly between Madero's shoulders and reached into the boot top, flicking his own small sheath knife into view for the first time. Kneeling with much of his weight on the defeated Madero, Elath reached a hand into the man's thick mop of hair, lifted his head, placed his blade tip just beneath Madero's jaw, glanced up toward the balcony, then withdrew the knife and drove Madero's face against the stone with all his shoulder behind it.

Madero had not cried for mercy, and he was incapable of asking now as he rolled onto his side. David Elath thrust his knife back into its boot sheath and stood up, backing away from Madero. His voice was unhurried, almost calm, as he called up: "A good fighter, but not so good when he is drunk and on uneven footing."

Vega called for a mozo to carry away the unconscious man and another to care for the victor's arm. As the cartel lords filed back into the great hall, fat Bermudez muttered briefly to Torres, who nodded and went on to reclaim his chair.

The younger Palacios mopped his face with a silken sleeve. Voice shaking with adrenaline, he said, "Brother Torres, your Jew had good luck."

"The Jew has patience and guile," his father corrected sternly, with a nod toward Torres that contained a sort of benediction. Vega then called for coca tea, a mild nonaddictive brew traditional in Colombia, perhaps thinking they could all use its mild settling effect. Torres sipped the warm stuff, enjoying its familiar spinachlike odor, and managed to keep half of his mind on the business at hand. With the other half, he thought how his plans might have bled away with Elath, and how important it was that his man stay alive for—it was now discussed in the great hall as if it bore capital letters—the Big Shipment.

LATER, THE DISCUSSION ended, Torres called for his weapons and then his car. He found Elath in the villa's huge kitchen, entertaining a pair of servants while he consumed sweet flan and coffee, wearing the same shirt that had been cut and bloody scarcely more than an hour before. "Can't complain about the service," Elath joked, leaving the place as jauntily as he had arrived, his shirt freshly washed, ironed, and mended.

Once in the black Mangusta Elath became more subdued, mostly responding to Torres only in monosyllables as the car rushed around the lake toward Torres's own villa in the heights, modest only in proportion to Vega's. Finally: "Tell me, David; was Madero really drunk?"

"No. But he had whiskey on his breath, and he was an offensive fool."

"Did you actually apologize as you said?"

"Yes, but it did not stop there, and he surprised me. I had noticed a flagstone that tipped a bit; I was suckering him toward it when he began to shout, and that brought us all the attention." Elath raised the bandaged forearm in a gesture of apology. "I wanted to take him quietly without my own knife because I had no intention of getting into a real brawl in such a place as Vega's."

"You were right about that. A tippy flagstone, eh? And all that clumsiness of yours was just to get him placed where you could level him with a tablecloth! You honored me, David. But if you were going to cripple Bermudez's man, you should have killed him."

Torres swung left into the throat of his own driveway, then stopped by the trunk of a huge palm and spoke as if identifying himself to the night itself. That intercom was known to few and, Torres felt, was a nice high-tech touch. He moved ahead more slowly.

"I would have made you an enemy of that senderista commander, Bermudez."

"Won't you ever understand, friend David? A man with a bad knee is useless as a bodyguard, and Madero had no special use beyond that. Bermudez complained to me that now he will have to see to Madero himself."

Almost laughing: "He wanted me to save him the trouble?"

"Call it that," Torres said, as his automatic gate swung open in the light of his high beams. "He does not relish the retirement of a good man. We South Americans are passionate people, David. You certainly made poor Madero lose his head, whatever you said to him."

"Poor Madero? Poor Madero warned me that I had fouled a good buffet with my dirty Jew fingers."

Torres stopped the Mangusta, turned off the ignition. "And?" He prompted.

"And I made a suggestion. I suggested if he did not like the taste of my fingers, I could pull his dirty Medellinista thumb out of his arse and suck on that. Perhaps he took it as an order," Elath finished, levering his door open.

"Now I understand," Torres replied, getting out with a wave toward the dim figures of his own men nearby, laughing at his discovery. "Madero is not from Medellin, he is a Peruvian. Perhaps I should say, *was* a Peruvian. I think, David, you got two insults for the price of one."

"I will never understand you people," Elath said.

Still laughing, Torres flung an arm about his friend's big shoulder. "Just understand this: You were my surrogate tonight, and you did me honor. Soon it may be my turn to do you honor."

"You honor me enough," said Elath, in apparent discomfort.

"Not as much as I could. I have not yet placed my life in your hands," Torres said.

TEN

Monday, May 1

At KINGSVILLE NAS, near the Texas gulf coast, the Nemesis ready room was deserted except for the two men. "Look, are you sure you want to do this? I'm not trying to tell you your business, Dr. Sheppard, but—"

"I'm certain, Mr. Hardin." Bill Sheppard, in a flight suit, knew that he did not seem the most prepossessing of men, but he had not risen to the upper echelons of the NSA through cowardice. "Now that I've been fully briefed, I want the feel of a Nemesis mission."

"What happened to that Aldrich guy? Not that I'm complaining," Hardin added quickly.

"He's still in the loop, but certain, ah, new facts have come to light, and a decision-level man may be needed as a comm-and-control link if—well, let's just say in case a lot of U. S. citizens are ever at risk. Fewer delays in the system, you see. The truth is," he said with a guilty smile, "I volunteered. I like the work. Believe me, Mal Aldrich was happy with the charge."

"You're saying this operation has suddenly developed a higher priority?"

"If you like," Sheppard replied. "And I needed a civilian pilot, and you were elected."

"Didn't win any Brownie points with my boss," Was Hardin said with a rueful headshake.

"When was Ben Ullmer ever happy?"

"Why, when he's pissed off," Hardin replied as if a child of five could have answered that one. He added, chuckling, "Which is most of the time. My grampa used to say a man like Ullmer is very even-tempered: mad all the time."

"Then," said Sheppard puckishly, "I must have made him very happy."

"Tell him that," Hardin laughed, checking the swivel of his helmet faceplate. "And run for cover. That ol' boy is independent as a bull in clover. But you know, I think he likes you. If he didn't, I'd have had a helluva time breaking my schedule for something you won't even tell me about beforehand. Speaking of which—" he let the sentence trail off, leaving his question unspoken.

"You were a good officer as well as a good pilot, according to your records, and you know how to deal sensibly with security matters. I promise you this: You'll understand quite a bit more in a few hours." Sheppard swung his own borrowed helmet under his arm and gazed through glass panes of the ready room below a sign proclaiming the room to be part of the Eighth Coast Guard District, though the base itself was a naval air station near Kingsville, Texas. Spook 2, the second of the Nemesis craft to have a Coast Guard shield painted below her cockpit, rocked gently in the hangar as a sneaker-clad mechanic secured a fuel filler cap and stepped onto a servicing ladder.

As if to himself, Sheppard went on: "I've flown in a U-2 and a Blackbird, and I never got to try a Hellbug, but by God, before they turn me out to pasture I intend to experience a Nemesis. You want the truth? I think every

ranking official should get hands-on experience in these vehicles before he makes national commitments with them.''

Wes Hardin, similarly clad in a form-fitting flight suit
that was almost a Day-Glo orange, checked a wrist chronograph two generations newer than Ullmer's. ''Well, you've
got the clout, sir. But this is a Coastie airplane now, and
you must have a reason for flying me here to Kingsville
instead of having a Coast Guard pilot take you up.''

''We have an excellent reason. I'll let you in on it when
we're on-station. Isn't it time?''

Hardin nodded and led the older man from the ready
room to the hangar, where South Texas coastal humidity
enveloped them like a warm, cloying, almost visible mist.
Here, Hardin's voice echoed as he spoke. ''You don't use
the hand and foot accesses up to the cockpit unless you
have to. Just follow me onto the ladder and do exactly
what I do. Remember, this is a tender beast.''

Sheppard astonished himself with gooseflesh in such
heat, the physical thrill of climbing into an advanced aircraft a treat he had almost forgotten at Fort Meade. As
Hardin mounted the ladder, more properly a wheeled platform painted buttercup yellow with expanded metal steps,
Sheppard noticed the pilot's footwear. *Even our boots say
"Hi-Tec." They sure don't weigh what hiking boots used
to.* He did not need to ask why pilots wore hiking boots;
he had seen high-speed films of men during parachute de-
ployment, and knew that ordinary shoes tended to fly off
during that godawful jerk as the canopy opened. Shoes,
false teeth, even wristwatches could be stripped away, lost
forever. And one might walk many a mile without teeth
or timepieces, but not too well without shoes.

It suddenly occurred to Bill Sheppard that the research
into these matters should make crews in military aircraft
feel safer, not more endangered. At least the military cared
enough to give the flier every chance *after* worse came to
worst. The builders and owners of commercial airliners
did not even care enough to anchor seats to sustain 30-G
crash loads, which were survivable if the seat stayed put,

or to replace the kind of cushions that generated poisonous gases while smoldering. In most respects, he recalled, designers of cheap automobiles do a better job of crash safety than commercial aircraft designers do.

Hardin, his hands now in brown unlined gloves of the finest, thinnest leather, made a show of placing his hands on the cockpit sill, his feet on a narrow yellow-painted area at the root of the little canard wing. Spook 2 nodded in a be-my-guest motion under his weight. Beyond that narrow area, the entire upper surface of Spook 2 gleamed the deep sinister blue of solar cells. Sheppard aped every move with care, noting how easily Wes Hardin could swing a leg over that cockpit sill when a man twenty years older had to work to keep from kicking that tender plastic hide as he stepped on.

His seat was like a couch, Sheppard found as he snugged into its embrace. Hardin swiveled, looked his passenger over head to toe, then showed him the harness drill. Only the submarine strap, which passed between one's legs to lock into the single-point release mechanism at his beltline, gave Sheppard any trouble. In crashes on takeoff or landing, pilots without those extra straps had been found huddled in broken bundles, tangled among foot pedals, the deceleration submarining them from under their seat and shoulder harnesses.

At Hardin's word, Sheppard found the handhold that pulled the canopy down. No extraneous motorized systems here; anything a small well-conditioned pilot could do was one less system to weigh down a Nemesis vehicle. Sheppard imitated Hardin's motions in hooking up his suit connections.

In his helmet, Hardin's voice, filtered slightly: "Try your pressure demand oxy now, sir. If you can inhale easily and it feels cool, you're set. Actually, you won't need it unless the cabin pressure fails."

Sheppard, closing his domelike faceplate, did as he was told and nodded, then remembered the intercom. "Feels good."

He found that the faceplate made him feel slightly claustrophobic, and levered it up again as Hardin had done. The pilot was flicking switches, tapping dials as pilots had done for generations, though Sheppard smiled to see it done here. Most of these dials were solid-state, and would not respond to any amount of tapping. *It's force of habit, but he'd claim it was for luck. Hardin's nearly forty; he didn't learn to fly with solid-states*, Sheppard reminded himself.

The wheel chocks were piled far to one side in full view and Hardin thanked his plane captain, an enlisted man's title Sheppard knew better by the air force term "crew chief." The first movement by the entire aircraft was startling only because Sheppard could clearly see that the tachometer in front of him read zero revolutions, and the wingtip walkers did not seem to be pushing all that hard. He saw that they were *not* pushing hard, but evidently did not need to. If a pair of healthy ground crew members could push a small car across a flat surface, they could push a similar weight that just happened to have ninety feet of wing on it.

Moving into the sunshine, the upper surfaces of Spook 2 glistened with purpose, and Sheppard could see the big hangar doors sliding shut before Spook 2 had rolled a hundred feet outside. Hardin used up her forward inertia by braking the left main gear. The right wing swung obediently around before he applied full braking, the great glistening bullet of Spook 2's nose now pointed toward the taxi strip. The plane captain cleared the pilot and Hardin began a ballet with his hands. His use of those controls reminded Sheppard of his oldest daughter answering the challenge of Liszt at a Bosendorfer piano: quick, graceful, unhesitating. *I'm beginning to see why they all give this little aw-shucks Texan such respect,* he decided. *All but that vest-pocket Venus at Aerosystems.*

When the shrouded rotary engine behind them started up, Sheppard felt the shudder and buzz through his back, scarcely at all on his rump because he was sitting on his emergency chute pack. He needed a moment to realize what bothered him: the odor. This kind of vibration was typical for a light aircraft during its startup, but because most of them had forward-mounted engines, the passenger usually smelled avgas fumes at such moments. In this creature of filament and superplastics, the engine was behind them and he detected only a faint residue of polymers, a scent reminiscent of leather.

The view, with the bulge of canopy swooping down to waist level, was excellent if you discounted the curve of canard wings that began just behind the seat backs. Hardin got eye contact with both of the ground crew, one a woman, who remained at the wingtips. His primary gaze, however, was for the plane captain who stood ahead and to their left, holding up a set of red canvas ribbons, each displayed separately for Hardin's view, each with a metal pin hanging from one end. As long as those pins were installed in the aircraft, the landing gear could not be accidentally retracted. Because all of the ground crew members wore minitel wireless mikes and headsets, the visual cues were redundant—but with redundancy came safety, and Sheppard appreciated that. The most peculiar facet of preflight checks was what Hardin did not do. No checks of flaps and ailerons for the spookship, because she had none. That mission-adaptive wing flexed as if muscles lay beneath its surface, every flexure meaningful but far more subtle than the whines and clicks of other aircraft. Sheppard grinned as he felt the hackles rise along his arms; he felt as if he were flying inside a live animal.

Hardin spoke with the tower operator, his drawl as unforced as that of Yeager, the man who made pilot drawls famous. Meanwhile the vibration of the engine faded as the tachometer reading climbed, Hardin checking his controls again before he began to taxi with a quick salute toward his ground crew.

Though Sheppard had once felt the pile-driver-in-the-backside surge of an SR-71, he expected this gossamer craft to accelerate gently. He revised his expectation as

300 horses sucked air through that prop shroud, the Nemesis careening toward the ends of the parallel runways of Kingsville NAS, and with all clearances in order, Hardin did not stop before making his quick turn onto the long ribbon with its hundreds of black streaks signaling touchdown by many an aircraft. With carrier landings in their repertoire, naval aviators sometimes touched down within yards of the Texas plain.

In Sheppard's helmet, that familiar drawl: "Maybe you can see the airfoil fattening in your rearview, Dr. Sheppard. You wanted to see that."

Though the rearview was jiggling a bit, Sheppard spotted a faint swelling along the upper surface of the wing that shifted to a subtly new contour and kept it. Though he could not see the underside, he correctly assumed it would be swelling more, with a gentle reverse curve toward the rear that aerodynamicists called undercamber. A hopeless drawback at high speeds, undercamber gave a tremendous improvement to lift at trifling speeds. And then Bill Sheppard laughed aloud, for he saw the runway dropping away, though they seemed to be moving no faster than a man could run. Hardin was not too busy to add, "This is a pretty smart beast; she'll fluff her airfoils automatically. You have to override her decisions if you want to do something abrupt, like a dive from high altitude or a Pougachev Cobra maneuver."

The airspeed indicator was reading forty knots, faster than a running pace but not all that much faster, their velocity rising as Sheppard watched. The separate thunks of retracted landing gear were validated by console lights, and now they were rising faster, the bullet nose of the Nemesis aiming higher, nearby buildings and the arm of the nearby salt bay growing smaller.

"Sharp left bank coming up," Hardin warned as they floated upward, now over the narrow bay with a thousand feet of air beneath them, and Sheppard felt that almost forgotten instant of panic as the left wing dipped in a steep bank. What might seem a gentle tilt to an outside observer became a slow, timeless, and dreamlike handstand to the passenger, the left-hand horizon tilting steeply upward, then gradually returning to the horizontal where, Sheppard's instinct told him, all good horizons should stay.

"Coasties don't fly spookships in or out of here much in daylight; too many curious airplane buffs might spot 'em," Hardin explained. "So we're climbing out over the bay. A Nemesis is so quiet with that shrouded prop, she doesn't announce herself. They'd have to be looking for us."

Sheppard estimated that their climb rate was at least 2000 feet per minute, a very respectable figure for such an ultralight brute. Presently they skimmed through wisps of cloud, emerging in sight of the Gulf of Mexico with an apparently endless strip of barrier island below them, the protected coastal waterway traversed by cargo barges that seemed frozen in place but for their wakes. Spook 2's airspeed was now over 100 knots but as they climbed ever higher, the sensation of speed diminished, the shrouded prop only a muted whirr. Bit by bit in impressive quiet, Sheppard felt himself joyfully freed from the planet, suspended in time and space, the earth becoming no more than a highly detailed map that slid inexorably past, far below. *And they pay people to do this*, he said to himself. *No, they get paid for what we'll be doing shortly. It can't be enough.*

The altimeter showed nearly 30,000 feet when Hardin urged Spook 2 into a gentle bank to the right, still climbing but now not as rapidly. He said, "Going to the electrics and max pitch setting. The prop needs more bite from here on up," and twisted a knob between the seats, then flicked an innocent-looking switch near the knob. As the propeller blades steepened their angle to the wind, Sheppard felt a faint new sensation of forward thrust; with the blades acting as rotor, and magnets in the shroud as stator elements, sixty more horsepower kicked in. Unlike the gasoline engine, this motor would not progressively starve for air as it climbed toward a region so high, with air pressure so faint, that the very blood in an unprotected human body would begin to vaporize. *It doesn't have to be hot for your blood to boil up here,* thought Bill Sheppard. *Thank God for pressurized cabins.* He gazed down at thousands of square miles of blue Mexican gulf and laughed again in sheer high spirits.

Presently, Hardin broke the silence again. "I'm on the one-seventy true heading you wanted, but you'd best break out a nav chart from that pocket at your right knee and advise me, Dr. Sheppard. Otherwise, in an hour or so we'll be over Mexican soil."

"Would you mind first names? Formality seems silly and pointless up here, Wesley. I'm Bill."

"Fine, but call me Wes."

"Right. And in an hour or so, I expect we *will* be over Mexican soil."

"No we won't," said Hardin firmly. "I may be a civilian, but if I got nailed for that in this airplane the FAA would jerk every license I've got right down to my Visa card."

"No they won't," Sheppard said just as firmly. "For one thing, I happen to know Mexican radar won't pick up a Nemesis. And the FAA is not a higher authority than mine, not today anyway."

"Shit," said Hardin. "I don't like this one bit, Dr.— Bill. Listen, my mother's people live in Oaxaca; yeah, she was born Mexicana," he said into Sheppard's quizzical glance. "You have no idea how many idiots there are who think you can't celebrate both the Fourth of July and el Cinco de Mayo."

Sheppard thought the pilot's command of Spanish was startlingly natural, and said so. For the next half-hour he drew Hardin out on his background; not the stuff he had already read, but a Hardin's-eye view of growing up near Abilene, Texas.

Evidently the place was a very big town keeping some small-town ways, a hundred thousand people gathered on the prairie for every sort of commerce, from aircraft parts to cattle and cottonseed oil. If your father farmed a half-section you grew up around machinery, and if you rode the bus to Cooper High School you tended to make alliances with other farm kids. It was a social problem if your mother was Oaxaqueña, no matter that she was a gorgeous creature from a good family. The name Wes Hardin was both an advantage and a goad, the legacy of a distant kinsman who was, by all accounts, the most deadly gunfighter who ever lived back before the turn of the century. Boys who liked young Wes treated him with foolish deference. Those who didn't, including the bigots, considered that name a challenge. It was easy to lean on a kid of Wes's small size; that is, until he learned to use his quickness— perhaps a piece of that genetic legacy, certainly a help in sports. Absolutely, Wes chuckled in telling it, a good way to lose some teeth because it taught that you didn't have to take bullying. But if you responded to it with a whirlwind counterattack, now and then you got nailed by one slow punch. Ultimately, he said, you learned to pick your time and place, and you never forgot a deceptive move.

By and large, however, Abilene seemed a good place to grow up: roomy, up-tempo, with a zoo, several good colleges, and an excellent civic center, to which he was always being dragged by his parents for some cultural function or other. "Real culture vultures, my folks," as Wes put it. "It took, I guess. My tape library is full of Gershwin and Rachmaninoff. No Willie Nelson or Richie Valens." Hardly the stereotype of the clodhopping dirt farmer Sheppard had first envisioned. But throughout his childhood, nearby Dyess Air Force Base never let Wes forget aircraft as long as B-52s came thundering over southwest of town, not many miles from the Hardin spread.

"You know why I picked the navy?" Hardin laughed again as he recalled it. "Two bozos I didn't like were service brats of Dyess blue-suiters, and I reckon I just figured any bunch responsible for them wasn't good enough for me. The navy didn't exactly dissuade me from that opinion," he finished with a wink.

By the time they reached 52,000 feet, Hardin had Spook 2 cruising at well over 400 knots with a brief, downsloping spurt to demonstrate that a Nemesis could go much faster, crowding the Machmeter's ''never exceed'' line while the airfoil shape flattened until Sheppard could see very little camber in it. With the main engine shut down, Spook 2 continued to climb with agonizing slowness, back up past 52,000, then almost to 55,000. ''This is roughly our ceiling today,'' Hardin acknowledged. ''It varies quite a bit depending on local conditions. By the way,'' he finished, pointing beyond the console above their feet, ''Mexico's dead ahead on the horizon—in fact, it's also over on your right. Veracruz must be over there, 'bout two hundred miles, right on the gulf coast.''

''Stay on this heading. Wes, do you know what's happening down there now?''

''Well, my mother keeps in touch by letters. They're worried down there, because their politicians are getting whipsawed between us and Mexican pride. They'd be touchy as hell if an obvious spy plane were caught south of the border.''

''I agree about the touchiness, but if you had engine trouble in the isthmus region we could glide all the way back to international waters in the gulf. And don't tell me about the handful of F-5s we sold to Mexico. I also happen to know they're on maneuvers somewhere else today.''

Hardin turned a calculating gaze on his companion. ''You guys gave a lot of thought to this,'' he accused.

''It's our charter,'' Sheppard said wryly. ''But what do you think keeps pricking Mexican national pride?''

''Machismo,'' Hardin said.

''Mexican media,'' Sheppard corrected. ''And by the oddest coincidence, a lot of Mexican dailies and TV stations are at least partly owned by a few very, very rich men.''

''What else is new,'' Hardin said.

''The fact that some are connected with Colombian drug kings.''

"Oh, JEEzus!" It was almost a cry of pain.

"Explains a lot, doesn't it," Sheppard asked.

"Starting to. You telling me that has something to do with us on a bearing of one-seven-oh?"

"It has everything to do with it, Wes. It's time to tell you a story, which you are to treat as Q-clearance stuff because it's true, and then I'll make a pitch to you, and even if you turn it down it's still black. You don't even talk to Coast Guard pilots about it. Fair enough?"

"Crap like this is never fair, but you have my word," Hardin said grudgingly.

"Good. Now let's swing over twenty miles or so off-shore from Veracruz, down the coast seventy miles or so to the Tuxtla volcanoes. They're right on the coast."

Hardin urged the control stick gently, the Nemesis answering with a sluggish motion that involved big deflections of the canard surfaces near them. Then he said, "How come you know the terrain so well?"

"I have a trick memory. I studied some charts last night, and what I need is in labile memory. I'll have forgotten it in a week," Sheppard smiled shyly. He pointed toward the video monitor, easily the biggest instrument in the console, which had been faithfully plotting their course with false-color imagery. The scale of its map mode was so large that the monitor showed both the main body of Mexico and the curve of the Yucatan, their course a languidly flashing black line between them. "We helped develop some of your hardware, Wes; set its specs, anyway. Move the gain up and find, uh," he closed his eyes, culling what was behind them, "nineteen degrees north, ninety-six west."

As though expecting a ruse, Hardin did so. The display shifted until their own path moved offscreen, and very near the crossing of those cartographic lines lay the city of Veracruz. "Cute. What's there?"

"A mole. Not the rodent; a deep-cover agent. When the Sovs catch one, they've been known to trundle him into an incinerator while he was still alive. The Colombians aren't that nice. Is my point made?''

Hardin made a facial gesture of revulsion. ''Good God. He's got balls, huh?''

''Or ovaries. Might be a woman,'' Sheppard said, because others had decided he did not have the need to know that detail. ''State Department has this mole, who rarely surfaces, among the cartel lords. Those people were setting out to buy the entire country of Colombia until their political leaders, with some help from us, bit the bullet and declared war on their richest criminals. It was a Goddamned civil war for a while.''

''I read about it,'' Hardin agreed.

''Things started improving after we nailed Gacha and some others, and the good word in Colombia is, Escobar and most of the other big fish have gone. The bad word from southern Mexico is, that's where they've gone to. And the toughest groups of the Shining Path guerrillas from Peru went with them.''

Hardin frowned in disbelief. ''How the hell could they just—pick up and set down like that?''

''It's Latin America, home of the bribe.''

''Mordida,'' said Hardin, validating the idea with the common Spanish word for it. ''Bribe a whole country?''

''Let's see: population ninety million, say a year's income for the cartel people, ten billion or so, that's over a hundred dollars to every man, woman, and child in Mexico just to look the other way. Of course the honest majority would have another Mexican revolution brewing, so that's not how it works. Instead of trying to buy ninety million people, you only buy a few key people, and remind them how easy it is to kill them in case they decide not to stay bought.'' Sheppard gazed down to his right, back at the console display, then watched the majesty of Mexico once more.

Compelled by her canards, Spook 2 had made that peculiar crabwise maneuver again, sideslipping gently to a new heading that paralleled the coastline. The city of Veracruz sprawled below, from this vast height not a place of buildings and streets but a scar primarily gray against earth's green hide, with scrawls of smoke and glints of glass suggesting that the ants down there were more high tech than most.

"From what the mole says, we believe that the cartel people intend to literally buy and terrorize their way to power throughout the entire Mexican isthmus," Sheppard said.

As the port city slid past ten miles below, Hardin adjusted the console video, lining up his heading seaward of a jagged ring of peaks to the southeast. "Tuxtla volcanoes ahead. You can see 'em already; don't look like much from here."

"Supposed to be one of Mexico's best locations for the rich," Sheppard replied, "perfect for cartel kings who feel quite safe in the isthmus region. We gather that's why tourists have been getting the bum's rush there for several months, and our State Department advisories now reflect that. We don't *want* Americans there. Hardin, can you picture what it will mean if those bastards effectively rule the Mexican isthmus? They can grow and process cocoa on the mountain slopes."

"Come on, Chiapas is coffee country," Hardin objected.

"And coca, according to our experts. There's a wild man of sorts, a renegade American archaeologist who thinks he's Indiana Jones, who claims he got chased clear out of the country recently. It was his bad luck to blunder into coca plantings in Chiapas that, he says, were tended by Peruvians: Sendero Luminoso. He believes they wanted to kill him. I ask you again: What does it mean if a drug cartel takes over the isthmus?"

Hardin nodded toward the console display, first magnifying the false image to the point where tiled rooftops and winding drives showed through the verdant slopes above Catemaco. "It means those guys know how to live," he said. He intensified the display's magnification and moved a roller control to bring crosshairs onto an object that moved along a winding road, then ordered a lock-on before bringing the magnification to its greatest. "Looks like a Rolls Royce to me," he said, playing with the display. "Maybe a Bentley; hard to tell. Sure ain't no Chevy pickup. I guess it means they intend to stay."

"Think bigger," Sheppard urged. "It means they get a stranglehold on commerce here. Now unlock that image and lower the magnification but stay on this heading. Take us to—seventeen degrees thirty minutes north, ninety-two degrees fifty minutes west. Give or take a second," Sheppard said, making light of it.

Hardin sighed. "You're sure about those F-5s? They could just about reach us at this altitude."

"Don't trust me, trust your sweep radar," Sheppard shrugged. "And I told you, their radar won't pick up a plastic albatross like this one."

The display now became a map again, the curve of coastline disappearing behind as another coastline appeared near the edge of the screen. Peering through the canopy Sheppard saw, more than a hundred miles ahead and to their right, the vague seam that was the Pacific Ocean between tumbled mountain peaks and the horizon. Spook 2 was now in violation of treaty, directly over Mexican soil that Mexico could no longer control. Tortuous threads of river broadened to thick cords as they neared the gulf coast, and a drunken checkerboard of cultivated lowlands split the mountainous spine of Mexico at its narrowest part. Spook 2 continued in a line that would take her over the range of mountains to the east, the rugged, rain-forested highlands of Chiapas.

"Maps are nice, Wes, but Korzybski said it: The map isn't the territory. This territory is terribly vulnerable. There are big oil pipelines crossing the lowlands, pumping crude oil from tankers on the east to tankers on the west. That's one reason why we didn't think we needed the Panama Canal anymore. A few little explosions at pumping stations and the cartel can hurt us. Same for the railroads across the isthmus, but that would chiefly hurt Mexico."

"There's the Panamerican Highway, too," Hardin added.

"It's there just as long as cocaine kings don't interdict it," Sheppard agreed. "The same for half of Mexico's hydroelectric power, which comes from this region. Wes, it's taken Mexico a long time to get all these modern additions. She can't risk having them cut to pieces, and she knows Uncle Sam plays a very gentle game. If you were a Mexican official and a murderous billionaire came to you with a bundle of dollars in one hand and a block of plastique in the other, who would you fob off with denials and empty promises?"

Wes Hardin shook his head, obviously refusing to voice an answer, responding with a question of his own: "Are you talking about an undeclared war with Mexico?"

"No!" Sheppard's own vehemence surprised him. "We won't even risk armed and deniable CIA aircraft—at least that's what I'm told. The only reason you and I are risking a Coast Guard aircraft today is, Spook 3 and 4 aren't ready to fly. When they are, they'll be sold to a civilian dummy corporation called Agrimap. Bet you didn't know Ullmer had that connection."

"Nope; I didn't."

"Well, he doesn't, but he will. A civilian operation, not NSA and not CIA. In fact, its corporate headquarters will be in central Oregon, which is about as far from us as a man can get in this country. We've got to keep an eye on what's going on right—down—there," he finished, straining his left arm out to put a finger within inches of the video monitor.

Sequestered in foothills between the lowland jungle and Chiapas peaks lay two ruler-straight lines, crossing near the southern ends. Hardin increased the magnification until the lines became runways flanked by low structures, and at maximum gain the display revealed a group of men. They seemed to be unloading a truck under the supervision of a figure nearby, carrying their loads into a building of warehouse size.

"What do you suppose they're doing," Hardin mused.

"Bringing chemicals in; sulfuric acid, acetone, something like that," Sheppard replied. "Whatever they need to process coca. You're looking at what we believe to be their center of operations, judging from months of satellite surveillance. It's also a training center for guerrillas, so you'd need an army to raid it. The Mexicans don't want to. In some ways I don't blame them, but the phrase 'Yankee hostages' has surfaced very recently. Just in case, we need long-term video of this site, a constant eye in their sky so that we can learn every detail of this operation."

Hardin watched the display until Spook 2's progress, and their viewing angle, made the display vague. "No better time to give 'er a try than now, I reckon," he said, pulling back on the throttle lever. As he moved the controls, Spook 2 began to slide across the sky in that decoupling mode that made Sheppard's stomach want to jump ship. With his keyboard and the roller, the pilot found a menu on the monitor and made three choices, then recovered their false-image picture and locked his crosshairs on that unloading operation.

For long minutes, Spook 2 tracked a circle that was over a mile wide and eleven miles high above the unloading, while two legends flashed at the base of the screen. They read LOCKED ON and RECORDING. "How long you wanta do this," Hardin asked at last.

"Give us another few minutes. This extended loiter capability is what satellites won't do, and neither will anything else, at least not half so well. I just had to see for myself before making my recommendation. The photint analysts at NPIC will love us for this, if you'll forgive the jargon. We're looking right down the necks of the enemy, and with civilian crews we could do it almost indefinitely."

Hardin rubbed his neck and stretched, with a casual look at his wrist. "Well, loitering is what these birds were designed for. Now I see why you wanted a civilian pilot; staying as near to honest deniability as you could. Now let me guess: Ol' Ben has agreed to put me on indefinite leave so you can send me back here and bore me to death."

"Not quite. Ullmer thinks you're the one man he has to have on the assembly line. It's your own little nemesis we might ask."

Genuinely puzzled: "My which?"

"Morrison. She's a civilian too."

Hardin remained silent for a moment, then gave a faint headshake. "Morrison's good and she's resistant to boredom, but I think we need the little fart at the plant as much as we need me. Well, almost as much," he added with the ghost of a smile. "Who've you tagged for her copilot?"

"Jared Cutter, if you think he has enough hours in the aircraft," Sheppard said. "We don't want to decommission a Coast Guard pilot for the job if we can avoid it."

"Good choice. Morrison's already given him his final check ride. So what do I have to do with all this?"

"Somebody has to be chairman of that dummy corporation; a deniable civilian," Sheppard said. "I understand the pay would be very good, but you'd lead a double life, continuing to work for Aerosystems under your real name. Don't worry, the FBI knows how to handle that end of it. You interested?"

"Let me sleep on it. Have you got enough of this to make your people happy?"

"Plenty for a sample. We'll want much more, later."

Hardin recalled the monitor's menu to the screen with one hand while he set Spook 2's nose onto a northerly heading, toward the distant line that was the gulf. "Hey, we can be back at Kingsville for dinner. But something's bothering me about all this, Bill. If you guys have been watching this shit come down for so long, why didn't somebody start lining up civilian crews a long time ago?"

"Just a government snafu," said Sheppard, who then fell silent. *I wish I could tell you about the rest of it,* he thought. *But you don't need to know about the billion-dollar kidnaping we're trying to avoid.*

ELEVEN

Tuesday, May 2

GIVE ME THE old days, said Walt Hildreth to himself, *when lines were more clearly drawn.* It had not taken him long to fatten the file on "Indy," as they had dubbed Mr. Harry Rex Brown. By now the FBI had shared those files with CIA, State, and Drug Enforcement Administration, a sister branch of the Justice Department and bidding fair to overshadow the bureau. *Damn the complications that high tech has brought us; cellular phones, personal scramblers, Stinger missiles in the hands of drug runners, even air travel itself. You can't keep up with the suspects without a handful of federal agencies.* But that was an old man's lament, he realized. When you felt it too much, it was time to put in for retirement.

Hildreth knew damned well he wasn't ready for that. *But you think of it a lot when the DEA man liaising with you looks like a surf bum, and his agency jargon isn't yours either.*

Gary Landis, the bronzed, long-haired young specimen accompanying Hildreth on his morning constitutional through Liberty Park in central Salt Lake City, was a case in point. "I'm certain this 'Indy' guy is the same one we made in San Diego," Landis was saying. "He wasn't dirty in customs, but there was something about the dude that just didn't seem real, and I was the tail DEA put on him. I was the logical choice, I guess; cooling off from a deep UC. Turned out his contacts weren't drug-connected. A broker, an old movie actor, somebody else. Antiquities collectors is what they were. If you wanted him for that, you could probably score."

They fell silent as a pair of young strangers passed, then Hildreth resumed with: "Not worth it. What we do need is somebody to put the fear of God into him to make sure he won't refuse a perfectly voluntary polygraph."

Landis chuckled at that. "I don't think he'll be a problem there, sir."

He sounds like my son-in-law! "Look, it's Walt, okay?"

Landis's smile grew tentative, his gray eyes searching the FBI man's face for some clue to his truculence. "Sure, sure, no problem. But about Harry Rex Brown: The thing is, you're right about the nickname. I followed that guy for a week around L.A., and I recall it better than most assignments because it was a little unreal. For a perp he's straight as the edge of your ID. Runs every morning, damn' near wore me out; owns a piece, but as far as I could tell he only carries it to meet his clients, and get this: it's a museum piece, Enfield revolver; takes Webley thirty-eights, which is not exactly your modern round of choice. Does he still wear khakis and that stupid hat? Old snap-brim, looks like it was shot at and missed, and shit at and hit?"

Hildreth nodded, reminding himself that DEA hired a lot of young nighthawks for street work and that Landis was probably not as far off the wall as he seemed.

Now Landis laughed outright. "Man, he's *so* goddamn' obvious the way he wants to be admired. Nice guy, though. I tried to narc him in a bar, and had to listen to a fucking lecture on why I shouldn't be involved with the stuff. By the way, he was drinking a boilermaker, and I swear to God I think he hated the taste. It was the image, see? It's what he has to do, and he does it pretty well. Some street bimbos really go for that, but he never got laid that I saw. I think he pulls his pud a lot . . . anyway, tell you what: I'll get my notes from that surveillance, must've been in the summer of eighty-seven, faxed up here to refresh me, and then I can pay the guy a little social call. Use that surveillance schtick to convince him every time he's scratched his ass, we've known it. Let him think he's been shortlisted on Uncle's shitlist for years and now his whole world is just a skosh away from apocalypse, unless. Was that the general idea?''

"Pretty much the scenario.''

"Consider it done, Walt. But I really don't think you'd need to. As I recall, the only thing that guy needs is an audience and then you couldn't shut him up with a mouthful of Superglue.'Course, he might let you in on how he defeated the slime monsters of Mars, if he thought you'd go for it.''

"Now you have the gist of it,'' said Hildreth. "There's a very special datum we need, something about an airplane that was buzzing Indy and his people.''

"You mean was it real or was it Memorex?''

"Right. Did it happen, and if it did, what kind of airplane? Landis, you wouldn't believe the flap that's going on about an airplane from Mexico right now. Before we're through, Aeromexico and Mexicana will think we're trying to bar them from our airspace. And you know what?'' He waited for Landis to meet his gaze so that he could do his Jack Webb imitation. "We just might,'' he finished.

TWELVE

Friday, May 5

THREE DAYS AFTER the DEA's Landis braced Harry Rex
Brown with an either-or choice, two days after Harry's
polygraph and one day after Scott King's summons to and
from the nation's capital, the interagency task force became reality. "Well, this rips it," said young Givens,
flinging himself into a bureau chair infamous for its perilous tiltback. "Why Vegas? Why not just set us down on
a rock in the Mojave Desert and be done with it?"

"Not exactly Vegas," King corrected, just as unhappy
as Givens that he would be losing two of his men on TDY,
but always voicing his loyalty to the bureau as any good
agent-in-charge does. "You'll have ID as civil service employees at Nellis Air Force Base, which is as secure as
Fort Knox and only a few miles from McCarran International. As long as we're taking this thing seriously, you
couldn't ask for better facilities next door to where the
action is. Is supposed to be," he corrected himself quickly.
"If the cartel has the brains they've shown in the past,
their operation will look like a legitimate international

flight out of Vegas, and that means McCarran. You'll have to keep an eye on the other airports, just in case.''

Walt Hildreth's reaction was more predictable. "But Scotty," he said, holding out one palm as if to show it was innocent of wrongdoing, "why me? I'm not going to whine for a medic, but this sort of stuff hasn't been my style for a long time. You know that." Those last three words said it all, the way Walt said them: an SAC is supposed to exercise his best judgment with men of Hildreth's age, and to put them where experience counts more than derring-do.

King stood up and began to pace, a neat trick in an office of that size. "First, you already know pieces of this scenario; you too, Merle. That's the chief reason you were tapped for Task Force Enable. Second, Enable is starting as a paper chase with the bureau as the lead agency, and you're better at that than most, Walt. You're going to run this thing so I can run the office. Do me proud, okay? There'll be liaison with airline security forces, and CIA and DEA will be in on this.''

As Hildreth pondered his sudden promotion with mixed emotions, Givens looked up. "Landis?''

King suddenly recalled how quickly Givens had sized up his opposite number in DEA, and that they'd seemed to hit it off as if interagency rivalry did not exist; like Butch and Sundance; like Damon and Whoozis. "Yeah," he nodded toward the hopeful look in Givens's face, "that DEA hippie, Landis, is on Enable for the same reason. You're two of a kind—God help us," he said with a glance through the ceiling toward the Almighty.

The slope of Hildreth's shoulders said he had already accepted the inevitable: TDY for an unknown period, the complaints of his wife, an unfamiliar bed. "Who else from the bureau? Anyone I know?''

"Payson is the bureau's inspector assigned from Washington to head Enable. Four or five others I don't know, like the Miami man who helped collar those Colombians who tried to buy Stinger missiles for Escobar a year or so back. If he knows how they work smuggling stuff out of the country, he should be a big help. Two more DEA people; one's a woman, no doubt Landis will be happy to pave your way there, Merle. I personally hope she's mud ugly, so Payson can get your attention now and then. And three people from the Company, because CIA keeps tabs on nonscheduled flights and suchlike in Mexico. I'll have printouts for you both later today.''

Merle Givens got up, perhaps subconsciously impelled by the pacing of his SAC, but stood where he was when King caught his eye. *Room for only one pacer in here,* said that look.

Givens said, ''It's nice to be lead agency, Scotty, but why didn't that go to the Company?''

''You know as well as I do, CIA's charter is restricted to outside our borders, except in connection with foreign nationals. This thing is supposedly to be set up and sprung in Vegas, which gives us one nod, and for all we know it'll be done by hired Americans, and that's two nods.'' King's hands commented, *simple as that.*

Hildreth: ''My second language is German.'' He squinted across at Givens. ''Yours is—what, Portuguese?'' He got a nod from the younger agent and continued, ''I hope somebody is fluent in Spanish because we sure aren't.''

''I can get by,'' Givens objected.

''Our Miami man passed as Cuban. Two of the DEA people know Colombian dialects,'' said King. ''Relax, Walt, we've covered the bases.''

Hildreth looked away into limbo for a moment. Then, ''Bases. Right. They've got to have a base to land on in Mexico. What do we have on that?''

King stopped pacing and put both of his big hands on his chairback, nodding into his thoughts. ''Funny thing about that little item. Your man Indy was pretty positive they've got an old surplus T-33. That sure won't carry several dozen hostages, let alone a billion dollars in cash. But it'll carry fifty-calibers, they tell me, and it needs a fairly long runway. The cartel people have one down in the isthmus; in DC they showed us photo intelligence of the base and said NPIC will be forwarding more to you in Vegas."

Hildreth nodded. "They're using one of those, uh, KH-12s, is it?"

"That's the funny part. It wasn't still photography, it was live video and the Company people were surprised because it wasn't from one of those upgraded U-2s of theirs. I'm damned if I know how we got it, but we got it. NSA claims we'll have more assets in the region soon, with more video than analysts can use."

"Then we'll have guys right there on the spot," Givens said.

"Looks like it. Pure surveillance, and they tell me it'll be a civilian effort. Probably CIA proprietary," King shrugged. "Those guys don't always tell each other what they're doing. But some top people were in the strategy meeting with me, including an NSA bigwig named Sheppard, and if they're doing it, they sure fooled me."

Evidently, Hildreth had been listening with only one ear. He returned to his immediate concern with, "So Task Force Enable comprises fifteen men—and women," he amended quickly, "all under Payson. Is that the size of it?"

"Should be enough," King shrugged, "with typists and equipment and a few investigative aides. Oh, you mean for the showdown?"

"It crossed my mind," Hildreth murmured.

"If it comes to a crunch, the bureau will fly in an HRT from Quantico." *That's why we train hostage recovery teams, to make sure we have youthful muscle and good aim. Poor Walt, he's afraid he'll let the bureau down,* thought King, looking at the wall clock. "Okay, you'll need some time to pack. You'll be taking different flights out tonight."

"They're not wasting any time," Hildreth said, making it a complaint.

"We may have wasted too much already," King said, reseating himself to indicate that the meeting was over. "It'll be a tremendous embarrassment to the bureau if the cartel pulls this thing off while we're still setting up."

THIRTEEN

Saturday, May 6

A MAN NEED not spurn a newspaper merely because he once had its offices bombed for its impudence. Torres looked up from his days-old copy of *El Espectador* as if mildly surprised to see Billy Borges here in the dome at Base Ana, though he would have had to be blind and deaf to miss the unique buzzing drone of the incoming Pilatus Turbo-Porter. With wheeled floats, the Pilatus was capable of landing on land or lake surface. Many years after it first flew in Switzerland, the Pilatus remained among the world's best aircraft for moving a few men, or a few hundred kilos of cargo, to and from short runways up to altitudes of a mile and a half.

Basically a high-winged, single-engined craft needing only one pilot, the Pilatus had practical virtues that made it a favorite of the Catemaco group. Because it was neither fast nor pretty, Torres had hired men to operate it as a billionaire's taxi service, and flew it only when he needed to. This suited his colleagues perfectly because, as he knew very well, it took a jungle-wise pilot to enjoy the way

Simon Torres could swoop a tail-dragging hunk of aluminum vertically upward at the edge of a jungle clearing without trading a wing for a tree trunk. If his colleagues failed to appreciate this, he felt, then let them live out their days in boredom.

He folded the Colombian newspaper away. "Hola, Billy, and how does our export business fare?"

Old Palacios, using his cane today, entered the big room in time to hear Torres's question and answered for Borges. "We had a good day, thanks to Guillermo. And the Big Shipment can go ahead if you have no objections."

Torres shared abrazos, Latin hugs, with the two newcomers. His fellows seemed to understand that he, who spent more time at Base Ana than any other cartel lord, treated the big pleasure dome as a second Torres villa. Servants appeared noiselessly and took fresh orders: whiskey highball for Borges, cafe sin crema for Perez Palacios. Torres, playing the considerate host, asked whether they intended to stay for a few nights.

"Only if necessary," said Borges, swinging an attaché case into view and pulling the knees of his trousers to preserve the suit's creases before he sat. "I would like to be on a flight to Los Angeles by morning." This, in common understanding, meant a transfer from the Pilatus to a Mexican jet out of Veracruz International. That might involve a sleepless night for Billy, a modest inconvenience for a man who could watch a gaming table for twenty-four hours without losing the sparkle in his eye.

Borges, like Torres himself, boasted a passport and ID that gave him free access to the United States. Some of their colleagues—Escobar, for an outstanding example—could not have risked that without extensive cosmetic surgery. Too many yanquis had memorized Escobar's features, the better to apprehend him under almost any pretext. But Billy Borges moved easily across borders, and his false Venezuelan papers lent him special respectability because Venezuela remained an important source of oil. The yanquis did not strain too hard to impede a man who kept them mainlining gasoline. Billy had been known to further this image with a tiny, hand-crafted tie tack of solid gold in the shape of an oil derrick, and could trade wildcatter jargon in Bakersfield.

Torres ran a simple equation through his head. The Pilatus had seats for eight, and if old Palacios had expected any problems in negotiating a tactic he would have brought young Gaitan along. Not because the son was expert in these matters, but precisely because he needed seasoning. The fact that the old man and Borges had come alone meant that whatever they had to say was probably cut and dried. "Well, then," said Torres, "let us see what it is that I should not object to."

Borges opened the case and withdrew one of several slick, four-colored brochures folded to the size of business envelopes, handing it over with a modest flourish. "Our colleagues in Catemaco are comfortable with this. I am almost tempted to invest in it myself," he said with a liquid chuckle.

Torres, impassive, looked at the thing for a moment before opening it out. He had seen many a brochure when studying havens for his millions. This one, mostly devoted to photographs of beaches and swaying palms, seemed typical of the breed, with the exception of several prominent mentions of the weekend for site inspection, all expenses paid. "It does not look much different from others," he said, careful to avoid outright offense.

"Exactly," said Palacios. "And developers have been doing it for decades. This should look like any other such scheme."

"As a sales technique, I am informed, it has had limited success," Borges admitted. "But the developers have never had much trouble filling the hulls of old airliners with customers. Keep the brochure," he said grandly. "You will notice that the offer is only for married couples, the flight contingent on both spouses going. We bill the place as luxury condominiums on long-term lease; no children, no pets, with a fat down payment. But that payment is advertised as half of the entire price, and prices begin at thirty thousand dollars. It follows standard practice except for the low prices, and should appeal to any number of middle-aged yanquis.

"That is the good news, Simon, and if you see no problem here, management internationale will do a mass mailing to a thousand potential clients within the week. They have the demographics well understood; it seems that practically every magazine and salon catering to middle-class, middle-aged Americans will happily sell its list of clients. You understand, we do not want to appeal to the very rich; some of those might be our friends."

"It looks like a go to me," Torres replied. "I gather there may be other news, not so good."

"Ah," Palacios said, smiling as the drinks arrived. They remained silent from force of habit until the servant woman padded off, silent in bare feet. He ahhed again upon tasting the coffee.

Borges took so long with the first sip of his icy concoction that Torres began to worry about the bad news. Finally, "I am afraid the Douglas aircraft you wanted is no longer on the market," Borges said, pulling a set of folded pages from the case.

"The Bristol would have done just as well," Torres said curtly. "If we are ever to do this thing, we should move on it."

"Then there is no bad news," Borges said, with the air of a comedian delivering a punchline. He opened the papers, spreading them for Torres. "Our firm is already the owner of one four-motored Bristol Britannia, originally purchased from the English by, I believe, Canadian Pacific."

Torres took the papers with a muttered malediction, and followed it with, "I have little disposition for your games, Billy." He read for a time, nodding his approval at the Proteus turboprop engines and the maintenance summary. Apparently this old horse of an airliner had never been relegated to cargo duty, hauling hay to snowbound Canadian cattle or palletloads of supplies. Its present equipment included reconditioned seats for sixty-four passengers.

When he looked up, Borges's glance sought approval.

"I will not keep you waiting, Billy," he said, taking Palacios in with his smile. "It will be necessary for me to check it over personally, but it looks good; very good."

Palacios had been holding his shoulders quite straight until this moment, but now he released a sigh and sat back with his coffee. "I believe we will see our money soon," he murmured.

Torres: "Have you given any thought to the schedule I suggested?"

"Oh yes. The date of the flight will be prominently stamped on the application blank of the brochure, if you agree. We selected one of your two suggestions, holiday weekends when so many yanquis are rushing here and there, to and from airplanes, we should have less trouble than usual with officials during the rush," said Borges.

Torres gave the man a level look. "Games again, Billy?"

"The Friday before the yanqui Memorial Day, the end of May," Borges said quickly.

"Good," Torres said. "I agree. Perhaps I should follow you to the land of the addict, the home of the foolish." He stood up; clapped his hands for a servant. To Palacios he added, "I should be back in a few days. I do not want to board an aircraft, ever, to find any unpleasant surprises in its cockpit." As if he had just this moment considered another thought, he muttered, "And that being true, while I am in Los Estados Unidos I should probably find a facility to overhaul my T-Bird."

Torres still proudly used the old U.S. Air Force nickname for his T-33 jet. With this offhanded acknowledgment, he would avoid arousing suspicions when he flew his unmarked silver bird away from Base Ana. They would have no way of knowing his choice of a maintenance facility was a place like San Pedro Sula. The Honduran airport was not as large as Tegucigalpa's, but he had known for a long time that it would suit his purposes with the T-33—or with a Bristol Britannia.

FOURTEEN

Wednesday, May 10

ELATH KNEW BETTER than to ask about the comings and goings of the Pilatus; until that little scrape with Madero had been forgotten, he did not want much to do with those men—always excepting his sponsor, Simon Torres. It was likely that Torres would satisfy his curiosity through oblique hints anyway, and besides, Elath was too busy instructing senderistas. The Peruvian guerrillas rotated in and out of Base Ana on the orders of their commander, Bermudez, for a combination of advanced training and relaxation. They left Base Ana for the coca plantations with better understandings of small ordnance including shoulder-fired rockets, thanks to Elath, but what they brought in—partly processed coca—was even more important. Peru might still have more senderistas than the isthmus region, but more arrived at Base Ana every month or so. Elath judged that he had given the basics of his craft to 500 men, and thought there might be 300 more spread across the Chiapas highlands. Without that training, they should never be allowed within a hundred meters of high explosives.

One of the new arrivals, a big fellow called Teniente, had the hands of an ordnanceman: slow, gentle, without a tremor. Such things counted for a lot when a man crimped blasting caps or wired a mechanical timer into a circuit that involved a mound of Semtex. It was in Elath's mind to requisition Teniente for further training to the status of an instructor, if Bermudez would go for that. It had not occurred to Elath that, among these irregular troops, a fighter might refuse to leave his unit.

Elath did not get the summons until his trainers had been dismissed for their evening meal, long after the Pilatus climbed out of sight over surrounding jungle; and he did not understand why Torres had summoned him until the two men had strolled in early twilight to the shallow slope of creekbed that wandered from nearby heights.

"You must understand," said Torres, speaking softly against the plash and burble of the stream, "that my colleagues can afford the very latest listening devices. A rushing stream is one of the few things that defeats those gadgets."

Elath sat down on a boulder, placing his big feet on stones to keep them dry, and grinned, arms folded. "But so can you," he replied. "And if you use such things to monitor them, my friend, please do not tell me about it."

Torres chose a boulder of his own to lean against, and peered at his friend in fading light. "If I did, why should I not tell you of all people?"

First a snort. Then: "Did you think, because I can take care of myself, that I would be immune to the persuasion of pliers against my fingernails? Then bolt cutters on my fingers, then a meat saw on my arms? I am only a man, and I have seen other men after questioning by your people. I could not have withstood what they suffered."

"Those are not my ways," Torres said. "Bermudez and Solano take care of that sort of thing."

Elath did not comment on the fact that Bermudez and Solano would not do those things without general support. He said, "Once, many years ago, I was questioned by Arabs for a short time. I scream and tremble and capitulate like anyone else; it just takes longer to reach my limit.'' For perhaps half a minute, David Elath stared into the stream as if reading his personal history there, or perhaps his future. ''You should tell nobody anything that could be extracted by methods that, to my certain knowledge, some of your people have already used. Me, of all people; oh yes, especially me. If you want my opinion, Simon,'' he said, standing erect, placing a hand on Torres's shoulder, ''our friendship is too obvious. It might be better if I became conspicuously busy away from your side for a while.''

A long silence. ''Better for you, or for me?''

''For myself,'' Elath said without hesitation.

''If you're going to lie, then do it less transparently,'' Torres said lightly. ''Now then, David: the truth. You may be a mercenary, but I know you are not the sort who expects to grow old in our service. You are too intelligent to imagine that you could simply walk away with the blessings of the cartel. No, you must glide away unseen, at some turning point of your choice.''

Elath, almost in a laugh: ''Apparently you already know the truth.''

''What I do not know is this: Where is your turning point?''

An even longer silence. *Be damned careful here,* Elath thought. *Whatever Torres is up to, he does not want it to go beyond the two of us. I think,* Elath added the final caution, *the plain truth may be easiest.* ''I don't know,'' he said at last. ''I enjoy what I do. I do it well, and it is interesting to see a small country being carved out of a big one.''

''Money is not a factor in your decision?''

''Certainly,'' said Elath, almost in exasperation. ''If I had your money, do you think I would be here tomorrow?''

''Easy, David,'' said Torres, laughing at the reply. ''Very well: I could pay you a half-million yanqui dollars. Promised that, you would not be here tomorrow. Correct?''

''Depends on who promised. And how it was promised,

and—talk of this kind makes me uncomfortable. Could you just get to it, Simon?''

Then Torres told him, without any mention of hostages, and promised that sum.

Elath refused. "I will not help you condemn yourself to death. They would find you, even if they did not find me," he said.

"This is not a matter of 'could' or 'would,' " Torres replied, now with naked urgency in his tone. "I am going to do it, David, with you or without you. And no, they will never find me."

I know that tone. He hides his passions well, but he will do this or die. And he is not so stupid as to let me live if I refuse, and—and half a million dollars? "But why, Simon? Are you in trouble?"

"Why?" When Torres spoke his mind earnestly, as he seldom did, he could speak almost like a lover, or perhaps a brother, "Because I will have enough and I am growing bored with this life, and finally because it will be *el mas gran travesura*, the greatest joke, ever played on men of limitless power!" Torres rarely guffawed as he did now, the laugh beginning softly, building as he spoke, virtually swallowing his last words.

Elath began to laugh with him. "Now, that is a reason I can accept," he said into the near-darkness, as if Torres had given the most rational of answers. "Yes, I accept; why not? You're going to do it anyway. I wouldn't last ten minutes with the cartel afterward." *I probably wouldn't last until tomorrow morning if I refused, unless I killed you first,* added his silent obbligato. *Or would I?*

"You must remember how I lived as a child," Torres said more soberly. "I wanted riches, yes, but more than anything on earth I wanted to outwit and embarrass the mighty. They respect no one as much as the man who hands them a defeat. I have begun to realize, now that I'm one of them, that there might be a goal beyond money—any amount of it. I can reach the goal by the end of May, and I may never have such a chance again. Do you really understand?''

"Quite well," said Elath, "It's plain machismo in clown makeup. As it happens, I have a fair supply of it myself.''

Torres, enthused as though he had snorted a line of his own product, began to outline Elath's role. Flying into San Pedro Sula on the following night was only the first act of it.

Though no jet turbine mechanic, Elath could oversee all stages of the T-33's overhaul, then await Torres's call. Knowing as little as he did of the plan, Elath vaguely imagined the cargo aircraft as a small executive jet. *At least,* he thought, *I know Simon Torres will help me stay alive until the end of the month. What more could a mercenary ask?*

FIFTEEN

Monday, May 15

COLLEEN MORRISON WAS mad as hell and thirty miles from almost anywhere as she confronted her colleague on the warm macadam of Agrimap's airstrip, between the fuselage of Spook 3 and a free-standing ladder. "Even though you trusted me to flight-test this new bird, you bastards won't even tell me all you know about this weird business, Hardin. I'm gonna be a goddamn spy, I know that much, but I'm second-class. Right?"

"Give it a rest, Morrison. Agrimap promised you the same hazard pay as Cutter yonder." Jared Cutter, who knew them both, had wisely decided to shake out the kinks of his recent flight with Morrison by jogging to the other end of the runway; transparently, Morrison thought, just to get out of earshot. For an ex-marine, Cutter seemed extraordinarily mild in manner. *Rather attractive, actually,* she thought. Morrison recalled the slender, crewcut, red-headed Cutter having complained that, when she was truly browned off, she tended to cuss whoever might be handy.

"The pay is not the issue and you know it," Morrison snarled, unheeding of the breeze that ruffled the hair framing her face. "Cutter's okay, but I was in line for what they gave him. It's because he's got a pecker. Admit it!"

"A dummy position in a dummy corporation? That's because Cutter was military, I suppose," Hardin replied. "I didn't invent this paper empire, Morrison, you should've bitched to Ben Ullmer if you didn't like the setup."

"I told him," said Morrison. "I explained in terms he couldn't misunderstand. He claimed the decision on who got to be Agrimap's president and treasurer and so on what was out of his hands. According to Ullmer, he didn't even know what the corporation's name would be. Said he thought it sounded shitty."

Now Hardin grinned, a lopsided whatthehell look she had learned to loathe. "Lucky you're a woman. If you'd been male he wouldn't have told you that much. He would've reamed your butt 'til you could hide that stepladder in it."

That ladder and the runway were, at the moment, the only visible assets of Agrimap except for the Nemesis craft itself. The four-place Cessna nearby was not an asset, but a rental in which Hardin had stowed the ladder because, he'd said, they would need the damned thing when they met at the airstrip and it wouldn't fit in a spookship.

For a newly formed Oregon corporation, ostensibly for aerial analysis of agricultural lands, Agrimap would not have impressed many investors. Not a hangar, not even a tent impaired Morrison's view of the Three Sisters wilderness area that glistened against blue sky over Hardin's right shoulder. The idea seemed to be that legally and factually, Spook 3 must begin her mission from Agrimap's own private airstrip here, some miles from Sunriver, Oregon, in splendid isolation. To the west their sky was full of rocks, at two-mile altitudes some of the most towering hunks of stone in the Cascade Mountain range. But Morrison had seen the Three Sisters before and was in no mood to admire that trio of snow-mantled crags that, for outdoor enthusiasts, characterized Oregon better than Mount Hood.

Perhaps because he saw the flames he had rekindled in her face, Hardin raised his hands as if to ward her off. "Okay, forget the figure of speech."

"You don't even know what's sexist," she raged, clapping her hands to her head, looking into the sky. "It's not your goddamn figures of speech, it's the way I'm treated."

"Not by me," Hardin said. "You think you'd have been chosen as Agrimap's number one pilot if I hadn't agreed?"

"No," she said, blinking hard as she made the concession, searching for reasons to explain it, finding one instantly. "Now you get to take credit for Spook 4. It was me who ramrodded her ahead of schedule, but a week from now wonderful Wesley gets to sign off her delivery papers while Cutter and I play Allen Funt over fucking Latin America."

She also hated the look of sufferance she saw on his face now, the same why me, lord grimace that Cal used to give her before The Crash. Whatever Hardin started to say, he didn't say it. And how the hell could she riposte if he didn't lunge? *I get it now; actually, I guess I got it a long time ago. This is really a military operation, and that's an old-boy's network. Nobody with tits need apply to the inner circle. But you'd never admit that, you scruffy Texas rednecked flyboy.* "Okay, I take your silence as assent," she said with a decisive nod that could have broken bricks.

At least he seemed to remember what she had once told him about how she could read his opinions in his face, and how that bugged her; he turned away, thrusting hands into pockets of his old, cracked, avaitor jacket. She saw his shoulders rise and fall with heavy breathing for a moment, saw his head jerk as he noted Cutter's approach.

When he spoke, he was almost inhumanly calm, she decided. "I'll see that you get full credit for Spook 4, Morrison. Now, whatever anybody did to piss you off like this, rest assured that I've paid for it and you can take off feeling good, because I sure as hell don't.'' He turned, trying to put on a toothy smile for Cutter. ''Well, Jarhead, ready for a couple of weeks in the pipe?''

Jared Cutter, doomed by his marine aviator background to wear that nickname, shook the fingers of both hands in a final limbering-up exercise. ''Mr. Treasurer to you, sire,'' he grinned back. ''We plutocrats like our respect.''

Cutter did not see Morrison's momentary glare. *Hell, Cutter didn't hear us,* she thought. *It wasn't a deliberate taunt. Besides, as long as we're flying this mission, I out-rank him.* The thought was a comfort, and she let it buoy her spirits. On her way up the ladder she said, over her shoulder, ''I expect Spook 4 to relieve us in less than two weeks. Don't let me down, Hardin.''

Clapping Cutter's shoulder, steadying the ladder with his free hand, Hardin said, ''You're really a piece of work, Morrison. And remember, you're flying a bird I built. Try not to bend her up too much, okay?''

Morrison waved in answer as she donned her helmet, settling into her harness, Cutter easing into place beside her. Though Jared Cutter might move back into the pipe once they had gained altitude, the crew stations for takeoff and landing were always in the cockpit.

Then, at Morrison's signal, the president of Agrimap became its ground crew. He pulled the ladder away and extracted the locking pins from Spook 3's landing gear, canvas streamers flickering in the breeze as he held the pins up one by one for Morrison's inspection. She nodded and waved, checking her systems while Cutter attended to the checkoffs, ninety feet of gossamer wing shuddering faintly as the rotary engine huffed to life.

His own headset in place, Hardin pulled folding plastic chocks from around the wheels, clapped them closed, stretched high to hand them to Cutter. The pins followed into their stowage pocket behind the cockpit, with Hardin's voice in her helmet: ''Ever think about the symbolism in the pins and chocks?''

''Educate me,'' she said, without enthusiasm.

"They're with you, Morrison, not at home base, because a Nemesis doesn't have one."

As Cutter lowered the canopy, Morrison pointed straight up through it. "Our home base is up there," she replied.

"You take my point," Hardin said.

"Not in a million years, buddy-boy," she said, hoping Hardin would grasp the innuendo, and made him duck as she urged Spook 3 forward. The full fuel load stabilized them despite a choppy breeze across the airstrip, and Morrison was very good, and knew it. Within two hundred yards she had cleared the runway, doing it by the book, holding the bullet nose at the precise upward angle to minimax the event, minimizing time to altitude and maximizing climb in the process.

The last thing she heard from Hardin's short-range tranceiver was a fading, "Like I said, Morrison: a real piece of work. Good hunting, you little fart."

Instead of replying aloud, she made Spook 3 nod, nose bobbing twice in the midst of climbout, because she knew Hardin would still be watching. And because, dammit, she could do it as deftly as any man alive.

IT WASN'T MUCH as tail winds go, but she got a modest boost ten miles above Nevada, running from the sun. Cutter played with the video monitor; serious play by a man who wanted more experience with the navigation gear every Nemesis carried. It was user-friendly, very sophisticated stuff with its own map displays and simulated beams from the microwave beacons that guided air traffic. "Ever been to Elko, Morrison?"

"Once, when I was little," she replied. "They've got a municipal airport."

"Well, you've been there again," he said, with a sideways nod of his head to their right.

She glanced across him, squinting at the broad arcs of color that defined earth's vast horizon, the almost-black of space, and the sea of air between. Astronauts, she decided, could claim a broader view, but no better one. Still, for Morrison it was a view that was never quite right. "Hey, Jarhead: paint us a thirty-degree relief, will you?"

He did so, probably thinking it was a test to see how quickly he could comply. Moments later the monitor, fed by Spook 3's side-looking radar, built up a series of lines that became a "virtual display," a copy of the real world on a video monitor, in this case a relief map of the terrain below as seen from a thirty-degree slant. Directly below lay jagged peaks with one striking feature that sliced down between them: a mountain pass, faithfully reproduced by the cockpit's display. While the cartoonish lines of terrain were displayed in brown, oblongs of blue splotched the lower right-hand portion of the monitor. Morrison hmphed to herself, mildly surprised because she had not remembered lakes of that size in the Nevada desert. Comforted by the display, she hummed to herself.

A paradox lurked at the edge of her awareness until she pinned it down. Though Colleen Morrison had never deluded herself that she was Olympic material, those solid little bones and close-coupled muscles of hers had helped her become a good college gymnast; and a gymnast either developed a special awareness of herself moving through three dimensions or eventually she missed one too many dismounts. Near-perfect timing and that heightened awareness, a sense of where you were, helped make you better than most. And with a sinus infection or any other situation where you lost that sense of position, you became uneasy.

Those same intuitive abilities, tuned far beyond the norm, helped in some kinds of flying too. Not up here, though. The paradox was simply this: Skimming across wavetops on the ocean of air, she was so high that even with their shadows clearly showing, ground features seemed flat. She could maintain that perception of three dimensions only by an effort of will, or by calling up a bit of help on the video monitor.

No matter how acute, human eyes are less than three inches apart. Depth perception becomes iffy when one is trying to estimate relative distance of objects two hundred thousand times as far away as that distance between the eyes. Morrison glanced at the display and smiled, pleased with a system that kept her world in three dimensions.

With twilight came a greater sense of peace, the hard points of starlight unwinking and serene above. She kept the engine tachometer on a steady 2000 revs and the altimeter on 40,000 feet, continuing to "run in" the new engine at an altitude where it was still strong. By using the electrics as well, she boosted their airspeed, and Kingsville had facilities to fully recharge the accumulators. Morrison did not like the idea of extended shakedowns of a new aircraft over a foreign country. It had not been her decision. The fact that Ullmer had backed such a decision meant that this mission was far more important than anyone was willing to admit to Colleen Morrison.

Less than three hours after Sunriver disappeared behind them, Morrison identified the sprawl of Albuquerque by its own lights, a ghostly glow that became brighter until she could pick out the freeway arterials crossing in the city's heart. "Two hours to Kingsville," she told Cutter. "Want to take it from here?"

He readjusted his seat, scanned his instrument cluster, and nodded. "Sure. Hit the pipe if you want to."

She stretched arms, shoulders, legs, and lifted her helmet so that it perched more atop her head than on it. "Nah. Talk to me, Jarhead. What's a boy like you doin' in a place like this?"

She could see his smile in the reflection of virtual displays. "Orders, ma'am, by your leave. And all that spit 'n polish crap," he said. "No, really. My dad was a Coastie. Hell, I was born at Cape May while he was flying short-range SAR choppers."

A good mimic, she aped the stereotypical sound. "New Jersey? You shuah missed dat Joisey accent."

"Service brats do," he said, "unless the old man's an

admiral. You get moved a lot. I started school in Petersburg, but I set the North Carolina high-school mile record for Elizabeth City—except that it was a meet in Raleigh. Then I applied to the Corps. I'd seen too many jets swooping around to want the kind of duty dad got; but try and tell him that. And you know how it is: the Corps gives you that stuff about needing a few good men. I figured I'd find out if I was one of 'em.''

"What was your verdict?"

"The commander was satisfied. At least he didn't tell me otherwise.''

"The hell with your father's verdict, I asked about yours," she said.

She could see his helmet nod in silhouette. "Yeah, that's right. I guess whatever his was, was mine.'' Silence for several beats. "Christ, do you know how hard I tried to make basketball teams just because he was a fan? Me, five-nine and a hundred-twenty pounds. But he was big on running folks into the ground with sheer stamina. Track was my way of doing it. My nickname was Coast Guard Cutter then," he admitted, and Morrison saw his teeth flash. "The commander saw to it that I got As in math and sciences.''

Morrison, slyly: "And what if you hadn't?"

"Don't ask. Listen, the time Lieutenant Martin told him I was making out with Mary Beth on the porch swing, my old man confined me to quarters for a month!"

"How old were you?"

"Sixteen. No, seventeen. Wasn't as if she complained.''

"Your commander ran a tight ship," she said.

"Yeah. Told me a man doesn't get his meat where he gets his bread and butter. If you know what I mean.''

Morrison laughed. "Right. I take it Mary Beth was a service brat, too.''

"Sure. Bobbysocks and lace, a perfect little lady. Until she got out of daddy's sight." Another pause. "Well, it could've been worse. I was an overachiever, and I can't

complain about that. Engineering degree from Rensselaer;
a tour in a Phantom; and a guy in our outfit turned me
onto sailplanes. Jeez, what a kick. I came close to an
altitude record in, uh, eighty-five. With some time at Pax
River testing carrier moods and a lot of soaring time, no
wonder Ben Ullmer liked my application.''

"He liked it well enough to make you secretary-
treasurer of Agrimap," Morrison said.

"Hey, that's just paper, Morrison. Now you."

"Me what," she asked, genuinely perplexed.

"You Tarzan," he said, making it light, "me Jane. You
were a gymnast at Oregon State, right? You didn't get to
be Tarzan by accident, but outside of your work at Aerosystems I don't know much about you. C'mon, it's your
turn."

Oh shit. Well, I asked for it, didn't I? "First off, I wasn't
in the service."

"Whoa. You weren't born twenty years old, so that can't
be first. Most important, maybe, but not first."

She let that sink in, stung by Cutter's accuracy. The imp
of competition made her say, "While I mull that over, you
can think about why you never once mentioned your
mother. Any sibs?"

With patience she found irksome, Cutter said, "Mother
raised me the way dad wanted, and if she didn't like it she
never complained. And no brothers or sisters. And you're
diverting the topic, ma'am."

"Touché," she said through a sigh. *Can't be bitchy with
a nice guy I'm spending weeks in an airborne conduit pipe
with,* she reminded herself. *Even if he has a million dollars' worth of military flying education I would've killed
for. Good place to start.* "Look, Cutter, they don't take
flight officers my size. That's something I can't help, God
knows I hung myself upside down on parallel bars until
my ears popped trying to stretch my spine a few inches.
Anyway," she went on, ignoring his chuckle, "I was born
in Stanford Hospital because mom thought that was the
place to do it and my dad let her make such decisions.

"My dad was a pilot for United, used to do overnights in Medford, Oregon and when he found a little town called Rogue River a few miles away, he flipped out. Mom was watching Palo Alto become a yuppie's slum, Stanford or no Stanford, and living alongside a quiet piece of a wild river sounded good, I guess. So that's where I grew up. Jerry was a year older and Cal three years older, so I was the baby. Shit, they called me Babe until I graduated.''

"Which didn't thrill you," Cutter put in.

"Aah. I didn't give it much thought, in those days; not 'til my size kept me out of military aircraft. But mom must've guessed I'd wind up a head shorter than everybody else. She was subtle about it, but she steered me toward gymnastics and let Cal teach me some of the martial arts stuff he was learning in Medford. Until I enrolled there, too. He quit a year later. I didn't.''

In the ensuing pause, Cutter vented a faint whistle under his breath. "Sweet shit—beggin' your pardon.''

"Never apologize for cussing as long as it's fluent,'' she said. "Jerry taught me that very early. So: sweet shit what?''

"Little bitty curvy thing, two big brothers, and martial arts, is what. You must've been a land mine for every boy in town.''

Now Morrison laughed, too, that giggly sound that was one of the things she most hated about herself, but whatthehell. "Very perceptive,'' she agreed. "Jerry and Cal were jocks for the Rogue River Chieftains, but they used to say once I was in high school, they were just regular Indians. Of course girls dated guys in higher grades if they could.''

"And you could, of course.''

"Of course.''

"Your modesty is most appealing,'' Cutter remarked.

"Anyhow, I was dating guys in my brothers' grades. They used to say if Little Chief couldn't handle it, whatever it was, she could send her Indians on the warpath.''

"And?''

"So they never had to. Those two were six-footers."

For a few moments they sat companionably silent, and Morrison was considering a move back to the lounge when Cutter spoke again. "Something you said about Elko, Nevada; you flew with your father on commercial flights?"

"No, he built an experimental. When we were kids, it would take us all."

"Jeez; not many experimentals that size."

"A Dyke Delta. Whopping big wing area," she said, and felt herself smiling. "Dad said as long as we all helped build a flying flapjack, we should all get to enjoy it. Enjoy it," she repeated with sudden bitterness, and spat out the last word: "Christ!"

"You didn't?"

Delivered very quickly: "I could keep 'er level at eight, navigated cross-country at ten, soloed on my fourteenth birthday. I'm goin' back to the pipe, Cutter," she said suddenly.

"No, wait, there's got to be more." She thought his pleading tone grotesque, under the circumstances. "They don't just hand out A and P tickets like party favors."

That was later. No pain in that, she told herself, repinning her seat. If Jared Cutter wanted to know where she earned her federal license for aircraft and power plant mechanics, the least she could do was tell him. "Oregon State has a great gymnastics program, and it turns out a lot of engineers. I got half a free ride on scholarship. But I got my mechanic's ticket at San Jose State afterward."

"Afterward?"

"After the fucking crash, Cutter!" She unpinned her seat and began to swivel toward the rear.

He would not leave it alone, damn him. "You?"

Halfway into the pipe, she threw it back at him. "Everybody but me! Both parents, both brothers, en route to Iowa to watch me compete. Insurance money got me through San Jose, goddammit, have you had enough? I fucking well have!" She left him before he could hear the tears in her voice. She knew it sounded childish; for one thing, you didn't say "crash"; you bought a plot, or augured in, or deep-sixed. But those were impersonal phrases and there was nothing on earth so personal as the loss of your entire beloved family, instantaneously, in a context in which you felt somehow the guilty party.

She did not need a light to find her handholds but used it anyhow as she moved into the lounge. She strapped into the couch harness, doing everything by the book as usual, vaguely aware that her guilt encompassed more than closed-casket funerals for four people on the way to see Babe perform. *I should have been with them*, she raged at providence, or sheer luck, whatever it was toward which she could direct that rage. *But no; when I buy it, I'll be alone or with people I don't give much of a damn about. That's the way it's supposed to work, isn't it? Isn't it?* A woman fated to become marmalade against a mountainside should not leave anyone grieving as she herself did, every day, after all these years. And she was not about to go willingly, not ever if she could help it, and to beat that hellish face of providence she must master the art and science of flying, absolutely and forever. *You can't beat fate. But goddammit, you can make it wait, frustrate it, for a hell of a long time.* It was the only possible way for Colleen Morrison to punish providence, and she would bear her guilt for a thousand years if that meant she could punish it that long.

Her father had always said, if you follow procedures you may just live forever. He also admitted, later, that nobody memorized the book, or flew by it, any better than Babe Morrison. And after The Crash, God help anyone who ever, for whatever reason, called her Babe. It was presumptuous beyond forbearance, of a loving closeness lost forever on a missed approach to Cheyenne Municipal, by an old pro with thousands of hours behind him.

"Cal, Jerry, you bastards! It should've been me," she whispered. Momentarily, the face of Jerry Morrison imprinted on her mind, a year her senior and the only one she could really compete against. That blond mop of hair, the sturdy legs and long stocky body, the lopsided grin that said "aw, whatthehell" clear as day. Cal reminded her of someone; didn't matter who, she decided, beginning to leaf back through fond memories. She had found it possible to calm down from one of her rages within a few minutes, if she could tie into the right memory of Jerry and Cal and Rogue River. That time they set off the fireworks at Gold Hill, for example . . .

Morrison was snoring lightly when Cutter called her on the intercom. "Present position: twenty-eight thousand feet above Uvalde, Texas, bearing one-three-niner; estimated time of arrival at Kingsville, zero-hours, fifteen minutes." He sounded subdued, almost apologetic. Her wrist chronograph said they would be wheels-down in less than half an hour. Morrison promised herself that she would try to be extra nice and let Cutter get in another night landing. It would be weeks before he'd get another chance—or else they'd both be up to their collective ass in trouble.

SIXTEEN

Tuesday, May 16

THE FIRST DAY of the Nellis operation had its rough spots, as Inspector Payson had expected. He simply ground them smooth, as always. Marvin Payson had known since childhood that he was different from most, but only began to suspect how different when his junior high football coach pulled him out of the line where, in the fullness of his thirteen years, Marv had thought he belonged. His coach was also his math teacher. Marv, who already looked like an offensive tackle, was the only kid on the team who could keep track of quadratic equations in his big round head—and once he saw an offensive play diagrammed, that play and all its permutations were his just as surely.

Young Marvin, as a quarterback, later proved an inspired choice through Massillon High, where opponents found him roughly as easy to stop as an Erie ore barge. Ohio State made him a fullback, but no one could make him truly fast through the line and, though it pained his family, Payson was secretly glad when the NFL draft ignored him. He did not want to have to explain why he'd majored in accounting, why he would have turned down pro sports anyway. Payson could not recall when he didn't want to be FBI.

His junior high coach, the FBI recruiter at Ohio State, and Payson himself had pegged his abilities with precision: The bureau had a career with Marvin Payson's name on it. Twenty years after he left Ohio, Payson was a full inspector with a premature bald spot and several careers behind him. Each task force became a small career for Payson, in the way that each chess game became a small life with a birth, growing to its own unique maturity, and finally a regicide to end it. Payson's loathing for stalemates was cool and determined, and he did not suffer them often. That was why the bureau had placed him in charge of Task Force Enable.

Some task force leaders led from behind doors that were often closed, maintaining a certain distance from other members. As a result, sometimes they did not know where all their people were going at a given moment. Payson could switch off a surrounding hubbub like a man with a hearing aid and switch it on again just as easily, often at the exact moment when his agents had concluded he was on a brief mental vacation. It worked for him.

The trouble was, agents were all sharp enough to think of using him as an encyclopedia when he needed his mental circuitry for planning the next four moves and calculating where each move would lead. This was the risk he ran in a bullpen office, but Payson had his own way of reminding them who was the bull.

Merle Givens was first to try the lazy way, calling across an aisle on that first day at Nellis, "Mr. Payson, what's our zip code?"

The big head came up slowly. With luck, he might have to do this only a few times. Two hundred and fifty pounds of Payson came to his feet; six feet, three inches of him gazed smiling across the tangle of hanging phone lines to the men and women settling into this wing of an air force office building. Still smiling, he brought his thumb and forefinger nearly together between his lips, and four liters of Payson lung capacity blew a blast that, judging from the face of Givens, might have been Gabriel's.

All activity stopped. Payson usually spoke high in his throat, a husky nonthreatening baritone; but he knew how to rumble from the gut, and he was doing it now. Astonishingly, his tones were dulcet as a schoolmarm's.

"Team, Mr. Merle Givens of the bureau brings up an interesting point of research." He had everyone's attention and, still smiling at Givens, Payson went on. "Mr. Givens asks me for our new zip code. This is not a trivial question, for it is quite possible that a piece of correspondence may eventually be directed to one or another of our little band during our months, or years, of residence."

Now Givens began to turn a vivid hue, close to cerise if Payson's memory for rare stamps was any guide, and from moment to moment as he spoke, Payson's gaze would meet that of Givens. "As always, your Federal Bureau of Investigation is ever vigilant in an unceasing effort to bring you the latest technical breakthroughs. And it employs men of the very highest caliber for the express purpose of training such operatives as yourselves in this modern wizardry."

Two of the dozen team members, the older Salt Lake City guy and the Miami man, were struggling to make their smiles stillborn; and to them Payson made nods with the kind of lasered eye contact that suggested stillbirth was a very good idea for any competing smiles at the moment. "By great good fortune, I am one of those men empowered to train you in the more arcane nuances of our profession. Rest assured, I will always be ready at a moment's notice to bring Task Force Enable to a screeching halt to share these advanced techniques with those who perceive themselves less fortunate than I.

"Now then: I would like to direct your attention, each and severally, to this device. It is known in the vernacular as a telephone book." He had already noted that everyone else had an identical tome, and now he lifted the big flaccid directory from his desk between his phone and computer terminal, brandished it, let it fall to the desk in a tornado of dust motes from a slant of Nevada sunshine.

Givens was now past magenta on his way to maroon, his eyes searching for some crack in the floor small enough to hide his ego. The smile unimpaired, Payson wrapped it up. "There are thousands, perhaps hundreds, possibly even dozens of cities involved here. There are white pages, yellow pages, green pages as well, with more information than even I can recount verbatim. The process is called printing, and I will be happy to discuss Johann Gutenberg at length unless one of us can think of something more important, like an airplane with a billion dollars in cash and dozens of hostages. And I almost forgot: Yes, it gives zip codes too. Ours is eight-nine-one-one-zero, Mr. Givens." And he made the faintest kind of bow toward Merle Givens before sitting down, and *still* he maintained the smile of Buddha.

Givens waited until the others, with suspicious coughs to hide more amused noises, went back to their work. "You didn't have to do that," he said.

"Yes I did," Payson replied, unperturbed. "Just as surely as you had to ask me a dumbshit question when the answer was ten seconds away from you." Givens had already turned away when Payson, speaking softly, added, "Don't worry, Givens; somebody else will do it tomorrow, but nobody will do it often. All you have to do is be sure your question is worth my time. That one wasn't. Okay?"

Givens nodded, and then shook his head. His color was almost back to normal now. "I wonder if—uh, never mind," he said quickly.

"Okay, this'un's a freebie," Payson said, and his real grin was almost friendly.

"Thank God," Givens said. "Well, we seem to be started on McCarran International, but there are two other airports around Vegas. North Las Vegas, and Sky Harbor to the south."

Payson replied, "Neither of the local airports normally handles aircraft big enough to carry that much cargo and that many passengers. Still, it's a possible. You already know the details we have, scanty as they are. Work it out and give me a rundown on the possibilities of those two airports. Ten hundred hours tomorrow morning, conference time."

"With that schedule, I could use help. Landis okay?"

"If you need him, but first check with Christiansen for some initial guesses; he was a United pilot before he joined the Company. By the way, it was a good question, Givens. And in case you think you're getting a shit detail, two other guys will be at McCarran for the evening shift until relieved by Calvin and Dorman. I won't get much sleep either."

Givens let his eyebrows ask the question.

"Oh, I'll be in bed, Givens. But what if our nightmare comes true right under our noses while we're still setting up? I'm not going to call Quantico for a hostage recovery team on a hunch, but how'm I going to feel if I have to call in the HRT after the fact? That's a little sleep-robber, I can tell you."

―――――――――――――

BY MIDMORNING OF the next day, Enable's aides had done much of the scutwork, setting up partitions to keep echoes down, moving secretarial desks as necessary. The aides and secretaries were all dedicated staffers, most of them experienced in task force work. With nine bureau agents and three each from CIA and DEA, this compact little army had flown its own equipment in, creating not so much as a ripple in the daily operations of their host, the air force. Nor did they need special cover on the base, beyond civil service IDs. Their teletype machines, which bore the same relationship to ancient teletypes that an Indy car does to a Model T, were already running. Payson believed that he would be patching into mainframe computers for exhaustive answers to several questions before the day was out and, as usual, he was right.

Opaque projectors throwing images on screens suspended from partitions were Payson's version of a blackboard. He had long ago realized that an agent's memory of a "chalk talk" improved markedly if the agent had an exact copy, smudges and all, of what went onto the wall. He began their meeting by slashing three lines on a page, followed by an arrow indicating north. The longest line was east to west. "McCarran is a major terminus," Payson said, "for travel to and from Mexico City; also to Cancun." A few groans met this news; the more direct flights to any place in Mexico, the unmerrier. "Longest runway is over twelve thousand feet, and they can take anything in commercial service. They also cater to nonscheds, and for a city of this size, well, you can appreciate that one way to prove you're a high-roller is to have your own aircraft. Swarms of those infest Vegas," he added laconically. "That's the bad news. Hildreth, your paper chase on schedules is as near as we have to good news. Tell 'em—our assumptions too."

Walt Hildreth shuffled papers before sliding a map of North America onto the projector's surface. "The good news is, just about all flights to other Mexican cities, Acapulco, Guadalajara, Pueblo, Los Cabos, and so on, can only be reached by connecting flights out of some other U. S. port of entry; L. A., San Francisco, San Diego, Houston."

One of the DEA men said, "Question," and waited. When Payson did not interfere, he went on: "I take it we're assuming once the aircraft clears the runway, it won't touch down again on U. S. soil. Should we assume that?"

"We think so," Payson said with a nod toward Hildreth. "A connecting flight means they'd have to transfer the cargo as well. Even if the passengers were still unaware of what was happening, to transfer that particular cargo on U. S. soil is a complication no one in his right mind would entertain. And since we have to make a few very basic assumptions, we also assume the passengers won't be willing hostages. So, wherever they think they're bound, according to our information, they'll all be boarding in Vegas and the cargo will be loaded here, too. Go on, Hildreth,'' he suggested, and fell silent.

"Okay; McCarran security has a list of us,'' Hildreth resumed, "so just remember to check in with them for the color of the day until they know us by sight. And they're checking closely on every massive air freight load that goes aboard, especially if it's scheduled to cross the border. We're taking the informant's word as gospel: if it isn't carrying our cargo, it isn't our target aircraft.''

Meanwhile, Hildreth had jotted down their assumptions by the numbers. *Those Salt Lake guys are thorough,* Payson told himself. He nodded to Hildreth and gestured for the ballpoint, starting on another page with the adjoining overhead projector. "About twenty flights a day begin here,'' Payson said, "direct to Mexico City. Another twenty to Cancun. All these flights are on U. S. carriers: Delta, American, Continental, United. But if you've read your abstracts, you know that our target aircraft won't land either place.''

With labeled circles and long lines, he indicated a flight path from Las Vegas to Mexico City and a longer line to Cancun. "People fly to the capital for lots of reasons, and you don't have to be rolling in money to stay there. The Cancun route is different; it's French Riviera time on the tip of the Yucatan. Folks headed for Cancun are generally flush, and they'd better be if they're going to stay long. For that reason, they might make juicier hostages, and I've heard it argued that we should give priority to the Cancun flights.

"But we won't,'' Payson went on, extending the Las Vegas-Mexico City line further to the southeast. "Because we know where that aircraft intends to land, and they wouldn't have to deviate from a standard flight plan until they're over Mexico City. Four hundred miles further is where they intend to land. That's less than an hour by jetliner, and by the time the Mexican authorities got their thumbs unplugged from, ah, wherever they had them, target aircraft could be on the ground. Their own turf.''

From the CIA's leggy Eulalie Calvin, whose eyes showed faint circles from her recent night stint at McCarran: ''Question. We give both routes the same priority?''

''We have to, at this point. In some ways, they're the simplest scenario. McCarran's already beefed up their security staff. You realize there are about two jetliners an hour out of there for Mexico, some of 'em with bulky air freight. McCarran security is checking that freight very closely. First one that looks like a real possible, they hotline it to us.

''As for the mechanism of deviation: There are three people in a cockpit: pilot, copilot, and flight engineer—sometimes called the second officer. If any one of them is working for the opposition, the deviation could start with a hostage situation right there in the cockpit. That's why we need data on every one of those officers flying those routes. It's a stone we can't leave unturned. Hildreth, you and your staffers can get on that right away.''

Walt Hildreth made a note, nodding before he asked, ''And the stews, uh, flight attendants? Why wouldn't it be simpler to grab hostages in back, and give coordinates to the pilot?''

''It might be,'' Payson admitted, ''and that's another stone for you. I needn't tell you to flag any scheduled flight with two or more close friends on the same crew.'' Responding to the raised brows around him, Payson stared back. ''Look, team, this isn't some minor scam with a few bucks or a plea bargain on the line. It's the biggest, most tempting caper any criminal could imagine. It's so big, the bureau tended at first to dismiss it as wild fantasy. But State Department's informant was correct in every detail before. The word is one—billion—dollars in large U.S. bills. They could buy a few normally honest folks for a hundredth of that.''

Eulalie Calvin shook her head and squinted. "Let's see, a bill weighs a gram," she said.

They're loosening up, not waiting to be called on, but not showboating. Payson thought. *Good.* "Works out to ten million grams of hundreds," he said. "Or ten thousand kilos, if you prefer."

The DEA's Gary Landis suddenly burst out laughing. "Ten thousand keys of hundreds," he said softly, as if repeating the punchline to a wonderful joke. Then, as the professional sector of his mind processed the notion of half a roomful of hundred-dollar bills, he added, "This isn't a load they can tuck away in a short-haul commuter aircraft. Gonna take a big airplane."

"Exactly. Now, State's informant only referred to scores of American hostages. If we take two score as a minimum, we have forty Americans, probably with luggage, plus twenty thousand pounds of money—maybe several times as much if the cargo is mostly in twenties or so."

With her big rawboned frame and the face of a handsome farm wife, Eulalie Calvin should not have been that attractive. Perhaps her fine carriage and open smile had something to do with it; the CIA had found her able to disarm men with a laugh or, if it came to that, with a kick from one of those long, long legs. Calvin drawled, "Nah. These are Colombians, guys; they try to deal in biggies. If thousand-dollar bills were still in general circulation, I'd expect them to do it that way. Best bet is hundreds and maybe fifties. I'd defer to DEA, of course, if I'm off base here."

No one disagreed. The Miami Man, long familiar with busts involving money as bulk cargo, stopped chewing on a thumbnail. "Charter," he said abruptly. "This is a natural for a charter flight."

"A very strong possibility," Payson said. "And since somebody was awake in Washington, the Company has added Curt Christiansen to our roster. When you list all the perks of a United Airlines captain, you'd think they'd add up to a pretty good life. But Mr. Christiansen quit that perfectly sensible job to work for Evergreen—which a few of you may have heard of.'' Payson's fey little smile suggested that any of the group who did not know of the extremely cordial relations between Evergreen International Aviation and the CIA did not know anything of importance. "Mr. Christiansen, you have the floor."

Curt Christiansen, tieless in a raffish sport coat, came forward with a nod toward Payson. Of medium height with close-cropped, thinning hair and high cheekbones, Christiansen moved with economy. He might have been a stockbroker retired in his late forties instead of a man who had flown arms into Africa and evacuees out of Pakistan.

"I've been thinking charter all along," he said, measuring his words slowly. "It fits, but it's a pain in the backside to start up a new charter service. I mean, there's a lot of paperwork and a lot of time involved. The initial application to FAA takes months. There are lists of manuals you must have on hand; engines, avionics, all that. You have to submit a minimum equipment list and prove your maintenance facilities. Somehow," he allowed the corners of his mouth to twitch, "I don't think that's a very likely scenario.

"What's more likely," he continued, "is a contract with an existing FBO—that's a fixed base operator away from the main terminal with its own hangar and taxiway, such as Butler in San Francisco and Reno, and Hughes here at McCarran. Big active terminal like McCarran usually has several FBOs on airport property. The big ones like Hughes can provide anything from avgas and sandwiches to a multiengine jet with catering for a hundred passengers. You pay for all that competence, but they're worth it.''

Gary Landis, experienced in shadowing people who favored chartered flights, raised a forefinger. "And from what I've seen, an FBO doesn't X-ray luggage or run you through metal detectors.''

"Too right," Christiansen shot back. "Take a charter

flight between a couple of FBOs and you think you're back in the days before airport security."

"Think, hell; you *are*," Landis insisted.

Christiansen shrugged. "Everybody in commercial aviation knows it; the public wants to see big, high-tech efforts to keep flying safe, and that's what they get. Not on most chartered flights, though. Can't be any big news to DEA that a tremendous amount of contraband can be moved by charter flights. If it's flagrant, an FBO might inform on them, but basically an FBO is a private commercial firm, like a common carrier. They just have to meet FAA criteria—and there are lots of those."

Walt Hildreth said, "I heard you saying a charter flight is a stronger possibility than a regular commercial airline flight."

With a glance toward Payson, the CIA pilot inclined his head. "That would be my guess. By the way, our assumptions pretty well rule out other local airports. Our target aircraft has got to carry fuel for over two thousand miles, plus something like fifteen to thirty tons of payload. That takes a lot of airplane. It might land and take off from Sky Harbor or North Las Vegas under ideal conditions, but neither one has an asphalt runway much over five thousand feet or over a hundred feet wide."

Payson: "Isn't that enough?"

"Not really. Altitude and temperature make a lot of difference; after midmorning in Vegas, the air gets so warm it robs you of a lot of lift. Takes higher speed to get airborne, and that means a longer runway. McCarran's long leg is two and a half miles, remember. Sometimes they need it all."

"So a big aircraft flying into either place would be very unusual," Payson suggested.

"A sore thumb," Christiansen agreed, "but it could be legit; one of those forest service borate bombers on a cross-country, something of that sort. Christ, they fly *every*thing, and when it's stripped and empty you can grease a DC-7 onto a smaller runway than that. All I'm saying is, it'd stand out. I can't believe the people we're up against are that stupid. Nobody that dumb would ever get his hands on that much money."

"All right, then, we concentrate on McCarran and put an aide at Sky Harbor and another one at North Vegas with FAA cover," Payson said. "And God help whoever leaks this. The opposition would just pull back and try again in a few months. We want to be their roach motel; we let 'em check in, but they won't check out."

A few smiles and nods ensued, Christiansen donating another lip twitch. "There's another base to cover," he said; "it's the aircraft type. Let's call the passengers and cargo the payload fraction. Very few airplanes can carry more than thirty percent of their gross weight as payload fraction. I'd suggest we run an exhaustive check on all known aircraft that can haul that payload that distance. It'll be a whopper of a list," he added. "But I'm guessing there'll be a few charters involving such aircraft at one of the McCarran FBOs. Servicing and maintenance and paperwork might take a week or so prior to takeoff."

"How would you like to handle that list, Christiansen?"

"Consider it begun," the pilot replied.

Lucille Dorman, who had kept her rosebud lips sealed until now, surprised Payson by raising her hand. *That's not the DEA we know and love,* he thought, nodding toward the pretty agent. "So far, nobody's mentioned the piece of the scam that interests me most," she said. Silence, but interested glances. "How the hell are those perps going to sucker forty people onto a one-way flight to nowhere?"

"Forty or more," Payson reminded her. "I can think of a few ways, but I'd rather you made the initial list. If you canvassed the FBOs, you might have a good start on what's likely."

"That's been worrying me too," said Givens.

"I thought it might," Payson murmured with a glance that added, *and Dorman's cleavage has nothing to do with it, I suppose.* "Dorman and Givens, then, on working out the sucker bait. Meanwhile, we keep teams of two on duty at the terminal. Next chalk talk in forty-eight hours, and if you need me, I'll be here. If I'm not, Hildreth will be." He snapped off the overhead projectors; looked around him for more input. "Okay, go for it."

The teams began to pair off as Payson gathered up the pages for Xerox and distribution. He found Hildreth standing beside him, rocking on his heels, hands thrust into pockets as he gnawed his lower lip. "Hildreth; problem with the assignment?"

Hildreth shook his head. "Just something for you to chew on. You said we're the roach motel, so they don't check out?"

"Don't take it personally," Payson said.

"No. But we may be missing a bet." Hildreth waited until his task force leader was fully attentive. "If we spot our target in time, Mr. Payson, we might win a lot bigger by letting 'em think they've checked out."

Payson locked gazes with the old pro for long seconds, nodding to himself. "A sting they carry home with 'em, you mean."

Now the nod, and the smile, were Hildreth's. "It might be a long shot," he said.

"Grab a chair," Payson invited, "and let's talk about long shots."

SEVENTEEN
Wednesday, May 17

STANDING IN THE shade of a mothballed C-82 with Denver's skyline in the distance, Torres watched his big Bristol flare out for its landing until it disappeared behind other aircraft. "I told you to dress lightly," he said to the sweating Borges beside him.

"I thought we would be in an air-conditioned airplane," Borges protested, "not broiling on an airport runway."

"This is not a runway," Torres replied patiently. "Most of these weary old birds exist for spare parts; they will never see a real runway again." They spoke quietly in lulls between the thunders of big commercial jets during takeoff. A jackrabbit paused beneath another derelict transport, a hundred meters away. Torres let his gaze travel over the acres of Stapleton International Airport's sequestered storage area, distant aircraft shimmering above the hot surface. The faint sound of gigantic fans swept across the open airfield ten seconds later as the Bristol's propeller blades reversed to test the system, and perhaps the pilot as well. "A check ride is no place for passengers, Billy. I just hope Orozco gets his type rating for the Bristol without delay."

It may have been the heat, or merely the naiveté of Borges, that put Torres in a foul mood. Borges could not seem to encompass the thousand details necessary for putting an old four-engined turboprop liner on a McCarran runway in seeming innocence by the end of May, less than two weeks away.

The mere fact of the Bristol's flightworthiness was a miracle, performed by hired maintenance crews. The Bristol's last previous flight, for storage in the high, dry air of Denver, had been over a year before. Torres had been dismayed to learn that its last commercial service had been between Miami and various Caribbean airstrips, because that kind of salt-air service often left an aircraft hopelessly corroded. However, his own inspection of the staunch old British liner had lifted his confidence somewhat.

Now, as the Bristol taxied the two miles back toward their storage apron, Torres felt a rising anxiety. If the Mexican, Orozco, could not pass his type rating for the Bristol in time, many plans would go awry. The cartel had the services of numerous pilots, but only a few commercially rated, whose records were still above suspicion. With a promise of $200,000 to let himself be "overpowered" by his first officer, Orozco did not mind coming under suspicion; and only Simon Torres knew that once on Honduran soil, Orozco would be both suspect and buried.

Borges seemed more curious than anxious, and proved his ignorance yet again. "This type rating; when will you have to do it?"

"I won't; as copilot, I only need a multiengine rating, which I have had for years. That medical exam I had two days ago updates my certificate. You see, because we are not charging our passengers, *ours will not be a charter flight*. I will need no commercial rating and I'm fully legal to fly beside Orozco."

"But if you don't know how to fly this type of—" Borges began.

"Orozco will have over a week to teach me," Torres interrupted. "For the love of God, Billy, trust me to know my business." *Perhaps his own problems will divert him.* "How will you take the cargo from storage, once we have flown to Las Vegas? Surely the fewer of your local people who know what they are moving, the less opportunity for trouble."

Now the pudgy Borges smiled as he mopped his brow. "None of this was the sort of thing I wanted to entrust to low-level people, so I sealed it all myself, inside ratproof five-gallon metal cans, four cans to the pasteboard carton," he said. "I must have sweated off two kilos in that week, loading and labeling. The cartons are labeled aniline dyes, and the cans clatter very convincingly inside. You will see; I will need you to drive one of the trucks and to help me load."

Torres imagined himself thrusting carton after carton of cash into the Bristol's belly. He would not mind that at all, but better that Borges should think otherwise. "Damned beasts of burden, is what we are," he growled. "How much in terms of volume?"

"Our cargo takes up eighteen cubic meters of space in that warehouse," said Borges. "It would fill a small room as high as a man's waist. I even have an extended lift-gate on my truck to raise the cargo—and I can see that it will be needed," he finished, nodding toward the approaching aircraft.

Torres let his eyes roam over his Bristol Britannia as it taxied to the edge of the apron and turned with a final surge from its nearside propellers. Unlike many aircraft of its time, the Bristol sported a low wing, its huge four-bladed props sweeping near the ground. Each of its main gear put four tires on the runway, retracting into an engine nacelle for flight. Torres liked the sudden downslope of its nose, a feature that gave unobstructed vision ahead and below. A Britannia rode lowslung against the runway, bringing its big straight wing low enough to steal extra lift from ground effect. It would be a lumbering brute, but while swilling jet A fuel its turbines would push it at over 350 miles per hour. *All the way to San Pedro Sula,* he reflected. *Too bad about Orozco, but I cannot have him running loose afterward. I shall worry not at all about that fumble-fingered pair training as flight attendants in Veracruz, but it is always a shame to waste a fellow pilot.* He had not decided yet about the passengers. It was clear that one or two might be sacrificed if necessary. Yet Torres was not a man who enjoyed killing noncombatants. Once he and Elath got all that cargo transferred to the truck Elath was providing, he might send most of the hostages scattering for cover. Or perhaps better still, simply leave them on the Bristol under cover of darkness with dire threats should any of them consider an escape.

Waiting for the jury-rigged ladder to descend, waiting more impatiently for a view of Orozco's face, Torres said, "Our cargo will fit in the luggage area in the belly of the beast, my friend, and it is not all that high off the ground. We can do all that the evening before the flight. I suggest we sleep in the aircraft that night."

"Rest assured," Borges answered, watching closely as the forward cabin door swung open.

The check pilot made his way down first, lugging a battered attaché case. Pablo Orozco followed, stuffing a clipboard inside the unzipped breast of his flight suit, showing his fine teeth even before he spotted his employers.

"*Gracias a Dios,*" Torres breathed. With that sunlit grin of his, Orozco had announced that Simon Torres was one step closer to a billion dollars in cash.

EIGHTEEN

Thursday, May 18

"I CAN'T LEAVE like that, Mr. Payson," Hardin protested, nursing a Sharp's as he leaned against one of Ben Ullmer's file cabinets. His stance suggested that he needed only a word or a gesture from Ullmer to walk out of the office, away from this impeccable FBI hulk with his startling offer.

To Hardin's surprise, Ullmer did not seem in a mood to give that word. Instead, the old fellow simply looked into the distance as if regretting a bad decision. Hardin shook his head at the solemn, silent Payson and tried again. "I'm scheduled to test-fly Spook 4 tonight. That's all we do here: build aircraft. We're busting our butts to get another aircraft flying and diverted to something you've set up, and—"

"Not us." There was no way Payson could force Wes Hardin into deeper involvement, and everyone in the room knew it. But among Payson's abundant talents was one for knowing when to listen, and when to argue. At the moment, it seemed a prudent move to make the Nellis part of the operation seem more distant from its roots in the nation's capital. "I know what you're talking about, but the people responsible for that are above my level. I'm just a cog grinding along with the multiagency task force in Nevada.''

Hardin had watched the bureaucratic chess before, and blocked the move. "You want me because of the spook-ships; right?"

A cautious nod.

"If it deals with these Nemesis missions, it's all the same big game, and we're running out of substitutes here at the factory. The woman who ought to be test-flying this bird is off somewhere boring holes in the air for you or your bosses, same difference, and, believe me, she'd rather be here." He turned toward Ullmer. "Ben, tell him!"

Ullmer pulled himself back to the present. "He knows, Wes. But there are only so many people who have your background."

"One, to be exact," Payson put in, using his patented gut-rumble. "This comes from above the bureau. Above the NSA. Above the CIA." In a bewildering change of pace, he tried a New York garment-district accent for comic effect: "You want I should draw you a pictchah?"

"Might help," Hardin admitted, amused in spite of himself. "What I've got to have is—" he paused, studying his watch—"twelve hours. Sixteen," he amended quickly. "It takes several hours to put Spook 4 through her paces; over an hour just to get up where she belongs. She can get down a lot faster."

"I have a watch too, Mr. Hardin" said Payson. "It tells me I've spent three hours away from where I belong at Nellis, and another hour or so before I get back. I can't afford it, but I did it. You're the reason. I saw that weird, wonderful airplane downstairs with claws on its wingtips and your people all over it, and I have to take NSA's word for what it does, but you're the man who knows its real limits. The reason I'm here is you, Mr. Hardin. We need you. People who will never even know your name need you."

"And you can't even tell us why," Ullmer injected. "That's the goddamn' gummint, all right. I oughta be building crop dusters!"

"I can tell *him*," Payson said, pointing at Wes Hardin, "once he's on board. I'm sorry, Mr. Ullmer."

Hardin had seen that hand-wave of Ben Ullmer's before; it said I hate it, but it's out of my hands. "You're screwing up your own delivery schedule, you know," Ullmer said. "And don't forget, Memorial Day weekend involves an extra day off for my people. That's a week from now, in case you need reminding."

"There is that," Payson muttered, then brightened. "Damn my stupidity! You can finish your shakedown flight and come to Nellis tomorrow, too, Hardin. I got here in an F-14 Tomcat, which is a shoehorn fit for me but it sure got me down on a short field, and if it doesn't get me out again, my wife's going to give somebody hell. But now that I got it requisitioned, I can keep it for a day. I could have a Tomcat waiting for you in North Bend sixteen hours from now. That'll put you straight into Nellis in the morning. Maybe you can catch a few winks in flight," he said, "if you like the idea of snoring at fifteen hundred miles an hour."

Wes Hardin shook his head sadly, crumpling his empty can, then managed a wry smile for his boss. "Ben, can we pull everybody off of Spook 5 to get Number 4 in the air?"

Ullmer, his chair swivel squealing, turned his back on them both and raised his outstretched arms to heaven. "Take 'em! Take Marie too, take my car, take my dog, if I had one. You realize I'll be running all three production teams myself? I've got a schedule here, and I don't intend to let it slip. Now both of you please just getthefuck out of here."

Hardin was out of the office, the big FBI man on his heels, when he heard Ullmer's chair squeal again. "Hardin! One question, just to humor me."

Hardin peered around a man who could have made two of him. "Let's have it, Ben."

"It was that ride in the Tomcat that did it. Wasn't it?"

Hardin glanced at Payson, then at the floor. "Aw hell, Ben. I've never flown an F-14," he said.

"Neither have I, but when this is all over, you button-down bastards owe me one, Payson, you hear me?"

''You'll get it,'' Payson called back. Wes Hardin was already halfway down the stairs.

———————

WES HARDIN MADE his accelerated schedule and flew to the North Bend facility in midmorning. Changing from a Cessna to an F-14, he found, was a little like stepping from a skateboard to a rocket sled. If he'd had any idea of catching a short nap, twin afterburners and that awesome vertical climb changed his mind for him.

Shortly before noon, he checked his watch again as an aide ushered him into Payson's bullpen, and found he had lost a bet with himself. It had not quite taken him longer to get from the Nellis runway, through the pass and ID section, to Payson's digs than it took an F-14 to fly the 700 miles from the Oregon coast to Nellis. Close, though. He decided he owed himself a beer.

After the fierce light outside, he blinked away his sun-blindness, ready to respond to smiles and nods by the staff as he approached Payson carrying his two-suiter. In this he was disappointed; the men and women in that big room seemed not to have noticed him at all, engrossed with their computer terminals and telephones.

Payson, at least, greeted him warmly, though he wasted no time in formalities. ''We need you fresh,'' he said. ''We've got a few daybeds in the next room if you need a nap.''

''I'm too wired,'' Hardin replied, looking around him. ''When I start feeling stupid I'll say so. Or maybe you'll tell me,'' he finished.

''Count on it.'' Payson turned to the aide. ''Pull the strategy group over here.'' To Hardin he said, ''Take a seat near that wall screen; your friend Morrison is getting some interesting pictures.''

My friend, hm? I reckon the bureau doesn't know everything, Hardin reflected.

While waiting for the group to assemble, Payson put a

map of Mexico on the screen and recited the bare bones of their problem: Task Force Enable not only had to identify a big airplane well before it took off from McCarran; they also needed to know if a Nemesis could ghost onto an enemy airstrip undetected. "And get out again with an extra aircrew of two or possibly three," Payson was saying. "There's just a chance that we might fly the target airliner down there ourselves, but not unless we can airlift our crew back out in one hell of a hurry." Payson craned his neck as a portly, aging man pulled up a chair next to them. "Wes Hardin, here's Walt Hildreth, the bureau man you can blame for this cockamamie scheme. Walt; Wes."

While Payson gave the two a moment to shake hands, he exchanged the map for a photograph. Hardin recognized its origin by the telltale crosshatches, part of the digitalizing process in sending a photograph by microwave from a Nemesis in flight. "This," he was told, "is a combination guerrilla training base and processing center fifty or so miles west of the Palenque ruins. It's—"

"I've seen the place," said Wes. "Runway altitude? Any prevailing winds?"

"Roughly a thousand feet," said a voice from behind Hardin, who turned to see an outstretched hand. "Curt Christiansen. If this comes off, Hardin, I may be flying our big Trojan horse into there. Sure hope you can get me out again. Oh, and from photint, we think you can count on light winds from the south over the runways."

Faint curved traceries on the photo provided a relief map showing local heights in forty-foot increments. "Just tell me we won't be dealing with choppy winds," Hardin pleaded. "That can happen at the edge of a mountain range."

"It's pretty well protected in that valley," Christiansen said, looking up as a stocky, tanned, blond man pulled up a chair near them.

Payson introduced the man, who Hardin guessed was pushing forty, as Lloyd Meacham, another of the three CIA agents dedicated to the task force. Meacham, it turned out, had a multiengine rating too—in addition to special training in light weapons and explosives. "This is the flight team, Hardin," Payson said with a circular wave of his hand. "There might be another man, depending on how much needs to be done at the last minute. We've got to know whether we have a prayer of pulling off our sting, and how good our prayer is; and we've got to know yesterday."

Hardin nodded, returning to his scrutiny of the photograph. "I can't tell you diddly-squat about the airliner's chances," he confessed.

"I'll have to make a go or no-go decision on that," Christiansen said. "But *if* we can put it down here, and *if* we do it before dawn, can we count on one of those forever-fliers of yours landing near the runway intersection to pick us up?"

"I don't see why not, unless there's some problem about the timing of all this. A Nemesis lands like a Schweizer sailplane, you know. Only you'll need two spookships, not one, especially if you have three crewmembers. Maybe you'd better firm up that crew list."

Christiansen drew in a breath and held it, with a long glance toward Payson. "Getting complicated," he frowned. "And my feeling is, we'd need that third man."

"Look, you'll have two deniable, privately owned spookships because I just cleared the second one," Hardin reasoned. "We give the crews a day or so in Kingsville, then fly each Nemesis in with a single fresh pilot. They're two-place aircraft, very sensitive to additional weight, but you *could* stash a third person in by doing some fuel transfer tricks. You want to bring three guys out? That's the only way to do it, unless you can get an SAR helo to come in from a carrier or a Coast Guard cutter."

"No way," Payson said. "Orders from 'way up; too much heavy politics involved, and they tell me nobody's flying a chopper yet that doesn't sound like God paddling double-time up shit creek."

"Now there's an image to ponder," Christiansen said, grinning. "But as for the timing: Uh, well, we're considering some options after we touch down. After all, our

Trojan horse is supposed to be theirs, so it's goddamned sure deniable. If you were the Company," he twitched a half-smile at the thought, "what would *you* like to fill an airliner with as a surprise for cokerunners?"

"Christ! the mind boggles," Hardin replied. "You haven't decided yet?"

A negative headshake from Christiansen. "It might be that we'll do a touch-and-go landing, and not even call the Nemesis ships in at all. But if we park that big sucker—whatever type it turns out to be, we know it'll be big—we have to know your assets will be out of the way when we come in, but in position to pick us up with exact timing."

"Say, right about here," Meacham put in, with the slow deliberation of a man who thinks twice before speaking once. On the screen, Meacham's finger was three inches wide, and its tip spanned the intersection of the two runways. He looked at Christiansen, then at Payson. "Well, if we're going to stop, there's no place half as good. Taxi toward those hangars, turn around, goose it back away from all those structures and crap where there's likely to be small arms fire."

It was Hardin's turn to consider the added complication. "Listen, a Nemesis has a ninety-foot span. You don't suppose you could go just past the intersection? You'll be blocking both runways."

"You just bet we will," Meacham said, and paused. "Curt, you might hang a ground loop and get your wings out of the way. That's a very narrow strip of runway."

"Yeah. But we're just playing with ourselves here. All we have to know from Hardin right now is this: Can two Nemesis craft land in tight formation, at night, timing it plus or minus ten seconds from my radio signal and stopping at a given spot?" Christiansen sat back and spread his hands as if to add, "This is the crux of it."

After a long pause, with four sets of eyes drilling into him, Hardin replied, "Only if you give us that signal three minutes or more in advance. A Nemesis comes in very slowly, Christiansen."

Hildreth: "Three minutes could be a lifetime, once they break radio silence."

"No hay problema; habla su frase in Español," Hardin said.

Christiansen: "Say what?"

Meacham, pointing a finger pistol-fashion at Hardin: "He said, 'No problem; say our code phrase in Spanish.' You rattled it off too fast for me but that's what you said, wasn't it?"

Hardin nodded. "And if you're bringing a big clumsy cargo plane into a place full of small arms, you damn well better have a good frequency and a Spanish-speaker on board. But that's your end of it," he added with a shrug.

"Hey," said Meacham, "you think that's all that's down there? There's some asshole flies a T-33 into there now and then. I just hope we catch him on the ground."

"If you don't, and he's there with any kind of radar or night vision stuff," Hardin said, "you can just forget about our spookships. Even without weapons, he could fly right through both of 'em and never feel it." He fell silent, studying the screen, thinking that it was Colleen Morrison who had sent them all that photo intelligence; wondering whether she would agree to pilot one of the spookships, and how Jared Cutter would respond. When no one broke the silence, he said, "So when does all this hit the fan?"

"That's problem one," Payson admitted. "We've had a false alarm already, Hardin, and I almost tipped our hand. One flurry of overt action from us and word will get out to the media. If we show our hand too soon we may as well pack up and go home."

"You've just got to be sneakier than they are," Hardin said, and winked.

"That's our charter," Payson agreed. "By the way: I knew you had some Spanish, but I didn't know you had it with the music. Let's talk about that."

NINETEEN

Saturday, May 20

BILLY BORGES DID not need an orientation to Las Vegas, having wasted many a month there; but even though familiar with Cartagena fleshpots, Simon Torres found the scope of the yanqui variations literally breathtaking. Where Denver's heat had been bearable, Torres found that his first noontime breaths in Las Vegas, minus air-conditioning, were like inhaling a blowtorch. Also, in blistering, nonmagical daylight the famed Las Vegas Strip seemed absurd to Torres, who had an informed layman's eye for architecture. The Holiday Inn reminded him of a highway collision between a Mississippi steamboat and Philip Johnson. The new Excalibur, where fake knights on real horses pranced across the lobby, he found too outré for comparisons; one horse, rumor said, had made a critical statement of sorts. The Mirage, at least, had some of the clean structural brio one found in Caracas or Bogota— if one could forget the six-story volcano that barfed perfume on a set schedule. Torres did not want to forget; it was the sort of display to make the poorest Colombian feel superior.

Torres coped by staying aloft in the big four-engined

Bristol Britannia or inside the motel at nearby Henderson until the evenings. That was when the lights of South Las Vegas Boulevard officially, magically, made it The Strip. He soon found more serious stripping on nearby Industrial Road, where escort services openly advertised beauties of many nationalities, with extremely personal service on a moment's notice and no obvious pimps. He spent a week that way, and managed to complete three calls to a San Pedro Sula number without making Borges any the wiser. In Honduras, Elath said he was ready with a truck, the T-33 almost ready. In Henderson, Torres was readier.

Henderson, Nevada is the little tail that swings discreetly in the wake of Las Vegas. It is home to croupiers, showgirls, and the honest workingmen who maintain enough marquee lights to illuminate Alaska, the glow visible across a hundred miles of desert whenever Torres practiced night flights with the Mexican pilot, Orozco. Most of Henderson's motels bear little resemblance to those twenty-story cultural tombstones a few miles away, and it was here, not far from his leased warehouse, that Borges had taken their rooms. During breakfast six days before takeoff, Borges first mentioned his problem at the warehouse.

"I did not want to mention this in Orozco's presence," Borges began, and paused. "Where is he, by the way?"

"Romancing a shill who has the morning shift at Vegas World," Torres replied, proud of his new jargon. "You know: two little skyscrapers like slot machines?"

"Ah. Well, I believe our warehousemen may be helping themselves to our cargo. At least, someone is."

"Spare me that calculating look, my friend. I do not even know where the damned warehouse is. Nor want to, until the time comes," Torres added, smearing a gobbet of rare steak in egg yolk.

"That time has come. For what we must do, I must have help."

"We? Billy, this storage business is your end of the shipment. Enlist your Mafia friends," Torres said, scowling at the coffee, which was a poor substitute for good fresh Chiapas stuff.

A firm headshake. Borges was ignoring his buttery pancake, and that meant it must be quite serious. "We cartelistas are like England," he said. "Outside our circle we have only interests, not friends. Our cargo is far too tempting, and I have stayed away from The Strip to avoid being seen."

Torres employed his napkin and sighed. "Our flight attendants will arrive here in a few days' time. Wait for them. They may look effeminate but—"

"They will not know our cargo either, and should not discover it. And what is happening to that cargo in the meantime, Simon? No, I need what the locals call a stand-up guy, while I ask those two picaros of Vega's a few questions. The man who helps me must be one of us." Silence, as the two regarded the ruins of their breakfasts. "Must I call Catemaco for help when you are already here?"

He must not think I fear their scrutiny. "Please yourself," Torres replied, raising his coffee cup without tremor. "Do you imagine our colleagues will praise you for letting your part of this operation get out of hand?"

Borges reached for his own cup; thought better of it; wiped a bead of moisture from his upper lip. *He would spill that swill all over himself if he tried to sip it,* Torres thought with satisfaction.

As the challenge died in Borges's eyes, he asked, "You are familiar with my Catemaco housekeeper, Simon?"

"The rubia, blonde, with the tiny waist and the ass you think is solid gold? I have seen her," Torres admitted, knowing how much Borges valued her many services.

"She is yours, my friend. But only if you are my friend," said Borges.

After a moment to let Borges sweat, Torres manufactured a smile of pure sweetness. "Friends can share," he said. "And so I suppose I should share in solving your little problem." And so, on the following morning, Simon Torres carried a little Skorpion machine pistol slung beneath his sport coat.

The Skorpion is a Czech weapon, quite small without a suppressor, carrying a twenty-round magazine. Borges produced a pair of them in the footwell of his rented Mercury Sable, and that made a point to Torres. If Billy Borges spent so much of his time in Las Vegas, and if he could produce such illegal firepower any time he needed it, then probably Borges had some permanent base nearby that was far more secure than a motel. But if Borges had a home there, why had he not invited Torres to enjoy his hospitality in the Latin tradition? Orozco, perhaps?

Yes, the Mexican was a complication, a man the cartel needed to use exactly once. *Borges does not want to show us his place, because he would then be obliged to move. If I were in his position, I might do the same,* Torres decided. He asked a few intelligent questions about the Skorpion's fire selector and its vertically folded wire stock, and chose to ask Borges no questions about where it all came from as he entered the passenger's side of Billy's blue Sable.

After Borges drove the Sable across railroad tracks in the general direction of Las Vegas, they approached a vast area of Henderson's outskirts given over to rectangular structures, a few with windows, some without. The Sable veered down a broad street faced by loading docks, and Torres watched as two men with forklifts ferried pallets of cardboard cartons from one warehouse to a waiting eighteen-wheeler. He entertained a fantasy that all those cartons, too, were full of yanqui hundred-dollar bills, and he smiled.

"I wish I had something to laugh about," said Borges, seeing the smile. A few hundred yards along he nosed the Sable into morning shadow between two warehouses and killed the engine before, very deliberately, unwrapping and lighting a cigar.

The air-conditioning had died with the engine and Torres was opening his door when Borges pointed to the glove compartment. "Por favor, Simon; my fireworks."

Torres, nonplussed, found two green-wrapped packets of Chinese firecrackers in the compartment among rental papers and maps; held them up. Borges's nod and gesture said that Torres was correct, and Torres tossed them over.

Borges, grinning, peeled away the translucent paper with its bright label that identified the contents at 20 Celestial Salutes, teasing the fuses apart with sausage fingers that became stained, as he worked, with a silvery gray powder. Then, sitting with his rump in the Sable, feet on macadam, Borges touched his cigar to a firecracker he had separated from the two rows in the packet.

Borges glanced at his companion and winked, holding the firecracker between thumb and forefinger, waiting until the silver of the fuse became gray at the tip of the paper tube before flicking it away. It became confetti in midair with a report that returned sharp echoes from nearby structures. Borges pulled another firecracker from the packet, lit it as before, tossed it farther this time. It hit the macadam, hissing, then became more confetti. Meanwhile, Borges was lighting a tangle of fuses without separating them, tossing them beyond the second firecracker.

The heat, Torres decided, was already becoming oppressive and the games of Billy Borges idiotic. He shut the Sable's door, checked the hang of his sport coat, and watched, impassive, as the Celestial Salutes evaporated in a series of small peppery explosions.

"Keeps them on their toes," Borges said, seeing his companion's expression. Torres watched a man walk from a distant warehouse and stand on the lip of the concrete dock, looking in their direction, and Torres shook his head, unamused. That was when Borges rolled back translucent paper from the second packet and lit the entire bunch at once, tossing it high into the air a fraction of a second before it began to disintegrate into twenty bursts of paper fragments and smoke.

Keeping the distant warehouseman at the edge of his vision, Torres walked around the car, squinting against brilliant reflections. "No roquetas or smoke bombs to amuse yourself, Billy? Then let us get out of this furnace." He still did not know which of the buildings to enter, nor how, but Borges settled his unspoken question as he flicked his cigar away and hopped, with surprising agility, up concrete steps to the nearest warehouse.

"Many fireworks are illegal now," Borges said, bringing a tagged key from his vest pocket and fitting it to a metal-faced door. "So they become contraband. And the laws against them are so unpopular that one can use them openly without fear. What better way to signal Vega's men inside?"

Torres said nothing. His combative juices were stirring but, as he reached inside his jacket, Borges stopped him with a muttered, "No show of force yet. Only if necessary," and stepped into semidarkness with a hearty "Hola."

Torres blinked, trying to see the source of the answering hail from somewhere above: "We knew it must be you, jefe." He thought he recognized the voice, and became certain when the man trotted down the last few steps from a second-story office inside. Yes, it was Acosta, one of the Medellin English-speakers. Torres knew him slightly: an obedient soldier with some education, but without enough imagination to be worrisome.

Recognizing Torres, the wiry Acosta stuck his pistol into his waistband and, hands at his sides, made the faintest of formal bows. "A sus ordenes, Colonel," he murmured.

"Be at ease," Torres replied, always pleased when a man reminded him of his old title. Then he looked toward Billy Borges. This was Billy's show, but that glance said *get on with it*.

"The colonel has asked to see our dye shipment," Borges said, mopping his neck in the stillness. Somewhere an air conditioner hummed, but the air in the warehouse was still at blood temperature. "If it is cooler upstairs, go. We will call if we need you. And Cordero—he is with you?"

"Si, jefe," said Acosta, and slipped upstairs to the offices, each step a tiny explosion of dust from the steps into a vagrant sunbeam from window slits near the roof.

Borges grunted as the man disappeared. Then, "There

is a window overlooking us from the offices. It will be interesting to see if they are watching,'' he added, walking toward an electric forklift attached to a wall plug.

Torres hated to sweat, and he was sweating as he watched Borges disconnect the forklift and test its buttons. Soldiers of the cartel were trained to remain incurious about the actions of superiors. If Acosta or his colleague watched them, that fact alone would be enough to raise suspicion. Torres kept the window at the edge of his vision as he moved about, avoiding Borges, whose forklift whined its way across concrete, Borges walking behind to steer with the control handle in both hands.

Until now, the dimness and his own caution had kept Torres from paying overt attention to the palletloads of cargo stacked near the back wall of the warehouse. But his vision had cleared quickly and now Torres frankly stared at those stacks with stencils in two languages. Borges jockeyed the flat steel arms of the forklift into the wooden pallet beneath one stack and selected another button, the man-high stack tilting toward him slightly, secure against the forklift. *A hundred million yanqui dollars on wheels,* Torres thought, watching Borges tow the stack a few yards away. *Or is it?* Aloud, he said, ''Can they live up there? Toilets, food, telephones?''

''No telephone. They do live there,'' Borges panted, hauling the control arm around as he swung the forklift toward another stack of cartons.

As the second stack trundled away under Billy's control, Torres noticed smears in the faint patina of dust that covered the third row of those cardboard containers. He stepped aside as Borges maneuvered the forklift again, finally to tilt the third stack. The forklift whined in a new note, the stack slowly levitating until the pallet base stopped at the height of a man. Then Borges came forward, breathing heavily.

After a moment of silent scrutiny: ''You see it,'' Borges said, pointing at those smears, leaning forward. ''No fingerprints. Gloves, no doubt.''

"How did you know?" Torres asked.

"The light happened to fall just right the last time I checked the shipment. There is not enough room between those stacks for a child to squeeze in, let alone a man," Borges said darkly. "Someone used the forklift and swept the floor afterward. He just forgot to wipe down all the faces of the cartons."

Now Borges was testing the cartons, thumping, peering, sneezing at the dust. It was Torres who stepped beneath the pallet and saw the space between wooden slats where a hand might be inserted—in fact, *had* been inserted. "Under here, Billy," he said, pointing toward the place where cardboard had been sliced away to metal, the thin metal of the canister bottom cut and torn, then pressed back into place.

Borges said nothing until he had used his pocketknife to pry the metal open. His hand protected from sharp edges by his sweat-damp handkerchief, he reached up through the hole in the canister's bottom and vented a curse. He pulled back and gestured to Torres. "Feel for yourself. The damned canister is empty."

Torres borrowed the lighter from Borges and flicked it to life, feeling only metal. He saw faint flickers of light through the hole, reflections of the flame from the inside of the canister. He handed the lighter back with, "And how many others, I wonder?"

Borges shrugged. "Only one canister was cut here. Stupid bastards! But cautious enough, I hope, to have left the rest alone."

They lowered the stack to the floor, Borges using his knife to open the tops of several containers. In each, they pried up wide circular lids to reveal banded groups of bills, some of hundreds, some of fifties. Both men were drenched with sweat when Borges, with a heavy sigh, pronounced himself satisfied. "We must check under each pallet, of course, but that will not take long."

Yet it did take long, and not once during this process, insofar as Torres could see, had the men upstairs passed that window. But surely, surely they would be in fear of discovery. At least one of them knew that this mountain of 'dye' was a staggering fortune in money.

In another twenty minutes, the two men had looked beneath every stack, finding no more pilferage. By this time the pallets stood in disarray across the warehouse floor, and Torres was wondering how fat Billy was still on his feet. "I say we find a cooler place," Torres said.

Borges, wheezing too hard to speak, nodded and motioned him toward the stairs. Simon Torres had never before wished for an escalator on a single flight of stairs.

They found Acosta squatting at the refrigerator of a kitchenette, pouring cola from a plastic container. Cordero, a thickset man pale and heavily muscled, sat alert on a futon watching television, so positioned that he could see the street through an outside window. Neither man showed fear, and Cordero seemed impressed to meet the famous Colonel Simon Torres of the Cali cartel. Billy's first move was into the walled-off bathroom, where Torres saw a shower stall before Billy closed the door. The office smelled as if no one ever used that shower, and while washing his hands and face at the sink near the refrigerator, Torres realized that he could not remove his coat without revealing the kind of weapon that was never carried casually. Though the office was comfortably cool, he felt as if someone had dipped him in thinned mastic and then forced him to run ten kilometers uphill.

And when Borges came out of the bathroom, he came with his Skorpion unlimbered, its stock against his arm. His field of fire put both Cordero and Acosta directly in line, and though he was well out of the line of fire, Torres was furious because he was dripping wet, his own weapon still compacted under his coat.

Because Borges said nothing, Acosta needed two seconds to realize his predicament. His "Jefe! Why?" and the raising of his arms made Cordero look around, and when Cordero came up from the futon he did it as if scalded, his hands a blur.

Torres would never know exactly what Cordero intended with his hands because, for all his flab and soft living, Billy Borges was not slow. A Skorpion can be set for full auto but Borges squeezed off three single rounds that caught Cordero high across the back, the multiple impacts hurling him forward on his face. While Borges stepped nearer to Acosta, the dying Cordero rolled onto his back, mouth working silently. His face did not show fear; only rage.

Torres needed that time to bring his own Skorpion out, training it on Acosta, who was either genuinely astonished or a masterful actor. "No, jefe, no! I am your man," he stammered, looking into the eye of Borges's weapon, then turning a beseeching gaze on Torres.

"Then you will have to prove it," Borges replied. "Turn around. Simon, take his weapons. Por favor," he added in afterthought, stepping sideways. Torres was relieved to note that Borges kept his wits, moving so that he could fire on Acosta without hitting his own colleague.

Torres, the barrel of his own Skorpion jammed into Acosta's side, found the man's S & W automatic in his waistband, a four-inch switchblade in his right hip pocket, and a snub-nosed revolver in an ankle holster. With the faintest of smiles, he asked, "Anything else?"

Acosta swallowed hard. "A little trick knife in my belt buckle, Colonel. Nothing more."

"Let him keep it," Torres said to Borges, and moved back.

"Face us again," Borges ordered, and Acosta complied, hands still raised. Cordero was still breathing, but in liquid rasps, a bright crimson bubble forming before it burst at his lips. Torres placed Acosta's weapons on the futon and knelt by the fallen man, rolling him over. "You will not live," he said to Cordero. "You may as well tell us about what you stole."

Cordero tried to speak but only coughed blood, his torso jerking in spasms as he inhaled. Torres tried again: "Was it both of you?"

Cordero's headshake was clear. Torres: "You, alone?"

Cordero's motion may have been another headshake but it ended with a violent fore and aft spasm, spraying blood onto the linoleum floor. Torres stood up then, moving away, and watched Cordero die. It was not a process he enjoyed but, in the Colombian way, it demonstrated to Acosta that life was fleeting and that death could be exceedingly painful.

When at last Cordero lay still, Borges pulled up a folding chair and sat down, his Skorpion still pointed at Acosta. "Simon, cover our Señor Acosta for me." As Torres recovered his weapon and held it at ready, Borges removed his tie, already loosened during his sweltering work below. "Down on your face, Acosta," he said, and then proceeded to bind the man's wrists behind him.

Torres could see a very special kind of fear in Acosta's face now, not the fear of death but of the kinds of things Colombians did to a man before his death. All Acosta said, his mouth against linoleum, was, "But Jefe, I am your man."

When Borges was done he said, "We think you are your own man. Sit in that chair and tell us about your theft."

Acosta struggled to his feet and did as he was told. It occurred to Torres that the man had probably witnessed such interrogations before, perhaps even conducted them, because this nasty business was usually turned over to cartel soldiers, sometimes with a physician nearby to keep the prisoner awake and able to answer questions. Acosta watched Borges light a cigar. Shaking his head, he said, "Jefe, I have stolen nothing. I do not think Cordero has, either. If he did, what was it?"

"That is for you to tell us," Borges said, inspecting the glow of his cigar. When Acosta only shook his head in bewilderment, Borges said, "How many times have you left Cordero alone here, and for how long?"

Acosta tried to ignore the movement of that cigar past his eyes, but blinked at the smoke. "Once a week, one of us replenished our food and made the telephone call you required. An hour, more or less. Sometimes Cordero, sometimes myself. Sss,'' he finished between his teeth as the cigar touched an ear.

If he were smarter, he would not show such bravery, thought Torres. "An hour might be enough," he said to Borges.

The fat man took a thoughtful drag on his cigar. "Perhaps. Tell me, Acosta: Has anyone else been here, anyone at all?''

"Only you, jefe. Our only problem was boredom," Acosta replied.

"Can you operate the forklift for me?''

"Yes, of course, jefe. At least I think so, *creo que si.*''

"But you are not certain," Torres put in, despite a hooded look from Borges.

"I have never done it, but I think I could," was the reply.

Borges again: "Did Cordero know how?''

A tortured look from Acosta, then: "I could lie and say yes, jefe, but I do not know. Truly, I think Cordero, he was loyal also. But I still do not know what was taken.''

Acosta gasped as the cigar entered his ear; cried out, shook his head as sparks flew from the ear. Torres saw something, then, that gave him new insight to the ways of Guillermo "Billy" Borges. Whatever Acosta might have done or not done, he had been loyal for many years. Left to his hobby, Borges might learn where roughly a million dollars had gone, but Torres thought not. In any case, Acosta would never again be dependable. As Borges opened his little knife and moved back to their captive's hands, Simon Torres made his own decision. He took Acosta's switchblade, flicked it open, and while using his free hand as a splash guard he made a single sweep across the man's unprotected throat.

Acosta's lunge brought him to his feet, the chair falling with him, and Borges needed an instant to see what had interrupted his little game. Torres controlled his rage at

Borges only with great effort. "You were wasting time, Billy. And liking it."

"Acosta lied. I have seen him use a forklift in Medellin. Now we will never find the rest of the money."

"It could not have been over a million, Billy. I will make it up myself," Torres said, closing the knife, trying to ignore the noises near his feet.

"Acosta's life was worth that much to you?"

"He was a soldier," Torres shrugged, avoiding the kicks of the unfortunate Acosta, who was bleeding out on the linoleum. "Not a very smart one, but a temptation of that size might overpower many a loyal man."

"So you will make it up," said Borges, leaning forward to retrieve his tie. "Of course, you realize that one or another of us must stay on these premises until we move the shipment."

"Yes?" Torres's raised brow asked why.

"In case they had help, my friend. For these last days and nights we must be very, very careful. Those two will begin to stink before that, so I must dispose of them in the desert tonight. I will take the first watch now, and you can make some excuse to Orozco. But do not forget me tonight," he said almost gaily, handing the car keys to Torres. "And bring me a pair of shower curtains. We will need them to keep the car's trunk clean."

Torres nodded, then washed his hands again in a muttering fury before he left the office. He did not care that his disgust showed. By his acts Billy Borges had made it necessary for Torres to spend much of his remaining time waiting in a damned warehouse office.

And Billy's acts had not been due entirely to necessity. Torres's new insight had come when he saw, during Acosta's interrogation, a nice little erection at the crotch of fat Billy Borges.

TWENTY

Monday, May 22

LAURIE IRVINE SLAMMED her armload of assorted documents down with a report Cam heard all the way from the garage. He was not surprised to hear the sound that followed: "Ca-am! Can you come here?"

"Oh sure," he muttered, struggling to lift the old Evinrude into the boat. "Can't find your ass with both hands so I—"

"Ca-a-am!" Then, loud enough to be heard by their neighbors in suburban Redding, California: "CAM!"

"Okay! Just a minute, for Christ's sake," he called, dropping the little outboard across the boat's transom harder than he intended. He stomped into the garage passthrough, letting minor irritation raise his blood pressure as usual, exactly the way their family physician said he mustn't. Laurie's study was at the other end of the house, sunny and bright and, as Laurie often reminded him, too small. Cam pushed her study door open and tried to make his face neutral, failing miserably, knowing it. A single word escaped him, managing to carry abused patience, an attempt at sweet equanimity, and truculence all at once: "Yeah."

"Our birth certificates aren't where I put them, and the brochure said we've got to have 'em or we don't fly to Condo Vallarta on Friday. If you're going to make me the keeper of records in this goddamn broiler, stop moving everything around when my back is turned." Angry or in repose, Laurie had brains aplenty, but even an idiot could see that Cam was ready for a fight before she said a word to him, his graying hair askew from whatever the hell he was doing, his belly tight against size forty jeans. She knew he was readying the boat for a couple of days on Lake Shasta, and that meant it was play, and if she had to work she could damned well call him away from his play.

Which Cam always resented, and often said so, and after thirty-five years of wrangling it was obvious that neither of them was likely to change. Cam Irvine, knowing damned well he hadn't moved a scrap of those mare's-nest records of hers, shut his eyes in silent concentration.

Because Laurie paid more attention to their grown son's needs than to her own, and because young Robbie knew it, it was always Laurie he asked about such details when he called. Cam adhered to the proposition that a grown man should keep his own records, while Laurie would turn the bungalow upside down to find an errant slip of paper for Robbie.

After a moment, Cam's eyes snapped open. "You had all three birth certificates in the usual wrong envelope when Robbie called last month for his. Does that help?"

"How can that help," Laurie snarled, "unless I put our records back in his file?"

"It can't, unless you did," Cam said with preternatural calm. She walked to her file cabinet with a fine bounce of tits, which intrigued him now as much as they ever had, and jerked the top drawer open—the "Robbie" file—and Cam made the process worse. "If you'd get this paper tsunami cleared up in here, instead of filing like old folks fuck, in fits and farts without result, you wouldn't have to yowl at me every ten seconds."

"Shit, piss, and vinegar," Laurie said, her cursing always a bit askew from other people's, as she drew an envelope from Robbie's file. The heavy flowpen legend on the envelope said, "Social Sec. cards" but both of them knew she kept the birth certificates there. "And if you're so bitching smart, Mr. Irvine, why don't we have enough money to extend this room enough for more files?'Cause no effin' engineering firm that checks past your resumé wants to put up with your shit," she answered herself.

Cam felt his bile rising, and she had the documents, so he found two reasons to escape and none to stay. As he stomped back through the house he could hear, "And I'm tired of putting up with it too, buttbreath, especially when you start something and run away before I have my say—" She was not through, but the slam of the pass-through door gave them both an exclamation mark.

They hadn't always fought this way, Cam reflected as he stowed the Evinrude properly. It had started when they were fortyish instead of sixtyish, about the time Cam decided he'd had it up to his eyeteeth with the aerospace industry. Didn't matter whether you invented a new injector nozzle for the company or a hairpin for your wife, you signed away rights to *all* your ideas, and if you pursued that hairpin idea on your off hours, the goddamn company could take the royalties away from you after you got the patent anyway. It was like the articles he sometimes wrote for magazines, as he was fond of saying: There were a dozen people in the loop between the initial "aha" and the final payoff, and the only sonofabitch the company dared to withhold payment from was the poor slob whose idea it was in the first place.

Cam had been forty-four, Laurie forty, and little Robbie all of five when Cam Irvine gave notice for the last time. Laurie had a good job with Allstate, even then; they'd saved enough for the endless maneuvers of patent attorneys; Cam brought in some money writing articles on technology; and one of these days the construction industry would realize that glass cable could beat steel in sev-

eral ways. It was that cable anchor of his that would make
glass cable practical, and this time the company would
consist of Cameron Donald Irvine.

Back then, when he explained it all to Laurie, she'd
given him one of those delirious kisses of hers, had gone
back to work that bored her silly, had in fact become the
main wage-earner while Cam wrote a lot and got paid a
little. Not until the patent became his after its third pros-
ecution did Cam Irvine begin to realize just how conservative the construction business could be. By the time the
glass cable anchor began to sell, Cam's old engineering
pals back in Sunnyvale were taking early retirement and
Robbie's after-school job kept him from trying out for var-
sity football. And somewhere in there, Cam and Laurie
had begun to supplant kisses with curses.

The truth, Cam knew, was that Laurie was a workaholic
while he was a playaholic. Oh, he could build the best boat
trailer in Redding from odds and ends—but only because it
was fun. Laurie, on the other hand, would put in hours without overtime at the office simply because the work needed
doing. She no longer tried to enjoy his hobbies—fishing, golf-
ing—and he still bitched when she came home five hours
late, bleary-eyed from overwork. He would call her "biga-
mist" and ask when she'd actually married the company. She
would call him "genius" and ask where he was hiding all
the money from Irvine Glass Anchor, Inc.

Though Cam had long since concluded he was merely an
adequate engineer with slick new solutions to old problems,
he knew Laurie did have a particular genius of her own. It
had been Cam who chose Redding as a place for Robbie to
grow up, but it was Laurie who found a repossessed three-
bedroom bungalow and bought it from the bank for a really
paltry down payment. "On a frigging credit card," he muttered to himself, recalling it now, lost in genuine admiration
for the way Laurie could work a system. Cam didn't work a
system, he fought it. And he didn't merely burn his bridges
behind him; he detonated them.

He opened the garage door and backed their Voyager

van to the boat trailer, determined to get a couple of days on the lake before the summer heat got truly fierce. Ordinarily he could have picked his days but, thanks to Laurie's sharp eye, not this time. She'd heard friends talking about some brochure offering an all-expenses trip to, of all places, Puerto Vallarta. And once Laurie saw that brochure and determined that she and Cam met all the qualifications but the fact of being solicited, nothing could have stopped her short of a federal injunction.

She got the telephone number of that ritzy L.A. bunch that liked to lower-case their name, management internationale, and convinced them that Cameron Donald Irvine, president of Irvine Glass Anchor, was a prestigious candidate they'd simply overlooked.

"Jee-zus; if only she really believed it," he mumbled, knowing that in some hidden corner of her heart she did believe it, lowering the garage door after he'd towed the boat into late morning sunlight. They weren't about to buy a goddamn condo at goddamn Puerto Vallarta, noooo *way*— unless, of course, his business took a sudden skyrocketing upturn. It could happen; it should happen; and Cam felt certain that, sooner or later, it would. Meanwhile, he took his vacations whenever Laurie wangled specials from the airlines, and treated life as a hobby, and never once wondered if maybe their only mutual hobby was verbal war.

Cam was in the kitchen, fitting the top on his Styrofoam cooler, when he heard the clip-clip of Laurie's heels on hardwood flooring. Not many women her age wore high heels; but very few women her age had legs that invited attention. He turned, seeing her poised in the doorway, probably ready for another battle, and though he knew she would not have gone fishing if he asked, he felt a pang of guilt.

"Thanks for taking the morning off," he said. "I wouldn't have known where to find all that shit we need for your vacation."

"Our vacation," she corrected. "I think of you too, you know."

"I know you do. Funny, you have so much patience

when you're finagling somebody else's system." He did not have to add, *and so little dealing with ours.*

"I guess I can jerk 'em around because I don't care about them much," she said. She did not have to add, *and I care about ours a lot.*

He picked up the cooler under one muscular arm; moved to encircle her with the other. "Don't wear yourself out so you fall asleep on the plane," he said, and kissed her forehead.

She patted his broad back, gave it a brief scratch. "Hell if I will," she replied, getting her slang faintly wrong as usual. "I've taken the rest of the week off. You just be sure you're here Thursday before noon; they won't hold up that Friday morning flight in Las Vegas for the likes of us."

"Serve 'em right if I bought the whole outfit and fired 'em," he grinned. "Take my calls, okay?"

"Fart on that," she responded. "I may drive the Chevy to Sacramento and stay with Minnetta a couple of nights."

"Hold it. Why not just pack a few things for us both and I'll drive down there day after tomorrow and pick you up on the way to Vegas?"

"Fine, but don't you puke and moan over what I pack," she replied.

"So long as you pack the documents, Laurie. I wouldn't want you to screw yourself up."

Thus challenged, she set her jaw. "You just be there, buster," she said.

He wedged the cooler in place, let the Voyager's oil pressure stabilize as all sensible engineers did, and pulled out of the driveway with a wave.

At the pass-through, Laurie waved back. In a half-hour, she intended to be on the way to Minnetta's. "Take his calls, poo," he said aloud. "Let the genius buy us an answering machine."

And that is why the Federal Bureau of Investigation failed to find either of the Irvines by telephone or stakeout team.

TWENTY-ONE

Tuesday, May 23

AT NOON ON Tuesday, Lucille Dorman sipped her iced coffee in the Omni Lounge, annexed to the Flite Deck Restaurant, and watched a business jet taxi away from the executive terminal of Hughes Aviation Services. "Too big for a Lear," she said, pointing with her glass. "What is it?"

"You've got me," Merle Givens admitted. "Cessna Citation? Too small for us, anyhow." He downed the last of his orange juice with a lip-smack and an "aaah" before checking his wrist. "Sure beats hanging out with Hughes Security," he said.

Dorman nodded. While the Hughes people had no hard data on what the pretty DEA lady and her attentive bureau friend sought, they knew it pertained to a medium-sized airliner, probably a charter flight. The previous Friday, their alertness had put Dorman and Givens in overdrive: an old Boeing 707, chartered to take a large group of teachers to La Paz, near the tip of Baja California.

Nearly a dozen task force personnel had converged on

the Hughes facility that Saturday morning, some in work clothes, all of them packing hardware that would have sent metal detectors twittering. The food and beverage group at Hughes had orders for two meals and snacks for seventy-nine people including the airliner crew. The beverage list had made Walt Hildreth ask jokingly whether college professors could possibly down that much booze in one flight, and whether MLA meant Modern Language Association or Major League Alcoholic.

Every detail unearthed by Payson's team seemed to endorse the MLA charter as an innocent vacation where teachers could brush up on their conversational Spanish—until Mapes, the black bureau weight-lifter, spotted a cargo tug positioning its string of trailers for loading. John Kennedy Mapes checked the MLA manifest. Those teachers had not brought four dozen brand new, boxed-in-carton Macintosh computers on the trip, but stencils on the cartons indicated that the charter outfit was carrying all those computers to a firm in La Paz.

Another bureau man, with perfect Miami Spanish, put in a call to the La Paz retailer while Mapes, in the guise of a Hughes loader, managed to rip the corners off two cartons by a judicious miscalculation with a forklift. While repairing the cartons with duct tape, Mapes found them both to be full of Macintosh, and got their weights on a bathroom scale he had borrowed from Hughes security.

Every last carton weighed within ounces of the others, as Mapes learned while positioning the cartons in the Boeing's belly. They found that the charter outfit had indeed made a last-minute deal with a La Paz retailer. At that point, Payson made a command decision and took an option he had worked out with the help of the MLA. Eulalie Calvin, Lucille Dorman, Lloyd Meacham, and Merle Givens were added to the passenger list, carrying Ingram submachine guns with brittle plastic slugs in attaché cases. The frangible slugs, said Quantico, were far less likely than lead to penetrate the fuselage wall of a Boeing in flight.

The Boeing took off an hour late with its four extra teachers, all four accepting aisle seats with good grace. Jump-jets from San Diego paced the big airliner at distances too great to seem suspicious, turned to the transceivers carried by Givens and Meacham.

Once the big aircraft flew into Mexican air space Payson could only wait, not knowing which scenario even to hope for, until he received a call from Givens in La Paz. The flight, said Givens, had been innocent, barring Dorman's problem with the half-smashed Lothario sitting next to her, a linguist who did not seem to understand ''no'' in any language. The only problem remaining to the Baja Four was in chartering a twin Piper across from Baja to Mazatlán, to place their attaché cases in the hands of the American Consul there. Mexican airport inspections on flights back to the U.S. could be only too thorough in these ticklish times, and the team could not risk alerting authorities to their presence on Mexican soil with four very special weapons. It wasn't that they feared the Mexicans would not understand; they feared just the opposite.

At first, Merle Givens had feared another of Payson's little lectures for having bayed at a false scent. But Payson, in a plenary session at Nellis, had singled him out with Dorman for acclamation. ''I've been all over it, and I agree that it smelled wrong. This may have been the best thing that could've happened: the charter people still don't know they put us through this drill, and next time we'll be more streamlined. Especially Mapes,'' he said, deadpan. Everyone knew Jack Mapes had sweated off nearly five pounds while flailing around on his knees with that bathroom scale in the guts of the Boeing.

Since that false alarm, Dorman and Givens had turned up nothing of interest. Dorman was not even interested in the fact that Merle Givens dressed better and better every day, ever since he learned that she favored a snappy dresser. Now he adjusted his tie, checked himself in the bar mirror, and said, ''Do we make a great couple, or what?''

"We're dynamite, Merle. But try to remember my guy's an orthodontist in North Hollywood," she said, standing up. "You think we should call in to Payson now?"

That might mean a split in their duties; and every hour with Dorman, he felt, was another hour to infect her with his charm. "Tell you what: Let's do it after we check with Hall Aviation. I know it's hot," he apologized, seeing her grimace.

Hall Aviation, a small fixed base operator some hundreds of yards distant, catered chiefly to smaller aircraft. They had virtually written it off after their first visit, and where Hughes was thirty degrees cooler inside, Hall seemed to be ten hotter. Lucille Dorman sighed and agreed on the visit, careful to pocket the beverage receipt because government reimbursements covered only expenses she could prove.

Their unmarked Pontiac was a sauna but the trip was short, only as far as the one-story offices grafted to Hall's big hangar. Givens beat Dorman to the door; held it open; hurried in to escape the Nevada noon.

The cheerful matron who retailed air charts and hangar space from the Hall counter had seen the nice young couple before, but still had no idea what flight the young lady's brother had spoken of in such vague terms. Without a strong security section, Hall Aviation was not the sort of operator that rated the show of ID and the long explanation. "Let's see," the matron said brightly, "he's the one who wanted to get experience as a flight steward with a charter flight, isn't that right?"

Dorman nodded while Givens, with a sad little smile, said, "He's given to flights of fancy, ma'am, and all we want is to talk him out of it. He's only eighteen."

"Still nothing, I'm afraid," the woman said. "And if he'd been asking around, I'd know about it."

In turning to leave, Dorman found her eye speared by a glint from a single tail fin, so high that it could be seen above Hall's modest hangar. "Gee, what's that behind the hangar? I've seen it taking off so often, it must be a trainer or something.''

"No, dear, just a transient," said the matron. "Owner of record is a Los Angeles firm."

"Ah," said Dorman, halfway out the door.

"Scheduled to fly about fifty people to Puerto Vallarta late Friday morning," the matron added. "They have their own flight attendants, though."

Dorman stopped. Givens bumped into her. Dorman: "Then it's a charter."

"No, dear, not unless the passengers pay. As I understand it, they're investors in a real estate scheme, so the flight is free. That makes it not a charter. All quite legal," she added.

Merle Givens had not imagined he could feel gooseflesh in such heat. "But that's just the sort of thing young Jimmy would like," he said. "Who did you say was the owner firm?"

"Oh, that's pretty farfetched, I'd say," said the matron, rummaging through a pile of papers. "They're from L.A.; management internationale, with little letters. Like this," she said, showing him.

"I'm sure you're right," said Dorman, flashing the woman a smile. "Thanks for everything."

"Come back anytime," said the matron to their backs.

"Lady," Givens muttered so only Dorman could hear, "you can truly depend on that."

All Dorman said, entering the car, was "Bingo."

TWENTY-TWO

Tuesday, May 23

"IT'S GETTING TOO close to call," Payson murmured in early afternoon, staring with Hardin at a wall-projected photograph of the Bristol. The photo was crisp enough to show faint outlines of a removed logo, Bahamasair, on its fuselage. "So far, Evergreen hasn't turned up another Bristol Britannia that we can use."

"They've only known about it for an hour or so. The Brits should have records," Hardin said.

"MI-5 is on it," Payson replied. "But even if we found an identical plane now, there might not be enough time to do a spittin'-image copy job with suitable mods before noon Friday. But you'd know that better than I would, Hardin. Your assessment?"

Wes Hardin rubbed his chin, looking again at the photo. "You'll need a big paint crew on site, for starters, with stencils ready-cut. Marana, you said?"

"Can you think of a better place to decorate a big airplane without drawing the wrong attention?"

"Nope; hell, it's made to order." The Marana airfield,

between Phoenix and Tucson, was known by other names as well, but a CIA-friendly aircraft storage depot by any name was sufficient. "Marana's practically on the Bristol's flight path, if it's heading for Mexico by the shortest route. I hope somebody's getting more shots of that old bird from every possible angle," Hardin added.

"Meacham just called. He got some half an hour ago while Christiansen played student pilot, shooting landings at McCarran in a rental," Payson said. "Meacham had some queasy moments with Christiansen's imitation of a student, he tells me."

Hardin shook his head and grinned, thinking how a canny old pilot could parody an incompetent landing, and of the discomfort another pilot might feel while trying to peer through a viewfinder. A stunt pilot himself, Wes Hardin did not envy Meacham. "And how about photos from beneath? That's the view that counts, if anybody's monitoring it in daylight hours," Hardin reminded him.

"According to the FBO the Mexican pilot, Orozco, is slated to go up again early this evening," Payson answered, miming a shutter-snap with both hands. "Meacham will get the shots. What worries me is all the changes Meacham will want in our substitute aircraft, if we *do* find one. Anything final from him yet?"

Hardin shook his head. "He's talking to armorers at Eglin; doesn't know what he'll need, but he knows you can't just start hacking holes in an old airplane to retrofit a Gatling gun. Whole goddamn fuselage could fold up in flight."

"Well, you're the aircraft designer," said Payson. "I'm giving you the go, no-go on whatever Meacham wants . . . yes, Walt?"

Walt Hildreth had scooted his swivel chair the few paces from his desk to where Payson stood and was waiting, telephone cradled on his shoulder. "L.A.'s transmitting everything they have on the passenger list; fifty-two middle-aged innocents, all told."

"We've got to make sure those folks won't be so innocent in a few hours. My compliments to the Los Angeles man, and get a confirmation that management international-ale knows its licenses are hanging by a thread," Payson responded, then raised his voice: "Muller! Let Quantico know we need twenty males and twenty-two females, or reasonable facsimiles thereof, by fourteen hundred Thursday. We should have a workup on most of the passengers by then."

"Can do," was the reply from ten yards away. Eric Muller, on loan from the FBI center at Quantico, looked as if he belonged there: tan, rawboned, with a hawk nose and hair barely long enough to part. It was Muller's boast that some of Quantico's best men could teeter on heels and apply cosmetics well enough to get their bottoms pinched, if the culprit was only a wee bit nearsighted. The balance of substitute passengers—ten of them—was to consist of task force members, including Givens in drag.

Curt Christiansen, who evidently hated to shout across office hubbub, strode up as Hildreth moved away, and Hardin caught his eye. Hardin: "Any luck on our ringer aircraft?"

"Doesn't look good," the CIA pilot said. "There never were many Britannias built; jetliners came along just in time to put 'em out of the running and most of 'em were junked out long ago. We're getting near a drop-dead time, Marv. I'm starting to lean toward the DC-7 solution, personally."

Payson thrust his arms out in a mighty stretch, sighed, sat down. "State of California, you said?"

Christiansen nodded. "Based in Chico; bunch of borate bombers for forest fires. I know one of 'em is a DC-7, which looks pretty similar to our target aircraft. You said we'll be coming down in darkness, and the engines will be doing very low revs so the difference in exhaust sound won't matter as much."

"Yes, and for all we know, a doper's T-33 will be escorting you into Mexico in daylight," Payson retorted. "You couldn't even fool *me* with that one, Curt."

"It really does have to be another Bristol, you know," Hardin put in.

"I'm willing to chance it," Christiansen said quietly, not looking directly at Hardin but speaking only to him.

Payson intervened quickly: "I'm not willing, and that's final. Thanks, but we either make that flight to the guerrilla base in a ringer that would fool an expert, or we just fill up that airplane of theirs with our people and wait to see if they're going to make their move." He cocked his head as if expecting a response from Christiansen, who only chewed his lip for a moment and then, with a short nod, walked away.

"I don't get it," Hardin said. "Why wait for the dopers to make their move, if you know it's them?"

Payson leaned back in his chair and looked up at the little Texan. "You know how we turned that false alarm into a dry run?"

Hardin nodded.

"Maybe they're making a dry run, too. Maybe, for a billion in cash, they'll make a couple of dry runs, including cargo that turns out to be innocent. According to the honcho in that L.A. management firm, there really is a place down near Puerto Vallarta that looks like a legitimate condo development starting up," Payson said. "As long as the dopers play it that way, so do we. A lot of guys from Quantico would have runny makeup by Monday morning, but that's the only way we can afford to play. By the way: have the Coasties left Oregon yet with the whatchacallit?"

"Spook 4. Yeah, they'll have it here at Nellis in half an hour. You sure you want to ferry it to Kingsville with me?" With Payson as passenger, Wes would be playing fuel-transfer games with the Nemesis onboard pumps.

"I have to make a pitch to other people, if we locate a second Bristol. And I want to know what I'm talking about when I do. Besides, I wouldn't miss it. I get to miss sleep instead. It's a bitch, isn't it," Payson asked softly.

"You chingada betcha," Hardin muttered. "Listen, I'd like permission to talk with my boss."

"I'm your boss," said Payson, and managed to make his correction sound more wistful than stern: "Try and remember that, there's a good lad."

"My real boss," said Hardin. "What Ben Ullmer doesn't know about airplanes isn't worth knowing. If anybody knows where there's another Bristol Britannia that's outside the usual lists, it'll be him."

"Permission denied. That's such a good idea, I'll ask him myself. You can talk on the extension, Hardin, but keep the protocols: I tell him what he needs to know. Neater that way—and when this is all over and Washington's looking for somebody to sacrifice, you don't want it to be you."

He could have sat and fidgeted, but Hardin knew he could burn off much of that nervous energy by standing. He waited on the extension phone while Payson got through to Marie Duchaine, waited another five minutes while Marie chased her old curmudgeon of a boss down somewhere in the plant, and finally let Payson announce his presence to Ullmer, who sounded a little breathless. "Hardin's on the line with us, Mr. Ullmer. He's got this fixed idea that you're a walking encyclopedia on aircraft."

"He does, huh? Hardin, you're hired. I fired you for handing me a fuckin' Chinese fire drill, but I just rehired you." The gravelly voice softened. "What's the problem, Payson?"

Marvin Payson told him only that a Bristol Britannia had to be on the deck at Marana early the following morning, in condition to fly again as soon as it was refueled.

Ullmer needed little time to think it over. The remaining Britannias, he said, were popular as island-hoppers for their ability to grease in on short runways with eighty or so passengers. Especially the long-bodied versions.

Hardin: "Damn! They made different versions?"

Ullmer: "Stretched the fuselage. Which version did you need—because it matters," he said.

Payson said, "Wait one," and left the phone to Hardin while he went back to the overhead projector, pulling a small measuring tape from his pocket.

"Hardin?"

"Yeah, Ben," said the pilot.

"How long those flatfoot bureaucrats gonna keep you there?"

After a moment's hesitation: "I can't tell you. Not very long," Hardin promised, wondering how bad a prophet he might be.

"You're missed," the old man said, his voice gruff, and Hardin found inexplicably that he could not have answered around the obstruction in his own throat. "Nobody else around here knows how to tell me to go fuck a duck. They try to do it nice. Shit, Wes, you can't do it nice!"

Hardin grinned and turned away as he saw Payson returning to his telephone. "Who taught you that: Morrison?"

"Naw, but give 'er credit, she can use her smart mouth like a busted bottle in a bar fight. With both of you gone, I—"

"I make it a bit over a hundred and thirty feet from nose to tail, Mr. Ullmer," said Payson.

"That's the stretched model. Forget it, I don't think you have a prayer of finding one."

"We already located one," said Payson.

"Well, I'll be dipped! Then what's your problem?"

"We need another one to send in as a substitute, a ringer that looks exactly like it. And that is for your ears only."

A snuffling laugh like a rusty pump from North Bend, Oregon: "Well, why not just get a CL-44?"

Hardin: "Come again?"

"Canadair CL-44, the one built in Canada."

"Sorry," Payson cut in. "It has to be identical; another Bristol Britannia."

The tassels at the tip of Ben Ullmer's short temper smoldered briefly. "Jesus Christ on Kaopectate, it *is* a Britannia! The stretch version was built under license by the

Canadians, most of 'em for cargo. The CL-44 has a tail like a barn door, opens to the side for big items, but it's a Bristol Britannia all the same.''

Hardin, sharing a smile with Payson, pursued the similarity one further step. ''Could you tell the difference if you were flying around them in an old T-Bird?''

''Not with fairings over those hinges on the cargo door. Engines aren't quite the same but they'll look and sound the same. There are prob'ly twenty of 'em looking for buyers in Canada. RCAF used 'em for—''

''We're on it already,'' Payson said, gesturing madly for Curt Christiansen's attention. ''And Mr. Ullmer?''

''Yeah.''

''If I have anything to say about it, we'll *give* you an F-14 when this is over. But don't discuss this call even with your secretary.''

''Assistant. Marie's my goddamn assistant,'' Ullmer growled.

Payson: ''I sit corrected, Mr. Ullmer. You'll hear from me again.'' Christiansen was rolling up as Payson placed his phone in its cradle. ''Curt, you ever hear of a Canadair CL-44?''

''Sure. Flew one out of Anchorage once; strong old brute—''

''Well, you're going to do it again, if we can buy one quick. And we need it at Marana with a modification crew, *now*. It's the Canadian version of a Britannia,'' Payson told him, and Christiansen slapped his own forehead.

The wall clock said that within an hour, Payson would be stuffing his girth into a cockpit designed for people half his size.

TWENTY-THREE

Tuesday, May 23

LESS THAN THREE hours after the summons reached them on-station over the Mexican isthmus, Morrison and Cutter urged their spookship from the taxiway apron to their hangar at Kingsville, Texas. Such was her concentration in keeping her bird unbent that Colleen's mind did not completely register the second aircraft in that hangar until she was removing her helmet, all systems off. When it did register, she gave a whoop. "That's mine," she exulted, pointing.

Cutter, levering the canopy up, tucked the flight logbook under one arm, anxious to feel concrete under his feet. "Spook 2? Make sense, Morrison."

"No Coastie shield or numbers, Jarhead, and almost no bug strikes on it yet; that's *my* bird!"

"Not so loud," called a familiar voice as its owner emerged from beneath their wing. "You'll wake the ground crew."

The plane captain's wry retort was lost to them as Colleen, laughing aloud, tossed her helmet down to Wes Hardin. "Brought it here yourself, did you? Then I'm almost glad to see you, Hardin."

"Don't worry," he said with a half-smile. "You'll be back to normal in no time."

Deplaning moments later, Colleen slung her bagful of necessaries—sneakers, personal laptop computer, and toilet articles—over a shoulder and hurried toward Spook 4, its safety streamers brilliant streaks against the prussian blue of solar cells. "Somebody, could I have a ladder over here?"

"No time to pet your bird, I'm afraid." Hardin's voice echoed from the metal roof, and unless she was mistaken it was the timbre of a man on his best behavior. Then she saw Jared Cutter shaking hands with a big fellow, really a Kodiak bear of a man, who stood near the ready room door beside Hardin. Muttering to herself, she walked toward them while zipping down, the hangar heat still oppressive though the sun was near the horizon. The big man turned out to be as impressive as he looked, a full inspector in the FBI no less, with an eye that sought everything and a mind that missed nothing. Colleen worked hard to keep from being slightly in awe, noting that poor Jarhead, puppy-friendly, had given up on that immediately. Though Payson made it evident that time was precious, he deferred to Colleen's urgent, almost sexual desire for a shower. She spent five minutes lathering under a hot spray and took more delicious minutes beneath a cool one. *The hell with those guys, I've spent too long twelve miles up in a broom closet,* she told herself.

She chose high wedge heels, no stockings, thin cotton skirt and blouse from her locker and, with short hair that needed little attention, made it to the waiting men moments before Cutter did. She saw something in Hardin's glance that might have been naked male appreciation. *Tough shit, buddy. Eat your heart out.* She'd let herself have a private thing for Hardin when she first hired on with Aerosystems, but not the sort of thing from which he could ever be allowed to profit. Fluffing her hair: "So what's the drill," she asked brightly.

The drill, Payson said, was dinner on the bureau, someplace where they might talk. He plainly hoped that Kingsville NAS might have decent fare in officer country, but Hardin was not so easily deflected. "There's not a mesquite tree on the Oregon coast," he said cryptically, "and I know this town pretty well."

With Wes Hardin driving the Chevy rental, the four of them showed their IDs at the gate, Payson drawing a respectful glance from the guard. Ten minutes later the Chevy's tires scrunched gravel in front of a clapboard shack with no advertisement other than a peeling, paintbrushed sign with three letters, BBQ. This would be Hardin's speed, she decided: a roadside ptomaine palace that looked, to Colleen, like a woodshed out of *God's Little Acre*.

Payson, too, seemed to have his doubts. Gazing at a diesel locomotive that passed along tracks within fifty yards of them, he said, "I'm not sure we're on the right side of the tracks—or does it matter out here?"

"You won't be sorry," Hardin rejoined. "The place doesn't start to fill 'til late, and we can sit out back. No waiters, either."

Colleen, snippishly: "With a view of the passing parade, courtesy of Southern Pacific?"

Hardin nodded. "You won't be sorry," he said again, and Cutter was already getting out, inhaling like a man readying himself to shout from one mountaintop to another.

Colleen got out too. *Let the poor redneck embarrass himself. This might be fun.* Then she inhaled, and found herself salivating.

Standing at a wooden counter with sawdust underfoot, they gave their orders to a villainous-looking fellow who, nonetheless, had the manners of a duke. Hardin enthused that the place had something called Shiner Bock in addition to Longhorn and Pearl; the men ordered the bock but

Colleen liked the sound of Pearl, and following Hardin down a short hallway with a full paper plate topped by a thick slice of homemade bread, she stepped onto a wooden deck into the year 1935. Colleen never did decide whether the ancient Coca-Cola and Burma-Shave signs were deliberate decoration, or simply castoffs. And once she bit into those barbecued ribs, she forgot her surroundings. The flavor, Hardin told them, was unique to mesquite smoke. As he explained it, the trick was in smoking a good cut of meat below sizzle temperature for a full day. If the stuff ever sizzled, he claimed, the chef got deported to Oklahoma.

They sat in the light of a dim porch lamp, theirs the only occupied table, once an AT&T cable spool, and as they ate Inspector Payson made his pitch. He said that an old civilian airliner would be landing before dawn on Saturday morning at the same Mexican airfield they'd been surveilling . . . "And what is this beer we're drinking, Hardin? Tastes like that dark Bavarian Kulmbacher nobody can get anymore."

Payson told them the airliner was a friendly, yet would have a mission anything but friendly to billionaire coke-runners, and "I thought I knew what barbecued brisket was, but this is unbelievable."

The crew of that airliner needed to be picked up with split-second timing and flown back to American airspace, and the only suitable aircraft for that were the two machines owned by an Oregon company.

"Agrimap," Cutter said around a mouthful of chopped pork. "Hardin, why didn't you tell me about this Texas food? Lord, I may go into the export business."

"It doesn't travel," Hardin answered. "But Payson thinks you might. Listen up, Jarhead."

Payson said they would have to pick up three men, none over 170 pounds. "Hardin tells me a Nemesis could take a third passenger strapped into the back," he added, "by monkeying with its fuel load. We've decided to do it."

Colleen discarded a meatless rib and thought about that,

studying Hardin's face. "With two-thirds of a fuel load and the aft fuselage tank pumped full; was that the idea?"

Hardin nodded. "And there might be somebody shooting at you, Morrison. For damn' sure there's gonna be some serious fireworks."

"And of course, you'll be flying the lead spookship," Colleen said to him.

Payson shook his head. "We really need Hardin for another part of the mission, and he agreed. You'll be senior pilot, Miz Morrison, with Cutter on your wing. If you agree."

"Me, senior pilot? Whose idea was that?" No one replied, but she saw a guarded glance between Hardin and the big man.

Cutter, wiping sauce from his cheek: "Anybody work out an estimate of our chances?"

"Seventy percent—give or take thirty," Payson replied. "I won't kid you."

"If we should get taken," asked Colleen, "what do we do? Carry a suicide needle?"

Payson registered something like disgust. "I doubt it would come to that. You're legitimate, deniable civilians, and you'd be worth a lot to the other side in good condition." Pause. Shrug. "Of course, I could be wrong about the good condition. There are Peruvian guerrillas down there. You'll be provided with kits designed to let you walk out, if it comes to that."

Colleen: "If I turn this down, then what?"

Hardin merely shrugged. Payson, with a sideways nod of his head toward the Texan: "He goes, in your place."

"I'm in," she said. "He weighs half again what I do." She knew, and surely Hardin knew, that the gross wingloading was not her primary goad.

"Well, hell," said Cutter, pausing to belch. "Sounds like fun to me. If this comes down before dawn Saturday, we'll be wheels-up late Friday night. We won't have a lot of time for R and R before the briefings."

"None," Payson agreed, studying the pathetic remains

in his plate. "There'll be other folks flying in here to update you as we firm up details. CIA, most likely. Hardin, do they allow second helpings in this joint?"

"As long as you'll stomp your foot to Roy Acuff," Hardin said, and left with Payson's plate for a refill.

Colleen Morrison studied Hardin's back as he disappeared into the shack. "One thing I don't get," she admitted to Payson, "is why wonderful Wes didn't want the job. He's not turning cautious in his old age." It was nine parts assertion, one part question.

Payson shook his big head. "I wouldn't say that, ma'am. He's perfectly fluent in Mexican Spanish."

"So?"

"So we'll need a man on that old airliner who can transmit over Mexican soil in perfect Spanish and, ah, do some engineering on the airplane in flight. And because there may be small arms fire, it'll be nice if that man can also pilot a Nemesis, should the need arise."

Cutter, who had been ruminating quietly, now expelled a satisfied, "Huh! So one of the guys we pick up will be Wes Hardin?"

"I thought that was obvious," Payson said.

"Son—of—a—*bitch*," said Colleen.

TWENTY-FOUR
Tuesday, May 23

"**. . . N**OT GOING TO work," Christiansen finished with some heat, thumping the big air navigation chart that lay unfolded across Walt Hildreth's desk. "Everybody assumed the airliner's ETA on that isthmus airstrip is in the dead of night because props mean piston engines and slow airplanes; am I right?"

Hildreth: "Yeah. So?"

Christiansen: "Dead wrong. The Britannia's props are the size of palm trees and they're cranked by whopping big turbines. I finally put on my doper hat and filed myself a mental flight plan for what's supposed to be a slow prop-job, and guess what: That old Britannia is a quicker machine than I remembered. Even if they plan to stay off the Pacific Coast until they can swing straight inland, which would be safest for them, that's only a twenty-one-hundred-mile flight at, say, three hundred knots—make it three hundred fifty miles an hour. Six hours to touchdown, Hildreth; they'd be on the ground by dark on Friday evening."

Hildreth's upward gaze had *why me* in it. "If it's not a dry run after all, we'll just have to create a delay somewhere along the line. Take off your doper hat for a minute and remember who we're putting on that plane. It may take off from McCarran on a doper schedule, but it's gonna land on ours. One thing I do know: Payson would be crazy to endorse landings by our people in broad daylight."

"Not to mention my endorsement. I'll be flying the Canadair, remember, and I'd better be at Marana when it gets here from Calgary. All we have is a lot of maintenance record faxes and the seller's word that it's a clean machine. If I don't think it's up to the mission—well, I'm not a kid and this ain't Laos, I won't kiss my ass goodbye. Meanwhile, Meacham and I will be out of here within the hour with those stencils for the aircraft, but don't expect me to come lazing down on a doper's nerve center in daylight." Hildreth saw him pinch the bridge of his nose; from now on, they'd be on No-Doz time. The younger agents seemed chipper enough, now that they all had plenty to do as simulated employees of Hall Aviation, but long hours could play hell with a mature guy. When Christiansen opened his eyes again, he seemed a little older. "Any word from Payson?"

"It's a go in Kingsville," said Hildreth, stealing a glance at his wrist. In a few minutes it would be Wednesday morning. "Payson will be here by dawn, and I told him about the buy in Calgary. He says that little Texas hotshot will be flown straight to Marana with his flight gear to meet you two." With a sudden smile, he added, "Also wants me to be sure there are plenty of Tums in his top right desk drawer; says if he dies of indigestion I'm to pin it on Hardin. What d'you think he meant?"

"Beats me. Oh: If we don't keep our dedicated comm links open, Payson will never let us forget it. I'll get a link to you, up to TEMPEST standards, from Marana." The CIA pilot turned away.

"If I know him," Hildreth said, "he'll want to know exactly what munitions are going into that Canadair."

"See Lloyd Meacham," Christiansen called. "Oh, man, he's going to love it."

Hildreth would have asked for particulars if his number one line had not lit up at that moment. He lifted the receiver and identified himself, and the weight of long hours began to peel away as his expression changed. "Hold it, Givens; you didn't tap phone lines at Hall Aviation without a court order, did you? . . . Oh. Sure, what NSA does is something else entirely. *What?* You'd think it would've been that Mexican pilot instead of his copilot. I hope they got it on tape. . . . *Dyn*amite, Merle; any Catemaco telephone number is a nail in his coffin. Payson will want a dub of that tape by dawn, but give me that translation now."

Hildreth's shorthand was far from the Gregg system, full of abbreviations and mental shortcuts, but it worked. When he had filled half a page from a yellow-lined, legal-sized pad, he spoke again: "Sounds like they don't know diddly-squat about us, but I don't like the part about the new personnel they expect. You did put smooth tails on him, I take it. . . . Mapes I like. I don't know how good Calvin is." Sigh. "I didn't mean it that way, Merle; I just know these CIA people can go weird on you. . . . No, I'll get on their channel and tell 'em myself: better to lose the bastard than take any chance on raising the slightest suspicion among those sleazeballs. . . . Yeah. Good work, Merle, this pretty much tips the scales away from the dry run scenario, but who knows? Maybe that call was a deliberate tripwire." The surest way to abort a good sting, Hildreth reflected, was to underestimate the subtlety of the other guy.

He listened for another moment. Then: "Well, not quite, but we've checked off twenty-one couples and we have the descriptions and license numbers of all the others. If we have to, we'll put a road crew on the perimeter road and watch for them, pick the rest up on their way in. Those perps won't have a clue that every last citizen who

climbs aboard is one of ours. Right. Get back to me,"
Hildreth said at last, and put down the phone.

He nodded at that yellow pad with massive satisfaction
before moving to the desk of the absent Payson. To the
pensive aide monitoring radio comm links, he said, "I
need to raise units three and five." He was soon in contact with Jack Mapes, glancing now and then at one of
Payson's wall maps. Calvin and her partner had driven off
toward the north, the only reasonable direction, before the
sturdy compact Latino got into his blue Mercury Sable.
Mapes had begun tailing the man in fairly close proximity,
informing Calvin when their man headed east on Tropicana toward Route 95.

Calvin's partner, with an extraordinary talent for surveillance, had a special trick with an alligator clip and a
single wire leading from his trunk to the driver. He could
short out one taillight while driving, so that the character
of his car would be subtly changed. With that single taillight, they passed both cars after the Sable took Route 95
to the southeast toward Henderson, accelerating out of
sight while maintaining radio contact with Mapes. When
Mapes took the Sunset Road turnoff, the Sable continued
into the town of Henderson, eventually passing Calvin,
whose taillights were now both brightly shining.

Walt Hildreth listened to the surveillance as it pro-
gressed. Mapes entered Henderson from Lakeshore Boulevard but finally parked near railroad tracks on the edge
of town. The blue Sable, said Calvin, had turned near a
region full of warehouses; and to her that meant the driver
might be suspicious. Instead of following further, they
stopped and switched seats, with Calvin's partner dropping low in his seat, Calvin pinning her hair up to change
her profile.

It was a half-hour later when Mapes spotted the Sable
on its way back to Vegas, and Calvin passed them again
on Route 95. She could not be certain, but thought the
driver might not be the same man.

Somehow they lost their quarry in North Las Vegas after

the man turned off at Lone Mountain Road. "Not to worry," Hildreth told them by radio link. Stakeouts near both approaches to those warehouses, in the next two days, might pinpoint one doper haven, and they had the Sable's treadprints back at Hall Aviation. Privately, Hildreth worried anyway. You always started a task force wondering if you had too many people, and ended wishing you had twice that many. Hall Aviation now had five new employees, all bogus, which Hall's real staff had accepted with every indication of joy. Given the blessings of the owner, they were perfectly willing to take two days off with pay.

Hildreth took off his glasses, crossed his arms on his blotter and rested his forehead on that fleshy nest to catch forty winks. It hadn't been a bad day, considering that Payson wasn't even at the center of his web. They'd got an NSA recording of a suspect and both ends of his conversation with someone in Catemaco, suggesting that a big shipment of some kind would reach Ana—whoever that might be—on schedule. With candid photographs and treadprints, they now had a firm line on that copilot and a general idea where he might be staying. If all went well, that scutwork would come to nothing. But if this sting operation went balls-up at the last minute, at least they might be able to sweep up something of value: weapons, illegal aliens, maybe even the money. Hildreth found sleep easily, imagining that Task Force Enable had the situation well in hand.

TWENTY-FIVE

Wednesday, May 24

OFFICIALLY, THERE IS no longer any such thing as the Marana airbase. A vast, fenced stretch of Pinal County desert the color of antelope hide, it sprawls some fifteen miles from Tucson within sight of jagged peaks that emulate sculptures in raw concrete, all of it swept by breezes as hot and dry and peculiarly scented as a bedouin's backside. The most identifiable odors in the breeze tend to be rubber and plastic slowly oxidizing in the heat, aircraft fuels, and smokeless powder residues. The several square miles of Marana once served as a USAF training base before its outright purchase by the CIA, which later sold it to a firm known today as Evergreen. Because Evergreen actually comprises several privately owned companies, its financial statements need not be made totally public. And because those thousands of acres of desert are used to train smoke jumpers, State Department diplomatic service operatives, police groups, navy SEAL teams, and reportedly certain foreign nationals, it is not unusual to see parachutes over Marana or to hear the coughs of special weapons borne on the wind.

Officially, Marana is now Pinal Air Park and, as the old hands are replaced, it is becoming known as Pinal with the same insiders' shorthand. It even has well-kept grass here and there; a chapel; a swimming pool; good food at Elinor's place; and liquid fuel for the tired airman at the democratically named Everybody's Lounge. All of which does not mean it is healthy to drive inside this particular park without a pass dangling from the rearview mirror and another clipped onto clothing. The chapel is now used for hand-to-hand combat training and if the green-clad guards are not quick enough, their German shepherds will be.

Wes Hardin had arrived at Marana in darkness, but he had overflown the famed complex before and he kept his sunglasses handy. From dawn to dusk, reflected sunlight from the skins of Marana's scores of parked aircraft can cause a blistering headache, and more exotic aircraft can be found under hangar roofs in the maintenance shops. The aircraft maintenance capacity of Marana's shops can be matched by perhaps three other depots in the world; most of its mechanics boast college degrees. Given a decent budget and such ungodly time constraints, Task Force Enable could not have chosen a better place to cobble up a copy of the cartel's old Bristol Britannia, which was now under round-the-clock scrutiny in Las Vegas.

Hardin napped for three hours before Christiansen and Meacham found him snoring on a cot beneath the newly-arrived Canadair CL-44, and while a paint crew swarmed quietly over the barrellike fuselage, the three men began to study their old bird. When someone snapped off the hangar lights soon after dawn, Hardin did not know it. He was inside the Canadair, checking its fuselage for window frames. The Bristol had three dozen passenger windows, but in its cargo version, the Canadair had only a few. Somehow, this obvious discrepancy had to be fixed.

Lloyd Meacham expected his munitions by noon; the minigun pods from Eglin in Florida, the still more lethal stuff from several locations, including a direct shipment from McDonnell Douglas and another from Wang Heating and Air Conditioning in Tucson. Hardin had seen those minigun pods before, slightly over a foot in diameter and a man's armreach in length, and envisioned no insurmountable problems with them. A pod contained its own ammunition and everything else but the business ends of a half-dozen gun muzzles. While rotating in Gatling-gun fashion, those muzzles would pump 7.62 mm. slugs, roughly thirty caliber, at the rate of 6,000 rounds per minute.

Some of those pods had been in storage since the Vietnam war. Meacham had used them then in a Dragonship, and had ordered eight of the pods "for our little senderista friends. We won't be aiming, so we'll install four on each side and mount each one so it fires a little lower or higher than the others. Better too low than too high; ricochets will bag as many casualties as clean rounds do."

He claimed nothing had been developed in the past twenty years that was more likely to keep an entire battalion of guerrillas scrambling for cover. It was the heavier stuff, he promised, that would make that cover useless.

"Okay," Hardin said, "we have enough windows to mount your pods, but we can't afford to slide those muzzles through the windows until dark. They'd be a complete giveaway to anybody flying near us."

"But they've got to be mounted as soon as they get here," Meacham argued.

"Fine. We lay the pods on sliding mounts bolted to the cargo floor at window height. The pods can be slid forward and locked by hand so their muzzles poke through window holes a few minutes before the apocalypse. We take the Plexiglas windows out now, and replace 'em with gray-painted aluminum panels that look as if a passenger pulled down a shade." Hardin was sketching quickly on a clipboard, making secondary dashed lines with arrows so that he could add exact dimensions later. "We can keep each panel in place with a quarter-turn fastener so removal takes only a second or two," he added, displaying his sketch to Meacham. "Can the shops turn those out fast enough?"

Meacham squinted; nodded. "You kiddin'? Marana could turn 'em out like aspirin. Hey, you're good with a pencil. They can work from that." Meacham pointed a finger at Hardin in sudden surmise: "We don't need every window to be real; we can do some of 'em with paint, maybe with silhouettes of heads on some of 'em, huh?"

"Sounds good to me," said Hardin, "but how many holes d'you need for the heavy hitters? Sheet metal guys need to know quick, and I've gotta run some stress calculations before I start making dotted lines with chalk."

Meacham's heavy hitters were known better to the Marine Corps as SMAW units. To his credit, Meacham knew that McDonnell Douglas had developed a lightweight, throwaway version of the SMAW launcher, so he had insisted on those simplified versions. To his debit, he had never seen one up close. "Look, we're just gonna have to wait for some of our stuff before we start bending metal."

"Shit we do," Hardin said, folding his arms. "We're counting down the hours, Meacham. Make a decision; tell me how big a hole, and the minimum number you need."

"Yeah, you're right," said Meacham, looking down, combing a hand through hair damp with sweat. "I *think* we can fire four SMAW rockets through one window."

"Simultaneously?" Hardin pursed his mouth in a silent whistle.

"Unless you think we should shoot nice and slow," Meacham replied, with hellish mirth in his eyes.

"I take your point. If push comes to shove, we'll just have to go with fewer munitions, so tell me, dammit: How many do we expect?"

"Sixty-four," said Meacham, as if admitting a felony.

"My God," Hardin said softly, looking at nothing for a moment. "A feller might think you don't like those dopers much."

Shrug. "Each SMAW, including launcher tube and

warhead, weighs under thirty pounds. I figured, whatthe-hell.''

"We're not going to leave a tree or a monkey, are we?"

"Dead monkeys tell no tales," Meacham said, and moved forward, his heels echoing on corrugated aluminum, voice a heavier echo. "Curt, we'd better crank this 'chine up to see about those gauges. I don't wanta get on the horn to Payson before—" The closing of the cockpit door muffled the rest.

For the next few hours, Hardin was too busy to think about Payson. He designed doubler flanges, flat doughnuts of aluminum to encircle the rounded rectangular holes they needed for windows. He located window holes with chalk, careful to note nearby spars and wiring. He conferred with sheet metal specialists to decide the quickest, lightest ways to build structures that would bolt to the Canadair's cargo flooring. And he found the trapdoor that led him below the floor, flashlight in hand, to see what might interfere with Meacham's simplest and scariest idea.

He traversed the belly of the Canadair until he was slick with sweat, tracing cables, bundles of wire, and hydraulic lines, deciding at last that a few perforated sheets of aluminum could be riveted like shallow trays a few inches from the Canadair's thin belly skin. Then, knowing that complicated plans were the first to develop glitches, he climbed out and ordered three items of equipment: a hand-powered nibbling tool capable of chewing through metal too heavy for shears, a battery-powered hand drill with bits, and a manual pop-riveter with rivets in varied sizes. He would not know for two days just how prescient he had been.

Lunch became a rubber chicken conference in an air-conditioned room annexed to the hangar. In answer to Christiansen, while chewing what seemed to be a piece of innertube, Hardin said, "Nothing we can't handle. As soon as those window flanges start coming out of the shop tomorrow, a courier will shuttle over with 'em. If you really want to watch vandals at work, they'll be punching holes in the bird later today." He swallowed, lubricated his grinders with tepid ginger ale, and turned to Meacham. "Haven't seen hide nor hair of your shipments. What's happening?"

"Some kind of contract bullshit from Mac Air; Payson says he's got somebody in D.C. to roast their butts and get 'em in gear for a shipment tonight," Meacham replied, counting the details off on his fingers. Touching his middle finger, he went on: "Marines can't seem to *find* their ordnance stores with both hands. I don't know, man, they keep saying no sweat, they'll locate the SMAWs. Our silly putty is on the way but it's just plain fuckin' late," he said, swatting his ring-finger. "You know who's the only guy on time? That Chinaman in Tucson with his two sizes of galvanized stovepipe. It was at the gate when these bungee-cord sandwiches got here; should be with us any time now."

"Sure ain't Texas barbecue," Hardin muttered, and wrenched at another bite. He half-listened as Meacham and Christiansen wrangled amicably over their cockpit arrangements, beginning to suspect that it wouldn't matter what Lloyd Meacham wanted. Most likely, Meacham and Hardin would both spend much of their flight working like galley slaves with touchy munitions back in the cargo section. Christiansen had already pointed out that if the Bristol actually got off the ground on schedule, those dopers would expect to see it lumbering in before dark. Conclusion: Somewhere between Vegas and the isthmus, a convincing delay must be manufactured.

But Christiansen had spoken to Payson just before lunch on a secure line, and had recounted the latest news to Hardin. A nice clear tape recording existed of a phone conversation between dopers in Vegas and Mexico. "Curt, about that doper phone call," Hardin said, interrupting. "I'll need a copy of it here, you know."

Christiansen blinked. "You mean a transcript?"

"The tape itself, as good a copy as Payson can get. I've got to hear their accents, Curt. If somebody challenges us

in flight, I just might have to imitate the one who called
from Vegas—unless you can do it yourself.''

"That's a fucking fat negative,'' Christiansen snorted.

Meacham: ''And my best effort sounds like Jose Jime-
nez, man. You're elected.''

Christiansen, scribbling a note on his clipboard: ''I'll
pass that on to Payson. Listen, Hardin, I'm hanging me
out on a long limb promising that the Canadair will be
ready. From what mods you know we need, what's your
real assessment?''

Hardin fixed him with a level gaze. "Just between us
wing-flappers?''

Meacham nodded. Christiansen, unpredictable in his
ways, solemnly crossed his heart. Hardin said, ''I think,
if we go at all, we'll have to bullshit the big chiefs about
our readiness. We're going to be wheels-up with the job
half done.'' He put up a hand, stopping Meacham between
a frown and an utterance. ''I think we can finish it en
route, but you'll have to let me use PERT and go with my
engineering judgment.''

Both CIA men together: ''Pert?''

"Program evaluation and review technique. All it really
means is, somebody works out what absolutely, positively
must be done in what order to get the best result, the
soonest, even if it means we don't get everything done;
and you do what he says.''

"What you mean is,'' said Christiansen, ''if we go,
you'll have to lie while we swear to it.''

"No,'' Meacham countered. ''What he means is, if we
turn into a cubic mile of guts in midair, we can blame him
for it.''

"Nicely put,'' said Christiansen, denying it with a
glance. ''Hardin, I hope you know your munitions as well
as Lloyd does.''

"Nope. He's the boss on that. It's the time and motion
sequences that worry me; for instance, I'll give you odds
that what Lloyd so charmingly calls his silly putty will
have to wait 'til we're in flight. But I know it can be done

last, and it won't matter whether it's day or night because it's dark as a doper's heart in the cargo bay.''

"Plus, I could set it up right on the cargo floor if I had to," Meacham put in.

"You might have to," Hardin warned him. "So: What do you say?''

"Personally, I think you're a world-class bullshitter with that PERT stuff,'' Meacham confided. "You're so good, I'm gonna go for it.''

Christiansen, to Meacham: "That's what I like about you, Lloyd. You say what everybody else is thinking." To Hardin: "I'll tell you why I'm buying it, Wes. 'Cause you'll be right there with us—and correct me if I'm wrong but you don't seem the suicidal type.''

"We'll know by Saturday, won't we?''

"To Saturday," Christiansen replied, raising his cola as a toast. Gravely, they touched their aluminum cans together.

TWENTY-SIX

Wednesday, May 24

BY WEDNESDAY AFTERNOON, Torres could have thanked Billy Borges for maneuvering him into so many hours in that stinking loft where he could do nothing but think. Blessed with a fighter pilot's eye, Torres also had an excellent visual memory. He smoked two Marlboros as he replayed that foolishness with the firecrackers which, he now decided, had been more than a signal to Billy's own guards. It had made muffled gunfire unworthy of attention nearby—and because he had used firecrackers in the past, Billy Borges had probably decided some time before that he would do some killing in that loft.

As he paced the room, glancing through the inside window at palletloads of money below, Torres called up recollections of Billy with the forklift, Billy working hard and single-mindedly (and uncharacteristically), Billy so intent on his own agenda that he never once glanced up to see if his men were watching. Almost certainly, Billy was playing for an audience of one: Simon Torres. Billy probably knew that money was missing because Billy himself had taken it. By killing his guards, Billy had given himself freedom to concoct any story he wished without fear of contradiction.

But why take so little? Perhaps the sum was merely symbolic, something to justify the killings. Or worse, and more likely, perhaps a complete count would show that far more was missing. The only evidence the cartel had that those pallets contained a thousand million in cash was Billy's word on it. *Billy's word!* Perhaps—many things. One of the possibilities drove Torres from his air-conditioned loft down to the pallets of money. Though not a true expert, he had seen bad counterfeits and very good counterfeits, and in his awareness grew a hideous suspicion.

He brought a stack of cash upstairs to better light and stared for long minutes at individual bills: the flawless engraving of clear-eyed, imperturbable Franklin; the perfect clarity of the clock numerals on Independence Hall; tiny threadlike lines of red and blue that signified the highest quality paper; and all the serial numbers were different. If those bills were funny money, they were better than any Torres had ever seen, good enough to pass anywhere, good enough that their value was unimpeachable. *I'm sure this is all legal tender,* he thought as he replaced the stack and retaped the cardboard container, perspiring not so much now from the heat as from the growing certainty of Billy's betrayal.

And if I had known when I called old Vega in Catemaco, what could I have said? They have trusted Guillermo Borges as they trusted me. I fear that Borges had personal plans similar to my own. God knows what, but I do know this: The first person I shoot once we are off the ground will be our fine Señor Borges.

He sat down on the futon and lay back, eyes closed, trying to purge the beginnings of a sensation he had not known since he had been trapped in an alley as a child; a surge like lava, starting at the back of his neck, flooding up and forward over his scalp, prickly, hot, terrifying.

Then he commanded his inner vision: *Bring me Guillermo Borges,* and with that fat face in his mind's eye, he found at last a focus for something other than panic. For most of his life, Torres had fought to become passion's master, not its slave. But he had never mastered his passion for winning, for ultimate victory. That passion made him formidable, his determination limitless.

If Borges meant to kill me, he has wasted good opportunities. That is not like Guillermo Borges, he told himself. Far more likely, Borges needed him for something. To fly the Bristol, of course; but Orozco knew their real destination and could perform that vital service alone, with Borges beside him lending credence to the kidnap plea Orozco intended to use later.

The most likely scenario that fitted the mind of Billy Borges, insofar as Torres could see, was that Billy had taken fifty million, perhaps more, hiding it elsewhere. He would have Torres to verify that he had tried to recover the stuff; could Billy help it if killing the traitorous guards became necessary?

And since Borges had driven off the previous night with two bodies wrapped in shower curtains, Torres did not even know where those bodies lay. *If Borges has turned informer to the yanquis, he may have put those two poor bastards in my motel room. If so, they will have been found by the cleaning staff, and I can expect police there, or even here, at any moment. Billy will point to me, and I am the only one who will know who really stole cartel money.*

Galvanized by these thoughts, Simon Torres fled downstairs, pausing to withdraw two pocketsful of cash before resealing the carton. Then he ascertained that the outside door would not lock behind him and took a bracing walk down the street, paying particular note to every railroad boxcar, alleyway, and structure where he might find cover at the first sign of trouble. The temperature climbed fifteen degrees during that morning while Torres walked, and watched, and waited.

He was almost disappointed when, around noon, Borges tooled his blue Sable into sight. Torres took long, seemingly unhurried paces on his approach from across the street, expecting to see sedans with flashing lights converge from both ends of the thoroughfare. But Billy, encumbered with a big grocery bag, remained alone and let himself in with his key, obviously realizing that the door had not been locked anyway, pausing inside the doorway to sweep the street with his gaze. That was when Torres stepped into the street, fighting the temptation to hurry, making himself stroll as if adrenaline were not singing in his veins. When he knew Borges had seen him, he even managed a smile.

The fat man did not seem disconcerted about that stroll and held the door open. "Bored with the television, I take it," he remarked as he offered his broad back to Torres on his way up the stairs with a sack redolent of food.

"When I get bored, I seek action," Torres replied. "All went well?"

Billy began to stock the refrigerator from the sack: deli sandwiches, bottles of Anchor Steam beer, a still-cold bottle of Mumm's. The Fritos and the girlie magazine he dropped on the table. "Our flight stewards have not arrived at the motel, but never mind; I do not expect them until Thursday. Orozco is too busy spending our money and romancing his gringita to develop a case of nerves, I think, and I would rather see him this way than the other way. He says he will be in his room this afternoon if you need him." With this, he handed the car keys over.

Torres grasped at two suspicions simultaneously. *I might be more easily taken while driving a bugged car, if it is not my Mangusta;* and *Billy is not perspiring as he does under pressure. I wonder if he is wearing a yanqui transmitter. As to the second matter, perhaps I can make him sweat with innocent conversation.* "That poor pendejo you killed: If he stank up your trunk, I may want to park your car and rent another."

"No problem, but by all means do as you see fit. A great shame that I had to do it, Simon; but Cordero was a mercurial sort, and a brute, physically. What would you have had me do, under the circumstances?"

"Cut him down as you did, I suppose," Torres replied, relieved at Billy's admission yet somehow disappointed. He persisted: "You buried them in the desert?"

"In a culvert. They may show up during the next rain, if it ever does," Borges replied.

The body-taped transmitter no longer seemed a viable suspicion. *I am almost convinced that Billy is committed to our flight, after all. I am even more determined that he will not survive it.* "This will be my last night on the town, Billy. Will you mind if I use it pleasantly?"

"If you must," Billy grumbled. "I realize that this," he took in the killings and the primitive amenities with a single wave of his arm, "was my fault. Lo siento, it is regrettable," he finished.

Torres opened the door, then paused. "Get a good night's sleep, Billy. Tomorrow night we will be loading a lot of cargo."

He saw Billy Borges nod and then trotted downstairs.

IN EARLY AFTERNOON Pablo Orozco, slender and erect and deferential to a fault, made a point of folding his arms throughout the short flight, and kept them folded while Torres brought the big Bristol down onto McCarran's shortest runway, 19R. Though no one had told Orozco exactly who was behind his employers, he would have been stupid beyond belief not to have a strong conjecture. "The only runway at Ordaz terminal in Puerto Vallarta is over nine thousand feet long," Orozco said after Torres felt his tires rebounding, ever so slightly, from the runway. As Torres reversed the pitch of his props, Orozco went on: "If my opinion is of interest, let me say you can land our Bristol in half that distance." He was showing those beautiful teeth as Torres glanced at him. Hinting for information, certainly, but happy to give some as well.

Both pilots knew that the brakes had only a few more landings in them, only one or two if savagely applied, so Torres made his rollout a gentle one and let the reversed thrust of those huge propellers do most of the work. In some ways, he exulted, this turboprop aircraft was superior to jets. Thrust reversal of a jet aircraft, for one thing, was not very efficient, while reversed props could virtually pull a man from his seat. He could not resist saying, "We can count on a nicely surfaced runway, Pablo, though not overlong." And he smiled back thinking, *you poor opportunist, if only I could afford to let you live.*

The taxiway from the end of Runway 19R to Hall Aviation has its kinks, and Torres navigated them with ease before cutting his switches in the Bristol's reserved space outside the hangar. No doubt remained in the mind of Simon Torres that he could set the big craft down on a short runway at night. Fifty yanqui hostages thought they would land on a long Puerto Vallarta strip in daylight; Borges nursed the illusion that they would find Base Ana's shorter strip about dark. Torres and his only confidante, David Elath, had San Pedro Sula in mind, on a runway shorter still and after dark. The amusing thing was that only their official pilot, Orozco, frankly admitted to Torres his total ignorance of his real destination. To Torres this fact was such a great joke, and the Mexican such a friendly victim, that he began thinking of ways to let Orozco live.

Orozco walked back to the main passenger exit directly behind the left wing; opened the hatch and kicked their short rope ladder out. By now it was understood that, for these short training flights, Pablo Orozco would perform such menial tasks as securing wheel chocks and stabilizers after a landing, and the Mexican did it with courtesy that said *I am your man.* Just as plainly, he hoped for future employment. Torres deplaned and followed the fuselage shadow to Orozco, glancing with concealed interest at the few workers in sight, all wearing Hall Aviation logos on their overalls. None of them seemed familiar nor even faintly curious but then, they never had.

"You may as well see to our fuel, Pablo," he said as Orozco dusted his hands. "I think we need no further check rides. But be sure you are every inch the flight captain on Friday morning, clear of eye and well rested."

"Not hungover and fucked into exhaustion? Ay de mi, the sacrifices I make to my patrons," Orozco said with a comic grimace. "I wonder how my first officer will look."

"Frustrated," said Torres in the same vein.

"In this town? My friend has friends."

Torres found himself tempted before he decided that he did not want such favors from a man he would still, in all likelihood, have to kill. The idea of dalliance with a woman, though: That had even more appeal than usual. Not so much for a quick ten-minute writhe in a pricey whorehouse, but something different; something fleetingly romantic, perhaps with a bedroom tussle to cap it, or perhaps not. He finally declined Orozco's offer with thanks and they walked together into the office of Hall Aviation, where Orozco sought someone to fuel the Bristol.

It was there that Torres saw the woman with the Hall logo on her crisp blouse and the Hall attendant's cap and the skirt that seemed a bit too short for her, and she returned his smile with what seemed to be shy interest. It was not the skirt, but what it failed to hide, that made his decision for him. Simon Torres was a leg man.

When flying, Torres always liked to dress for the occasion. Orozco invariably wore military shirts with epaulets and little wings—not too little to be overlooked by an alert woman—gabardines, and black oxfords. For his grand deception Torres had bought a similar outfit, almost the same shades of tan but with black Italian loafers, and unlike Orozco, he preferred to leave ties to those required to wear them, or who were too stupid not to. It was an expensively dressed, smiling, attractively casual Latino who confronted Eulalie Calvin.

Torres engaged her direct attention by asking her opinion of French restaurants in Las Vegas. At first her reply faltered, her gaze registering something like apprehension, but that was quickly replaced by what he inferred was a look of riposte to challenge. Though not a beauty, she glowed with the health, and the deep roan hair, of a thoroughbred. Her cheekbones had the leanness of a fashion model, but her lines were not anorexic. Her name, she said, was Eunice Kaltenborn. And her smile, Dios mio, when she finally give him one it was a grin that shaded that of Orozco! She stood nearly as tall as Torres, and her carriage was proud as that of a contessa. Her forearms, tanned and whipcorded as her lower limbs, were those of an athlete. He made a silent wager that she knew her tennis, and other sweet spots that did not imply tennis rackets. Had she been an entry in a crossword puzzle, Torres would have admitted it was too early to fill in all the blanks; but when he did, he thought it might spell "rough sex."

He sensed in less than a minute that she had decided in his favor, but Torres knew better than to rush it. Conferring over a telephone book, they veered toward Armand's at first . . . "and it's not all that far away," he observed.

Then she spied another ad and her, "Gee, it's not too far either, I've seen it in Flamingo West Centre," was so wistful he agreed on Greek food instead. For a wonder, she did not play the coy virgin when he asked her to share that meal with him. They had both known that he would ask, and that she would consent.

She agreed to let him call for her there at six, but vetoed the idea of leaving Hall Aviation early; not very smart for a working girl, she explained as she picked up her sheaf of papers and disappeared into Hall's offices with a swirl of skirt that set Torres's glands ajingle.

His pleasure was all the greater that Orozco had seen the encounter and, as they climbed into the Sable, pronounced himself envious. "I might have known," Orozco sighed, "you could make any selection you liked on a moment's notice."

I really must find a way to let you live, Torres replied silently, and they completed the drive to their Henderson motel largely without conversation, Torres thinking furiously how he might use the Mexican to check his own room. Borges had said the bodies were in the desert—but Borges might say anything. He did not get it worked out until he was swinging the blue Sable into the motel entrance, but Torres always thought more quickly under stress.

He parked and reached as if to shut off the engine, then swore softly as Orozco opened his door. "Mierda! What if Borges is waiting in my room?"

Orozco paused, his whole body a shrug. "How would he do that?"

Torres made his smile apologetic and implied that Borges was the real boss with his first phrase: "He has my spare key, and he may insist on my time tonight. And I have sweeter things in mind, my friend. Wait, I have it," he said, digging for his room key, handing it to Orozco. "I shall drive around to the back. Go to my room. If it is empty, bring back my key. If Billy is waiting, tell him I asked you to say I shall be back late, and you were to leave my key at the office."

Orozco's glance was puzzled but, "Why not," he asked rhetorically, heading for Torres's room.

Simon Torres backed out; drove around to the rear of the motel; backed into a parking space without shutting off his engine. Scenarios of dead bodies or even some of Billy's yanqui gangster friends in his room tumbled over one another. After thirty seconds of waiting, he was surprised at the immensity of his own relief when Pablo Orozco ambled into the endless, unspeakable sunshine holding the room key like a dead mouse.

"Your room has no passengers and you are cleared for takeoff," said the Mexican, his teeth outshining the sun, and handed the key over.

Torres remembered to thank him before driving away. He felt considerable relief that his fears were coming, one by one, to nothing. *So why,* he asked himself as he turned onto the highway toward the southeast and Boulder City, *do I feel like a bug under a burning glass?* He settled back and drove at the minimum speed, adjusting his rearviews carefully. He saw no other traffic imitating him. Then, skirting Boulder City, he stepped up his pace before turning off from Route 95 toward the great, pure, sunblasted desolation that lies beneath everything else that is Nevada.

One car followed him to the unlikely hamlet of Nelson. It continued when he stopped and fed a cola machine, but he etched into his memory the image of two men in a tan Chevrolet Caprice with Arizona plates. He drove behind the lonely store, parked with the engine running, then walked back to stand seemingly idle, swigging cola, watching the silent dusty road.

When no Arizona Caprice returned and no other traffic passed in several minutes, Torres tossed the cola can aside, regained the cool haven of the Sable, and acquired Route 95 again by another route. *No one is hagriding you,* he told himself furiously. *You are an old woman, startled by every creak of the stair.* That helped; but he did not entirely shake his paranoia until he had nursed a scotch for a half-hour in Circus Circus, watching the show. He was assessing the legs of the aerialist when he commanded his mind's eye: *Bring me the charms of Eunice Kaltenborn.* After that, he rode the broad afternoon as a cowpoke rides a brood mare, lounging in comfort, only half alert.

Torres arrived back in the parking lot of Hall Aviation at five minutes before six, not so late as to seem inattentive, not early enough to suggest anxiety. He nodded toward a muscular black whom he had noticed earlier in the day, wearing a Hall logo. He pretended to study the panorama of air maps someone had pasted, an age ago, to a wall. Someone else had penciled new features in: here a smokestack, there a row of high-tension electric lines. It was cheaper, Torres supposed, than sticking up new charts every six months.

The woman he knew as Eunice murmured a greeting as

she passed him, adding, ''Just let me freshen up and change my blouse,'' and in another five minutes she was back in a sleeveless white blouse that complimented her tan and without that silly institutional hat, taking his arm without hesitation. It was the first time she had physically touched the man who called himself Simon Aguilar.

He found the Greek cafe less expensive than he might have wished, and soon learned that ouzo could be had without the retsina that had made him hate it years before. He enjoyed the coarse salad with its feta cheese; Eunice surprised him by denying she had ever held a tennis racket. She loved bicycle touring, however, which set his mind to rest on the matter of her fine, lean racehorse body. Though the place had been empty when they arrived, it began to fill as they sampled dolmades—which tasted of weeds, he thought—and tiny deep-fried rings which turned out to be calamari, and finally a multilayered main course of ground lamb and eggplant that had them both exclaiming. It was near the end of that moussaka course when Torres, checking his surroundings between ferns that hung before their mirrored wall, noticed the man.

In a dark suit, tall and as swarthy as Torres and perhaps a few years younger, the man had ordered appetizers but did not seem to attack them with much gusto. He was facing away from them but used those mirror tiles in much the same manner as Torres, whose favorite explanation for the fellow's interest was the athletic sexuality of Eunice. His paranoia had a better explanation, however, and though she seemed rapt with Torres's fanciful tales of his ''Bolivian'' cadet days, Eunice glanced at least once toward the stranger.

Torres pressed his left arm to his side, feeling his little sidearm, as a passenger might check his safety belt, and broke off a story in mid-lie. ''Do you know the short-haired man across the room?''

Eunice frowned; put down her fork; looked at Torres without expression.

"Gray suit, black tie. By himself near the corner," Torres went on to eliminate any misunderstanding.

She paused before she reached some internal decision, her gaze judgmental and unwavering on the tall man in the corner. Beginning with a small sound of exasperation: "I've known him too long," she said. "Wait," she added quickly, her hand beseeching on his wrist as he started to turn. "Please, Simon: If you like me, don't embarrass me. I'll handle it later, but I can't have someone from my past disrupting such a wonderful meal. Please," she said again.

He placed his free hand over hers, lightly, then withdrew his hands and pursued the last morsels in his plate. *If this man were of much importance, she would have denied knowing him*, he told himself, assuming that Eunice Kaltenborn was only, after all, that simple creature all women were.

From then until their last sip of rich Greek coffee and their final scrap of baklava, Torres laughed more often, with more expansive gestures. It was not a thing he had to think about, but the sort of thing one did when being watched by another suitor.

Torres took the check with scarcely a glance, held Eunice's chair, and started toward the cashier.

She put a restraining hand on him a second time, said, "Please wait here. I won't be long," and then walked the few paces toward the startled fellow in the gray suit. Though she spoke quietly, Torres could hear her every word as she leaned forward near the man's head. "Reuben, this is the third time you've done this, and it will end by making me hate you. It's over, Reuben. You'll simply have to accept that and get on with your life, and let me get on with mine." The man tried to meet her gaze, but failed and nodded. "And please don't call me later at home, I'll probably be at Hall catching up on paperwork. I wouldn't have anything more to say, anyway. All right?"

The man nodded again, looking away, a strong-looking specimen reduced to jelly by soft words. She took Torres's arm then, and did not speak again until he had paid with a single hundred-dollar bill, not waiting for change.

As they walked outside, she only said, "I met him at work two years ago. We were together until recently, Simon. I feel sorry for Reuben but I can't have him asking my other friends where I'm going and who I'm with so he can ruin my evenings, can I?"

Torres agreed that she couldn't, making small talk, reflecting silently that, without meaning to, she had answered a few very important questions. *She knew where we were going, and was pleased enough to mention it to her friends.* That must have been how poor Reuben knew where to find them. Aloud he said, "I hope you did not mean what you said about ending your evening with paperwork. I think you might find it far more pleasant to end it with me."

"Another time, I hope we can," she replied with an altogether different kind of smile; slow and slumbrous, and full of promise. "But Reuben brought back too many memories. I hope you can understand that, Simon."

He thought he did, and talked her into a nightcap that stretched into three at a quiet bistro off the strip, and at the gentle urging of alcohol and the woman he found himself recounting some of his real exploits, none of them pertaining to his current business. When at last he saw her to the door of Hall Aviation, it was after midnight. She waited for him to kiss her and returned it hungrily, pressing herself against him with a murmured, "I'm sorry," and then he thought she had walked out of his life.

He drove back to a familiar place and requested a long-legged woman who would accept a few bruises for a thousand in cash, and got exactly what he asked for; but it was not really what he wanted.

TWENTY-SEVEN
Thursday, May 25

THE CATNAPS MUST be working, Hardin figured, because he did not really need the caffeine in Marana's coffee during their Thursday midmorning break. He couldn't fault the help they were getting. "Marana's sheet metal guys are artists," he replied to a question by Lloyd Meacham, who sat across the table nursing his Jolt Cola. "They're even leaving us crawlspace beneath the backflash pipes in the fuselage. Any word yet on those runway mines of yours?"

"The MIFFs? They're promised absolutely, positively by tonight," Meacham responded. "And they're not exactly mine. You know who makes 'em?"

"Picatinny Arsenal," was Hardin's guess.

Meacham shook his head and grinned. "Germany; Messerschmitt, in fact. Ain't that a bitch? Now we're ordering wonder weapons from those swell folks who gave us the London blitz," he said wryly, and broke off to wave at someone coming through the door. "Curt; you reach Payson?"

Hardin raised a hand in greeting as Curt Christiansen nodded and swung a leg over a wooden bench, protecting his coffee and bearing the smile of a man with news to impart. Hardin primed his pump with, "What'd Payson say?"

"He got a go from Washington." Christiansen watched his two colleagues slump with relief, then resumed. "Since the Canadair was bought with cash and the new owner's untraceable, we can claim the cartel bought it. Gun pods like ours are in the hands of several countries, and the launch tubes from Mac Air have no serial numbers or anything else; 'without provenance,' as Payson put it. All our other stuff will leave nothing but debris. What's so funny, Lloyd?"

Meacham was chuckling, a slow "huh, huh" full of evil mirth. "I'm just thinking: if those fuckers start checking into what's left down there, they may figure it really *was* an inside job by a rival! Don't you love it?"

"Ask me again on Saturday," Christiansen replied. "But you haven't heard the latest, gentlemen: One of the doper aircrew wangled himself a date with one of our people."

"You mean Dorman," said Hardin, recalling the DEA agent's voluptuous profile.

'No, when I said ours, I meant *ours*," Christiansen said, taking a sip, watching the others.

Meacham, who was CIA himself, reacted first. "Not Calvin! Good God, she could tear a man's head off."

"Or kick it off. But she didn't," Christiansen said. "She took him up on it. And get this: While they're eating at some Greek place, the doper spots a bureau guy surveilling them in the same cafe. Calvin played him as an old flame. You know the rube code?"

Hardin looked blank. Meacham caught it. "Old carny call for help, Hardin: They used to call 'hey, rube!' but to us it just means, 'I've got a problem here.' So Calvin called him 'Reuben,' thinking he'd understand. Payson says his bureau man didn't pick up the allusion, but he got the gist of it and played along; got a water glass for prints later. So Eulalie Calvin shows up at midnight with some stuff we can check; the doper says he's a Bolivian—and get this: He *says* he has his own T-33 back home."

"That's great," Hardin said. "If it's the same T-Bird we were warned about, he can't be both places at once."

"And there's only one Latin doper in the world who can fly one, hunh? Dream on, pal," Meacham said, upending his can of Jolt.

Hardin glanced at his watch; sighed. "Twenty-six hours from now, we've got to be ready," he reminded them.

Christiansen: "What do you think now?"

The little Texan stared at their tabletop, seeing instead the forest of big metal tubes taking shape inside the Canadair; the monster stainless steel bands that kept launchers grouped in sets of four; the metal stanchions that must support gun pods that could each spew one hundred slugs per second; and the additional tubes that had not yet been fabricated because they could get no exact dimensions on those German submunitions. "It'll be a tossup. I still think we're looking at several hours of work in flight, Curt, so I've had some more structural bits and pieces crated in the plane; 7075 T3 alloy braces and so on. Still, we may have to land without everything in place."

"I don't want to hear that," Christiansen warned.

"Then I didn't say it," Hardin returned equably.

Meacham: "Take it easy, Curt. Even without the MIFFs, nobody will be using that airbase for some time to come, and we can make it to those little spookships while guerrillas are still dodging shrapnel." He glanced toward Hardin: "You're sure your civilians won't come unglued in all the commotion?"

"I've told you."

"Tell me again."

"Cutter was military, and Morrison has more balls than a gum machine," said Hardin.

Christiansen: "But neither of 'em has ever taken hostile fire."

"Neither have I, since I left Abilene," Hardin said.

Christiansen's expression said "I didn't want to hear that, either," but after a moment he simply took another sip of coffee. "What about Abilene?"

"Fifteen-year-old kid with a watermelon, farmer with a shotgun."

"And?"

"I dropped the melon, and a load in my pants," Hardin admitted. "But it was gone by the time I cleared his fence."

"You didn't freeze, then." Meacham's tone was hopeful.

"Feller can't very well freeze and clear five feet of bob-wire at the same time," Hardin grinned. "Actually, I went back the next night."

Christiansen maintained that look, one of withheld judgment. "What for?"

"*Two* watermelons."

Slowly, the CIA pilot's eyes closed, and when they opened he was smiling. "You'll be okay." He pushed his cup around with a forefinger to no particular purpose as he continued, the smile fading. "It's got to worry you, because you're bright and you have a good imagination; and of course there's no perfect guarantee, but look at it this way: You lost your virginity in a watermelon patch. All the same, when we put our boots on that runway I want you to go first."

"To make sure I don't freeze?"

"To put my foot up your ass in case you do," Christiansen corrected. "It works wonders. You'd be surprised."

"You've been under fire, then."

"I've taken the odd round, now and then," Christiansen confided.

To this, Meacham gave another cynical laugh. "Stopped a few, is what you did," he told his companion. "I've seen you in the shower, man, you didn't get those scars in divinity school."

Hardin studied the senior CIA man with interest. "Mind telling me how it felt?"

"Sure, but it won't make much sense to you. Both times it was more like an electrical shock, whacked and numbed me. Gave me fits later, why deny it? Did I cry, you mean? Yes; later. I might cry after this is over and we're wheels-up, but not until then. Goes with the territory," he said more softly. "I just hope you're right about those civilians."

"And I'm glad you can fly those things yourself, just in case," Meacham said.

Hardin nodded. "In case Morrison or Cutter gets hit?"

"That doesn't worry me a lot," Meacham explained. "The opposition is gonna be stoned on concussion. And I'm not worried about that Cutter guy. It's the woman, Hardin, this little tiny broad who prob'ly thinks an incoming round is a waiter bringing the drinks and a deflection shot is when you spill your bourbon. I mean, what if she freezes?"

Hardin thought about that for perhaps fifteen seconds while the others regarded him gravely. "I can unfreeze her," he said at last.

"You mean, kick her butt?"

"Easier than that," Hardin promised. "All I'd have to do is let on that *I* can't handle it."

"That's weird," said Meacham.

"That's also Morrison," Hardin said, and stood up. "Come on, let's get those wiring harnesses rigged."

TWENTY-EIGHT

Thursday, May 25

A LOT OF government employees had left Nellis Air Force Base by eighteen hundred hours on Thursday but few of them were attached to Task Force Enable, and those few were pulling surveillance duty. To the assembled group, Marvin Payson first recapped recent history, bringing them up to date with, "Take a good look at Captain Ryan Spannier of Quantico, because you may not recognize him tomorrow morning."

All eyes turned toward the sweatsuited man at Payson's right who came halfway out of his chair, raising a perfunctory hand, before resuming his seat. Payson went on, "Cap, the floor is yours."

Ryan "Cap" Spannier stood up again, pulling a clipboard from the zippered nylon bag at his feet, and passed his free hand across a scalp as clean-shaven as his jaw. Of medium height and in his early forties, Cap Spannier might have weighed 160 pounds, half of it evidently gristle. His eyebrows suggested he would have been blond and his stance was relaxed, in the manner of a man who saved his adrenaline for necessities. His general demeanor was that of a two-legged anvil, but instead of barking out what he had to say, he spoke in a bass that was almost sweet.

His Quantico people, he said, were barracked nearby for their own briefing. "We studied the emergency exits for a stretched Bristol; you never know how the opposition might want to use 'em. With that in mind, our hardware includes some little handheld Taser units that will stun a dray horse. We've got ID packets on the pairs of citizens we're standing in for, including photos, and by zero-eight-hundred tomorrow we'll begin showing up in Hall's parking lot with boarding passes, looking very middle-aged and vulnerable. Don't expect a color of the day; if we did that we might as well wear armbands, because we assume these dopers aren't stupid. I gather that a few of you folks will be on board, despite my recommendation. Just remember, especially once we're aboard, to take your cues from the old fogey in the green double-knit leisure suit— that'll be me, by the way."

He consulted his clipboard; looked up again. "Three couples are still not accounted for, so we'll have a road crew digging a trench in the access road. Our flagman knows which vehicles to watch for and will divert the DeLongs, the Satterfields, and the Irvines. That failing," he said, and shrugged, "you'll have to divert any last-second arrivals. Our road crew will be in radio contact with the Hall office, and I think we can cover all the bases without letting any innocent lambs get aboard. Questions?"

Eulalie Calvin, one of four task force members slated for the flight, raised her hand. "Worst case: Those missing couples do show up, and somehow get aboard. Do we abort the flight?"

"That's a command decision; I can't tell you how happy I am to turn that one over to Payson," Spannier said, and glanced at the task force leader.

After a long moment of nodding to himself, Payson replied without getting up. He spoke slowly, as if still measuring the idea. "If it were a dozen couples, or even half a dozen, I'd have to call an abort. But if it were only one or two—well, won't some of your people be wearing flak jackets, Cap?"

He waited for Spannier's nod, but got more than he expected. "We can physically interpose a couple of warm bodies wearing Kevlar skivvies, if it comes to that," Spannier said, ignoring the chuckles from his audience. "There are lots more of us than there will be of them, even if they bring a dozen more aboard. That's always a possibility," he said over the sudden muted buzz. "We just don't know what they might have in mind. I gather we intercepted a phone call suggesting this won't be a dry run, and unless it's disinformation, at some point they'll most likely show their doper colors. If they do, NSA will blanket their signal before they can warn their people about it. We could sneak a tech into the cockpit with a radio-activated guillotine switch, but Marvin vetoed that, and I have to concur; there could be someone on the opposition who hasn't surfaced, watching the airplane for exactly that. In case you're wondering: My attaché case will be full of microwave gear, so I'll be in touch during the flight. Anyone shadowing us in our own airspace will have to do it at three hundred and fifty knots, and NSA will be flying high cover with jamming equipment."

Merle Givens, who had made a strong case for himself the day before while wearing makeup and a wig supplied by Lucille Dorman, stood up. "So we'll be somewhere over Mexico while another Bristol shadows us; correct?"

"Twenty minutes behind, if you get that far," Payson said. "An hour ago, our aircrew at Marana swore they'd be ready, but they shouldn't be in sight of you at any time."

"I'm just wondering whether there's any possibility of us actually landing at that doper airbase. If so, we should be carrying heavier ordnance than sidearms."

"You'll be monitored on radar," Payson replied. "Assuming you get as far as Puerto Vallarta without entering a landing pattern, Cap will get the word. No way you're going inland toward the isthmus.'' Payson released his droll half-smile. ''But we know some folks who will. If the dopers fool us and land you at Puerto Vallarta after all—well, our guys at Marana will have enough fuel to return home.''

Cap Spannier glanced again at his notes. ''Marvin, it isn't clear to me just how many dopers will make up the flight crew.''

''Nor to us either,'' Payson admitted, ''but now we think it'll be five. We knew there'd be three Latin males, but we've got a 'round-the-clock surveillance on them, including a van full of optics and electronics. Subject One is the listed pilot, a Mexican national named Orozco. Spends most of his time on the Strip making Latin time with his girl. No other known associates besides Subjects Two and Three.

''Subject Two is the hotshot who bought dinner for a pretty lady who just happens to be part of our operation,'' he went on, with a nod toward Calvin. ''His prints match those of a Colombian cadet this country once trained, before he became a colonel down there, before he disappeared one jump ahead of a court-martial. Name, Simon Torres. He may not be an Escobar, but we think he may be the cartel's top flyboy.

''Subject Three is one Guillermo Borges; he's left a lot of prints around Vegas the past few years consorting with Oh Cee,'' he said, using the short term for organized crime figures. ''All three of these guys have rooms in the same Henderson motel, but Torres and Borges have taken turns, the past couple of nights, occupying an air-conditioned loft in a Henderson warehouse. No phone, and they aren't connecting with anyone else local; the cartel money is probably there. Believe it or not, if we got in with a search warrant and found the money, we probably couldn't make any serious charges stick. Not until they actually cross the CONUS border, so their loading cash on that airplane does not, in itself, give us an ironclad case. They could claim they were going to make a stop in Tucson or you-name-it and forgot to change their flight plan. Sure it's thin, but it could throw doubt on our case. But if our Bristol ever crosses the border, U.S. and Mexican Customs will get word to do a subtle toss of whatever cargo it carries.

"Now to your question, Cap: A couple of hours ago, another pair of males showed up at the motel in Henderson; described to me as a couple of ballet dancers, though I haven't seen 'em. They had a face-to-face with Borges—the spiffy dresser in size forty-eight pants. We put an agent on the motel cleaning staff and she activated his phone speaker, so we have the whole conversation. Like Two and Three, the new pair speak Colombian Spanish.

"Subjects Four and Five say they're looking forward to the flight, and we figure them as attendants, no doubt heavily armed. By the way: We've put detectors in the wall at Hall Aviation, so we'll know who's packing heavy metal," Payson finished.

To which Cap Spannier raised his hands in mock surprise, making his eyes wide. "Surely," he said, "You don't suspect *us*?"

Payson waited for Spannier to get his laugh before reading out the duty roster for the next shifts, not missing the fact that some of his people threw envious glances toward the four who left without waiting. Those four already knew when they would next pull duty. They would pull it as middle-aged tourists aboard a Bristol Britannia; two from the bureau, one each from the other agencies. Politically it was his best choice. As for the tactical side, he would know by Saturday.

And so would every reporter on Planet Earth.

TWENTY-NINE

Thursday, May 25

THE LIFTING TAILGATE on Borges's truck made their loading job merely difficult instead of impossible. Every time Borges cursed a concrete lip or a leaning pallet, Torres wondered whether fat Billy was also cursing himself for disposing of the men who would have made that job simple. Shortly before 11:00 P.M., Billy Borges trundled one more palletload of cash across the loading dock and maneuvered it into place near the tailgate of the truck. "That's more than half of the shipment," Torres said, securing the vehicle's cargo door as Borges jockeyed his forklift back into the warehouse. He lowered their chain-driven warehouse door as well while Borges connected the forklift's battery charger. "A great pity we must leave the rest without a guard, even for an hour or so. I wonder if you have considered putting Orozco upstairs, merely as a tripwire. He would be better than nothing."

"We would waste time bringing him, and I have taken responsibility. We do what we must," Borges puffed, checking the lock of their smaller door, testing its latch after they stepped outside. He did not speak again until they were underway, Billy driving while Torres adjusted the big mirror outside his window. "I need that mirror," Borges complained.

Torres mastered an impulse, now constantly bubbling just beneath his surface, to backhand Billy, and did not readjust the mirror again. "You have one for driving, and I have one for watching, Billy. Let us imagine that your Vegas friends have somehow discovered what we are doing. Can you imagine a better target for a hijacking than we offer?" He said nothing about that neck-prickling sensation that had ridden him for the past day and a half, a sense of being shadowed by some unseen presence, an intelligence both patient and hostile. He simply placed Billy's little Czech burp gun across his lap and studied the road ahead when he was not watching behind.

Borges only grunted in answer to the suggestion of a hijack attempt, driving at a legal pace as they retraced the now-familiar highway, taking the Tropicana turnoff with a load that pendulumed on a fully loaded suspension. Billy overcorrected, cursed, straightened with a low moan of tires that was not quite a howl. *"Falta de mi,"* Billy apologized, and it was Torres's turn to grunt.

Because Las Vegas does not sleep until dawn, Torres spread his suspicions among many following headlights and welcomed Billy's decision to take the less-traveled Industrial Road to McCarran. The lights he worried most about belonged to a sedan that swung past them shortly before they reached the airport entrance. He had just commanded his arms to relax when Borges, guiding them along the perimeter blacktop, braked with an oath but did not stop.

Limned by floodlights, a road crew could be seen placing cones of bright orange plastic in the roadway. "If you trust this, Billy, you are a fool," Torres hissed.

"I know," said Borges, gearing down, flicking his lights as he proceeded. Torres knew that no one could see over his window ledge without climbing up, and resolved to fling his door open if that happened. He saw Billy Borges's hand stray from the gearshift selector to the second Skorpion lying in the seat between them.

Their salvation appeared suddenly, magically, in the person of a tall fellow in overalls who swept the beam of a big flashlight to the left of the cones, squinting into their headlights and waving them around. If he had any special interest in the truck or its contents, he kept it well hidden, turning away as Borges navigated the left lane, giving a final sweep of his beam ahead of the truck as if to hurry them on their way. Billy Borges accelerated up through the gears, his precious load shifting, a heavy thump from the cargo section making a sound like a falling body.

Neither man spoke until, two minutes later, Billy drove behind chain-link fencing of a parking lot to the Bristol that sat in majestic silence, and mostly in shadow from sodium arclights that bathed the parking area of Hall Aviation. "What in God's name were those obreros doing at this time of night," Billy asked as he positioned the truck for backing.

Torres, poised in the doorframe with Billy's flashlight in hand, said, "Yanquis are crazy; that is all I know," and dropped to the concrete, trotting off toward the low-slung fuselage of the Bristol. As he inserted his simple, almost comically ordinary key into the flush handle of the aircraft's cargo bay door, he reflected that aircraft—even very large ones—are notoriously easy to vandalize, given such poor security locks. *Another need for a guard when we cannot even tell Orozco why we need one,* he thought, swinging the door away to reveal the cavernous cargo interior. *Perhaps when I shoot Guillermo Borges I shall not kill him with the first round.* He knew that was subdued rage talking; no matter how most of his colleagues enjoyed themselves, Torres kept a small scruple against torture.

Because the Bristol Britannia was designed for first-class transatlantic flights, it has ample seating for fifty lords and almost as many ladies, and cargo space for a wagonload of luggage for each. Torres had flown cargo loads through rotten Andes weather; though not an expert cargomaster, he knew that the luggage of those silly yanqui hostages would not begin to match the weight of his money, and in any case he wanted the money to be readily available when the time came for him and Elath to unload it. He juggled these priorities quickly as he guided Borges in backing the truck. He would simply tell Borges it was necessary to load that luggage ahead of the real cargo, for reasons of balance. It would be those two palo blanco flight stewards who had to do it, in any case.

Without a forklift, even though the liftgate helped, the two of them slaved for nearly an hour to empty that truck. The wheezing of Billy Borges grew almost to a snore, echoing through the Bristol's big cargo bay as he shoved cartons toward the waiting hands of Simon Torres. Without room to stand in the Bristol's cargo tunnel, Torres scrambled and shoved, readjusted and shoved again until, to his amazement, he actually lost count in that stifling, flashlit tunnel of aluminum. When Borges announced that they were ready to return for the second load, Torres could only peer down from his hands-and-knees posture and blink stupidly. "Cargo net," he gasped. "Rig cargo net. Momentito, Billy." Then he forced himself to secure the load with hefty nylon net, using tiedowns almost as old as he. Well, it would have to function only one more time. . . .

As they passed the road crew again, Billy stopped. "Digging for gold? What else could be so important at this time of night?" he asked with forced bonhomie.

The tall one with the lamp made a face that said "you know how it is" in most languages. "Old water main leaking. I'm not gonna roast a good crew in the middle of the day," he replied. "You must not be from around here."

"*Vamonos,*" Torres said softly, and with a carefree laugh Billy surged the empty truck away. Torres's wristwatch told him it was 1:35 A.M. Friday.

At three in the morning they locked a now-empty ware-

house, Billy driving away alone while Torres followed in
the blue Sable. His stated reason, a perfectly good one,
was that one of them should collect Orozco and the attendants at the motel. His more urgent need, left unstated to
Borges, was to hang back a half-mile and study other traffic more closely. Torres could not deny, by now, an almost
palpable sense of impending disaster. Even in the coolness
of the desert night, hot gooseflesh marched in phalanx up
the back of his neck to lodge in his scalp. Every set of
headlights became an undeclared enemy until proven otherwise. He tried to convince himself it was only the nearness of total success, on a scale beyond the dreams of most
men, that churned his guts this way, but bone-deep paranoia takes a lot of convincing.

This time, Torres approached the road crew several hundred yards behind the truck. As he drove near with a
casual wave, he saw that the men were using old gasoline-
powered jackhammers behind their bright barricades to
cut the roadbed, leaving a free lane. A sudden thought,
full of worry but also of happy surmise, made him stop.
*Too bad for the cartel if most of their hostages cannot get
to the airplane,* he thought; *but perhaps a great deal simpler for me.*

"Go ahead, Mac, it's clear," called one worker.

"Thank you. Will we still have room to pass later this
morning?"

"Oh sure, no sweat," was the reply.

Torres smiled as though pleased and drove on, parking
in the Hall lot. The office seemed to be staffed at all hours,
and he was tempted to enlist some help, but allowed good
sense to command him. A dropped carton, with millions
in cash spilling from a five-gallon can, could bring his
plans to a ludicrous end.

Thanks to his second wind and a welcome breeze, Torres found the energy to complete his part of the task, wrestling the last of the cartons into the cargo bay alone when
Borges finally reached his physical limits. *It's all on board
now,* he exulted, invigorated for the moment by fresh hope.

Let fat Billy go after Orozco and the others. Dios mio, what an ass I am! While I relax in the cockpit and pretend utter exhaustion, Borges will leave in the car, and who is to prevent me from taking off by myself?

Torres could see no flaw with this sudden, dramatic change in his plan. Billy could hardly complain to American authorities; in less than an hour after takeoff the Bristol could be over Mexican air space; and even if the aircraft were reported stolen, he could loiter over international waters and land in San Pedro Sula after dark, calling in false identification. Such matters were simple at many Central American airfields.

Beguiled with his fresh solution, operating on reserve strength at four-thirty in the morning, Torres locked the cargo bay door and allowed Billy Borges to help him into the rear passenger door of the Bristol, where he fell into the nearest seat and stared at the cabin paneling, eyes wide.

A moment later Borges was back. "Let us hope you do not need this," he said, placing a Skorpion on Torres's lap. "Would you like a few uppers?" He pulled a vial from his shirt pocket. Then, reading bewilderment in the face of Simon Torres, he avoided yanqui slang: "A stimulant, Simon. To keep you alert."

Artificial stimulants have killed a lot of pilots, and Torres knew it. He also knew better than to trust the effects of any pill Billy offered. Once he got the Bristol free of chocks and control locks, and cleared the McCarran runway, he would be alert enough. "No, gracias. Perhaps later." *Later, you will understand I have a billion stimulants beneath my feet. And you will still be alive only because I cannot risk gunfire here and now.*

Borges pocketed the vial. "I need the keys to the Sable," he said, almost apologetically, and waited while Torres produced them. "I will bring the others back, and then we can sleep a few hours."

Torres nodded and stared at the ceiling, breathing deeply. He made himself go limp to remove any slightest suspicion on Billy's part that the pilot might be considering more furious activity within the next half-hour as dawn approached. Billy snapped off his flashlight then and climbed down the ladder.

Torres stayed where he was, listening carefully to the whine of a liftgate, the rattle and bang of a truck's cargo door, the familiar slam of a passenger door, the grind and cough of an engine. He decided to give Borges five minutes to switch vehicles. In such profound, predawn quiet he was certain he could hear the Sable start up.

Resting his head on that airliner seat, racked back in comfort, he began to wonder why he had entertained such wild paranoid fantasies of hostile forces ranked against him. He must have been a little crazy, he thought, but now it would be all right. He would have the rest of his life to laugh about it, and to savor a billion-dollar joke on cartelistas who had absolutely no sense of humor. He laughed softly and closed his eyes for an instant.

And when he opened them again, Orozco was shaking his shoulder.

THIRTY

Friday, May 26

"O<small>KAY, READ IT</small> out to me word for word," said Cam Irvine, each word softer and slower than its predecessor. Laurie could hardly hear his last words over the song of Minnetta's little Toyota MR-2 at eighty-five miles an hour.

Of all Cam's irritating habits, Laurie decided, this was his worst: this big production of calming down and steadying up when everything went to shit, gearing his replies down until every word came ve—ry slow—ly, as if inviting some invisible third party to compare his behavior with hers. It had to be machismo, no matter how often he denied it. She gave him her hardest glare, knowing he was aware of it though he did not take his eyes from Interstate 15 as the white Toyota sportster climbed into high desert toward Nevada. Then she found their boarding passes in her purse and wrenched one of them open.

She read as if reciting to a first-grade defective: "Dumdadumdadum, 'standard luggage allowance of forty pounds,' dumdadum. 'You must be aboard the aircraft by ten A.M. on the day of your flight to Condo Vallarta to be assured of a seat. Your boarding pass is nontransferable and will not be honored by regularly scheduled air carriers.' In case you're too busy thrashing my sister's car to read a digital clock," she added, voice rising again, "it is now exactly eight fifty-one."

"Seventy-eight miles," he said, making it sound as though he was satisfied. "We can make it."

"Su-u-ure we will. How d'you know that mileage counter is accurate, in a car you've never driven before and wouldn't be driving now if you were as good a mechanic on both of our own cars as you thought you were?" Quite a nice list of charges for one breath, she thought, folding away the boarding pass.

"That little podunk a mile back was Halloran Springs, and the sign said seventy-nine miles to Vegas. Can you subtract one from seventy-nine? Try hard," he suggested.

"We're not gonna make it," she wailed suddenly, not wanting to cry, needing to, compromising with hot-eyed recriminations because if she didn't, she would start screaming. "I bust my butt to get a totally all-expenses flight to Puerto Vallarta for us, pack two bags for you so you could decide which stuff you want to take, and lug the damn' stuff to Minetta's while you go traipsing off to the lake, trailing that miserable little tub of yours. And you can't even bother to phone me when a breakdown makes you half a day late and my Chevy's brakes quit! I nearly went out of my mind," she finished.

"You're getting there. Wait, hold it; I didn't mean to say that," he amended, too late as usual.

"Syllables just fall out of your mouth accidentally, Cam? Wonderful how they fit together into cheap shots," she said.

"I mean if I'd thought about it, I mean I'm sorry, I just—ahh, shit, Laurie, I'm no saint when I lose patience, and I'm trying to apologize."

"Why not just say you're sorry?"

"I just did."

"Where was I when you did it?"

"God knows," he said in a martyr's tone. Then, bursting out: "God *dammit*, I'm sorry!"

"Why is it so hard for you to say that?"

"You make it damn' near impossible, Laurie. Tell you what: Give me a role model. Maybe if you can, I can."

She gnawed a knuckle instead of backhanding him as she fairly itched to do, watching the desert scrub sail by them. She wanted to remind him that one more speeding ticket would tack a fat premium onto their auto insurance but feared that, if she did, Cam was perfectly capable of slowing down to sixty-five just to spite her, and then when they were careening toward the airport and saw their airliner climbing toward Puerto Vallarta, he could claim it was her fault.

"Laurie, look at it this way: They aren't going to give out more tickets than they have seats," he said a few minutes later. "That wouldn't create much good will, and they're trying to sell real estate."

"I could use some good will in this car right now," she muttered.

"I'm trying to help. I'm telling you that even if we're a little late, there's a ninety percent chance there'll still be seats, and with all the air traffic on Memorial Day weekend, they won't leave the terminal on time. And anyway, we can just about make it so try and relax, will you?"

"Thank you, oh wise one," she said, biting back a more bitter response that would only have made things worse. Cam did have a blood pressure problem; he was the one who wanted to relax, trying to convince himself everything would be okay no matter how much he screwed up in the process.

The State of Nevada had a sign, but a better announcement was made by a group of casinos, Nevada's idea of Hollywood's version of a Western musical comedy, flanking I-15. The engine's soft whine rose a bit. "Nevada highway cops pretty much let you alone if you're not throwing whiskey bottles," Cam remarked. "You want to break out the California road atlas, honey? Won't be long now.''

"We're not in California," Laurie said.

"Would you just do it? Vegas might as well be part of California. Trust me, it's in there."

He was right, combining an irritant with a faint renewal of Laurie's hope. She turned spiral-bound pages to find both the segment of highway they were passing and an expanded map of the city. She hated maps; they always got a person turned around so, half the time, you turned the wrong direction. "What was that little burg we just passed," she inquired.

"Jean. Do we take any turnoffs?" The speedometer was reading ninety-five as he asked.

She found Jean on the map. "Not 'til we're in town. We're gonna get a ticket, you know."

He shrugged. The engine's warble did not drop a half-note. Presently he said, "Do we take the Henderson turnoff?"

"Never heard of it. We go into Vegas and hang a, uh, right on Tropicana."

The time was 9:43.

He wanted to take a turnoff that purported to lead them to McCarran International, but Laurie had three maps to contend with now, and the little one on her boarding pass showed Tropicana Avenue, endorsed by the road atlas in her lap. Laurie knew they couldn't go wrong that way, and said so in terms that carried a militant warning. At ten o'clock on the dot, passing casinos on Las Vegas Boulevard, she was directing him to turn off ". . . right, no no, left, left, shitfire, left," when she saw a big silvery tube climbing into the heavens on slender swept wings. "Ten o'clock and all is not very well," she remarked, watching the airliner and wishing that, wherever it was headed, she had been on it.

Turning hard left, Cam let the tires squall for him. "Which way now?"

She knew he was feeling the pressure because he was

talk—ing that way a—gain. She called out the next turn
and he took it, a right-hander that fishtailed the little
Toyota's rear end, and in moments they were racing along
the perimeter of McCarran, miles and miles of it, and she
looked for some sign of a big jet labeled 'management
internationale' among the hangars to their left, and before
she realized it they had gunned past a road to the left,
almost certainly the one on their boarding pass map.
"Left, you should've turned left," she said, maybe a little
too loud, and he braked so hard she felt the bite of her
shoulder strap. Oh yes, Mister Cameron Donald Irvine
hated loud voices, unless it was his.

Because an MR-2 is a yuppie's undeclared race car, it
tends to forgive orders that would put a Cadillac belly-up,
and through sheer luck Cam avoided stalling the engine
as the car swapped ends, peeling a month's rubber from
Minnetta's tires as he sought that side road. The clock said
10:05. Cam said, "Hall A—vi—a—tion," like a robot with
its "casual" knob turned up, nodding toward a sign.

"Don't you think I can read?"

"My opinion wavers," he replied, and that was the
capper.

If she hadn't screamed her wordless frustration, Laurie
would have burst. But she was facing him when she let
go, and the next instant he was braking savagely, the
Toyota's nose dipping. He simply got out; said, "That's
it, sweetie pie," and began to *walk* down that road.

She had not come this far to fail, notwithstanding the
fact that he might have made them fail already, and ten
seconds later she was scooting the driver's seat forward,
determined to make it even though she could feel hot tears
on her cheeks, her mascara burning her eyes so that she
had to keep blinking. She passed Cam, the bastard, without stopping. She would leave his overnight bag on the
car's hood is what she would do, even though he didn't
deserve it. And besides, he probably knew how to get into
a locked car anyhow.

A few hundred yards farther, she saw the painted barricade and the Day-Glo orange cones. Far behind, the rearview showed her, a panel truck followed and Cam seemed to be trying to thumb a ride. The road crew just ahead did not seem to be swinging picks with much enthusiasm. A tall man looked her way, motioning for her to slow down, staring hard at the car, and then bending down to peer inside. She tried to toss him a gay smile but knew it did not come off since her face was all squinched up from the sting of mascara.

As he waved her forward, he turned away. She distinctly heard the miserable sonofabitch say, "Singleton. My God, that face would stop a sundial," and she began to wipe her cheeks as she churned gravel in the Hall Aviation parking area.

She could see, behind the sheet metal hangar, dozens of people waiting in line to climb one of those adjustable stair gizmos next to a big airplane, not even a jet but a prop job, which meant it was probably left over from the last glaciation. *If it's free, it's probably worth half of what it costs,* Cam was fond of saying. That meant it was probably her flight to Condo Vallarta, stylishly late but definitely not a first-class accommodation. "Yeah, right," she said aloud as she hauled her bag out, Cam's too, realizing that she had plenty of time, half wishing she didn't because Cam Irvine would come swaggering up with a beatific smile that said "I told you so." If he did, she would hit him, swear to Almighty God she would.

She started toward the door with the Hall logo over it, then stopped. A well-dressed couple with little Gucci overnighters in hand and successful middle age written all over them stood to one side of the door, the man holding what appeared to be boarding passes exactly like those Laurie had in her purse. A big strapping guy wearing a logo like the one over the door was showing them his wallet, holding it near his gut as if fearful that someone else might see it, and Mr. and Mrs. Successful began to deflate like rubber dolls, and the woman looked as though she might start bawling. The big guy talked some more, with gestures, and soon the three of them were scrunching through gravel, Mr. Successful unlocking the trunk of a four-door BMW and tossing the Guccis in. Laurie did not like the looks of that, not even a little bit, and it was undeniably after 10:00 A.M., and damned if she intended to show her boarding pass to some officious asshole who had the power to turn her away when there was the plane right over yonder with twenty people still waiting to climb aboard, most with gray hair and one wearing, good God, a Nehru jacket that hadn't been stylish for thirty years.

Another Hall man stood inside the doorway. Laurie turned on her heel just in time to see her husband climbing down from a caterer's panel truck, and she dropped their bags into the gravel between two parked cars and met him with an embrace that took him by total surprise. "Look happy," she commanded, "or I'll kill you."

He let her talk, attentive to her face when she told him not to look around, and when she was through explaining, he did look almost pleased. "I'll be a dirty son of a bitch," he said as she picked up her bag.

"You'll get no argument from me," she said, and strode off alone; not into the Hall office, but in a purposeful march that took her into one of two doors set into the hangar wall. She saw Cam strolling in the same direction as the door swung shut, and then she was walking across the concrete floor, click click click, ducking beneath the wings of small airplanes in various stages of disrepair. Two men, obviously mechanics, paused to check the merchandise, as Cam liked to say, but no one said boo. Laurie kept walking, now into the sunshine as if heading toward one of the smaller airplanes moored by chains in the near distance beyond the airliner. When she doubled back, hurrying into the shadow of the big plane, she saw Cam following her example.

Ten seconds later he was beside her. "Take this," she said, "and don't ever say you don't need me." With that she handed him his boarding pass. Together, they brazenly walked over to the end of the passenger line. The woman just ahead of them turned, did a double take, and said in the voice of Gravel Gertie, "Oh Christ, there goes the neighborhood."

A slender little specimen dressed all in tan, smiling as if his face had been frozen that way, sashayed toward Laurie and Cam. The couple just ahead, now arguing in fierce whispers, calmed down as the little guy approached; no, said the husband, they preferred to carry their bags aboard. The little fellow turned to Cam then, asking in a Latin accent if they wanted their bags stowed.

"Sure," Cam replied, "as long as you don't work for United. Sometimes they send my stuff to the shredder in San Francisco."

Laurie handed her bag over too, moving with the line now toward the boarding stairs, the little Latin guy handing their bags to a sweat-streaked man in the cargo section who might have been his twin. Gravel Gertie's husband seemed to be talking to his own shoulder instead of to his wife, in a furious mutter. Without warning he turned to Cam. He said, "So who are you folks?" but his manner said, "White trash, go home."

Cam put his hand out. "Cameron and Laurie. Redding," he said.

The man shook hands quickly, brow furrowed. "Cameron and Laurie from Redding," he repeated, louder than seemed necessary. Then, more softly: "Listen, I think there's a message for you back at the office. I'll keep your place while you—"

"I know," Laurie said quickly. "It was nothing important." Most likely that message was that they were late and wouldn't be allowed to make the flight after all, but by God here they were, a few feet from the boarding stairs.

Gertie had moved ahead, talking to herself as her husband had, and now she turned back too. Laurie wondered who had taught her to apply makeup, if indeed anybody had. The woman had pores like the surface of the moon. "The phone call was for someone named Irvine," she said. "I gather it was very important."

"Maybe life or death," her husband put in.

Now a man in Hall uniform, perhaps the same one who'd turned away the couple in the parking lot, was striding toward them. The couple ahead seemed reluctant to start up the stairway. At the same time, someone was trying to get back out of the airplane and all of these events spelled fate to Laurie, who had battled most of her life to kick the ass of kismet and was not about to quit now.

Sure enough, the Hall man was the same one, wearing a smile but with concern lying beneath it, and as he neared them he called out, "Telephone for Cameron Donald Irvine. Is there a Cameron Donald Irvine here?"

If it were Minnetta, she'd ask for me, because she doesn't like the cut of Cam's jib anyhow. And nobody else knows where we are, was Laurie's thought. She took Cam's sleeve with a grip like pliers and said very softly, "They want to turn us back. You stay right here."

Cam studied her face, nodding, and ignored both the Hall man and the fellow in the once-trendy green double-knit leisure suit who had come slowly down the boarding stairs and was now standing near them but facing away—and apparently talking to himself. Was everybody on this flight a looney-tunes escapee?

The Hall man came up to them and said, "Telephone call for someone who fits your description, sir. Would you be Cameron Donald Irvine?"

"Smithers," said Cam; "Maxwell Smithers; and this is my wife, Gwen. Sorry."

The big dude ahead of them horned in with, "But you said your names were Cameron and Laurie."

"I lied," Cam said, bless his idiot heart, and began to expand on it the way he invented most things, not seeming to know what the hell he'd do next but usually managing to wind up with something useful. "Actually that phone call is a code. There's nobody named Irvine but we use the name for making reservations when we might not show. That's my sister on the phone; if I had missed the flight I would've taken the call."

The Hall man stood on one foot and then the other. "Look, why don't you just let her know you made it like a nice guy?"

"Because I'm not a nice guy," Cam said, his wrapper off now, staring straight at the Hall man. "Listen, Jack, in my family we've got more hard noses than Mount Rushmore. My luggage is on its way to Puerto Vallarta and unless this is United Airlines, where my bag goes, I go. Okay? Now, if you'll excuse me," Cam finished, trying to step onto the boarding stair.

Now the little Latin fellows were closing up that luggage bay in the plane and a further commotion, somewhat subdued, ended just inside the airplane when two more tan-clad guys emerged. One, a great-looking Valentino if you liked the type, clutched his belly. The other, wearing a tie and two chins, followed him down the stairs with a look that bordered on consternation but stopped there, watching the smaller guy shamble toward the hangar. The fat one then turned and said something to one of the little fellows, who gave him fast reassurances of the si, si sort and then followed Valentino at a trot.

"Well," said fatso in near-perfect English, "let us all get aboard," and put a pudgy hand in the small of Cam's back.

The other little Latino stood obediently to one side, looking alert and expectant, grinning as if his life depended on it. The old gent in the green leisure suit gave everyone a sad little smile and said, "May as well," and then hurried up the stairs himself. Laurie was well past the stage of nicing to these yahoos and put her hand on Cam's back. She would have carried him on her shoulder if necessary.

It wasn't necessary. Cam had an engineer's view of air travel and never, never sat any farther up front than he had to. When you hit the ground in an aluminum concertina, he would say, you always want to be on the end that hits last. Most of the seats were taken, but there were plenty of spares in back, Cam letting Laurie take the window seat, still breathing heavily after his faceoff with the Hall guy but settling down now, looking around, ignoring the curious glances of people nearby. Moments later, the chubby Latino hurried past them to disappear into the cockpit. The big airliner seemed to shake itself awake, one of the huge props on the right wing beginning to spin; not nearly as loud as Laurie had remembered from old prop jobs. Thank God for small favors.

All four of the propellers were circular blurs when the second of the little guys came trotting onto the airplane, doing little swivel-hip routines on his way toward the cockpit. "I thought I was beyond being fascinated by a stewardess's butt," Cam remarked with a wink.

"I'm sure you could have some of that one if you asked," Laurie returned, smiling. After all of their problems, all that last-minute bullshit outside the plane, she heard the passenger door close and saw a Hall employee wheeling the stairway off. It was going to be just fine, even if Rudolph Valentino hadn't come back aboard. She felt the forward surge of their airliner and sat back as one of the little fellows began to speak with a hand-held microphone. Laurie reached over and squeezed Cam's hand, and he squeezed back. She had a very special feeling; this was going to be a flight to remember.

THIRTY-ONE
Friday, May 26

Torres had spent too many years scuffling for his supper, and too many more around aircraft hangars, not to know about lockers and people who left them unlocked. Before that little flight attendant reached the Hall maintenance hangar, Torres was hunkered down behind a disconnected rudder with Cessna printed across it, his eyes alert for the nearest work clothing.

He had known from the first instant of wakefulness, with Orozco's hand on his shoulder, that he had actually slept through his window of opportunity. Rigid with loathing at himself for falling asleep, he had tried to tell himself he still had his original Plan A in place; could still put a few bullets in Billy Borges and land in San Pedro Sula after all. He had maintained that view until well after their hostages began to arrive, turning on his charm, giving a thrill to a few yanqui matrons, though he had never in his life seen such a concentration of frowsy women, most of whom let their husbands do the talking.

A few, however, had been worth a second glance. It

was one of those second glances that had shaken his paranoia awake again. The woman had been tall and willowy,
blond hair gone gray and piled atop her head, her posture
proudly erect for a woman he judged to be in her late
fifties. She and her escort had taken seats near the front
and because she always seemed to be turned away from
his lively smile, he had only glances of her face, not beautiful or unbeautiful, only a face—with a wide mouth and
strong cheekbones. She might never have been a ravishing
beauty, but—and then he walked forward toward the cockpit and Orozco, and saw her searching an overhead bin for
pillows, and flicked his glance at her legs.

They had strong, muscular calves with a special taper
toward the ankle, another toward the swell of her hips,
and even in sensible shoes they registered powerfully with
Simon Torres. They were the legs of Eunice Kaltenborn.

Torres continued toward the cockpit, mind whirling, and
checked those legs again before he shut the door. He had
studied Eunice's face long enough through an evening to
know she was not fifty-nine playing at thirty. For an instant he wondered how he could identify a woman from
her legs as easily as her face, but the fact was inescapable;
he had done it in years past without thinking about it. *That
woman is Eunice Kaltenborn*. Yet this Hall employee had
walked aboard the Bristol looking like her own mother and
plainly was avoiding his gaze. Hall's security service? They
had no such staff that he knew of. And if she was security
of any kind, but not Hall's, then she meant serious trouble
aboard. As soon as they were aloft, he would tell the attendants to watch her carefully.

Orozco, sipping coffee from a thermos, was particularly
offensive with his good humor. "Feeling better, I hope?
You wake with the surliness of a bear," he said brightly,
and offered Torres a cup of coffee.

Torres sank down into the copilot's seat, accepting the
brew, framing and discarding scenarios by the second. He
wondered how many other of his passengers might be thir-
tyish, dressed as sixtyish. He also wondered whether he

really wanted the money beneath their feet enough to ignore the evidence of Eunice Kaltenborn. Was she, perhaps, a cartel employee sent to study the efficiency of Borges and Torres himself? A Borges plant?

Cars continued to arrive in the Hall parking area, and couples continued to dribble out to the aircraft until shortly after ten o'clock. The last couple sent Torres's paranoia skating out on thin ice: They walked toward the line of private aircraft singly before doubling back, the woman ahead. They did not at any moment show confusion or indecision. Perhaps, thought Torres, they were completing a surveillance of the aircraft before stopping at the end of the line of passengers. He turned to Orozco. "Pablo, hand me your jet navigation chart of Mexico," he said quickly, producing his pen. "I want to show you an alternate field, just in case."

Orozco's smile was quizzical as Torres scrawled, but he took the chart without reply and Torres, peering over the Mexican pilot's shoulder through the side window, decided to look over those late arrivals more closely. He was halfway down the aisle when he heard a voice unlike all the others around him; stripped of overtones, all business, not a live voice but one typical of a very good radio. It was coming from the lap of an aging rake wearing a forest green leisure suit. Torres heard only ". . . but subjects went through the hangar. Probably Irvines, Cameron and Laurie. We're trying . . ." before the old fellow silenced the attaché case in his lap. Torres kept walking toward Billy Borges, who stood just inside the entryway, beaming good vibrations as the hostages came aboard.

If this is a trap, it will snap very soon now. And I have two pockets full of hundred-dollar bills. I must not have them if they stop me when I deplane, he told himself. Behind Billy was a single toilet cubicle, and Torres made a face as he stepped past Billy, locking himself into the cubicle, pulling those stacks of hundreds from his jacket pockets. *I have been seen entering here; flushing is the first thing they would expect. So I must put the money elsewhere.*

A first-aid box protruded from the cubicle wall, and Torres opened it silently. It held dusty packets of this and that, but it had not remained full over the years. Torres managed to cram the money into place, needing two shelves to do it, but when he secured the cover he felt one step closer to escape. He dampened a towel and patted his face before realizing that he had an excellent reason to deplane, one that Borges would accept.

He opened the cubicle door and took a few small, halting steps up the aisle before he gave a long grunt and sagged against the nearest seatback. "Señor Borges," he said softly, because Billy was turned away. Then, because Billy was slow to turn: "*Ayudame, Guillermo;* help me." He bent nearly double, then straightened once he knew he had Billy's attention.

Holding his stomach, face damp, Torres became the very image of a yanqui tourist in Latin America. A fact largely unknown to yanquis but familiar to many Latins, the same symptoms can scramble the innards of a tourist from south of the border. Billy closed his eyes. "Madre de Dios, not now," he pleaded a fickle providence.

"I marked Base Ana on Orozco's chart," Torres said, and managed to break wind. "If I am not back soon, do what you must." With that, he launched himself through the entryway to the boarding stairs.

Billy would have restrained him but the cut of Torres's jacket was good and Billy's grasp had not held. Still giving a convincing show of a man defying his bowels, Torres had stumbled down the stairs before he began to run toward the hangar.

Now he cursed the flight attendant whose "Señor? Señor?" echoed among the hangared aircraft. A hundred yards away, one of the Bristol's big props began to hum. He heard the attendant inquiring in broken English about bathrooms. Moments later, running footsteps and a slammed door signaled the man's exit.

Torres did not stir when he saw the attendant hotfooting it back to the Bristol while a Hall man stood by to remove the stairway. He waited and watched as three Hall personnel ran together nearby, jerking their heads around as they conferred. Then he edged away from his cover, squatting in shadow, moving toward a line of lockers nearby.

The unlocked bins, he found, held paints and aircraft parts; but a white coverall was draped over the top of one locker. The legs of the damned thing were too long so he turned them up. Battery acid had eaten holes in one sleeve, large enough that the tan of his shirt showed, but he rolled his shirtsleeve up and let the coverall sleeve down again, and knew he had done all he could. Grabbing a can of paint and a brush from one of the lockers, he walked out of the hangar through a side door toward those parked aircraft as he had seen two others do, a few minutes previously. Billy Borges had the keys to the blue Sable, and somehow Torres did not think that sedan would be unwatched anyway.

He heard voices; short, sharp commands. The Bristol Britannia trundled away under Orozco's control, a spasm of dust roiling behind. Torres knew better than to look back and continued his steady, unhurried stride past nine, ten, eleven tethered light aircraft. Then he began to check the security of the planes.

Three hundred yards away, men were beginning to search the hangar, which meant that no one had paid attention to the man in the white coverall. Torres worked his way back to the ninth plane before he found an unlocked door; a beige Piper Warrior, one of those smart little two-place craft that claimed to seat four and would do so if the two rear passengers would only remove their legs below the knee. He climbed aboard its low wing so that his feet would be hidden, and watched his Bristol taxi off with his billion dollars. As soon as possible, he would telephone Catemaco.

The Warrior's only entry door was from the right wing and it opened from the rear, not upward in gullwing fashion, so Torres was able to squirm across to the ignition lock on the lefthand side, expecting a major problem, becoming weak with relief when he saw the key in place. This kind of casual foolishness, Torres knew from long experience, was not uncommon even among people who removed keys from their cars. When only one out of a hundred people knows how to fly, the attitude seemed to be, theft of an airplane is almost unthinkable. Torres turned the key and listened to a fuel pump chatter, checking gauges, making a choice that was really no choice at all.

Because most light aircraft sputter and smoke for the first few clamorous seconds, he knew that he must be ready to roll when he hit the starter. That meant climbing out to squat below the aircraft, slipping steel hooks from the metal rings provided for tethering the plane. He knew he had absolutely no hope of powering away from those tether chains; he had seen tethered aircraft facing high winds with no one aboard, literally flying two feet off the ground while moving noplace at all.

Torres slid the first chain loose from the right wing, then duck-walked behind the nose wheel with a quick glance to make certain the tires were reasonably well inflated. The nose wheel looked half-flat, which suggested an owner who did not maintain his little Piper very well. Given time, Torres might even check the engine oil level.

Torres did not get that time. Loosening the final tether from below the Piper's tail, still squatting, he saw two men walking toward the line of aircraft so that one would pass ahead, one behind the line. They were less than 200 yards away when Torres jumped forward, kicking the paint can from the wing as he leaped for the left-hand seat. The engine did not so much as chuff until he found the prime knob, and then it blew a smoke signal back that no one could have missed.

By the time he shoved the throttle forward, one of the two men had sprinted within thirty yards of his left wing, and a dead cold engine does not respond with full power. Torres felt a thump from behind and saw, in his rearview, the second man hammering the thin aluminum of his rudder with a handgun, teeth gritted, eyes shut against the Warrior's dust wake. Torres stabbed at the right brake for an instant as the plane moved forward, bringing the left wing around like a scythe at the level of a man's head, and the man near the front sprawled on his belly, a handgun clattering onto concrete.

As the engine gained strength and Torres found himself accelerating beyond a man's best pace, something whipped through the aluminum skin of his engine cowl and a small hole appeared just behind his ankles a heartbeat later, doubtless from the man behind him, because his clever braking had sent him taxiing off at an angle. His airspeed indicator showed less than fifty knots, not yet enough to fly but perhaps enough to achieve a long head start when the engine faltered. With the little sidearm still under his left armpit, he might yet escape across the field.

Fleeing down the long taxiway, Torres realized that he was following the path of the Bristol Britannia, which, for all he knew, had already made its slow two-mile journey to the mouth of McCarran's Runway 25. Torres saw a twin-engined commuter craft far ahead on his taxiway, but he also saw seventy knots on his gauge. Torres knew that his airspeed, not ground speed, was the crucial item for take-off. That commuter craft was not going to take off yet but, if his engine did not fail, Simon Torres would be airborne in seconds. If the engine failed he would probably land atop those whirling blades. He pulled the control column to him, feeling that wondrous familiar tug on his backside, and broke enough safety regulations to ground him forever. He had a hundred yards of air beneath him when he saw, over the right center of his cowling, a four-engined turboprop airliner clear the runway, heading in his direction, and of course it was the Bristol.

The 150 meters between runway and taxiway prevented an outright midair collision but, with thousands of hours of air time, Torres had no illusions about the turbulence a big airliner generates in its wake. Torres had blown a man away from his rudder; the Bristol could turn a small airplane end over end.

Though he knew that a steep turn would drop one wing and bring him nearer the ground, he could not fly into that invisible maelstrom of clear air turbulence and hope to live. Yet that banking turn would also bring him in danger of a stall at such low speed; and at his altitude, a stall would leave him smeared across his engine in a meter-deep desert crater. His engine still firewalled, Torres dropped the Warrior's nose and in defiance of instinct, banked away as steeply as he dared.

An enormous shadow whisked across Torres's cockpit as he brought the little Piper straight and level, ten yards from the ground. He felt a shudder, as of a giant gently shaking his aircraft, for only an instant, and then the Bristol's passing was a memory, Torres turning toward the south away from the dry brown rocks that serried most of his horizon. Simon Torres had not read the manuals in the Warrior's pockets, but given four hours' fuel he thought he might approach the Mexican border. Even if he had to land and thumb a ride to a border crossing, his chances were good. The 2000 yanqui dollars he kept in pocket money would bring him home in style.

Rummaging among the maps on board, Torres found his bearings and pointed the Piper's nose southward, giving wide berths to such places as Yuma and Phoenix. Though he could not see the leak, he soon began to suspect that a bullet had found its way into the wing tanks. He was still an hour from Mexico, trackless miles west of Gila Bend, when the engine began to stutter.

THIRTY-TWO

Friday, May 26

Somebody, Laurie figured, had weird ideas about the magazines to stock on an airliner. The attendants seemed to have one of everything and no two of anything. She took a *Vogue* because nobody else had, and saw it was vintage 1987. The only thing left for Cam was *Pop Rock Blast*, but he took it anyway, letting it lie unopened in his lap.

Two men on aisle seats a few rows forward had their heads nearly together. "I can probably see better in back," one of them announced, and got up. Fifteen minutes into the flight and already people were bitching about the accommodations!

"Good idea. I'll have a smoke," said the other, and both men made their way back, one of them practically falling over Cam as the airplane lurched in some vagary of wind current. Cam helped steady the guy, who apologized before dropping into the seat across the aisle. The other fellow took an empty seat just ahead of Laurie. Five minutes later, a third guy made his way back to occupy the aisle seat ahead of Cam. No one spoke.

A moment later: "Got to find the can," Cam said, pretty loudly, though the engines were mercifully quiet, and started forward, turning back as though undecided which direction to take, and stumbled on his way back, catching himself but not before half falling on the guy ahead. He righted himself with a muttered excuse, and though Laurie prided herself on reading her husband's expressions, she found this one indecipherable. One thing sure, he wasn't happy.

Five minutes later he slid back into his seat. Laurie: "Everything come out all right?"

Cam: "Not yet," and after a silent moment, "I think we passed Kingman back there."

"So?"

"Means we'll be flying near Phoenix. Listen, kid, I don't feel so hot." He began to massage his left shoulder.

"Phoenix? Home sweet home," Laurie said, with sarcasm Cam would understand because, while she had grown up there, she had no urge to go back. "Looks like they're starting to pass the drinks up front," she told him. "Freebies, I bet." But while she could see the little miniature booze bottles on the cart, she noticed that people were only asking for soft drinks. Hell with it, unless the prices were outrageous. She'd order a . . .

"I mean it," Cam insisted, squeezing his bicep hard. "I'm feeling numb, Laurie." Then he stared straight ahead, with a heavy grunt, eyes closed tight, and made claws of his right hand as he gripped his shirtfront. For five seconds she watched as his face and neck grew choleric, his ears all but glowing a deep red. He let a long breath out and slumped toward her. "Phoenix," he gasped, then grunted again.

The long wild ride; Cam keeping himself steady as his tensions mounted; and then the almost unbearable tension as they bamboozled their way aboard: "Oh, God, you're having a heart attack," she yelled.

Cam only nodded, obviously awake, though he kept his eyes shut.

"Somebody," Laurie called, but they had already heard, and the big lanky character across the aisle was up and kneeling beside Cam in an instant, tilting Cam's seat back, genuine worry etched on his face. "Where does it hurt," he asked as others moved near.

Cam couldn't or wouldn't say, only rolling his head, gasping, rubbing his chest with his right hand, then making a fist as if describing the sensation. He managed to say, "Phoenix," again.

A man in the aisle said, very loudly, "This man is having a coronary. We need to land as soon as possible," and as if by magic both of the attendants were pushing through.

The nearest of the little Latin guys knelt down, putting his hand on Cam's forehead, patting his shoulder. "I will tell the pilot," he said, but by now Laurie was sitting with her knees in her seat and she could see that the other attendant was rushing forward, presumably to carry the news. "You've had first aid training," she bleated to the attendant, gripping his wrist. "For Christ's sake, *do* something!"

The little fellow said nothing but his gaze told her this was beyond him. "Bring him an oxygen bottle," someone said, "and give him room. *And get this thing down right now,*" he finished. It was the guy in the green suit, she saw, shaking his head in evident sadness, or maybe it was disgust.

Laurie kissed the top of Cam's head, caressing him, crooning as she had not done in longer than she could recall. "It's gonna be okay, Cam baby, tell me it doesn't hurt so much." She raised her head again and shouted, "Where the hell is the goddamn fucking oxygen, you morons? Doesn't it drop down?" With that, she twisted around, grappling for purchase, her nails scrabbling at seams near the little air outlets above their heads.

"I don't think they had it on these old airplanes," said the lanky guy who had been sitting across from Cam. He patted Cam's shoulder. "Hang on, buddy. It won't be long."

Laurie sat down again, trying to rub Cam's left hand in both of hers, not knowing anything better to do until she thought about oxygen again, and she yelled, "Oxygen!!" without looking up.

Now Cam's eyes opened. His voice was faint, but clear: "In my ear, Laurie?"

She turned away, fists against her mouth, feeling real panic on its way through her system. *Not yet*, she begged it. *Stay back.*

The second attendant rushed to them with an odd contraption, a small green cylinder attached by corrugated hose to what looked like a gas mask. "From the pilot," he said, handing it to Laurie instead of applying it himself.

She seemed all thumbs and could find no spigot, but a hand reached out and pulled on a tagged lever, and then they heard a welcome hiss, Laurie fumbling the mask onto Cam's face. She pleaded again, her voice rising, "Tell me you'll be all right, honey baby, oh, Cam honey, oh, God—" It was very strange the way he opened his eyes above the rubber mask liner, seeming almost calm, and nodded.

Someone, then a second someone, demanded to know how near they were to Phoenix. Both of the attendants, smiling their little heads off, began to sweet-talk everyone into sitting down, and presently Laurie realized she was counting Cam's breaths, willing him to keep doing it, with his head on her shoulder and her right hand keeping the oxygen mask in place.

A voice: "No smoking now, you guys. Oxygen."

Another, behind Laurie: "Oh shit, wups, okay, right."

A third, from the man who had taken the seat ahead of Laurie, as he stared out his window: "Funny-looking feature down there. Different color, like an octopus ten miles long."

"More like a hand," said his seat companion, peering past him.

Laurie glanced out and saw it, recognizing it instantly although she hadn't seen it for many years. When rock-hunting in western Arizona with her parents, Laurie had heard them call it by several names: Bouse Wash, Hand Wash, or merely The Hand. Its special color came from the occasional floods that leached its fingerlike extensions with mineral salts. The major highway that crossed the wrist of the hand was I-10, running between Blythe and, and . . . *"Jesuschrist, we're missing Phoenix,"* Laurie screamed.

Immediately, both of the Latinos were back, trying to talk to her though Laurie did not hear a word of it because she was screaming her head off now. "Too far west, goddammit to farting hell we're going north, no no, south, tell the idiot flying this thing," she yelled as the big chubby guy in tan came down the aisle looking like a storm was breaking over his forehead. Because she was inhaling at the time, Laurie heard him out.

Chubs said, "Please, you are upsetting the others. We will make a long circle and land in Phoenix very soon."

Something in his face had become very hard. This was a thing that Laurie dealt with every day of her life. Using her best killer look she gritted out, "Very soon's ass, buster, we're seventy miles west of Phoenix and I don't see us turning."

"That's right," said someone. "Why aren't we turning?"

Glitter-eyed, Mister Chubs stood up and nodded toward the two attendants who stood ahead of him in the aisle. "Because," he said, "we have changed our schedule." And with that, he pulled a wicked-looking little machine pistol from his coat.

Both of the attendants pulled guns, too, and then Laurie's panic burst its dam and she loosed the kind of shriek that had sent Cam running from the house more than once. With a fierce show of teeth, Chubs did something to his weapon as he turned it toward Laurie, but the sound seemed to come from everywhere at once, not click, but clickclickclickclick, and the three Latinos were staring openmouthed about them at dozens of handguns, at least two of them with muzzles buried in Chubby's fleshy neck.

The fight went out of Chubby like flies out of a shit-house, she thought, feeling faint. She watched the three men disarmed, and saw the green-suited man move back toward them, giving orders simultaneously that the pilot must be informed of the change in management but must not be allowed to radio for help. He ambled over, producing his ID. "Federal Bureau of Investigation, Mr. Borges. Man, are you ever under arrest."

But Laurie did not faint then, not for another five seconds, not until after her goddamned malingering fool of a husband sat up straight and said, "Oh hell, is *that* all? You guys had me scared to death."

———

SHE MUST HAVE been out for only a minute or so because someone was snapping handcuffs on the chubby one when Laurie managed to focus again. "You *turd*, you," she spat at Cam, who was cradling her against his chest.

"Hold on," he said.

"Get away from me," she said.

"Fine," he said, and took his hands away. "May I talk?"

"It better be really, really good," she warned, giving him the old hard eye.

"It's all I've got. Look, while we were getting aboard, you must've seen some of these folks were talking to body mikes. You know: wired for sound. How many average passengers do you know who go around on vacations with body mikes?"

"How would I know," she shrugged, but she listened.

"Guys were trying to stop us every which way, but we were a team, you and me. Who were they? I didn't care; it was you and me, kid, all the way. Until some guy fell against me when we were already in the air. Either that guy was made of solid wood, or he was wearing body armor, Laurie. And I felt a shoulder holster right near his armpit.

"So who was I gonna tell? You? My God, Laurie, you'd have been yelling your head off, tryin' to make him walk the plank or something. Maybe I tell the guy ahead of me—only when I fall against him just to check, he's packin' something hard under his arm too, and I figured it wasn't a Gideon Bible. So the next thing I want to do is just get off this airplane with you in one piece. I know we're heading generally south, and it's less than an hour between Vegas and Phoenix, and they've got to land and let us off.'' He began to laugh, shaking his head. ''But I was wrong; no, they didn't have to!''

The green-suited man had been standing near, leaning on a seat back. Now he said, ''You slicked us all, Mr. Irvine. That was a pretty convincing coronary. Now we can shut this operation down without crossing the border. Matter of fact, we'll probably be landing near Tucson pretty soon. We owe you,'' he added, and started down the aisle.

Laurie blurted it out: ''How'd you know his name?''

''We didn't until you spoke with one of our people in the boarding line. We intercepted everyone else and figured you for no-shows, but you made like old-timers who knew your way around, and we thought you owned one of the private planes there. Nice going,'' he said wryly. ''You two worked the system pretty well. By the way, please don't wander off after we land until we debrief you on all this. The last thing we want now is to have you talking to some TV reporter.''

''I must look awful,'' Laurie said, reacting to the idea of TV. ''Let me go freshen up, Cam.''

He stood up, holding her arm like a goddamn gentleman, and she walked none too steadily to the single toilet cubicle. It was stuffy in there, and she still felt as if she might barf or faint again whenever she thought of all those guns clicking into readiness. What she really needed, she thought, was smelling salts.

When Laurie Irvine returned five minutes later, she was as bright, as clear-eyed, as Cam had ever seen her. She rustled into her seat with a big smile and patted his hand. ''Never mind, honey,'' she told Cam. ''We'll go to Puerto Vallarta some other time.''

THIRTY-THREE

Friday, May 26

Wᴇꜱ Hᴀʀᴅɪɴ ʟᴀʏ on his back with a sheet metal gauge in hand, and broke into a grin for Christiansen. "A clean takedown in flight? That was mighty quick. Are we sure nobody transmitted a Mayday?"

"Not a peep," said the CIA pilot, pulling Hardin to his feet. He looked at his hand. "Hardin, how do you manage to get all greasy so fast?"

"Shucks, it's nothin'; I'm just a natural mechanic, I guess." All business again, the little Texan moved forward and called from an open door in the fuselage: "Make the stiffener plates of oh-nine-six sheet, age-hardened. And we've got to have 'em in a half-hour or we'll probably have to leave without 'em."

A voice from below said, "Then you'll have 'em," and a tiny, two-wheeled scooter took the man off with a chirp of rubber, thanks to an outrageously overpowered engine.

Hardin wiped his hands on a shop towel, then checked his wrist. "They're landing here, you said." He saw Christiansen nod. "That's the first piece of luck we've had. Marana's damn' near on their way. We'll actually be able to line the aircraft up and see if they're really twins.''

"We won't have time," Christiansen replied as they climbed down from the aircraft. "We've got to be on the move before some other people at Langley get an attack of the queasies. You know, that task force isn't in our loop anymore." The CIA pilot saw Hardin's quick inquiring frown and, without pausing in their walk to the showers near the ready room, gave Hardin the facts of life.

So far, the sting had become a classic, the FBI's role completed inside CONUS borders by fast preparation, a series of mishaps, and one unarmed civilian's suspicious nature. "The most multifarious fuckup you can have and still come out smelling like a rose," as Christiansen put it. Task Force Enable would be winding down inside Marana's security perimeter. From the moment of takeoff onward the Canadair and its crew were entirely a Company operation. With Washington's deniable blessing, Langley had taken responsibility for the flight, though NSA was furnishing some assets, including a ranking comm-and-control man. Evidently fearing that each minute of delay made a change of heart more likely, Control had reached Christiansen on their tieline. The Bristol's Mexican pilot was under orders to land without delay at Marana. This had all come about sooner in the day than anyone really expected. Best estimate of the Bristol's ETA gave the Canadair crew a bit over twenty more minutes on the ground, said the pilot, toweling off, reaching for a nondescript flight suit. "Lloyd Meacham knows; that's why he's rounding up everything we've ordered, trying to get it aboard right now."

Hardin, stepping into his briefs: "So we don't even wait for that old Bristol to land?"

"Barely. We line up just off Runway 30 and watch it come in, and then we try to punch the same hole in the sky it was punching," Christiansen said, "in case somebody in Mexican airspace has a stopwatch on the operation."

"I wish you wouldn't say hole in the sky," Hardin replied. "If Meacham doesn't keep his detonators separate from everything else—well, we'll never know it, will we?"

"Lloyd's good. Don't even think about it," Christiansen said, and punctuated it with the whine of a long zipper. "Take a hard look at your checklist, it'll be too late to order anything more once we hit the taxiway."

Hardin closed his locker, wondering whether he would ever see those civvies again, and hurried after the CIA pilot.

Lloyd Meacham was supervising a loading crew when the others reached the aircraft. He straightened, hands on hips, and faced Christiansen. "Okay, here's the bottom line: Everything we've really got to have is here, but we'll need hours more to finish the dispenser hardware for those Kraut munitions. They're an odd size."

Christiansen scratched his neck and squinted at Hardin. "Can you do it in flight?"

This is no time to waffle, Hardin reminded himself; *but don't promise what you're not sure you can deliver.* "Lloyd says he needs twelve dispenser tubes. I'm sure we can mount a pair, maybe four; six at the most. Something you may not have thought about, Lloyd," he went on. "Those tubes through the Canadair's belly will be like organ pipes opening against our fuselage skin. Unless we keep 'em filled or capped somehow until we land, we'll sound like all the banshees in hell coming in on that doper airbase. Do we care?"

"Hell yes we care," Meacham said, and Christiansen nodded vigorously. All three stood motionless, grasping for ideas. Meacham's glance was not admiring as he as he asked Hardin, "How come you didn't fuckin' mention this before?"

"Because," Hardin shrugged, "I didn't fuckin' think of it before."

Curt Christiansen, for all his casual demeanor, proved he could command when he needed to. Pointing a forefinger at Meacham, he said quietly, "Pinch it off, Lloyd. I didn't think of that either, and I used to come back to Nakhon Phanom with empty launcher tubes sounding like an airborne Wurlitzer. And,'' he added, checking his wrist for the nth time, ''I'm going for a tug to haul this goddamn pterodactyl outside.''

''Sorry,'' Meacham said as if fearful that someone would hear him apologize.

''You're entitled,'' Hardin said, then snapped his fingers and set off toward the hangar parts bin at a dead run. He had finally hit on a partial solution to their problem: simple, quickly applied, quickly removed.

Minutes later, receiving a taped stack of aluminum stiffener plates from his scooter-mounted courier, Hardin trotted outside where the big Canadair waited. He carried a set of stainless steel rings over his arm like huge bangles. A mechanic steered a tractorlike tug away with its towbar trailing behind. Meacham was waiting at the rear exit door, a short aluminum ladder locked into place at his feet. Both of the Canadair's propellers on the opposite side were windmilling now, the turbine exhausts a rushing whisper. As he helped pull Hardin into the aircraft, Meacham spoke quietly into his minitel headset. ''Crank 'em all up, Curt,'' he said. ''Securing the hatch now.''

Because a cockpit checkout routine can be performed while the aircraft is taxiing, Hardin hurried to one of the rear seats and strapped in while Lloyd Meacham made his way forward, squeezing between the mounts of gun pods, stepping over zinc-plated tubes that lay like huge jackstraws across the aisle. They all knew that their unfinished hardware was loosely secured by nothing more than tape in the passenger section, no real problem unless a major crosswind caught Christiansen with his Canadair in its slow, stately climbout. Hardin clasped his own minitel over his ears and plugged it into the onboard communication system, which worked like a party line. It would not transmit beyond the airplane, though all the men using it could hear the pilot's end of radio conversations. Curt

Christiansen was already getting his takeoff clearance as he taxied away from the shops.

Hardin looked down at his hands, shedding the adjustable steel rings from his arm, counting those stiffener plates brought to him on such short notice. *I've got a day's work ahead of me*, he thought, only half-listening to Christiansen's exchanges with airport traffic control. *At least I brought the necessary tools.*

The waiting, as always, was hardest. Meacham was first to spy the Bristol Britannia on its final approach; from his passenger window near the tail, Hardin finally spotted the craft with its landing gear down, floating low over the desert moments before touchdown. *Christiansen pegged it right. It's a pterodactyl, a flying dinosaur, and so is this old Canadair of ours.* During the few seconds when he could see the Bristol, Hardin studied the markings on the elongated fuselage and tail, markings identical to their own. "Are you sure that's not us?" He did not realize he had spoken aloud until he heard Meacham's reply.

"Hot damn, man, we're a dead ringer. Ain't that somethin', Curt?"

Christiansen's chuckle, and his advancing of the Canadair's throttles, became his answer. He guided over sixty tons of metal, fuel, and deadly munitions onto the end of Runway 30 and, after another brief wait with propellers revving hard, released the Canadair's brakes. Wes Hardin sat back, trying to ignore the tubes that buzzed in sympathetic vibration throughout the passenger area, and watched the edge of the runway pass by.

Only after they had cleared the Marana perimeter, nose at a modest upward tilt, did the tape fail to hold, and only one of the pipes came slewing around to fall in the aisle near Hardin.

Christiansen held the aircraft steady but his voice was intimate in Hardin's minitel. "Trouble in the loge seats, Hardin?"

"Naw. One of the backflash tubes is all. Might help if you keep this thing right side up," Hardin responded. He had stuck his foot out, pinning the lightweight tube in place.

Over ten minutes passed before the Canadair's nose settled into the horizontal, its gentle banking turn complete as they headed south, high over desert whose scrub was now so far below that it seemed only sparse patches of fur on a badly cured pelt.

Lloyd Meacham returned from the cockpit, wrestling the big tube out of the aisle with Hardin's help. "Curt's gonna stay down where we won't need to pressurize the cabin," he said. "When we cut those holes through the belly for our organ pipes, we won't have shit for cabin pressure anyway." The fanlike buzz of the engines was not too loud. Both men found that they could talk without shouting and, after watching Hardin for a moment, Meacham picked up a pop riveter. Needing no air or electrical supply, the plierlike device held one rivet at a time, deforming it neatly into place until a pop signified that the rivet was secured. During the next hour, both men proceeded down the aisle, accompanied by the snap of rivets and the whine of an electric hand drill.

———

THEIR IN-FLIGHT LUNCHES were welcome chiefly for the break they afforded, Hardin occupying the flight engineer's seat behind his colleagues. "The latest from Marana," Christiansen told them, "is that the flight was no dry run of any kind. They're offloading somewhere between ten and twenty tons of cargo out of that Bristol, so the dopers have got to be expecting that shipment."

"You mean dollars," Meacham said with a headshake full of longing.

"Mostly in hundreds," Christiansen said, and they all fell silent for a moment.

Then Hardin began to laugh. "It doesn't even compute, does it? I mean, just multiplying the weight of a little piece of paper until it reaches ten tons or so. Tell me:

What would we have done if our part of this included flying that much hard cash to somebody?''

"Let's talk about something else, shall we?'' Christiansen did not lose his smile, but his tone remained serious.

"Okay. Talk about how the hell we're going to finish this job while we bounce around in the sky in the next few hours, which we can't,'' Hardin replied.

"Or how we delay our arrival until the middle of the night,'' Meacham put in. "Look at the Jet Nav Chart, man; shit, if we were the dopers we could be on their airstrip before dark. This old bucket really hauls,'' he said.

Christiansen: "We've got fuel to burn. I could continue down the Baja Gulf like this and then orbit for hours off the Pacific coast.''

"But not for most of the night,'' Meacham objected, drawing agreement from the pilot.

"Also, we've got a problem working in flight,'' Hardin admitted. "Let's face it, we don't have a stable platform and that makes us clumsy. You know what we need,'' he finished.

"A skyhook,'' from Meacham.

"A scam,'' Hardin corrected. "Some justification for landing and keeping curious folks from coming aboard. Like Mexican customs officers, for example.''

Christiansen: "How long?''

Hardin: "Until after midnight, I reckon.''

"I'd better scramble up a call to Control, then.'' Christiansen adjusted his headset, then frowned. "I really don't like it, though, before thinking it out on our own. Listen, Hardin, they'll end up creating some master plan with fifty people in the loop, as full of holes as a goddamn butterfly net, and we'll have to follow orders unless we can come up first with a scheme we like.''

Meacham grunted assent. "And quick, too, 'cause meanwhile we're making tracks toward the end of Baja.''

Only the buzz of propellers broke their silence until Hardin swallowed the last of his potato salad and gave the others some basics to ponder. "We know this much: We've got to land, both to save fuel and to give us time to work on the ground. And not at some major port of entry where they have lots of folks with nothing better to do than check foreign aircraft. We're supposed to be a Bristol full of passengers, so we should keep up that pretense, aircraft ID and all, as well as giving a reason why we have to land. Tell me if I'm wrong.''

After half a minute of silence, the two CIA men shared a glance. "I'm buying it," said Meacham.

Christiansen adjusted his headset a millimeter and then began his response to someone Hardin could not hear, identifying himself, giving their position. "Little snafu in the timing, Control—not mine. We're to rendezvous with our people over the LZ at oh-four-hundred hours, but we don't carry enough fuel to stay up that long because you sent us off so early. . . . Negative, there are plenty of places we can land," he went on, with a masturbatory gesture for Meacham's benefit. Hardin grinned; no matter who you worked for, now and then you had to stroke the boss a little. At the same time, if you were risking your neck in the field and not a desk-bound bureaucrat, you needed freedom to make some decisions on your own. Christiansen gestured toward the map pocket near the knee of Lloyd Meacham.

Meacham opened the Mexican airfield listings on his lap as he listened in from the copilot's headset. Christiansen began to scan those listings as he talked. To Hardin it was obvious that the pilot was improvising. "Negative, Mazatlán's a port of entry, Control. . . . Affirm that, we need a simple hard-surfaced runway without a lot of officials hanging around."

Meacham suddenly stabbed a finger against the handbook, folding their big navigation chart while he followed the coordinates with his gaze. A moment after he tapped a spot on the Mexican mainland near the coast, Christiansen looked it over and then nodded. "Culiacán," he said, as if he had known all along. "Give us that discretion; we thought eighteen hundred hours would be late enough so

that any local customs officials would be long gone from
that little strip before we declare our emergency. . . . Not
Pacific time; Mountain time.''

He's quick, thought Hardin, with an OK handsign to
Christiansen, who managed to sign off without cursing
their mission controller for sending them aloft so soon.
Now that they had committed to landing on the Culiacán
strip at six in the evening, Hardin did not mind facing the
afternoon's work. He would be jounced and clumsy and
might have to do everything twice, but he could look forward to better conditions once they had landed at Culiacán.

THIRTY-FOUR

Friday, May 26

TWELVE YEARS OF hard work had taught Juano Benitez no more about civil engineering than he had known when he took his degree. On the other hand, it had taught him much about titles and what they meant. To Juano, acting chief maintenance engineer at Aerodromo Culiacán, his title meant that he got a telephone to his little home at his own expense so that he could take nuisance calls at all hours, and that he got to break his honest balls with repair crews to keep all 7544 feet of the little city's airstrip functioning. In short, it meant that Juano had all the responsibility and did all the work while his boss kept all authority and, whenever the slightest thing went wrong, had Juano to blame it on.

The airport's official chief engineer had no degree of any kind and could not have engineered his way out of a parallel parking slot. The man's chief success had been to marry the spinster daughter of an old Sinaloa family, and after that he had whatever job he wanted. He seldom ventured away from the air-conditioned comfort of his office on summer days, and left promptly at cinco en punto, five on the dot, unless he felt like leaving earlier. He had left very early on Friday afternoon, knowing that Juano, the dutiful family man with the civil engineering degree and no clout with city hall, would stay as late as necessary. That was how an honest engineer kept shoes on the feet of his four niños, and a decent shawl over the shoulders of his wife: He became janitor, garbageman, and yes, sometimes diplomat. Soon after the emergency call from that unscheduled airliner at half-past five, Juano realized he might have to polish up his rusty diplomatic skills.

Ten minutes ahead of time, Juano appointed a man with some experience in directing large aircraft to help him and drove down the runway in their sole functioning Ford pickup, the one without a windshield. Its two-way radio worked, however, and Juano knew when the Bristol Britannia's pilot lined up for final approach. Parked near the end of the runway on ground so bricklike that it would not take a tire imprint, he waited with interest. Juano did not know what a Bristol was exactly. He did know that its flight engineer needed to make immediate repairs, or so the pilot claimed.

It was among Juano's many duties to see that the aircraft parked safely, and that its passengers did not wander off illegally. That would probably involve keeping them in Culiacán's tacky little waiting room unless he could get some official to leave his dinner table and drive the fifteen kilometers from Culiacán to the airport. It would certainly involve making certain that the Bristol's crew paid for the use of the field, whatever that entailed. On this semidesert lowland airstrip between Culiacán and the coast the ground was baked so hard that most of the year, where irrigation did not reach, one hardly needed to surface a runway at all. Such were the thoughts of Juano Benitez as he saw the big airliner flare out over the green line of irrigated tomato farms in the distance.

Puffs of smoke signaled contact of wheels with the runway, and Juano judged that the pilot intended to use the

whole strip. The offices lay midway down the strip, and
that usually meant the airplane would taxi slowly back.
Maximum comfort for passengers, maximum trouble for
Juano. He pressed the transmit stud and identified himself,
the mozo in the yellow pickup truck. He spoke English,
in which he was reasonably proficient, because virtually
all pilots spoke English, the common language of commercial flight the world over.

The reply from the Bristol, now approaching him with
idled propellers, was in Spanish; not surprisingly, an unfamiliar dialect but as fluent as Juano's own Sinaloa
accent. Would it be safe, they asked, to make their turn-
around of the hardpan soil off the runway?

Of a certainty, Juano replied, since the sun of a million
years had transformed that soil into concrete, barring rain.
He told them to follow him back to the terminal.

To Juano's surprise, they preferred to do their repairs
here, at the end of the runway.

But, Juano said, as anyone could see, there were no
facilities whatever for passengers here, nor for fueling an
airplane, nor anything else. This deserted scrub land was
as innocent and naked as when Satan first created it, God
being occupied elsewhere at the time.

After a radio silence that lasted a minute or so, the voice
replied that their only problem with fuel was a transfer
pump inside the aircraft. If any fuel leaked during repairs,
was it not safer for all concerned for the aircraft to be
parked here?

Juano let his inner eye conjure up a pool of fuel igniting
near the terminal, the aircraft a ball of flame that consumed the entire building and, not incidentally, Juano's
job. He agreed then that theirs was an excellent decision,
except that the passengers would certainly want to deplane
for such dangerous work.

After another silence, they replied that they would certainly wake the passengers and deplane them if any fuel
got spilled.

Passengers all asleep at six o'clock in the evening, Juano repeated in wonderment.

Most of them, was the reply. The passengers were oil field workers from Alaska en route to a new work station, and had been working under a midnight sun until a few hours before boarding. And now, if it was not too much trouble, could they please, please shut down and get on with their repairs?

They were a kilometer from any larger cover than tuft grass; they did not seek fueling; they did not intend to have their passengers spilling out to complain loudly about the facilities. And even if they flew out again without paying, they had cost Aerodromo Culiacán precisely nothing. As Juano told his assistant to get back in the pickup, he reflected that this, as an emergency, was almost too trivial to be true. While driving back to the office, he transmitted again to ask how long their repairs might take.

The reply was long in coming. They thought it might take a few hours, no hay problema, unless they had to keep coming back into the cockpit to answer his transmissions.

Juano thought about that until long after he had left the pickup, called his wife, and explained that he would be late. This emergency was not enough trouble to be real and so naturally Juano thought of emergencies that were, perhaps, not real. Perhaps, he thought, they intended to offload someone or something after dark, depending on the naiveté of Juano Benitez. And though Juano had been known to inhale from home-rolled cigarettes that unscrewed the top of his head a bit, he knew about his country's trouble with more serious drugs. Knew, and was unalterably opposed. Juano did two things then: He had the pickup loaded with floodlights and a portable engine-driven Honda generator, and he called his wife's youngest brother.

Lucas Morelos, Juano's brother-in-law, was the part-time lawman in the nearby village of Las Puentes. Because the fisherfolk there were mostly law-abiding, Lucas continually complained that he never had any need to draw his nickel-plated pistol, let alone fire his rifle. When Lucas arrived at the airport in his old VW Beetle, he had both weapons with him.

Juano explained his suspicions to young Lucas. It would be dark within the hour now, and they could prevent any illegal traffic from that old airliner by lighting the entire area around it; and in truth, who knew when another aircraft might need to use the Culiacán strip? He, Juano, would inform the crew of the Bristol that an aircraft parked near the runway must be floodlit by night in the interest of safety. Lucas would drive out following Juano; they would position the lights to illuminate the surrounding hardpan and start the generator; and then Juano would return in the pickup, leaving Lucas on guard in the darkness.

Wonderful, said Lucas, and when they jump out I can shoot them.

No, said Juano, probably they will give up the idea as long as those lights are on.

Ah, Lucas replied, and when I turn off the lights for a moment they will jump out, and I will turn the lights on again and *then* I can shoot them.

It took Juano quite a while to convince Lucas that he would be much more a hero by preventing crimes than by punishing them, and the sun was nearly gone when the two drove up to the old airliner. The fellow who fitted an aluminum ladder and came out to watch them place the floodlights was smaller than Lucas, and from his accent might have been the one Juano had spoken to.

"My friends call me Condor," said the little man. "Many thanks for the lights."

Juano introduced himself and Lucas, who did not seem happy at Condor's good cheer. "We do need to know how soon you will be finished," Juano added. The man calling himself Condor gave the matter some thought as small ticks and creaks emanated from the aircraft. Juano smelled the kind of fuel that was sometimes pilfered to fill coal oil lamps, and thought about leakage. Lucas, meanwhile, tried to pull-start the generator's engine.

"Perhaps a few more hours," said Condor, wincing at

the sounds of drilling from somewhere inside the airplane. "A good thing our passengers were so very, very tired. Why do you need to know?"

"They must sleep like the very dead," Lucas muttered.

"We must charge you for parking by the hour, plus landing and takeoff fees," Juano said reasonably.

The Condor fellow wanted to know how much it would cost if they left, oh, say around midnight, and Juano quoted him a figure.

The man said he thought that figure muy caro, but Juano replied that negotiations of the old sort were becoming a thing of the past. It was not his place to bargain, but merely to collect the fees. At this point the little engine began to fire, the floodlights bathing them in hard glare.

"We have been paid in dollars," said the man. "Tell me the amount and we will pay you now. It will go more quickly now that we have plenty of light. I and my assistant may be working below the aircraft for a short while."

Juano could figure a rate of exchange in an instant, rounding it off in such a way as to leave something for Lucas. "Two hundred and forty dollars," he said.

The little man shook hands and began to walk back to the airplane. "You shall have it," he said.

Juano could not see the eyes of Lucas in the hard shadows, but he could almost hear the young idiot thinking. "Please do not leave the vicinity of the airplane," Juano called. "This is very important. For safety," he almost pleaded.

Condor turned long enough to wave, and then Juano was left standing near the runway as Lucas turned to face him, and the look on Lucas's face was the look of a man betrayed.

———————

DURING THE NEXT several hours Juano endured the fears of the recently damned, sitting in the pickup outside the office, listening for gunfire and praying that he would not hear it. He had made a mistake in calling Lucas because the trigger-happy young fool needed watching, yet would have deeply resented Juano's constant presence. Juano could now ridicule the old paradox a professor had presented his class: Who watches the watchers? The answer was all too obvious to Juano, who had driven out to the runway's end twice before midnight, once on the pretext of getting fees: The watchers must watch one another.

Juano found himself dozing in a welcome sea breeze when he was wakened by his radio, and wondered if Lucas had finally opened fire out of sheer boredom until he realized that Señor Condor was asking a favor. For a small gratuity, which he was giving their watchman, said the man, would it be possible for Señor Benitez to make a telephone call and send a message forward to the airplane's destination?

Juano would have said yes to almost any request by now. He took down the message carefully, the number as well, and agreed, hurrying inside to the office telephone. Five minutes later he was driving back down the runway. He was not about to clear that airplane for takeoff until he could see the hands of Lucas Morelos without a gun in each one.

While a surly Lucas piled floodlights into the pickup illuminated by the airplane's landing lights, Juano spoke by radio a final time to Condor, who had already removed the boarding ladder and closed the door. The call had gone through to the Catemaco number, Juano said, though the old man on the other end seemed to have an army of secretaries. Juano had repeated Condor's message: the Bristol had mechanical problems, but repairs were being made there at Culiacán and the Bristol might arrive an hour after dawn. The passengers were getting proper attention. Their only other problem, hardly worth mentioning, was the Bristol's radio, which was no longer operating properly.

As the big airplane's propellers began to inhale the world, Condor asked about return messages.

Why, none at all, said Juano. The old man had merely laughed before hanging up.

It is difficult, said Condor, to know what an old man finds amusing; and thanks for your help. And that was that, as the bleary-eyed Juano waved good-bye, watching the looming dark mass of airliner hurl itself down the runway to become a set of diminishing lights in the night sky, never to be seen again.

Juano was warming his dear wife's backside a half-hour later, satisfied with a day's work well done. Of course Lucas had mentioned nothing about the little gratuity mentioned by the Condor. Juano Benitez, content with things as they were, never asked.

THIRTY-FIVE
Friday, May 26

COLLEEN MORRISON TENDED to the crucial bits first, once the NSA patched in direct communication links with the Canadair. She thought Control's voice suspiciously like Dr. Bill Sheppard's but made no effort to acknowledge the fact. She and Jared Cutter had left their Kingsville base minutes after receiving word that the Canadair would soon be aloft again. Their spookships, each with a lone pilot, would be on-station above the doper airbase an hour before the Canadair. She finished her location report with, "Tampico lights off my starboard wing unless I'm mistaken. You copy, Sleeper Three?"

"Roger, Sleeper Two," said the voice of Cutter, five minutes behind her over the Gulf of Mexico. "My one o'clock low; has to be Tampico. How'd it go in Vegas, Sleeper One?"

"We heard it was a Chinese fire drill," said the laconic voice of Curt Christiansen from high above the Pacific, across the entire breadth of Mexico. The digitalized transmissions, via satellite link, scrambled their signals into mush to any listeners other than Control. "The good news is, there were no casualties and we had a Culiacán official telephone the dopers for us; they'll expect us after dawn."

"So drop the other shoe," Colleen urged.

"Say again, Sleeper Two?"

Theirs was a protected frequency and Colleen knew very well the CIA pilot had heard her. "The bad news, god-dammit," she demanded.

"Well, well," Christiansen murmured; "I hope you're this feisty under tracer fire. The bad news may not change anything, but one of the dopers got away in a single-engine Piper. Task force knows who he is now, they just don't know where. You better believe the SIGINT people are blanketing the isthmus in case he calls home and lowers our credibility."

Though she had her gloves on, Colleen felt her fingers begin to go cold. "Can't they disrupt his signal or something?"

"It's not easy if he calls by ordinary land line, Sleeper Two. But we can monitor the calls. By the time we locate him, the damage would probably be done. If he transmits by radio, we might have a shot at jamming him. We're going on the premise that he's too busy saving his hide to make that telephone call. If he does, though, we'll be warned immediately; and he hasn't done it yet."

Now Cutter joined in with, "I don't want to sound like a spoilsport, boys and girls, but if we haven't got a Plan B for that telephone call, we've *still* got a Chinese fire drill. Make me happy, Sleeper One."

Christiansen, as though discussing matters of no importance: "If that call goes through the bigwigs in Catemaco, it'll have to be relayed to the airbase. If it goes straight to the telephone feed to that airbase of theirs, we've got no time buffer. And if that call reaches the airbase too soon—well, Plan B is to abort the isthmus landing. We've all got the fuel to land back in Texas. Last I heard from your guy Hardin, the Lone Star State was still in friendly hands."

To Colleen, that sounded as if Hardin had not made the trip. *That should make me delirious with joy,* she cautioned herself. *Why doesn't it?* "Don't tell me you left Wes Hardin behind."

"You guessed it; about fifty feet behind," Christiansen returned, evidently enjoying himself. "Hardin and Meacham are still in our cargo section, poking holes in this old bucket, because we had to leave Culiacán before they were done. And Hardin had to stop several times and sweet-talk some Culiacán official. Hardin's the only one who could pass as a Latino. That doper who flew away is a Colombian, calls himself Condor in telephone calls, so Hardin had to put on his condor suit. Never mind, it's all a little confusing," he finished.

"It sure as hell is to me," Colleen said.

Now the pilot of Sleeper One reacted to her, as a person, for the first time. "Young lady, I don't know how many hours you've logged, but I'm coming up on nine thousand and in that time I've learned to live with a little uncertainty now and then. I'm forty-seven years old and I'm still here, and that means I'm not the kind of risk junkie who will step out of a perfectly good airplane if I think I might get bagged for my trouble. You two won't hit the runway until after I do. If there's a welcoming committee, you'll have more warning than—"

"Stuff it, buddy," Colleen fired back. "I don't need your patronizing, old bold pilot routine. You think I'm looking for an abort excuse? Stuff that, too."

For a long moment, silence. Then, from Christiansen: "Roger that, Sleeper Two, that's what I was thinking. You have to understand, we've been holed up in Arizona for days and I don't have all the answers you want to hear."

"You might've said that up front," Colleen charged, yielding not a millimeter. "The people you work for have a reputation for using contract people like mushrooms." *If he doesn't know the line about keeping mushrooms in the dark and covering them with shit, that's his loss,* she thought.

But he laughed as if he knew, all right. "Touché, but we're all working for them equally tonight. I've told you what I know; you've just got to get used to not knowing everything. Coming up on a course change; Sleeper One out."

Cutter gave her some minutes of blessed peace before contacting her. "Hey, Morrison, can I make a suggestion?"

"You're not in my cockpit, how can I stop you?"

"Ease up a little, okay? We're on the same side."

"Okay," she said. "So long as they don't try to sound like my father." *Why did I say that? Cancel that, forget it.*

Cutter understood better than he should have. "He doesn't know how many triggers that pulls," he said.

"Screw off, Jarhead," she spat, "let's have a little radio silence." She could have changed channels, but that would have been unprofessional. For the next few hours, the lives of all of them depended on the professionalism of each of them.

A tiny imp of inquiry posed the question in her head: *Do you still want to do this, or would you rather hear that some doper has made his telephone call?* She answered it immediately: *Whatever these military-trained males can do, I can beat. Especially Hardin.* She willed that telephone call into limbo. For almost three more hours, it seemed to be working.

THIRTY-SIX

Friday, May 26

IN COMMON WITH most foreign pilots trained in the United States, Simon Torres knew something of Arizona and desert survival because he had trained out of Luke Air Force Base near Phoenix. Torres had waited in the shade of the Piper's uptilted left wing until almost sunset watching for scorpions, dozing fitfully in the heat, too wise to remove his bloodsoaked coverall or to leave his cover in midday, and much too canny to radio for help. His dead-stick landing up a gentle arid slope had ended with his right main gear snapped off, slamming him against the side window, but his injuries were slight. Though his nose was undoubtedly broken, he thought his wrist might merely be sprained. Very late in the day, he set out on foot toward the dry riverbed he had seen before his forced landing. Without water, guided only by the ball compass he had wrenched from the Piper's cockpit, he took his bearings often for an approximate course. Finally in full darkness he trudged toward the gleam of lights some miles to the east and, a few hours later, saw that he was approaching a surfaced road. By the light of his cigarette lighter he read the legend on a sign; he was walking toward Painted Rock Dam.

Moving lights to the south had told him he had come within walking distance of a major highway; long experience following geographical features from the air reminded him that a road to a dam often dead-ended at the dam. Torres turned southward and continued to walk, letting his feet find the edge of the roadbed.

When he saw his shadow, he realized that headlights were approaching from behind. By the time that wheezing old Ford stopped to pick him up, he had hurled his coverall into the scrub. To the Indio driving the Ford, he thought, a bit of blood probably would not have mattered.

The man seemed no more interested than a bus driver in his solitary passenger, and his accent was that of any other yanqui. Torres decided that the man's profile, his checked shirt, and the body odor were those of a man who cared little for yanqui values. But it was his willingness to pick up a total stranger without a volley of questions that said Indian to Torres.

They exchanged hardly a dozen words until they reached the highway. Then the man said, "Turning left to Gila Bend."

"Good," said Torres. "Do they have bus service?"

"Drop you at Greyhound," were the man's final words on that or any other subject. He looked to Torres like the kind of man who would not quail before an automatic pistol, and even if Torres shot him for the car, the damned old Ford strained every bolt to reach forty miles an hour. When the Indio stopped at a self-serve convenience store on Pima Street inside the township of Gila Bend, Torres saw that the store was still open, and a sign with the slender silhouetted elegance of a Greyhound dog dominated the place next door. Torres stepped out. The driver did not wait for a thank you or a *hijo de puta*, but churned away into the night leaving Torres at the Greyhound station. To his disgust, the station was closed.

Between the gasoline pumps next door lay a bucket half full of soapy water with a windshield squeegee. Torres tried not to think about the bug fragments in that bucket as he washed his hands, then his face, so that no one would remember the swarthy man in expensive tan clothing with blood caked on his mouth and chin.

He might have saved himself the trouble. The sunburnt youth behind the store counter popped his gum as he totaled up the Cheetos, two cans of 7-Up, Mars bars, and Beef Stiks that Torres chose and then, when Torres offered him a twenty, said, "Sure you don't want some aspirin?"

Torres looked at himself in the mirror over the sunglasses display. The flesh across his cheeks was a study in purple and blue, puffed to the point where his nose seemed hardly to protrude, and both of his eyes had been blacked by that crash. And no wonder his jaw ached; he had taken a cut just below his lip. Torres selected the pair of wraparound sunglasses that best hid the damage and placed them with the food. "This will do," he croaked, and forced him to open a 7-Up as if he were not dying of thirst.

The youth counted out his change. "How does the other guy look?"

Torres drained half the can before he replied, "Much the same," took his change, and started to ask for quarters to feed the telephone he had seen outside. *Mierda, in this town of two thousand or so, there can be only a few pay telephones. If I am to use a telephone, it must be from a much larger town than this. Those armed yanquis were almost certainly federales, and they have ways of tracing many calls at once.* Emptying the can, he opened the second and said, "Tell me, what is the next city to the west?"

"Yuma—if that counts."

"And how far?"

"Couple of hours. You driving?" The youth's flickering glance said that he doubted it.

"I may need an autobus," Torres said, then damned himself for using that giveaway word.

"You missed the twelve twenty-five. Next one's about nine in the morning." The gum popped again.

"The bus stops even when the office is closed, then?"

"Sure. Not for long, though." The youth looked away, through the front window. "Like that'n."

Torres looked around to see the bulk of a Greyhound bus pull off the road. "You said nine in the morning!"

"To Yuma, man. That's headed east; the twelve fifty-five to Phoenix, right on time." Then, as Torres bolted for the door with 7-Up in hand: "Hey, you want this crap or don't you?"

But Simon Torres wanted more to be on that autobus to the biggest city in Arizona, a city he knew from times past. He had nothing smaller now than hundreds to pay his fare, yet the uniformed driver showed no surprise while counting out Torres's change. For the next hour and a half, Torres listened to his empty gut rumble, and wished he had carried all of his purchases with him.

Phoenix had continued to spread since his cadet days, but some things never seemed to change: The city's anglo heart was still an entity apart from its multiracial body, and the San Carlos Hotel still stood only a few blocks across the civic plaza from the Greyhound depot on East Washington. An historic structure in the shadow of towering newer hotels with shinier bells and sharper whistles, the San Carlos had managed to become second-class without losing some of its old panache. Torres had spent whole evenings there; could almost recall the names of some of the Latina staff; asked as he registered whether the place still operated its vintage London hack as in the old days. Told that the antique taxicab sat entombed now in the basement, Torres beamed a genuine smile. As long as they kept that relic, he felt, the San Carlos might become third-class while remaining first-rate.

He stayed in his room for only a moment before leaving again by the stairs, noting that it was nearly three o'clock in the morning and that the telephone he used must be anonymous. At least now he had a hideyhole for the night, registered to one Jaime Mendoza, the name on his Bolivian passport. He hurried back across the breadth of the plaza, peopled at this hour only by monumental bronzes, to the Greyhound depot and its pay telephones.

At 3:00 A.M. he was bringing David Elath fully awake in his San Pedro Sula suite, using innocuous phrases to give the briefest outline of their mutual disaster. "I am not certain which corporation won the contract," he went on, "but we are left out in the cold. I walked out of the negotiations but I can tell you, there were some who wanted me to stay. Some of the process might interest you, my friend; I will tell you about it later."

From far away, with a poor connection, he heard Elath curse. "What I want to know is: Are we still employed, you and I?"

"Oh yes, but I suggest that you hurry to my Catemaco villa to wait for my call. I must make travel connections and will call you there as soon as I can. For all I know, our big shipment may have arrived already."

"My God, don't you know where it went?"

"Not even that," Torres admitted. "I was in a hurry. For that matter I am still in a hurry." He rang off a moment later and realized he would need another five dollars or so in quarters; that and a different telephone across the depot.

When the Catemaco call went through to Vega, Torres thought the old man must still be half-asleep from his answer to Torres's first question: "Has the shipment arrived?"

"Why would you ask, of all people? Have you managed to leave it since Culiacán?" The old man's voice was steady, but cynical.

"I know nothing of Culiacán. I am calling at great risk from los Estados Unidos and will be flying out shortly," he said for the benefit of other potential listeners. "Our people flew out with the dyes but left me behind, so I am not certain whether our friend Billy is still our friend. If he is, surely he has arrived by now."

"Then," Vega said slowly, "you did not cause an airport official to call me from Culiacán last evening?"

Further confused now, his wrist throbbing as he gripped the receiver, Torres replied, "I did not. I have survived a crash to make this call, brother. And you still have not told me if our dye shipment has arrived."

"It is expected sometime after dawn," Vega told him. "Perhaps I should make special arrangements for friend Guillermo."

"His story should be interesting," said Torres, "if indeed it is our friend who is coming."

After a brief pause: "I see what you mean," Vega replied. "I fear my sleep is done, and I have calls to make."

Torres replaced the receiver and hurried from the depot. The time in Phoenix was 3:14 A.M. The time 900 miles to the east in Catemaco, and at Base Ana, was an hour later.

THIRTY-SEVEN
Saturday, May 27

With his initial low pass over Base Ana, all lights blazing, the Canadair pilot deliberately announced his arrival for several reasons. It was the proper maneuver to maintain the ruse of an airliner certain of its welcome; it gave him a real-world view of the field at low altitude; it might prod someone to turn on the runway lights; and any winking of gunfire, barring severe damage, would warn Christiansen while he still had enough velocity to abort the landing.

Hardin, the only one aboard who could pass for a native Spanish speaker, took the copilot's seat and broadcast their intentions broadband while toggling his transmitter off and on to surrogate a defective radio. He had listened repeatedly to the recorded voice of Simon Torres, and knew he could not give a convincing imitation of the man; but according to the FBI there had been other Spanish-speakers aboard that Bristol Britannia. It might work; it *should* work. . . .

Lloyd Meacham remained in the main passenger compartment, scrambling from window to window as he opened the aluminum ports they had installed at gun pod and launcher windows. Their jury-rigged electrical control panel was taped beside the starboard emergency exit, scant yards behind the crew compartment bulkhead. If all went well, Meacham would be back with his control panel shortly after their landing. Moments after touchdown, Hardin would be hurling himself aft to help Meacham with the gruntwork.

Christiansen completed his broad turn over the jungle, making his downwind leg a long one. On their dedicated channel, Christiansen then informed the Nemesis pilots: "Sleeper One on base leg, descending to six-zero-zero feet. You should see our lights on final; over."

"Sleeper Two on final approach, a mile out. You're on my radar, Sleeper One," Colleen replied. Their instructions from Control had left little to the imagination, and both of the Nemesis craft ghosted forward now, barely maintaining their lowest flight speeds, their wings cambered to simulate lazing hawks. If a mishap or a bullet caused Sleeper One's munitions to cook off too soon, Bill Sheppard's voice informed them, its blast and debris radius would not engulf Morrison or Cutter. That was the theory, anyway. . . .

"Sleeper Three on final, in formation," said Cutter, seconds behind her in both time and space. "Your landing lights at my eight o'clock, Sleeper One." Without warning then, a set of blue lights flashed on ahead and below them, outlining the huge scissors of crossing runways.

At that instant, the transmission they had dreaded became a fact. "Sleeper Control to Sleeper Flight, a warning call from Catemaco is in progress. Repeat, in progress," said Sheppard.

Christiansen did not so much as glance toward Hardin as he increased his flap setting to thirty degrees for the most gentle landing possible. To Wes Hardin the huge Canadair seemed to be hanging almost motionless in mid-air though its airspeed indicator read roughly a hundred knots. Christiansen, quickly: "Do I have an abort order, Sleeper Control?"

A seconds-long pause, then Sheppard's voice again. "That call still in progress; they're calling a full alert but they don't know what to think. Touchdown within sixty seconds or abort, Sleeper One."

"Sleeper Two at two zero-zero-zero feet from touchdown, Runway Three-Two, at thirty knots," said Colleen, voice tight but steady.

"In your slipstream, Sleeper Two," said Jared Cutter, exaggerating very little. With this geometry, the gossamer spookships would land with no lights of their own at the scissor-end of the runway while the Canadair swept past ahead of them at a shallow angle and three times their speed to land on Runway One, its lights spearing ahead.

Hardin, in the cockpit, had seen the gear down-and-locked indicators and stayed in contact with Meacham. "Greasing it in now, Lloyd. The runway intersection's in sight." As their main gear duals chirped against the runway, all three men felt the jolt throughout the big ship, its nose settling with ponderous grace until the nose wheels made contact, and then Christiansen thrust his power levers past detents into a setting labeled BETA RANGE. The reversal of all four multibladed props created a braking force so powerful that Hardin felt some part of their cargo shift. He had never flown one of these old brutes, and almost certainly no one would ever fly this one again.

"Start portside munition drop," Hardin said to Meacham, changing headsets as he saw the runway intersection flash by. In seconds, as the braking diminished, he fled from the cockpit. He knew what he would see in the main compartment but the noise was overwhelming: the howl of wind past holes in the fuselage, the chatter of big thin pipes that he had assembled stretching belly-high across the entire compartment, and the curses of Lloyd Meacham as he kicked at one of several vertical tubes.

Hardin duck-walked frantically to Meacham, halfway back in the compartment. "Fucking Kraut mines hung up,'' Meacham shouted, trying to dislodge the tube's contents.

''All of 'em?'' Hardin barely made himself heard.

''Just this one!'' Another kick did no good.

Hardin's wireless headset was now picking up Morrison and Cutter, who were remarking about those runway lights. A glance outside proved that the runway lights had been shut down again; not a good sign, but perhaps good for the spookships. ''Go to the next one,'' he shouted to Meacham, hauling on a long wire designed to dislodge the lower plug of a delivery tube. He felt vibrations within the tube as a dozen small mines began to drop out of the aircraft. They had known those vertical tubes were a slipshod dispenser system, but at least some of them worked. Meacham ducked under more horizontal tubes and tugged at another protruding wire. ''Mines away,'' he called, and moved on.

Christiansen: ''Give us portside rockets in five seconds.''

''We need ten,'' Hardin panted, scrambling on all fours toward the front. If any of those rocket exhaust tubes failed, he did not want to be among them. He felt Christiansen's braking maneuver, a desperate move to give them that five extra seconds.

''People are running out of barracks. Gotta hang a left,'' Christiansen announced, now using wheel brakes. ''Do it!''

Meacham was waiting, eyes hard, fingers poised, as Hardin dived to the forward bulkhead. He waited no longer than that but dropped to a crouch and, one by one, began to salvo their portside heavies.

The SMAW rocket, a shoulder-fired round of some 500-yard range, has folding fins and carries a warhead over three inches in diameter. Lloyd Meacham had called for simple, disposable launchers from McDonnell Douglas so that they could be bound in groups of four. Each group fired one shaped-charge antiarmor round, one fragmentation round, and two with delay fuses that would penetrate a building before exploding. It is the exhaust of SMAW rockets, searing backblasts of flame, that could incinerate everything inside an aircraft fuselage. Meacham and Hardin had spent hours assembling thin-walled conduit tubes that would direct that backblast out the opposite side of the fuselage.

Hardin saw bursts of light, but the tubes held as Meacham toggled his heavy hitters in rapid fire. The SMAW rocket exhausts, through transverse pipes, emitted a series of rushing *slamm* reports that deafened the men inside. Thanks to excellent photorecon by Nemesis craft on earlier flights, the Canadair's pilot knew where to aim his huge four-engined weapon platform. Christiansen simply had to position his craft and wait for Meacham to fire. Meacham clapped his hands to his ears, evidently to hear the pilot, then began to fire the starboard rockets as well, the equivalent of a light artillery barrage. Hardin thought he heard the pilot whoop, and darted a glance outside. A half-dozen wooden buildings were erupting from within, and some of the flying debris seemed to have arms and legs.

Now the big ship was turning, props biting to accelerate again, onto the taxi strip leading to the other runway. Hardin screamed for Meacham to toggle the gun pods and could barely hear his own voice, but Meacham was already reaching for more toggles and, a heartbeat later, the real racket began. From the right side of the Canadair, six-barreled miniguns began to whine as their barrels rotated, followed by a sustained and almost unbelievably rapid hammering roar. They did not sound to Hardin like machine guns because, with each pod firing 100 slugs per second, the hammer became as constant as the snarl of some enormous chainsaw gone berserk. Meacham had not ordered any tracer ammo, because the aim of the pods had been preset and tracers would have pinpointed their source better than muzzle blast alone. Wes Hardin's view was filled with light all the same, some of the guns firing ricochets that sparked from the runway in a fireworks display that fanned low across the terrain.

Somehow in all this pandemonium, Curt Christiansen managed to sweep the Canadair hundreds of feet down the taxiway toward the second runway. Meacham's eyes had gone wild, face contorted, mouth open wide as he silenced the portside pods. This interruption of fire on the port side had been stressed over and over again by Hardin because, he had pointed out, while taxiing between those runways their port guns would have been firing toward their own spookships.

Then Hardin felt the big Canadair swerve in a sharp turn, and knew they must be accelerating down the runway. The portside guns resumed like a belch from Almighty God. Hardin flailed down the compartment again, feeling the residual warmth of tubes against his back as he pulled himself erect to tug on the wires of the vertical dispenser tubes for those MIFF runway mines. Then he stared in disbelief as a finger-sized hole appeared in a transverse tube near his face. Somebody had their range; maybe a lot of somebodies.

"Starboard mines away," Hardin shouted, leaping for another of the vertical tubes, trying to distribute those MIFF mines down the length of the runway. If the delay setting of even one mine failed, and fragments entered the Canadair's belly, no one within twenty miles would fail to know about it.

The minigun pods, now raking down both sides of the runway, began to fall silent as they consumed their last rounds. Hardin found Meacham at the forwardmost mine delivery tube, and together they dislodged its load. At that point they heard Christiansen bellow for help.

"Flight engineer! On the double," the pilot called, again trying to reverse the propellers but without effect. Hardin burst into the crew compartment to find Christiansen jerking a thumb over his right shoulder. "Hydraulic handpump's behind the copilot seat! Give me some pressure," called the pilot, and Hardin concluded that smallarms fire had seriously damaged the aircraft.

He found the little pump unit instantly, but the shudder

and weave of the big airliner made him clumsy. The pump handle, stored apart from the unit like a jack handle, would not fit easily into its socket and then Christiansen was shouting, ''Hang on,'' as he tried to steer the nose gear into ground-looping the big ship.

A ground loop for an aircraft follows some of the same dynamics as a spinout for an automobile, but imposes such stress that the landing gear may collapse. Christiansen had evidently seen that, without hydraulic pressure to his brakes, he was in danger of overrunning the point where the runways crossed. The Canadair's nose gear began to howl, then screech, the right wing coming around sharply, and that was when the tires blew out, the steel nose strut a plow that dug through the runway surface.

Hardin, with one knee in the flight engineer's seat, grabbed for something, anything, to secure himself; too late. He found himself flung headfirst toward the control console, seeing Christiansen's hands move in a controlled frenzy, and then Hardin was on his back. He felt a sheet of agony as it blanketed his left shoulder, his world a series of flashes strobing red and brilliant yellow.

When his vision cleared, he saw in the dimness of companionway lighting that Christiansen had already bounded over him into the aisle, turning to shout: ''Hit that hatch, Lloyd, go, go, go!'' The whole business seemed oddly distant to Hardin, lying face up near the copilot seat, but he raised his right arm toward the pilot. Somehow he knew that, even if he had not been lying on his left shoulder, that left arm of his would not have been much use. Still, his instant of pain seemed to have passed—until Christiansen, gripping Hardin's right arm with both hands, hauled the little Texan to his feet.

Wes Hardin would have yelled then, had he not fallen half conscious on his knees in the Canadair's sloping aisle.

It was Meacham who lifted him in a fireman's carry, stumbling back to the emergency exit, pausing to make one final manipulation at his taped control panel. With the aircraft nose touching runway, Meacham's downward leap was only a few feet but Hardin's weight was enough to send them both sprawling. This time, the pain galvanized Hardin fully awake. He staggered to his feet, blinking as he turned, and felt a hand in his back, urging him forward. "I said I'd be behind you," Christiansen told him.

Hardin could not imagine why he thought to ask such a question at such a moment, but asked it anyway: "How'd you know where that emergency pump was?"

"All else failed, so I read the manual," the pilot said, trotting behind. "Three days of it. Fucking lot of good it did me. Hey, are you okay?"

"Got my chimes rung. Used my shoulder for a clapper," Hardin said, and kept shambling along though every step was an aching throb.

As the three men pelted away on foot, a series of explosions began to erupt down the runway, each detonation a *thump* through bootsoles simultaneous with the flash and only a fraction of a second before the sound reached them. Those flashes, German mines with preset delays cratering down the length of the runway, said that no one would be landing anything heavy there for awhile.

In the distance, buildings blazed merrily. The thin whistle in Hardin's ears began to recede enough so that he heard faint sporadic pops and hammering far away, and several times the bee hum of a small slug touring the night. *It's all so fuzzy,* Hardin kept thinking, propelled forward by Christiansen as he held his left elbow with his right hand. *All but the pain.* That was sharp enough. Then people were calling back and forth, familiar voices, and he saw the low silhouette of a spookship lit by distant fires of retribution. Those runway detonations seemed to be a steady march back toward them now, and a flashlight played across him, and one voice asked why the hell the side of his head was all bloody, and he tried to tell her it was his shoulder, not his head, but something like paint seemed to be crackling over his left cheek and he could not grin no matter how hard he tried, and then he knelt like a praying Moslem too dizzy to stand and half heard her arguing about where they were going to put him if he couldn't crawl into the aft compartment of Cutter's spookship on his own, as they planned.

More bees were humming now, and Hardin clearly heard three quick taps on a hard surface nearby as if fingers had thwacked a snare drum. "You heard me," someone snarled—oh yes, a familiar snarl. "I'm flying the lead Nemesis and you goddamn do as I goddamn say."

Another voice: "Curt, somebody's peppering the Canadair. Let's go, man."

And then they lifted Wes Hardin like a toy, and when the bone ends grated he went limp.

THIRTY-EIGHT

Saturday, May 27

*G*IVE THOSE GUYS *credit for cool,* Colleen admitted, seating her helmet with one hand as she locked her canopy with the other; *they took care of our casualty first.* The way they had sprinted away afterward to Cutter's spookship made it clear that their anxiety matched her own. Maybe anxiety wasn't the right word; come to think of it, she had always felt the same rising sense of arousal just before her turn on the parallel bars, or the balance beam where she excelled and knew it. Maybe it was just heightened anticipation, pure and simple, of something you were good at. The notion of fear might be natural, but that's **what** training was all about. Maybe it wasn't natural to ignore the guerrilla bullets singing and spatting nearby, but there was nothing natural about a backflip on a balance **beam** either. *You don't think about it too much. You just do it. If you thought about it a lot, it would scare the hell out of you.*

She pushed the throttle of her idling Nemesis to military power, its maximum emergency setting, and centered her craft on the runway waiting for the satisfaction of a shove against her backside. In the thirty seconds it took for Cutter's two passengers to pile in, she could be wheels-up over Chiapas. Except that her shove was not satisfying at all.

Rev counter at maximum, control settings correct; but something in the whirr of her propeller blades felt and sounded subtly wrong. She wondered for a moment if her brakes were dragging because, goddammit to hell, she was hardly picking up speed at all and, while that thousand feet of runway beyond the intersection had seemed far more than enough, it was not going to be enough now. She aborted her takeoff in time to swap directions at virtually a crawling pace, watching Cutter in Sleeper Three through her night vision helmet. He was centered for take-off now, but he was not moving. "Sleeper Three, stay on the right verge and get your butts out of here. I'll give you room," she said, realizing that her brakes were working perfectly, steering with her pedals so that one of her main wheels was very near the runway edge. Cutter would have to take off on the same runway, but she was certain he could do it. A tiny demon of analysis in one corner of her mind said, *The rotary's running smooth and my blade setting's right, but it feels like half of my blades are missing. Impossible! This thing would be vibrating like a carnival ride.*

"Wilco, Sleeper Two, stay on your side. Sleeper Three rolling," was Cutter's reply. He was coming, all right, a green ghost approaching Colleen on a green strip in the green world of enhanced night vision. With his extra passenger on a runway a thousand feet above sea level, Cutter needed a longer takeoff run and well over thirty knots on his airspeed indicator—data that had been factored into the performance curves shown in each Nemesis operating manual. Cutter was confident enough that, before his main gear cleared the runway, he could say: "Want to tell me what in God's name you're doing, Sleeper Two?"

She waited until he was airborne, rising gracefully to

the height of surrounding palms and informing Sleeper Control of the fact, before she firewalled her throttle again. "Got us a power problem here, Sleeper Three. I may need all the runway I can find," she told them and added, "rolling—I think. Kind of hard to tell." Ahead to her left, one wing of the Canadair tilted high at an unnatural angle, protruding across the intersection. Her takeoff run would entail a pass literally beneath that wing, her airspeed indicator barely registering, directly toward the flames and debris of a guerrilla base.

She was passing beneath the Canadair's wing when she heard, "Sleeper Control to Sleeper Two: Give us your status, over."

"I have full revs but low thrust, and twenty knots on Runway One," she said, fudging the truth by four knots and making it as calm as possible, her mouth dry because she could see huge potholes now, the legacy of small mines sown minutes before by the Canadair. *My God, what a mess they made*. She felt her main gear bump lightly over chunks of crater debris. "Twenty-two knots," she added, truthfully this time, easing back on the control column, the nose canards tasting the wind as her nose gear cleared the runway. She knew that in cycling the gear up, her nose wheel would fold first, making a cleaner shape with less drag. The main gear would not retract until the weight of the Nemesis was taken by its wings—but for a truly aerodynamic, clean machine she needed the main gear retracted too. "Twenty-four knots," she managed to say as if abstracted from it all, fingers flashing to the Retract controls, knowing that if her Nemesis settled now it would be all over. Perhaps not for her, if she could grab that special survival kit and flee into the jungle; but the man in the seat beside her could expect no pity from enraged guerrillas.

Of course she could abort now and not risk a crash, but somehow that was not an option. *Hotshot, I'm going to get you out of here or bust an airplane*. She made the canards flex their polymer muscles; noted her nose gear indicator, and felt the little wheel thunk home. "Twenty-five knots, a-a-and rotating," she said, and felt her main gear wheels scrape laterally across the runway as they began to retract before the Nemesis was fully airborne.

"Gear up at three feet," she said. Cutter would know that the clearance of a Nemesis nose at rest was three feet from the ground. She let her airspeed build, bit by interminable bit, now all of thirty knots as she cranked in more rotation—elevating her nose. The belly of her Nemesis craft was now all of ten feet off the ground, and she could see the blink of small arms here and there. *Shit, a clay pigeon moves faster*, she thought.

She could tell without a glance that Wes Hardin was struggling to sit more erect, his harness restraining him. He groaned, and apparently read her instruments at a glance. "Bank left, stay on the deck," he called as if she were a hundred feet away. That was all she needed right now.

Well, she sure couldn't keep on at a bicyclist's pace, heading for the bulk of those burning structures. But she had misjudged her abysmal climb rate and certainly could not make a steep bank without catching a wingtip against the runway, and second by second it became more obvious that her only choice was which set of flames she wanted to fly into.

"Gonna have a momentary power loss," Hardin warned, as Colleen used aerodynamic decoupling to force the Nemesis crabwise over the blaze she judged to be lowest. By now she had perhaps thirty feet of altitude and needed twice that much to avoid the blaze of a burning warehouse. At roughly forty miles an hour, Colleen Morrison flew directly into a hell of rising sparks and flame, feeling the sudden bump of a rising air current first, and somehow she had known that would happen so she was ready for it, but the loss of power came immediately after that for a near-fatal two seconds, the engine faltering, but she was ready for that too—*thanks to Hardin, damn him*—letting the nose settle a precious few feet.

The uppermost fronds of a banana palm whispered below the spookship's belly and by then she was past the flames, the rotary engine picking up its tempo again, and she risked dropping below flight speed to gain more altitude because the dark humps of higher trees were approaching, and she was positively, absolutely *not* going to make it over them.

Even with the canards flexing, it helped to drop one wing if you were going to turn on a dime. She had perhaps forty-five knots now, but a turn like this was beyond anything Ben Ullmer had put into the manuals, and Colleen nursed her spookship around with one of those endless wingtips tickling grass until she was headed toward the wrecked Canadair again, though fifty yards to the right of it, a very good thing because she was back on the deck now and the airliner's tail fin was higher than she was as she passed it, seeing figures with weapons advance on the abandoned Canadair. Some of them looked up as her Nemesis overflew them.

"Christ, get away from here," Hardin gasped as something small and very fast entered the cockpit between them to exit through the canopy. "Stay on the treetops. Don't climb, whatever you do."

She made no reply, gaining altitude as fast as she could, knowing that with fifty knots now she could make it above the highest of the trees ahead, and then the Nemesis swept up to clear a slight ridgeline, trees and all, sacrificing some speed in the process, and she said so. "Sleeper Control, I have two hundred feet and thirty knots, bearing one-sixty true. We're out of there."

"Get down lower," Hardin demanded, then grunted in pain.

Cutter again: "Sleeper Three on the deck with eighty knots, bearing two-forty true. My passengers both say you'd best get your head down, Colleen."

So who the hell was Jarhead Cutter to give advice? Yes, they'd been briefed to stay at treetop height but with her power plant malfunctioning, she wanted all the altitude she could rake and scrape. She could glide all the way to the gulf with a few thousand feet of air beneath her.

"Morrison," said her passenger, in obvious pain. "The bloody airplane's a bomb. For Christ's sake *get us lower*!"

She needed a second or so for this to sink in, preoccupied with her efforts to coax more altitude from her misbehaving beast. When Hardin's words finally made sense, she traded altitude for airspeed, achieving sixty knots scarcely five yards above the treetops, and the white flash that burst across the jungle from behind them seemed to last forever, a flashbulb as big as all creation, and she could hear Cutter's "Great God almighty" more in awe than enthusiasm. She did not see the shock wave until it passed them, lifting the rear of her Nemesis so that it would have dived nose-first into the darkness below had Colleen not fought her canards to level the brute. Though the shock wave itself was not visible at this distance, its passage whipped treetops as if a huge invisible cable had been drawn across them at the speed of sound.

She had put a mile of distance between herself and that airfield, yet something back there had almost blown her out of the sky. Too astonished even to curse, Colleen turned to Hardin. "What—was—that?"

Hardin, with one hand gripping his other arm, did not answer, but Cutter had heard. "Five tons of plastique, Sleeper Two," he told her. "Those guys hand-formed the biggest shaped charge in the Western Hemisphere inside that old crate, and set it for a five-minute delay. If you couldn't drop a blimp hangar in the crater, I miss my guess."

"Now you can climb," Hardin managed to say, "with my blessings."

"Screw your blessings, hotshot, you might've told me ahead of time." What she wanted to say, but would not, was that she had even less power now than before. That would have been bad enough, but her lateral control seemed to be gone as well, and the nose of her Nemesis was pointed southwest, exactly the opposite direction from the gulf. If she tried a decoupling maneuver to turn, sure as hell she would settle into the treetops. If she didn't, she would have to deal with a mountain range before reaching the Pacific. If she lost no more power, it just might be possible to clear the high rain forest that clung to the mountain slopes of Chiapas. Having made her choice, Colleen began explaining it to Sheppard. In her rearview, the rim of the world showed a slit that might be the approach of dawn.

THIRTY-NINE

Saturday, May 27

CESAR MACHADO'S SQUAD had arrived at Base Ana a week previously. As it happened, both Machado and Teniente were awake when the big airliner thundered overhead, Teniente trudging a sentry path between the aircraft hangar and one of the coca refining sheds, Machado seeking sleep in their preferred bivouac near the training grounds. The orderly sent to wake Teniente for guard duty at half-past three had stumbled among the blanketed sleepers, earning a curse from Machado, whose hand the fool had stepped on.

Liquor in the senderista bivouac or barracks was, to be sure, against Bermudez's regulations but no disciplinary action was ever taken unless the drinker became unruly; and Machado had nipped at the tequila bottle only because it was a cheaply available aid to sleep. He did not even like the Mexican stuff much. Three strong swallows should have brought him the oblivion he sought, and perhaps it would have, given another few minutes of silence.

Several of the others in his company, men of Machado's

stripe who scorned the softness of cots and barracks, had
sat up abruptly when the aircraft droned over them, its
lights a swath of daylight that passed over the surrounding
jungle growth. When Machado heard the familiar mechanical clash of someone cycling a round into his assault rifle,
he felt only irritation. "It is just the one who thinks he is
a condor," Machado called. "You were told. Lie down
now; if the commandante thinks we are still asleep, he
will roust those ripe bananas in the barracks to unload his
damned airplane." A ripe banana was soft and rather
sweet. Machado knew that men who chose barracks life
had a word for the bivouac people, too: *ganado,* livestock
whose home was in the fields.

A few mutters were still rising from thin blankets when
alarm buzzers began to clamor among the barracks buildings across the airfield. Someone laughed. Someone else
honked an exaggerated snore. Machado was not much on
smiles, but in the reflection of barracks floodlights across
the field, his teeth showed faintly. Some of the senderistas
thought the condor and his people admirable, but in
Machado's group the Colombian pilot was merely a means
to an end; an overdressed, dandified Colombian at that.
In the perfect classless society of Guzman and Mao for
which Machado fought, men like Simon Torres would become extinct very quickly; and the road to that society
was the Shining Path. Meanwhile, if the elitists wanted
ganado help at four in the morning, they could damned
well come out and round up the cattle themselves.

Though the buzzers echoed clearly enough, the loudspeakers between barracks were, at this distance, a gar-
bled mess. Yet it sounded to Machado like the voice of a
man who was uncommonly excited over a call to work.
As he thought about that, he saw a star moving to the
south, no, three stars, moving in unison low over the jungle, becoming manmade beams that sought the far end of
the runways. That, in all probability, would be the airplane
on its final approach because the runway lights had been
energized. Well, no matter. Teniente, whose duty post lay

halfway between the barracks and their bivouac, would have heard and could explain it all later. Machado, a warrior and not a porter, composed an aphorism for himself: *One can always wait to hear news of hard work.*

Voices began to float across the airfield now, some as high-pitched as those of children. The lower registers of the human voice, Machado knew, did not carry as well, but he was hearing too much of the high-pitched stuff. Those bananas were excited. When a single burst from a rifle stuttered into the predawn, doubtless by some half-asleep idiot due for punishment duty, Machado decided he had gotten all the sleep he was likely to get on this night. It was two minutes before he realized just how right he was.

Machado had his boots on when the big airliner swooped low to settle on the far end of one runway, its engines surging for a long moment. Then he felt a big calloused hand on his shoulder, and knew its gentle pressure instantly. "Teniente; sentries who leave their posts catch hell, you know." As he spoke, the runway lights went out.

Teniente squatted, speaking low: "That airplane may not be friendly, Cesar. I was sent to alert you. We are forbidden to fire unless it does something hostile." Teniente, while speaking, followed the passage of the airplane with eyes that shone in reflection of barracks floodlights.

And then those eyes blinked as a flash erupted from the side of the plane, which had now reached almost to the taxiway that spanned the ends of the runways. An instant later, one end of a two-story barracks structure disintegrated in a series of greater flashes, all in utter silence until the sounds of obliteration reached the bivouac two seconds afterward. By this time, more flashes spewed from the airliner, and, for a moment, Machado thought the aircraft was taking hits. Already dressed, he leaped to his feet and shouted to his men.

Cesar Machado knew better than to go racing off alone when he could wait sixty seconds and have dozens of hardened guerrillas beside him. Shouting to spur his people, he stood beside Teniente and watched the airplane's progress, now a demon of aluminum alloy that poured sparks from the runway and fired warheads into most of the buildings of Base Ana. One wall of the hangar folded out with a direct hit; a few seconds later, as the roof began to drop, another hit blew out the opposite wall and, for one instant, the roof seemed to float above white glare before it collapsed into its own debris.

Woven through these sounds of destruction, audible between detonation waves, came the grinding roar of a thing Machado had never before heard in his life and hoped never to hear again; a sound as if a hundred truck engines without mufflers were racing themselves to death. One of the warehouses, miraculously untouched by warheads, began to melt into fragments of clapboard and metal as something invisible, yet producing sparks on impact, cut the little building down crosswise at window height. Machado realized that the airplane was moving at the same pace as that invisible chainsaw, and screamed for his men to get down as the airplane turned its broad hull toward them. Most of them dropped low, but a hail of sparks and a hive of blunted slugs careened toward them, and some of Machado's men cried out.

For a moment, as the airplane lined up on the nearest runway and began to gather speed again, Machado thought it had exhausted its munitions before trying to flee. He sprinted beyond his men, dropped to one knee, and squeezed off a burst from his Kalashnikov, knowing that he must aim high for a 300-meter target. He felt the nearness of Teniente and knew that he was not the only one firing as the airplane continued to accelerate, now away from them.

None of them even saw the rocket-propelled warheads launched in their direction, but suffered their effects when one of the rounds impacted among the abandoned blankets. Behind them at the treeline, more explosions, and a palm fell among the men in a flurry of fronds and, from

Machado's men, screams of agony. Machado shouted for his men to advance in line so that no one would shoot a man ahead of him by mistake. Running and stumbling toward a target lit by the reflections of burning buildings, firing without apparent success, Machado's group advanced, but far more slowly than the airliner retreated.

Machado had ordered them to cease fire, their target now hopelessly distant, when he saw the airplane slowing. He was the first to cheer when it yawed to one side more than halfway down the runway. He ordered his men to the attack again, but sent them into the depression of the shallow creek after one of his men fell, evidently shot by friendly fire.

When the airliner's landing gear gave a protracted squall and collapsed, Machado felt as if they had wounded some mechanical dragon from a child's storybook. Other squads of senderistas could now be seen streaming forward on foot, an undisciplined mob of 200 armed men lit by flickers as though marching through an annex of hell. Machado had already lost at least one man to idiots firing blindly, and called to his men, who flopped where they were, awaiting further instructions.

Cesar Machado intended to order his people to advance behind the others until the thump of high explosives and new flashes of light began to approach them in a steady progression up the runway like the footfalls of a vengeful giant. To Machado they seemed to indicate mortar fire, but in a procession far too fast for a single enemy, and with appalling accuracy. He gave no more orders for the moment, ears ringing as the footfalls crashed alongside, then past them toward a military base that was now a blazing shambles. The advancing mob had become a rout with men dropping everywhere and sporadic firing from a few who were intelligent enough to fire from a prone position. Machado could see no flashes of light from the airplane and concluded that the mortar fire was coming from elsewhere. And it kept coming, the giant now stalking up the runway Machado and his men had recently crossed.

It did not appear that his own men were targeted now, so long as they stayed in their shallow arroyo. When the last leviathan footfall had cratered the runway, Machado brushed hot shards of runway surface from his hair and called for a crouching advance down the creekbed, himself in the lead. He dropped on his face at the sound of an unfamiliar whirr, like the whisper of a huge incoming mortar round, but as it diminished he realized that something, perhaps a helicopter, had fled southward into the night. He was rising to his feet when something flickered beneath one wing of the silent airliner, something that moved toward him on the runway no faster than a man could run. And as Machado aimed at the thing, foreshortening seemed to make it sprout enormous wings, a hellish creature with a bullet's nose that sniffed the air like a live animal as its nose lifted. He fired, and fired again.

Beside him, Teniente's awed, *"Madre del diablo,* mother of the devil"; and then Teniente fired too.

They watched it together, a creature that needed only scallops on its wings to become a cave bat of unbelievable proportions, and in the dim light of destroyed buildings Machado saw another of his company cross himself. "Old ways die hard," he said, noting that the bat with whirring wings disappeared into the flames of a burning warehouse as if returning to its infernal maker. Some of the barracks troops were now advancing on the airliner, shooting as they went. Others ran toward it without shooting, without discipline, without caution.

Machado would have followed but for the "Ayudame" of a wounded guerrilla nearby. "Let the ripe bananas advance on the dead," he cried. "We have comrades to find!" With that, he led the company in finding their casualties in the arroyo, pausing only when that whirring whisper approached again.

Machado could not see it at first but one man did, or claimed he did, sending single rounds from his rifle up at a shallow angle. When Machado did see it, the bat thing flickered beyond the airliner so low that a man might almost have leaped up to touch it, if any man could have been so rash. More firing now, some from troops near the airliner, and then the thing was gone, and Teniente had found one of their company still alive, naked except for his boots, with blood pulsing from his thigh.

Cesar Machado continued to lead in a guerrilla specialty, almost a hallmark for the best of his breed: spiriting their casualties away from the scene without delay. He and Teniente were halfway across the training ground with their dying comrade when an incredible blue-white flash lit their entire world, but instead of dropping to the ground instantly they turned disbelieving eyes to face it, and the shock wave from ten thousand pounds of Czech plastic explosives slapped the breath from them, then hurled them twenty feet. Machado's first thought, as he regained consciousness, was that Base Ana had been leveled by a nuclear weapon.

FORTY

Saturday, May 27

"**A**ND TO THINK I had doubts about a woman under fire," said the voice of Curt Christiansen in Colleen's headset. "I owe you an apology, lady."

Colleen's laugh had little mirth in it. "If I were a lady, you might've been right," she replied, then returned to business. "Sleeper Two at four-seven-zero-zero feet, with a few hundred feet to spare over the, uh, Grijalva river valley at forty knots. Some heavy-duty rocks ahead and I've gotta trade speed for altitude again."

Bill Sheppard, as Sleeper Control, had spent the last half-hour trying to pretend he was calm and doing a passable imitation of it. Now he said, "You're a couple of ridges east of Sumidero Canyon, Sleeper Two. If you can put down in the lake there, remember the city of Tuxtla Gutierrez is a day's walk. Hardin's fluent; you're his wife, and he's had an accident. There's plenty of pesos in your kit. Stay at the Hotel Avenida downtown, it's a bug sanctuary but it's safe and we can exfiltrate you."

"Just like that, hm? And how'm I supposed to explain my ninety-foot wingspread?"

"Consider scuttling your machine in the lake."

"Negative, Sleeper Control, I can barely crab this sucker now, let alone bank it. And there's no way I could scuttle my bird. It'd float like a Ping-Pong ball. And who'd own it then?"

"Let us worry about that, Sleeper Two." A flash of irritation now from Sheppard. "We're trying to give you viable options."

"Me too. And since ours is officially a civilian outfit, it isn't your bird, guys; as far as I'm concerned, it's mine. I hatched it fair and square," she replied, feeling a welcome surge in the local winds that wafted her Nemesis a few yards higher. "Thirty-five knots and holding." Ten knots less at this altitude and she would be mushing downward helplessly. She was less than a mile above sea level, hardly aloft at all for a Nemesis, but with so little power the thinner air was making a difference already. She tweaked her canards a bit extra and soared over the nearby ridge with yards to spare, recognizing the shapes of pine trees among the palms, and then concentrated on her horizon; and at that point her hope, so carefully nurtured until now, shattered against towering stone escarpments ahead. The next ridgeline was five miles away, but nothing short of a booming thermal air current would ever get her over it—and boomers, she knew, seldom occur at dawn.

Moments later, Cutter put in his two cents' worth. "I've got you on visual, Sleeper Two. Forty miles more and you'll be in Guatemala."

"A better option," Sheppard put in, tight-voiced. "We positively can*not* risk any rescue by air in Mexico."

"Roger that," she said. "But there are more rocks ahead and if I can't get higher I'm gonna need machetes on my wingtips."

Suddenly Cutter's voice became animated. From 20,000 feet, still climbing, he had an infinitely better view of what lay before her. "Morrison, you've got a little lake two miles ahead. No name on my chart, but I make it half a mile long, a few hundred yards wide. Take it, Morrison. Take it,'' he repeated, pleading. "It's all you've got."

She swung her night vision away now, hoping to see what Cutter was seeing. Both pilots were ignoring the formalities of radio communication, their minds focused tightly on a high mountain lake too small for the charts. "I don't see squat, Jarhead, with or without enhancement. Just trees and slopes."

"Trees right up to the edge, Morrison. You won't see it 'til you're over it. But the nearest village is a couple of miles north of it. Nobody will get your bird, Colleen, and we can send help."

"That's affirmative," Sheppard added quickly. "If you've got a window, go through it. I show ridges over seven thousand feet in your path."

"I'm going to look for a boomer," Colleen said.

"At *dawn*? Even if you got one, you couldn't circle in it anyway," Cutter exploded. "Think about your casualty, you hardnosed little bastard; he's your hostage, you know."

Astonishingly—she had not seen Hardin fumble his headset into place—Wes Hardin spoke for the first time in twenty minutes. "Her passenger, Jarhead. I'll accept Morrison's decision."

"He's fucking right, he will," she said, aware that a boomer thermal was out of the question, merely a wild hope born at the cusp of panic; wondering if it was already too late to find that little lake. All professional now: "Sleeper Three, wilco; but talk me down, I still can't see water."

"Go to the deck, Morrison. Can you decouple and crab a few degrees to starboard?"

"Only when my descent rate is high. Don't drop me too soon," she warned.

"You've got a klick, but you're a hundred yards to port," Cutter advised.

A kilometer was roughly two-thirds of a mile. If she

stayed a few hundred yards above the treetops, she would see the lake sooner, but she might not be able to ditch safely before reaching its opposite end. *Trust your instruments*, she told herself; *and Cutter's your instrument now*. She lowered the nose of her Nemesis, gaining a little velocity, dropping toward a solid mass of greenery. Her canards flexed, one almost flat, one bowed in an outlandish curve, and then the entire aircraft was sliding sidelong without turning, and her first awareness of the lake was a hole in this little valley where treetops ought to be, and now a calm stretch of water the color of molten lead appeared beyond the trees, with grass-choked shallows. She saw the pine tree that would intersect her wingtip and rocked the entire airframe in a tilt that cleared the tree but sent her sliding faster, one wing near the water, before she brought her craft level again. She had ten feet of clearance now and did not need to risk a glance at her airspeed indicator because she could estimate her speed perfectly well at this proximity, and she did not have enough of it to win a footrace. "Sleeper Two on final," she said, a ridiculous statement under the circumstances, and aimed the nose of her Nemesis for the high tule grass interspersed with slender wisps of cane that stood higher than a man could reach.

Her gear warning horn buzzed in fury, exactly as it was designed to do when the landing gear was still up and airspeed dropped to virtually nothing, and that was when she switched off her main .power systems, silencing the horn. The whirr of the engine died and, for endless seconds, she felt her wings floating on the cushion of trapped air called ground effect, though it worked just as well over water.

She heard Cutter's excited, "She's down, looking good," while her canards were still scything cane tips, the trailing edges of her tail booms entering the water first, slowing the craft while inertia and lift kept its nose elevated. When at last the nose dropped, Colleen could see nothing but green and tan stripes whipping by because the grass rose higher than her head; Hardin sat with both feet against his control console in defiance of all good sense, though perhaps trying to protect his upper body against the same vicious bite she was feeling from her own safety harness.

She felt a single jarring surge of deceleration, the kind of jolt she had felt at the end of roller-coaster rides at Six Flags and Great America, and someone shouted from between clenched teeth. Colleen's next sensation was that of rocking in a small boat, going nowhere. "Sleeper Two in the tules at zero knots," she said, and then checked her switches. She should have had Cutter in her headset, but then rethought that. With her antenna loops underwater now, she was talking only to herself.

She turned to Hardin. "Well, hotshot," she began, then stopped. Hardin lay unconscious with blood caked down the side of his head, and his left shoulder slumped farther than seemed possible.

FORTY-ONE

Saturday, May 27

SCOTT KING ROLLED out of bed early Saturday morning in Salt Lake City to take an urgent call from his bureau chief in Washington, and was told that his office TWX machine was already humming. He hung up with an old question revisited: Maybe there wasn't supposed to be any rest for the wicked, but how about the good guys, for God's sake?

Fifty minutes later, three-piece-suited and nursing a cup of coffee over fresh TWX pages and a file he was learning to hate, King got Marvin Payson on the line at Nellis, heard the inevitable jibe, and made a suitable answer: "Where else would I be on Memorial Day weekend but at the office? By the way, if you're still in the loop you already know a couple of task force civilians wound up stuck in Chiapas about dawn this morning."

King doodled as he listened, impatient to get his people back, reluctant to interrupt a full inspector. "Well, I didn't need to know 'til now, but Washington called and my TWX machine filled me in. Seems that Langley is trying to put

a rescue team of deniables together, and they need some-
one we've already contacted here. . . . Fellow named
Harry Rex Brown, you may have run across the name. . . .
Right."

Listening again, he scribbled "commend Hild., Giv."
into the doodles. "Good to hear it, inspector; they're my
best men. Look, that's what I—yes, I will. But I need
Givens and another of your task force people here as soon
as you can break them loose from Nellis paperwork—yes,
today if possible. . . . Oh: Young buck with DEA. Landis, Gary. . . . No, this is from the AD in Washington. It
was Givens and Landis who sent a foot-long icicle up the
backside of Mr. Brown, and Brown seemed thoroughly
impressed, so we should let the same personnel carry on."

He grinned at the response, the same one he might have
made himself, and hurried to straighten Payson out: "Oh
no, we'll stay in our own bailiwick, but Langley's flying
a man here from Veracruz today to recruit our Mr. Brown.
The AD thought it'd be best if it's Givens and Landis who
hand Brown over to the lads from Foggy Bottom. It'll be
their show from that point onward. Langley will look more
like a juicy carrot to Mr. Brown, if our people start waving sticks. . . . Sure; who knows, Brown might even enjoy
it. From what I gather, Harry Rex Brown is exactly the
kind of guide the rescue team needs: He knows the region
firsthand, and even if he should talk about it later, he has
the credibility of Richard Nixon."

King winced at Payson's reply. "Duly noted, inspector,
but it was merely an old expression. The man hasn't been
our commander-in-chief for a long time now. . . . Yes,
you'll get a confirming TWX right away. Oh, and incidentally: my congratulations on Task Force Enable. Whatever
happens in Mexico now, you made the bureau look good."

The call completed, King picked up the file on Harry
Rex Brown and reviewed its pages again, sighing. Brown,
in King's orthodox FBI opinion, was perfectly matched to
the CIA: a compulsive tale-spinner a bit out of control,
making up his own legend and then coming to believe it.

King tried to imagine himself joining a CIA team into a Central American jungle guided by such a man, and laughed out loud. If there was one thing Scott King would rather do than that, it was to get a root canal job while on horseback.

King reached for the telephone again when it occurred to him that his Mr. Brown—or rather, now the CIA's Mr. Brown—might not be in Utah, or North America, or the solar system. He paused before dialing to sort out the best approach, and then smiled to himself.

The young woman who answered after six rings seemed to be somewhat out of breath. He gave her a cheery good morning and named himself, but not his title. "Mrs. Brown?"

She admitted it readily enough. Sorry, she added, but it was Saturday so she had two days' worth of weeding to do.

King recalled that many Mormons would not work, or even shop, on Sundays. If Sunday was the big day of their week, Saturday ran it a close second. "Sorry to bother you, ma'am. May I speak to Harry Brown?"

Her response was guarded. *With a hubby like hers, she must get some pretty weird calls,* King reflected, and then met the situation squarely—or almost squarely. "Mrs. Brown, your husband has been of great assistance to the federal government recently, and we think he might be able to help us again. . . . No, no, nothing like that," he chuckled. "Your Harry is something of an expert in Mexican affairs, that's all. Do you think we might reach him some time today?"

King wrote "dinner 6:00 P.M." on his pad. "Thank you very much, ma'am. If he should happen to come home early, you might ask him to call the Federal Bureau of Investigation. If I'm out, he might leave a message. . . . Yes, Scott King or Merle Givens. And thank you again, Mrs. Brown," he said before he broke the connection.

His watch told him there would be plenty of time for lunch before he met Miguel Contreras, the State Depart-

ment man, at Salt Lake City International. Contreras, a
career man with some years of experience in Southern
Mexico, was already en route from Veracruz—and almost
certainly he would be CIA. Scott King's experience was
broad enough to let him read between the lines of a TWX
message. Contreras would have to be a man capable of
posing as Latino—if not Mexican, then Nicaraguan or Cuban—and where he was headed, none of his team would
be wearing ties or wingtip oxfords. For a moment, King
allowed himself to imagine that he was to be part of that
team.

But only for a moment. "Those guys," he said aloud,
"will be blind men fumbling for a hornet's nest."

FORTY-TWO

Saturday, May 27

"AHHH, GOD," HARDIN muttered, trying not to gasp with the pain. "Not again." He found himself still in the right-hand seat but no longer encumbered by harness, and realized that Morrison had swiveled him to face rearward toward the claustrophobic Nemesis living quarters.

"Not what again?" Morrison had moved aft and squatted beside him, removing his headset with care.

He had never expected to see on her face such a mixture of concern and—what was it, pity? "Collarbone. Broke it once on a one-and-a-half gainer," he said.

"You were a diver," she replied, and somehow she made it an accusation.

"Thought I was. Anyhow, I know the feeling—Christ, it isn't getting any better!" He tried to elevate the left shoulder and shook his head to clear the cobwebs from his mind. That hurt, too. "How long have I been out?"

Now Morrison hunkered back on her heels, elbows on her knees. "A few minutes. Look, you'll have to tell me what to do. I was gonna drag you back here in the pipe—"

"Thanksbutnothanks," he said, his good hand warding her off. "I can do it. I think," he added, and slid his rump to the edge of the seat.

To keep from making tortured sounds, he talked his way onto his knees in the companionway, gripping his flight suit as high and as far back as possible with his left hand, which brought his left shoulder up and back. It hurt like a sonofabitch, but now he could work his way back to the adjustable couch in this tiny room they called the pipe. "Supposed to—keep your shoulder back—while the bone heals. Can you drop the—whew—arm support on—left side?"

"You're in the way," she muttered, but she managed by stretching across him. "Okay. Now what?"

He eased himself onto the couch. "Figure-eight splint," he said, and saw from her expression that he might as well be talking Swahili. "Doctor talk; that's what they called it. We need some straps, maybe belts—only we aren't wearing any, are we?" He tried to laugh, shook his head, blinked tears of pain away. Some evil homunculus inside his head was pounding to get out with a padded sledge-hammer, and his awareness kept waxing and waning in no predictable pattern. "You use adjustable straps, Morrison. How about the glass jock there? Scrounge, dammit, scrounge!"

Their exercise machine had a few metal parts but was formed chiefly of boron filament and polymer with little fiberglass, and it related to a Nautilus machine as a Cray computer relates to an adding machine. Its Dacron straps, with Velcro attachments, kept the user in place. No one had ever considered that those straps might have some medical use.

As Morrison removed straps, Hardin caught her studying him, her expression unreadable. "Say it," he prompted.

"You look like shit," she said, wrestling with a strap.

"And you, madam, are a goddamn vision of loveli-ness," he said.

"No, I mean you must've stopped a bullet with the left side of your head, you're all bloody down to your shoulder. You didn't feel it?" She was working on the second strap now.

"The least of my problems," he said, wondering if it were true. He tried to remember the word *concussion*, but gave it up. "Not a slug; I got tossed headfirst into the console when Christiansen stopped us. My own fault; I fetched my head a lick then, I reckon."

Briefly, she looked at him in surprise, then continued. "You fetched it, you reckon? That wallop must have sent you back thirty years, Tex."

Hardin sighed. "I've never said anything yet that made you happy. Why should I start now?"

She collected the straps and knelt beside him. "Try 'thanks,' " she said, with a lopsided smile. "Just 'thanks.' Let's see if you know how."

At a time like this, he thought, his eyes tightly shut, feeling something grate inside that left shoulder, *I have to kiss her butt. Well, she did a great job, at that.* "Thanks, Morrison. Nobody could've done it better."

As if she had not heard him: "What do I do with these?"

"Loop one through the other. Then pass one loop over my left arm to the shoulder." He watched as she did it. "Now listen: You pass them across my back so the other loop goes over my right shoulder—*not yet*—and then you tighten them 'till both shoulders are pulled back. That fits the ends of the collarbone where they should be, but I may not be able to help much."

"Shouldn't you have your flight suit off?"

"No, you'd have to cut it off. Hold it; can you pass your hand in there, nice and easy, and see if the skin is broken? If it is, better check our medkit." For the moment he felt fully alert, his agony slicing like razor wire.

On her knees beside him, Morrison slipped off her gloves and then, pulling his zipper down to his breastbone, eased her right hand inside the neck of his flight suit. The intimacy of these small motions, given different circumstances, might have been the high point of his season. As it was, he hissed an inhalation as the suit fabric tightened around his shoulder. To show her that he was still awake he asked, "How's it feel?"

"Not too exciting," she said as he felt her fingers cool and feathery on his flesh. "Blood's soaked in from your head, but the skin's not broken down here." She removed her hand, and he exhaled. "I feel a lump there," she added.

"Durn tootin' you do. When you tighten that figure-eight splint, keep the loops even and tighten 'til the lump goes away. I'm telling you this now because I'm 'bout ready to pass out on you." He leaned his head back on the semireclining couch, then opened his eyes wide in alarm.

The sound was unmistakable, a heavy thunk resounding from the cockpit. Morrison: "What's that?"

Hardin: "Headhunters, for all I know. Got a sidearm?"

In answer, she pulled a government-issue Beretta from her thigh pocket, nipping past him to her seat. He could see her swivel forward, away from him, and heard her open the canopy. A rushing in his ears seemed to dim the pain for a moment, and he leaned back, his left shoulder off the seatback while he tried to stifle a wave of nausea.

WHEN HE OPENED his eyes again, the pain was dull and he felt unaccountably mellow, and Morrison was dismantling the glass jock with adjustable socket wrenches carried in each Nemesis. She turned and saw him watching, and parked her rump on the exerciser seat. "Back among the living?"

He tried a deep breath; found it easy. "As I live and breathe. I fainted," he said.

"Girls faint. Boys pass out," she said, and grinned. "But have it your way. Oh: I tightened those straps while you were out, and something popped, and there's still some swelling but the big lump is gone. That little medkit has some interesting stuff, Hardin. You've got morphine sulfate in you; I was afraid it was too much 'til now.'' Her expression changed, eyes alight. ''You'll never guess what put a ding on top of our canopy when it fell on us.''

He knew his smile was foolish and didn't much care. ''Stars fell on Alabama. My guess is Meryl Streep.''

''My God, that must be great stuff I gave you. No, it was frozen food. Cutter came down on the deck and dropped us some CARE packages. And a note on his second pass,'' she went on, digging into her breast pocket, unfolding a piece of cardboard that, he saw, had been the back cover of a Nemesis maintenance chart. She read: ''Control demands we bug out. Figure your antenna's blanketed. Dropped all our food ahead of you, hope you find it all. Try and cover your bird. Will make more passes now, screw Control. If you're OK, wave. Jarhead.'' She lifted one foot and he saw, for the first time, that her boots and lower legs were covered with mud. ''He came over several times at about forty knots, and he dropped the note when he saw me, and you know what? It's not even knee-deep out there.''

''Remind me not to dive,'' he said, hoping that was germane.

For perhaps thirty seconds she just sat and studied him, refolding that note, putting it away. Then: ''Want the bad news?''

''Film at eleven,'' he said.

''Our skin,'' she began.

''Fingers like feathers,'' he said, recalling her touch on his injured shoulder. ''Cool feathers. Very nice, Morrison.''

''It's damaged inside the shroud, and the ripped skin fouled our rudder controls. I'm surprised we had any power at all.''

''Absolute power corrupts absolutely,'' he informed her. Abruptly, she gave him a laugh and a headshake, and stood up. "Crazy as a bedbug, Hardin. I'm going out wading again; turns out that our frozen meals don't float. Maybe if I take my boots off I can find more just by temperature differential before it warms up. I take it you're feeling no pain?"

"No pain, no strain," he mumbled, and winked. Actually, he thought, Morrison wasn't such a bitch when she was making intelligent conversation.

"If you had any idea how you're free-associating," she said, with a smile he thought had a little too much superiority in it.

He raised his good hand, shaking his forefinger at her. "Association is not free. All association is very, very expensive," he said.

"You make more sense when you're bonkers, mister," she said. "If you're gonna keep talking, talk to yourself." And she moved past him with care.

He followed her with his eyes as she made her way forward and out of his field of view. He thought she had left the aircraft until he heard another of those soft, musical laughs. "Give me a hint," he said dreamily.

"I was just thinking," her voice echoed back to him; "I like you better this way." And then he felt the gossamer hull of the Nemesis rocking, and knew that she had gone, and sleep became a warm cloud that enveloped him for at least a million years.

FORTY-THREE

Saturday, May 27

TORRES KNEW HOW to get to the border without using public—and therefore easily watched—transportation: He merely took a short city bus ride to the old part of town and asked the first three Latins he met. Street-smart from the cradle, he knew that anyone in the American Southwest who is fluent enough in Spanish can find a place that operates a kind of informal third-class bus service. In Mexico it is called a cooperativo; in the United States it is sought by the authorities and may be a decrepit sedan or a produce truck, and the passenger may have to cling to a spare tire, but these are inconveniences to be expected by those who would travel in Arizona's Latin infraculture.

The trip from Phoenix to Nogales, a border-straddling town, Torres endured in the back seat of a Pontiac with tires so bald they might have been innertubes. He simply walked across the border in Nogales, producing money, remembering to pronounce his intention—"tourism"—with a yanqui's short "i": "toorizm." Had he said, "tooreezmo," he might have been remembered.

At this point, once he was on Mexican soil, Torres could have simply found cartel people and made his needs known. He exchanged a thousand dollars for pesos and found his way alone for two excellent reasons: He did not intend, *ever,* to be known as a man who needed help from lackeys; and he could not afford to waste time getting back to Catemaco. His choice was a chartered Cessna from the little Nogales strip to the nearest Mexican jetport in Hermosillo, an hour to the south. From there he took commercial jets, which could cover the distance to Veracruz in under four hours, but interconnecting flights kept him cooling his heels in Guadalajara for nearly as long. Infuriated by the delay, he called his own Catemaco villa from Guadalajara and found that David Elath had not yet returned. He left a message for Elath to bring the black Mangusta to Aeropuerto General Jara near Veracruz to meet his eight o'clock flight. At least, in Veracruz he was practically in his own backyard.

He was striding toward the nearest telephone in the Veracruz airport when he heard a familiar "Hola," and turned to see Elath moving toward him. He gave his friend an abrazo with both arms, accepting the keys to his Mangusta. "I have no luggage. Which way is the car?"

"This way." Elath led him outside, studying Torres with morbid interest. "You could use a shave."

"And a better meal than I had in Guadalajara, and some answers," Torres retorted, spying the gleam of his toy under a coating of dust. "How long were you at the villa?"

"Ten minutes. There are calls awaiting you there."

Torres unlocked the doors and slid into familiar leather seats, the kind of Recaro Specials that cupped a man like a lover, and sighed. He was home again. Backing out, he asked, "Did you take any of the calls?"

Elath snorted. "Not I. The less I must talk with your cartelista brothers right now, Simon, the better I like it."

Pointing the Mangusta's snout toward Federal Highway 180 and Catemaco, Torres barked a short laugh. "It would be very dangerous for me to be heard agreeing with you, friend David, but I agree absolutely. Do you know whether the airplane arrived at Base Ana?''

"No. And again I must tell you, Simon, I am not certain that I want to know. I consider myself as good a man as the next, but I am not such a fool as to think myself invulnerable. I already know far too much about things that could have me separated from my fingernails, and then my fingers, then my hands, then my arms.'' Elath placed his palms up, shaking them as if juggling his explanation as he said, "I went to look after the overhaul in San Pedro Sula. I have been there ever since. Whatever tales you told me about what might have been, I have forgotten. Would it not be better if you left me in ignorance?''

Snicking the gear lever up to fourth, Torres pretended to consider the request of David Elath. Then he offered an excuse for what he intended to do anyway. "Do not be naive. I would not allow them to use you that way, but if they did it would not matter how much or how little you knew. And what happened in Las Vegas was a thing so far removed from San Pedro Sula, you could not have affected that fiasco one way or the other. You are at liberty to tell other cartelistas what you did, should they ask— providing, of course, that you say nothing about my intention to land anywhere but Base Ana.

"Besides, I did nothing there that the cartel could complain about. I am not so sure the same is true of Guillermo Borges.'' The thought of fat Billy Borges flicked the reins that controlled Torres's fury. In the World Cup of all deadly confidence games, he had watched himself losing, unable to change the outcome. He felt his honor deeply wounded, and only blood would atone for that. At the moment it seemed that Borges must be behind his defeat. Rage called out for a clear, unambiguous target.

"Perhaps when I tell you the story, David, you will have insights to share.'' With that, he turned south on the highway and watched his tachometer needle climb. "By the way, how did the overhaul go?''

"They were installing your engine when I left. Another day or so."

Torres thought about that for a moment. "Do you mean to say my T-Bird would not have been ready had I flown the Bristol in last night?"

"Correct, despite all the money I passed around. But the truck was ready, and so was I. You never told me where we would drive it; only that we might need bolt cutters for fences."

Torres grunted, only half satisfied. "Well, no matter. The T-Bird was my contingency plan, in case we had to fly out with our ammunition magazines full of yanqui dollars. It seems, friend David, that Borges or someone else had contingency plans too." And with that he began to give his version of the Las Vegas operation, including the fact that someone claiming to be El Condor had spent the previous evening with a planeload of passengers at Culiacán. There was reason to hope, Torres said, that the airliner had indeed landed at Base Ana with a very special cargo.

FORTY-FOUR

Saturday, May 27

IN SALT LAKE City's federal office building, lights burned
late on Saturday evening. Harry Rex Brown, at first an
extremely reluctant guest there, began to feel after an hour
that his halo burned as brightly as the lights on State Street
below. While the DEA's Landis made no secret of the fact
that he considered the halo somewhat askew, the strangers
with him in the FBI office seemed anxious to straighten it,
as though trying to impress the fellow called Mike. It
seemed that while Mike had interesting maps and a promise of an extremely urgent secret mission into Chiapas and
a peek into Harry's business, the man had no other names,
lending him a certain aura of the mysterious and wonderful. Harry began to wonder whether, in the future, he
should bill himself as just plain Harry, with no other
names.

Harry's major surprise came after Mike tested him with
a map of the region to the west of Lago Miramar in southern Chiapas, a region of limestone cliffs sometimes sunny
but often hidden by mist, of rioting vegetation too high to

be jungle, too rank to be anything else: the bosque. Mike's questions became more acute, probing like little needles into Harry's self-confidence. Finally, if Harry had explored no closer than thirty miles from the spot marked on that map, said Mike, was Harry absolutely certain that spot was reachable by men on foot when some spots in Chiapas were unexpectedly trackless, high mountain swamp?

Harry gave him a wise nod and decided to show off a little. *"In wohel be-t'-e,"* Harry assured him; "I know how to do it," in Maya, expecting Mike to ask him what the devil that meant.

"Tin t'sen tal," Mike replied; "I'm listening" in near-perfect Maya, but maybe in a lowland dialect. Harry gaped.

Mr. Givens of the FBI had been listening quietly, but now he exchanged a glance with Mr. Landis and sat up straight. "What's the matter, both you guys swallow your gum?"

"He speaks Maya," Harry accused.

"And Spanish too. Don't underestimate me," Mike said, only he said it very quickly in Spanish.

"That I can dig," said Landis.

Harry, trying to reconcile Mike's ability with what he knew of government agents, winked at Mike. "Why didn't you say you were LDS?"

"Because I'm not, Harry. I've just spent a lot of time in Mexico, much of it outside the cities. And I want to make sure the guy who guides us to that spot knows at least as much about the unpleasant details as I do. I'll ask you again: How would you go through a swamp where no swamps are shown?"

"You'll be part of the team I lead, then," said Harry, ignoring the question for the moment because its answer was so elementary.

"Not unless you can answer my question, Harry," said Mike.

Harry did not enjoy Mike's tone so much now; the man

acted as if he had Harry on a string like one of those mechanical monkeys, and Harry did not appreciate it. He tried to be polite, however, and recited for Mike. "You don't go through it, you go around it," he said. "Even if it's a greater distance. I always found it quicker that way. You could bring a rubber boat and pole your way through, but they're heavier than you think. Half of your porters would be lugging equipment you can get along without."

"Forget porters," said Mike. "Everybody on the team will pack his own gear. They might be toting something out, though."

Harry knew, somehow, that if he mentioned his good friend and guide Yaxpoc at this juncture, Mike's little band might run off seeking Yaxpoc, leaving Harry himself behind. Once there they probably would not find Yaxpoc, but that would do Harry no good. Time enough to let Mike in on the secrets of jungle travel—in some places even the guide should have a guide—when they reached base camp. "What might they be toting, Mike?"

"Sorry. You'll know when we get there."

"If I'm leading a team, I have to know what I'm doing it for."

"No you don't," Mike said easily. "Or let's put it another way, Harry: You're doing it for glory, or for ten thousand dollars, whichever sounds better to you."

This, to Harry Rex Brown, was beginning to sound like a test of wills. Harry had not been second-in-command of an expedition for some years, for reasons too illegal to mention; and Harry did not intend to be second again. Why do that, he reasoned, when he had enough funds to go again, his own boss, anytime he liked? Harry had sensed during the past hour that these government men weren't kidding about the urgency of it all but they had nothing on him worth their trouble, and that all this stroking and abrading on a holiday weekend meant that he had something they wanted very much and very, very soon.

Harry fairly salivated to lead a real team connected with a real government toward a real goal so that one day, one of his tales of derring-do would be based on a world everyone else agreed was real. But Harry knew something important about plans and repeated an old adage to himself: *When negotiating something important, try to find yourself an alternative so attractive you won't care much whether the negotiation falls through.* He decided on the instant that, if he didn't lead his team, he would go anyway, without them. Whatever they sought, Harry might find it first. He had, after all, committed that spot on the map to memory: Thirty miles in direct line from Lake Miramar, westward toward the village of Gonzalez de Leon.

Harry stood up. He spoke without rancor, in the tone of a man who knew he had an attractive alternative. "Fellows, I would not be leading the team, only guiding it. I was born to lead. Have a nice trip," he smiled, and reached for his hat, the smelly old snap-brim that looked so right with his khakis.

"Hold it right there," Landis snapped, standing in his way. "I've been waiting for a chance to nail you, and you know it."

"Then get your hammer, Mr. Landis," said Harry, adding, "Excuse me," as he stepped to one side. Now he clapped his hat on and reached for his bush jacket, the one with all the pockets and the epaulets.

"I tried," said Landis to one of them.

From Givens: "Can you afford this, Contreras? He's gonna walk." Harry made a mental note as he put on his old leather jacket.

Mike: "Let him walk; plenty of other guys we could get."

Harry: "Overnight? With recent knowledge of the region and the languages they need? I wish you the best of luck."

Mike: "You've taken your last little jaunt with a passport, asshole. We can do that, you know."

"If guerrillas can't catch me, how do you expect to?" Harry said, enjoying himself as he grasped the doorknob, fully intending to walk out. *Oh, what a story this will make,* he exulted.

"A man! A wounded man, goddammit," welled up from Mike as if pulled out by treble hooks.

Harry turned in the doorway. "Beg pardon?"

Mike's face, like the hide of a chameleon, had an interesting range of shades; now it made a segue from brown to maroon. "We might be toting an injured man away from that spot, if he's still alive when we get there. You fucking had to know; well, now you fucking know."

Harry stood in the doorway for an endless moment, thought about shutting it, then left his hand on the knob. Lifting a schoolmarmish finger toward Mike: "When I no longer lead, I tend to walk out. Here or in Chiapas. Understood?"

Mike's face had apparently decided to stick with maroon. "Understood," he choked.

Harry found it difficult not to gloat, but he managed. "My team members, whatever language they speak, do not swear. If they do, they must repeat the word five hundred times without stopping. Agreed?"

His voice failing him, Mike could only nod.

"I told you about this guy, you knew he was one of Mister Clean's Bobbsey twins, I put it down in black and white a long time ago," Landis was muttering softly to the others.

"And I intend to supervise each member's pack and gear. You'd be amazed how many old-timers don't know how to pack for the tropics," Harry went on, unperturbed, the finger still shaking. "Oh, and by the way: No one carries weapons. Weapons make people foolhardy. I carry a pistol for snakes, that's all."

Landis's laugh was downright nasty. "You find many venomous reptiles in San Francisco bars?"

"You bet I do," Harry replied, then snapped his fingers, an act that seemed to make his eyes light up. "I kept thinking I'd met you in another context," Harry said, smiling, nodding at Landis. "Now I remember: a bar in

San Francisco, a few years ago. Just for that, you can't be on the team.''

Harry thought he saw several emotions fighting for primacy in the face of Gary Landis. The one that settled in was contrition. ''Aww, Harry, don't be like that. I've been counting on it *so* much.'' Then, as Harry's steely gaze began to soften, Landis added, ''Come on, Harry, don't be such a cock-walloping, motherfucking asshole.''

''That's it, you don't go,'' Harry barked. ''I mean what I say, fellows.''

Landis turned away. The expressions of the other men, Harry thought, were passing strange. With a heavy clearing of his throat, Mike said, ''Uh, Harry, we agree to your conditions but we don't have a lot of time and we only had, uh, one extra man and you've just told him to stay home. You understand that you'll have to take the others.''

''I haven't met them,'' Harry said reasonably.

''What the fu—,'' Mike burst out, then resumed, his hands opening and closing rapidly—''the fudge can I do, Harry, the government has picked them. We accept your rules, but you don't get to make any more rules than those, okay?''

That seemed fair, and Harry nodded.

''And we need to be on the way Monday at oh-seven-hundred sharp. We've got an injured hero to rescue—and a pretty girl, too,'' Mike said in afterthought.

''I'll be ready, Mr. Contreras,'' Harry replied, and saw Mike's face go blank. ''Oh yes, and if it's Contreras, tell me: Is it really Michaelo or Miguel?''

''It's Mike,'' said Mike, with a look toward Landis that would have frozen hot coals.

''You must think I'm a credulous idiot full of schoolboy fantasies, Mike,'' said Harry as he started out the door. ''Pretty girl, my backside,'' he muttered to himself.

FORTY-FIVE

Saturday, May 27

Tᴵᴹᴱ ᴡᴀꜱ ᴡʜᴇɴ Colleen could spend hours at hard labor, even taking falls in practice, without feeling as though her arms were ready to drop off. That time, she reflected as she climbed aboard her Nemesis in darkness, was ancient history. She hadn't felt rosin on her palms or tried a tricky dismount for years; *no wonder I'm out of shape,* she thought. The aircraft no longer rocked like a winged canoe, now that she'd scavenged a hundred yards of cord from her parachute and had run it from a wingtip light bezel to the trunk of a lakeside tree. It still felt tippy, though, as she swiveled her seat to face the pipe. She had failed to budge the one-ton mass of her Nemesis an inch nearer to the shore, but maybe tomorrow, when she was fresh. . . .

" 'Zat you, Morrison?" Then, in lower tones from inside the pipe, "By God it better be."

She chuckled to herself, ducking for entry in total blackness. "No, it's a headhunter, and what're you going to do about it?"

Sigh. "Become a lively dinner, I suppose," Hardin said.

The poppy syrup has worn off. That's good—or is it, she thought. Colleen located a handgrip from memory; snapped on a twenty-watt reading lamp; directed it toward the floor. "Speaking of dinner, I found a bunch of 'em scattered out in the muck. God knows how many I missed and God bless Jarhead for dropping the dozen I found. You hungry, Napoleon?"

He had managed to put his left hand into his flight suit with the zipper locked at his breastbone to surrogate a sling, reminding her of the Bonaparte pose. He smiled at her allusion. "Try me. I'll fang it, plastic plate and all. We still have our electrics up and running?"

She tossed him a superior smirk. "Is this a bird I built? Hell yes, they're up and running! We haven't shipped an ounce of water yet."

She knew he was watching as she selected two of the most-thawed meals and placed them in the microwave heater above their toilet unit. *That shouldn't irritate me. Hang loose, Colleen, you're stuck with this pampered fly-boy for quite a while.* She knew, nonetheless, why his gaze had always made her irritable: because his judgment counted far too much with Ben Ullmer. *If I'd been a few inches taller, I could've had his training.* And his credibility.

She knew this train of thought always brought her to a boil, and deflected herself with the job at hand, peeling away plastic wrap, wadding it.

"Hey, save that stuff. We may need it," Hardin said.

"Shut up and eat your chicken Kiev," she replied, but of course he was right and she draped the flaccid wrap over a railing.

With their glass jock disassembled, she had room to sit cross-legged beside him, and watched as he adjusted the couch to a sitting position. Every so often his breath would catch during an inhalation and she knew he was hurting.

His effort to eat one-handed was almost comically pathetic. "Want me to cut it for you?"

"Nope. Gotta get used to it," he said, and then the plastic dish slid from his lap and would have dumped its contents had Colleen not been so quick with her free hand.

She had the meal away from him until he looked into her face. "You can't clean up a mess for a while," she said. "And I'm not the upstairs maid. Face it, Tex, you need to be spoonfed. That's a woman's job anyhow, right?"

He just looked at her, now unsmiling, and managed a one-sided shrug, and she alternated the spoons; a bite for him, a bite for herself, in heavy silence.

When he asked for water, she found a topic that carried less emotional baggage with it. "Yeah, but we'll have to conserve. Remember that our condenser won't work when we're not airborne to scoop a ton of humid air." She fitted a plastic bulb to the drinking water outlet and watched it fill. An outgrowth of space shuttle hardware, those little bulbs with their built-in straws saved a lot of spillage. They had not adopted NASA meals, she recalled, because the damned things took special warmers and were wildly expensive for a Coastie budget—*and Hardin didn't count on anyone having to eat with a broken collarbone.*

He insisted on squeezing the bulb for himself and sucked greedily. Then: "All I've seen from the rear canopy is sky. What's our situation here?"

"We're at the edge of this little lake, must be a seasonal runoff or something. Once you look into all the moss and creepers, it turns out most of the trees are pine and oak, and something else; cypress, I think. I had to climb a pine to anchor a wingtip so we don't bob around so much. I tell you, those creeper vines are worse than barbed wire."

"That means nobody will be nosing around without a good reason," he said. "How does it stack up for a rescue?"

"I wish I knew. Altimeter reading is forty-nine hundred feet, give or take. We won't freeze and we won't starve, not for a while anyway, but we can't raise anybody by comm set. They know where we are, and according to Cutter the nearest lights are a couple of miles down-slope.'' She fell silent for a moment. Then, as offhanded as possible: ''They don't have headhunters in these parts.''

Hardin handed her the empty bulb for a refill and then, as she was filling it, said, ''Was that a question or a statement?''

''Oh, unscrew you, Hardin.''

''I hope you've spread the blanket over our canopies,'' he said. ''What if they saw our light?''

The blanket, nothing more than silvered Tyvek plastic to protect transparent canopies during ground storage in the open, was stored beneath the cockpit where its paltry weight would add ballast forward. She started to scramble to her feet, skin prickling, and then saw him with his face studiously averted. ''All right then, it's a question.''

''No ma'am, there are no headhunters in Central America.''

''God *damn* you, Hardin,'' she exploded. Given the choice of tears or curses, she preferred the manly option, and exercised it with abandon. ''I'm no fucking expert on jungle natives, you smug son of a bitch! Stir that shit you use for brains and ask yourself who the bloody hell would have to protect your helpless ass out here! What a bastard,'' she finished, fighting tears anyway, hiding her face with hands that shook.

When her breathing steadied, she looked up and blinked a few times to clear her gaze, and saw the sorrow on his face, and if it meant pity, somehow that was even worse.

But it seemed to be simple guilt, and that was better. Guilt she understood very well. ''You're absolutely right,'' he said. ''You shoulder all the responsibility, and I wait 'til you're exhausted and then expect you to take some kidding. I was a bastard, Morrison. Maybe it's the morphine.''

''Don't blame it on downers, you're always a bastard.''

''That's a bit strong.''

''Somebody's got to be strong out here,'' she retorted. ''It sure won't be you.''

He bit back a reply. After a moment he said, ''I'll mend as fast as I can, Morrison. Meanwhile, we're making the worst of it. There's got to be some way we can kiss and make up.''

The look she turned on him was withering. ''I'd kiss a cockroach first,'' she said, moving forward toward the cockpit. Despite her comment about not freezing, the chill was now pronounced and their heating system used too much energy. She began to haul the canopy blanket from its stowage bin.

''It was just a figure of speech, Colleen,'' Hardin said mildly, with the suggestion of a chuckle.

''Figure this,'' she shot back, and thrust her hand toward the rear, middle finger up in the ancient salute.

''I can't see you, but I have a great imagination,'' he said.

''Hold on to it, Tex,'' she said, arranging the blanket and adjusting her seat so that it reclined. That had been another of Hardin's ideas, so an off-duty pilot could take a brief rest without going aft to the pipe. At the moment, she hated him for that, too. ''Your wonderful imagination may be the only friend you've got.''

For a time, after Hardin switched off the light, she thought weariness would bring sleep. Yet she kept hearing that catch in his breath, and his efforts to find comfort with occasional faint grunts that said he was not finding it. The blackness became suffused with dim light again. She tried not to listen as he moved around, undid the zipper at his crotch, used the toilet, closed the unit afterward. It was impossible not to guess what he was doing when she heard familiar snaps and rustles. ''Are you into the medkit, Hardin?''

No answer, but labored breathing and a change in the light level that said he was directing the lamp on something.

"Hardin, if you need morphine, I can help," she said, surprised at the softness in her own voice.

"Go back to sleep, Morrison," was the reply. "How many of these did you give me?"

"Just one. There were four in there, already loaded with about two ceecees each; I just pulled that rubber nipple off the needle and emptied the plunger into that big muscle near your neck."

"I know where you stuck me, for Christ's sake, a dead man could tell you. Go to sleep."

She said nothing more until he snapped off the lamp and, a moment later, released the ancestor of all sighs. "I wouldn't hurt you on purpose, Hardin," she said, still softly.

"I know it," he growled. Another moment passed. "And this," he went on, "was what I meant by kiss and make up. Beats going to sleep mad."

"Sweet dreams, Hardin," she said, putting saccharine music in it.

Evidently he missed the sarcasm. "You know it, lady," he murmured.

She lay still long enough to hear his snores before she would let herself relax, amused at her own reference to dreams. *I wonder what he'd do if he knew about my daydreams, for a couple of months after I signed on with Ullmer.* Her ploy had been standard practice for Colleen: pick an attractive man she knew and create a fantasy life about him, but never let him guess. She had a love life, all right; wide-ranging, sexually inventive, free from worry. But for several years now it had all taken place within herself.

And when at last the object of her sexual favors began to disturb her in one way or another, Colleen could dump the poor clod without explanation. A real affair, she knew from experience, was far more fraught with entreaties, recriminations, furies. She had found this way better, allowing her to people her short stories with complex relationships while she sailed through her solitary life without need to consider others very much.

For the past few weeks her fantasy partner had been Jared Cutter; not that she ever gave him so much as an inkling of it. She had foolishly let Jarhead peek into her life a bit—a mistake—and soon it would be time to leave thoughts of him behind. And on the day when at last she made her fatal mistake—in an airplane of course, how else could she tantalize and frustrate her fate half so well?—she would leave no loving kin to mourn her, certainly not the way she mourned for dad and mom and the Rogue rats, as her brothers had called themselves.

The trouble with all this, she realized, was that she tended to behave toward her rejects as if the affairs had been of the flesh, *in* the flesh. She had become so familiar with the virtues and vices she had given Hardin's alter ego that his every move fitted, in, or could be made to fit in, to what she "knew" about him already. All this, Colleen admitted to herself, could have confused a more sensitive male. *Damned good thing Wes Hardin is an unregenerate macho Texan,* she concluded, slipping toward sleep.

FORTY-SIX

Saturday, May 27

ALVARO BERMUDEZ, THE senderista commander, had been in residence at Base Ana on that fateful Saturday predawn. His anguished radio message to Catemaco afterward had seemed too apocalyptic for belief until old Vega and the young Gaitan Palacios had themselves flown there in the Pilatus. Their expectation was that the Turbo-Porter, with its wheeled floats, should be able to land. After one look at the savaged base, however, their pilot warned that the runway damage was too great to risk a landing. Vega ordered him to fly them home again, sick with rage at what he saw: fragments of bodies still uncollected, most of the buildings reduced to their concrete foundation piers, and a crater at the runway intersection that could have swallowed their Pilatus whole. Perhaps most telling of all, they could see palms stripped to bare trunks, and not one unbroken window. Their lodge on its higher slope was still habitable, but the processing sheds lay in ruins.

Nor did Bermudez like his position in the ruins of Base Ana. Some of his guerrillas were giving him hard looks.

Almost as bad was the rumor of a ghost aircraft that had flitted like a vampire among the flames, making ground-level passes over the devastation as if contemptuous of the men firing at it. That, at least, explained how the airliner's crew might have been spirited away. Another explanation, favored by Gaitan Palacios, was that the airliner had been remote-controlled. The ghost aircraft might have been pure imagination on the part of terrified Peruvians.

By the time Torres reached Catemaco on Saturday night, the cartel leaders had spent hours in council. Torres took an hour debriefing them before he learned, from his old mentor Perez Palacios, of the American news releases from Tucson. "I do not trust this," Torres muttered, scanning the front-page story in Mexico City's conservative *El Universal*. "They say Borges is held without bail, but I believe he was working for the yanquis."

Miguel Solano, whispery-voiced: "It is evident that someone was." His gaze did not waver from Torres's face.

Torres knew the signs. "But it is not evident to you who the traitor was? Then believe what you like, Brother Solano. Guillermo Borges could have been advising the yanquis for a long time. If I read your suspicions correctly, ask yourself why I would let our only military airstrip become a gravel pit."

"You removed your airplane from it in advance," said old Palacios. "Why, Brother Torres?"

"Shall I let you read its maintenance log? It was over-due for repair, and while I risked my backside among the yanquis I thought an overhaul would be appropriate. Make no mistake, I am relieved that our only armed jet was not destroyed." He tapped the newspaper. "I very nearly killed myself twice while escaping, brothers; the news story mentions only my takeoff in Las Vegas. My landing gave me this." He passed his fingers across the bridge of his nose.

"Yet you say, yourself, that we must not trust the ve-racity of a yanqui news release," Solano reminded him.

"Well, I am here," Torres said, now nursing a resurgent headache and still suffering from lack of sleep. "I even managed to warn you that someone pretending to be me was in Mexico with that airliner. I can only guess that they turned it into an airbase destroyer with the complicity of the Mexican government."

Perez Palacios, first among equals of the Cali group and the man who had brought Torres to the top, nodded. "That may have been your salvation, Simon; that call you made. If only you had made it ten minutes earlier," he sighed, and released a wan smile. "A man's intentions are often mirrored by his bank accounts. I am sorry to say we found it necessary to check your Bancomer accounts, but I was glad to see that you have made no large withdrawals recently."

Simon Torres harbored no illusions about his "brothers" in the cartel. *Perhaps I should bear in mind that Cain and Abel were brothers,* he thought. If they decided against him, he would have no warning, and David Elath would be of little help. "I did what I could. I am still ready to do what I can."

Into a deafening silence, Vega spoke. "That is good, because we will need every man to make our response to the Mexicans. You see, we have already agreed in council with your suspicion: The guilt for this is probably theirs, at least in part. Escobar is making his own inquiries."

Torres had not really imagined that the Mexican government had allowed this body blow. He had accused them only to deflect suspicion from himself. Now he asked for an explanation, and he tried not to show his horror when Vega complied.

It could be no coincidence, they had decided, that Base Ana had been mauled and half their senderista army killed within days after the cartel failed to make payoffs on the usual schedule. The Mexican officials were evidently running a protection racket and would doubtless admit as much to Escobar. It seemed clear that in helping the yanquis they had simply sent a deadly message to ensure that, in the future, payment would be more prompt. Bermudez had reported condensation trails over Base Ana and thought they might be Mexican photoreconnaissance; the Mexicans checking their handiwork. *And why not,* thought Torres, *after such a blast?*

Vega finished his explanation in tones befitting an elder statesman: calm, measured, inhumanly rational. "Had they rounded up some of our coca teams, even killed a few, I would understand," he said, his hands weaving gentle patterns in the air. "A small misunderstanding, easily remedied." The hands came down carefully to the top of the great council table. "But they have slapped too hard, and honor requires a response. Brother Perez," he said, and sat back.

The message in the face of Perez Palacios was, "I don't like this either, but for the sake of your skin don't argue." What he said was, "A score of highway bridges and three transisthmus rail bridges must go—and the dam at Chicoasen. All by Monday night. More than half of Mexico's hydroelectric power comes from the Rio Grijalva. We will need your man Elath for the dam."

Torres nodded as if this were a small thing and not a wildfire whipped out of control by winds of frustration. "He is waiting below," he said. "But let me suggest something to relieve Bermudez. The senderistas still in the field should stay there until Base Ana looks presentable. The federales may yet be planning to move on our coca teams in the field, Brother Vega. I think Bermudez should radio his senderistas in the field to make more use of the locals. Any organized groups moving into Southern Chiapas must either be our own or assumed as the enemy."

"A good point," said Solano, making a note as the others nodded. "But bring your Jew in now. It has been Sunday for half an hour, and Monday night we want the Mexicans to feel our response. They cannot hurt us with impunity, and it is essential that our guerrilla teams operate as one, to show that we are an organized force."

To show that we are one-legged lunatics goading a Miura bull in his own pasture, Torres thought as he rose, viewing himself as from a distance, a man striding toward his own destruction, compelled by his own passions as well as other men whose sense of outraged honor was leading them to suicide. "I will call David Elath now."

FORTY-SEVEN
Sunday, May 28

Sunday morning, Colleen made her first of several very special schedules, acutely aware of Wes Hardin's snores. She wanted to take that CIA survival kit with her, but knew she would wake Hardin retrieving it and decided to do without. She then made a circuit of the lake, boots squishing with every step, the Beretta snug in a pocket of her flight suit. Small mammals scuttled away, some on a spongy green carpet of matted vegetation, other creatures traversing vines the thickness of her upper arm; and the instant they quit moving through the sun-dappled gloom, they became invisible. *God, it's quiet,* she thought. *Even on the Rogue River you can usually hear a chainsaw or something.* Here, the loudest noises were rustlings of leaves, with an occasional bird call that sounded to Colleen like a parrot's orgasm. Twice she glimpsed shapes that fled through the high rain forest on silent wings, their plumage iridescent in blue, scarlet, and yellow. She had to admit it was all quite gorgeous, and the sooner she got away from it the better. At least the season was not advanced enough for mosquitoes.

During the next hour she found it easier, and somehow more comforting, to wade in sunlight through grassy muck than to fight the tangles of thorny vines that choked trees at the lake's edge, but near its narrowest end she discovered firm footing and a grassy verge that extended several hundred yards without trees or bushes. Evidently the lake level fluctuated enough to prevent the growth of trees or bushes over the limestone bottom here. This ankle-high variety of grass, however, seemed capable of growing on a hot stove. She spied a few breaks in foliage suggestive of paths leading from the lake, but *I'm not ready for that just yet,* she decided, patting the Beretta for reassurance.

Near the greensward, a quarter-mile from where her Nemesis had come to rest, was the primary thing she had sought—fresh water trickling from the heights into the lake. She returned with a quickened step, sucking a fingertip where a thorn had penetrated her glove, but stopped on rounding a lakeside bend as her Nemesis came in view, fifty yards away.

"And just what the hell do you think you're doing," she called, realizing too late that she sounded like a harried mother.

Hardin, in stockinged feet, had somehow managed to make his way outside from the open canopy, over the solar collector panels, and back to the rear surface of the wing. He sat near the shrouded propeller, facing rearward, and he turned at her hail. "A postflight inspection, what else," he called back, and continued to study the shroud.

She waded out to the fuselage and hauled herself up, sitting on the canopy still to remove her sopping boots and socks, placing the socks on a canard surface to dry. "Talk about wasted motion, I'll get wet all over again."

"Yeah, but you get dry in between. Good thing these boots dry so fast," he said.

"I guess I don't have to ask whether you're feeling better," she said as he edged forward toward her, his left wrist still slung in his flight suit, and squatted to face her.

He turned his head this way and that, stretching the neck

muscles near those binding straps. "It hurts, okay? I mean it won't let me forget it's there, Morrison, but it's not much worse up here than in the pipe, and the sun feels good. And that's not all," he added, waiting for her to respond.

When she didn't, easing herself back into the pipe barefoot for a spare pair of socks, he said, "I read your checklist on the seat."

"What's wrong with it?" she asked, collecting that spook survival kit, coming forward into the sun again.

"Nothing that I can see. But I notice you've listed rivets and epoxy, with big question marks."

"Sue me," she said, checking the ugly wrinkles across her feet, the result of sleeping in wet boots.

"Please cut it out, Colleen," he said softly. He resumed in lighter tones: "I know what you're thinking." When she only looked at him without a reply, he went on, "We took a couple of clean hits through a rudder, no problem, but one slanting round ripped the shroud skin loose near the propeller. Looks like the low pressure inside the shroud kept lifting the skin and started a peel failure, and it kept getting worse in flight 'til the skin's loose all along that trailing edge."

"Okay, you're a genius at failure analysis, and we're screwed. What else is new?"

"You think you might be able to fix it," he said. "You think maybe we can fly it out of here."

As if his guess was of no importance, she inspected a roll of monofilament fishing line. "Is that what I think?"

"Yep. And you know something, Colleen? I think you could be right."

For a long moment their eyes met. Without admitting anything directly, but with a hammering in her breast that made her feel giddy with hope, she pointed eastward toward the narrowest end of the lake. "There's a place over there a few hundred yards where the shallows become low grass. That's where I should've landed us, there's a little stream that trickles in there too. Fresh water. There's only a few gallons in our tank, you know."

He put his good hand out to steady himself and sat down, taking great care on those solar panels. "I know you're touchy as a ten-pound zit about taking advice from me," he said, and endured the hard look she gave him, "but if you haven't drunk the local water, don't start until you've followed the stream up a ways."

"Isn't there anything you're not an expert on?"

"My mother's people are from Puebla, so I've been there a few times. It's around seven thousand feet there and for some reason we gringos don't get Montezuma's revenge as much at higher altitudes where there aren't many people. So it may be okay, but then again, how'd you like to drink from that stream and then find a deer carcass rotting in it a hundred feet upstream? Right; me neither," he said, seeing the face she made.

"I think there are purification tabs in here," she replied, toeing the survival kit. "I fully intended to use 'em, Hardin."

He nodded, started to say something, thought better of it, then tried again. "Now, as for the epoxy and rivets, that's wishful thinking unless you brought some of both."

"I didn't, but as soon as we get my bird clear of the water we'll have our antennas out in the open, and then we can call for a CARE package." They both knew the antennas could not be reached from inside the fuselage. They lay under water.

She watched him chew his lower lip, gazing across the lake with the sun backlighting his tousled hair. *You're a good-looking sonofabitch, and don't you know it,* she asked him silently. *No wonder I made you my first fantasy on the job.*

Abruptly he grinned down at her. "So we rig slings and lift the bird enough to lower the gear, patch her up, burn the grass and clear us a couple of hundred yards, and go for broke. Right?"

"In principle, but wrong on most details." *I can't help it, I love wiping a grin off that face.* "I winch my bird onto wooden rollers and backward up the slope to the treeline. The landing gear stays up. We fix the bird, wet down the grass to lower its friction coefficient, and use a catapult rigged with 'chute cord and timbers to give us a kick.''

''You're nuts,'' he said.

''Worked fine for the Wright Brothers,'' she replied.

''Take you weeks,'' he warned.

She shrugged. ''What else is there to keep me occupied?''

''You think I don't know why you don't just walk down the mountain, today, right this moment?''

''Wounded man,'' she muttered, not very convincingly.

''Oh, no you don't. I speak the lingo, I could give it a go right now. You don't give a good goddamn about a wounded man, nearly as much as you want to bring our bird back.''

''*My* bird, Hardin.'' She was still taking stock of that survival kit, but paused to look up at him. ''Ben Ullmer hasn't turned it over to the Coasties yet, so it's still mine.'' She knew she was blushing as she made her outlandish declaration, but this was no time to deny how she felt about it.

''Your bird, then,'' he said, and she could have shoved him off his perch for the amusement she caught in his reply. ''You don't intend to, uh, try and hide it somewhere, I hope.''

''Give me a break,'' she said. ''I'm gonna get this bucket of polymers back to Ullmer and he can sell it or use it for a suppository, but listen to me, Hardin: *Nobody is ever going to say a woman wrote off Sleeper Two.* Is that clear?''

Silence, as he watched her attach the handle of a double-edged brush knife, almost a machete. ''Whereas a man, for example, would have walked away from it to save his ass,'' he said at last.

''For example,'' she said, mimicking him. ''A man who doesn't have to prove himself 'cause he's already God's gift to the military-industrial good-ol' boys' club. Go on down the mountain if you want to.''

His expression was at first disbelieving. ''Is that it? My service background? Is that why you've been so tight-assed all these months?''

"Don't call me that," she said.

"If it was any tighter you'd have to wipe it with a Q-tip," he scoffed.

The imagery struck her unexpectedly, and she burst into laughter before she could stop herself. Then she slapped him across the thigh with the flat of her knife blade, the way she had penalized her brothers for making her laugh through her anger. "If you're so damn' uppity, go nuke us some packages of ham and scrambles; one thing we're not short of here is electricity."

"Or little teeny broads with weird hangups," he said, twisting out of reach as she swung the flat of her weapon again. "You want to be careful with that knife, you could shorten a guy with it," he said more seriously.

"And don't you forget it, fly-boy," she said, putting the knife down. "Come down here, for God's sake, before you fall down."

She helped him lower himself, moving her notes and survival hardware from the copilot's seat, and continued to inspect the stuff as he made his slow progress into the pipe. "Ten thousand peso bills? Wha—*hundred* thousand peso bills? We're rich, Hardin."

"Sure we are," he replied. "A beer'll cost you a few thousand, if you can find a beer. Only it'd be pohsh, most likely. I hear the Maya learned to distill the stuff."

She could hear his progress with the food, and the ding of the microwave unit. "I thought the Mayans faded out centuries ago," she said, unwinding a ringsaw, which was simply a three-foot serrated wire with steel rings at its ends. Held with her thumbs and drawn back and forth, it might drop a big tree; stretched in a frame of bowed wood, it might make a dandy coping saw.

"Nope, the Maya just faded into the jungle for a while. They're still around. Damn' near threw the whites out of the Yucatan in a civil war a hundred years or so ago and now, little by little, they're coming back out of the uncharted areas with their old ways. My kinfolks in Puebla cross themselves when they talk about it."

Colleen had found the water purification tabs now, and was reading the instructions on a flaccid bag of transparent plastic. "What for? They're not devil-worshipers or anything, are they?"

Odors of hot breakfast, but no answer. "Look, I asked you a question. And don't give me any of that headhunter shit, okay?"

"Hot stuff," he announced, and passed her disposable dish forward with its plastic tableware.

She held the dish in her hand. "Are you going to answer me?"

"Didn't want to worry you," he said, coming forward with difficulty. When at last he was seated beside her, he continued: "Okay, no devil-worship exactly—but they speak a language that was old when Rome was new, and they pray directly to the sun and sacrifice live animals, and in some places they've thrown the Catholic priests out so they can burn black candles and make sacrifices in the old ways. I gather it's not healthy to spend a night in some of those villages unless you speak Maya. And from what my Mexican grandfather claimed, their shamans have ways of knowing things, ways that have nothing to do with newspapers or TV news. Personally, I think that part has the reek of bullshit. Satisfied now?"

"Not very," she said, attacking a meal she would have sent back had it been served at Krista's Korner in Rogue River. "We're spending nights here, in case you didn't notice."

"Could be that none of those types are in the immediate area. Have you seen any sign of people?"

"Not that I know of. Could be animal trails I saw," she replied.

"Just don't worry about it; it wouldn't help."

"It would help if I knew you speak Maya."

He chuckled at that, jiggling the dish in his lap. "It sure would, but I don't. Most of them speak some Spanish, though; or so I was told. Stop worrying and eat." He gave every indication of taking his own advice.

COLLEEN HAD NEVER forced herself to question the validity of the Wes Hardin she had thought she knew until late that morning. Texans were macho, pilots of military jets remain cocky, and Ben Ullmer's second-in-command would, like the old man himself, show little enthusiasm for other people's improvements to his designs and less sensitivity toward anything but the technical details of a job; those were her self-imposed guidelines and she fought her personal wars on that basis.

She began to reconsider after Hardin suggested a means of hauling the Nemesis to shore. "The nose gear tiedown ring is above the waterline, so you can tie a 'chute cord to it," he said. "Run the cord ashore, tie it a foot from the butt end of an eight-foot wooden pole, and dig a shallow hole. Then stand the butt end in the hole, twist it 'til the line is tight, and haul back like hell on the top end," he finished. "You can tow a pickup out of a mudhole that way."

"I drag the bird maybe a foot closer," she said. "So?"

"And then another shallow hole a foot away, and so on. With that mechanical advantage, you can haul it ashore by yourself and pretty soon the bird's nose is over dry land," he said.

"And where will you be all this time," she said, with an eyebrow arched. "Singing 'Tote that barge, lift that bale'?"

"I can be digging holes," he said, "If you want my feet to get wet so you have to change my socks for me. That and hauling on bootlaces is something I just can't manage yet. Somehow I, uh," he faltered, and gave her a one-shouldered shrug, "that didn't seem like something you'd want to do, and wet feet in the tropics is a good way to let your feet rot off. And if my feet aren't up to it, I can't go to the nearest village to see if they have epoxy, or something we can use for rivets. But I reckon if I come up with jungle rot too bad to walk, you can go yourself. It's your option, Colleen."

"Some option. I'll keep your little footies dry," she

muttered, refusing to look at him, concentrating instead on the sketch as she developed it in her spiral notepad. Because she had failed to anticipate his simple engineering idea of multiple pivot holes, it seemed important that she improve it a little. She tapped the elementary sketch. "I can get even more mechanical advantage if I leave a few branches on the pole. Then I can turn it like a turnstile and just wind you in."

"Capstan drive," he said, his eyes lighting up. "Better still!"

"Also," she went on, "I'd rather pull on the propeller hub. That way we pull the bird ashore backward and the comm set antennas will be above the waterline."

"Well of fucking *course*," he said, slapping his forehead.

"You know why engineers have hunched shoulders and headaches, don't you," she asked slyly.

"That's always bothered me," he replied in the same vein.

"Because when they're asked a question, they do this," she said, raising her shoulders in an exaggerated shrug; "and when you give 'em the answer, they do that," she finished, with a resounding slap to her forehead.

He laughed in delight, and winced because it shook his upper body, and as they continued to plan their counterattack on fate Colleen Morrison could not escape a twinge of guilt. *This is not the Wes Hardin I know and loathe. I'm starting to wonder if that one ever existed. . . .*

FORTY-EIGHT

Sunday, May 28

THOUGH SIMON TORRES was the one who called Elath into the war council, the others did most of the talking as they studied regional maps. Torres wished that he had been able to take David Elath aside beforehand, to counsel patience. It is sometimes difficult, he would have said, for a trained military mind to accept orders from men who have only the vaguest ideas about the waging of war. But at the top, military men must do exactly that: achieve a political end by force after the politicians themselves fail to do it by negotiation. The word from Escobar was that his Mexican connections denied responsibility for the raid on Base Ana—but judging by their reluctance to discuss it, Escobar believed they were lying.

Elath, to his credit, kept a respectful silence until he had a fair grasp of what they wanted him to do. Once he understood the sheer magnitude of the operation, Elath made one point clear: It was one thing to demand a general disruption of isthmus traffic and a blown hydroelectric dam, and quite another to make it all happen on short notice.

The cartel did not like what Elath told them about their decision on that predawn Sunday. Torres liked their response even less: essentially, do or die. Elath had supposedly trained those senderistas as sappers, bridge-blowers; and now was the time to test them. If most of the senderista teams failed to return, they would die doing what they liked doing most.

Elath understood, but pointed out that he needed the best-trained of those Peruvians for such work. Trucks and vans could transport them anonymously to their bridges, plastique and all, but Mexican federals might be watching their roads afterward. Without some means to get the guerrillas back to Base Ana, the cartel might be expending their best men.

It was the younger Palacios who suggested scrambler bikes, which could detour across a mile of open country to avoid a roadblock. "Those Peruvians are more crazy about lightweight motorcycles than Mexicans are," said Gaitan Palacios. "We could buy scores of them, one or two from every salesroom between Veracruz and Villahermosa. Each truck or utility van could carry an entire team with their getaway vehicles. Surely they are not too ignorant to use maps."

"Surely," Elath agreed, looking up from a map, using a tone that Simon Torres feared was dangerously close to insolence. "We would make a great mistake to underestimate the average guerrilla. He knows the chances he takes, and he reads a map better than he reads comic books. Your idea would have great appeal," Elath said, making the young drug lord beam. "They might even refuse without some such means of escape. We can expand the missions of some teams to blow more than one bridge. Could you provide twenty of those scramblers and a dozen enclosed trucks by, say, Monday noon at Base Ana?"

When Gaitan Palacios said he could, Torres began to breathe more easily despite his pounding headache. He knew that the responsibility for these coordinated strikes lay squarely with Elath, and that Elath was his man. *It's his neck and mine both,* Torres reflected, and then began to take more interest in the logistics.

When they had placed a red X on the last chosen railroad bridge, Elath gained permission to take that map with him. "We have much to do in little time. I must see the Chicoasen damn, for one thing, before I can know how my team must deal with it."

"It is festooned with lights," Torres said, massaging his temples.

"Then I could see it at any hour," said Elath.

"Why not," Torres shrugged.

"We should go now," Elath said simply, "and fly past the dam before we return to Base Ana. The sooner I arrive there, the sooner I can begin assembling the sapper teams."

"I will fly him there now in the Pilatus," Torres offered. Flying the float-equipped little monoplane was better than no action at all.

"But you cannot land at Base Ana," Vega warned him. "Our pilot said it is too dangerous before the runways are cleared and patched."

Torres waved away the objection. "For him, perhaps; not for me. Bermudez must know of these decisions right away. Please tell him to have his men clear the taxi strip for me, right now, even if they have to do it with flashlights." The sooner he got out of that meeting, the better. "If they surround the cleared area with any kind of lights, I can put down with room to spare."

As Torres and Elath prepared to leave, old Perez Palacios made it clear once again that he retained some doubt about the outcome of this revenge mission. "We might be wise to transfer certain of our personal funds, brothers, to accounts not easily reached by the Mexican government."

"We must do nothing of the sort," Vega snorted, "unless we want the Mexicans to think we lack confidence."

"I leave that to you, brothers," Torres said, leading Elath to the door. "I will be too busy making war." *Any-*

one who does not already have fifty million or so in some Bahamian bank is a fool, he thought as he strode out.

———————————

IN THE PILATUS, their roundabout flight to Base Ana took less than two hours. The dam at Chicoasen lay in difficult country, but Elath exulted when he saw it. "Since it is deep but not overly broad or thick, we will not need tons of plastique," he called over the turbine's whine, beginning to enjoy the challenge despite himself. "We can float almost to the spillway in darkness, and lower our charge like a fishing weight. The depth itself will help concentrate the shock."

Torres nodded and flew on. Benzedrine had done little for his headache but it kept him alert, even edgy, and he swore furiously as he approached Base Ana because at first he thought he had made a navigational error. Then he discovered that the pattern of mercury vapor lights outside the processing sheds, which he had always used to orient him at the airstrip, was nowhere to be seen. He was forced to make two passes over the base before he saw the torches resolve themselves into parallel lines.

One more slow pass over those torches with his landing lights boring holes into the night, and Torres saw that they had cleared only part of the taxi strip. He also spotted numerous craters, and knew that he needed more room than usual with those wheeled floats added to the Pilatus. "This may be a rough landing," he called to Elath.

It was all of that. Without lights to define the end of the strip, he overshot and then compensated so much so that he struck too hard on one side, rebounding unevenly. Elath cried, *"Look out!"* but already he had strayed to one edge of the strip, missing a crater partly filled with rubble but unable to avoid running off the hard surface. He saw the chunk of rubble he hit an instant before his float slammed into it, the Pilatus shuddering, almost nosing over, and then Torres swerved the aircraft back onto the runway. He admitted then that their Catemaco pilot had been right, but he had made some semblance of a landing after all.

He taxied all the way to the opposite end of the airstrip, his lights picking out crater after crater, a ragged line of damage that told him he would not be landing his T-33 there until repairs had been made. He snapped off his switches near what was left of the hangar, aghast at the little he could see, and noted with wry amusement that Elath piled out of the aircraft without a word and in a great hurry.

Alvaro Bermudez walked up while Torres was inspecting his floats. "And how do you like what the bastards have done to us here," Bermudez growled.

"Let me have your flashlight," Torres replied. After a moment he added, "I wonder how they will like our response. Vega must have consulted you," he said. He was peering at the underside of that float, the slender hull of aluminum that first touches down in a water landing. No longer smooth, it bore a deep gouge that became a hole like a sugar scoop. He would not be landing the Pilatus on water, either, until repairs were made.

"Vega told me," Bermudez said darkly. Then in quieter tones: "Listen, Torres, my people are spoiling for a fight. If we did not give them a set of targets very soon, we might have become targets ourselves."

"They will have their fight," Torres promised, and proceeded to outline the tactics by which the entire Mexican isthmus would become paralyzed in a single night. The very mention of such vengeance put a note of savage elation in Torres's account.

Elath stood by, listening silently until Torres had finished. Bermudez, who had learned to respect Elath's opinion, said, "And what is your honest opinion of all this, Elath?"

"It reminds me of another battle in World War Two," he said, "the Battle of the Bulge."

"You can be more specific than that," Bermudez prompted.

''The German counterstrike came unexpectedly, and worked without flaw for a time,'' Elath said, ''but it worked so well because the Allies were expecting the usual rational German strategy. Ultimately it failed because the underlying strategy was insane. And remember, you asked me.''

Bermudez flung his arms up and out. ''Look what they have done to us! You will see when dawn comes. What else could we do now?''

''My honest opinion,'' Elath said as if to himself.

''Naturally!''

''You are senderistas and Colombians,'' said the Mexican Jew, looking now into the eyes of Simon Torres. ''There is nothing else you could do now.''

FORTY-NINE

Sunday, May 28

Jared Cutter had done everything they told him to do; had brought his passengers back to Kingsville without a scratch; and finally, on Sunday morning, had learned from Curt Christiansen that Meacham had already left, furious because no one intended to airlift Morrison and Hardin from that lake in southern Chiapas.

"Other plans, they said," Christiansen told him, deep in disgust for the outfit he served, pacing the ready room of the Coast Guard hangar in Kingsville. He held up a hand to forestall Cutter's reply. "Let's take a walk, shall we?"

Strolling toward the taxiway, Cutter and the CIA pilot spoke quietly, earnestly, Cutter unconsciously walking with head bowed.

Five minutes later, Christiansen concluded their discussion by presenting Cutter with a wad of money and a handshake. Cutter, his back now somewhat straighter, strode fast to keep pace with the longer legs of Christiansen. "I hope you can come up with that hardware, Curt. You're a man after my own heart."

"I owed you," said the CIA pilot as they separated. Five paces away he added, "And never mind your heart; just try and stay one jump ahead of whoever's after your ass."

* * *

AFTER A LONG shopping foray to Corpus Christi, Cutter returned alone to the hangar. Because he thought the mountain air might be chilly, he had chosen inexpensive sleeping bags as drop containers; and because he was not an idiot, he made sure the zippers of those bags did not match.

No one had left any packages for him at the ready room. "C'est la guerre," he murmured, and carried one of the lump-filled bags to his Nemesis, which sat fueled and waiting for his departure. He found a duffel bag between the seats, scrambled in, lowered the canopy, and moments later found himself holding a little M1A1 Winchester, its wire stock folded flat. An unsigned note read: *Sorry, only one available, Mexican army issue. Lightness counts! Rumor says an LRP packing in to recover assets within a week.* Cutter, though too young to have had the Vietnam experience, knew Christiansen's acronym referred to long range patrols.

Christiansen's choice of radios, a pair of commercial units with hefty battery packs, was less satisfying at first glance but made sense; if Colleen and Wes had to separate, they could remain in touch. Cutter could pass the word that the downed pair just might have a walkie-talkie or two along.

When Cutter finished packing, the righthand seat of Sleeper Three was occupied by almost as much mass as Colleen's own. *Not as cute, though,* he reminded himself, and then checked his watch.

A sensible chief exec, he reflected, would be down the Oregon coast—Bandon, perhaps—with his family, enjoying the holiday; so he went to an off-base bar and called the factory, and identified himself to Ben Ullmer. "Why did I know you'd be there," he asked.

"Don't stroke me off," Ullmer growled instantly. "I couldn't leave 'til I knew my crews were back."

"Well, I made it, Mr. Ullmer, and the bird's still cherry. Little problem with Wes and Colleen, though. They took some damage, enough that she had to put down in a shallow lake near the Guatemala border."

"She? You mean she let Hardin into her bird and he let her fly it? Shit, that's not important," the old man berated himself, and started asking better questions.

Cutter answered in bright, upbeat tones, and knew that he wasn't fooling the old man. "By the way, I haven't called you, sir. In debriefing they mentioned my nuts and a vise in the same phrase, and I'm rather attached to 'em."

"God *damn* the bastards, I can't even use my contacts without putting one of my people in deep shit," Ullmer raged. "Well, I can start asking, anyhow. Come home, Cutter, I need you."

"No, sir. They gave me clearance to light out of here around dawn—but I've got to be straight with you, Mr. Ullmer. I've decided to take me a little detour."

"The hell you will!"

"Yessir, sorry, but yes I will. Sorry, sir."

"Quit saying that, Cutter, or I'll fire you here and now. Come home."

And then the old guy will be off the hook for this! "Yessir. And no, sir." Silence. "I said, no sir," Cutter repeated. Silence. "Well then: Fuck you very much, sir," Cutter said, doing the best he could on short notice.

In utter disbelief: "Jared gyrene Cutter, are you *trying* to get your ass fired?"

Cutter had to clear his throat before he could say, "No comment, sir, you old devil."

Another long silence. Then, in what might have been deep suspicion, Ullmer asked, "Where are you going to detour?"

"Thought I might go south a ways, look around, burn

up a little fuel, drop a few things, sir. In your bird, too.''
Trying to avoid a wheedling tone now, Cutter rushed on:
''I really think you better fire me now, sir.''

''What for? Not that I lack reasons, you understand,''
Ullmer said.

''Grand theft, aircraft,'' Cutter said; and, ''insubordi-
nation too, damn your eyes, isn't that enough? How about,
whatthefuck do they call it, emotional instability? You can't
trust a man of my stripe, sir, you old devil.''

''You already said that. And you don't have a stripe,
you have a dotted line, Cutter, and you're tearing around
it right now. And I think I understand, and you—are—
fired. Satisfied?''

''Thank you very much, sir. Just one thing: Would you
mind not calling anybody about me until maybe oh-eight-
hundred hours your time tomorrow?'' *Whatever happens*,
Cutter told himself, *I could be in the air before he gets
anyone down here to stop me. Unless he lies. And he won't
do that.*

''I can do that, Cutter. But I warn you, if you try to
come back to work for me it'll be at a higher salary. You
understand me?''

''Yes, *sir*,'' said Cutter.

FIFTY

Monday, May 29

Wᴇs Hᴀʀᴅɪɴ ᴅɪsᴄᴏᴠᴇʀᴇᴅ on Monday morning that by using one hand and his teeth, he could at last make use of his merit badge in knot-tying. Colleen, as she trimmed an oak sapling with its stub branches, complained to him that a ringsaw could give her blisters through her gloves. Though the cord and pole scheme brought the rear end of their Nemesis slewing around, Colleen could not make it drag the aft end of her bird ashore through all that tule grass until she had used her bush knife to scythe away many square yards of it.

Wes chose more of Cutter's defrosted meals for their breakfast, cursing the injury that kept him from work he wanted to perform. "Come and get it," he called as she stood, breast heaving, shin deep in water.

She waded around to the cockpit and reached up for the dish, too tired to climb to the cockpit sill, then made her way back to shore where she sat, only a few feet from one of the rudder booms. Wes put his dish into a zipper pocket, its film wrap protecting the contents, and negotiated the distance from the cockpit back to the wing. For a man with only one good arm this was a chancy maneuver, yet he did not want to eat alone. *Besides, little by little I'm almost learning to enjoy her company,* he thought. "You didn't think the help was going to eat in the kitchen?"

Her smile was abstracted as she stared at her meal. "Beef stroganoff for breakfast? Could be worse, I guess," she said, spooning into it.

"I kept the real breakfast for myself," he said. "Chicken à la king. There's coffee, but you'd have to come in and get it."

"Too damn' bushed," she said.

They ate in companionable silence for a few minutes. Wes gazing at the treeline hundreds of feet above them, catching a glimpse of a parrot's bright plumage through the treetops nearer. Finally he said, "I'm really sorry, Colleen. You shouldn't have to do it all by yourself."

Her response was typical of a gradual change in her attitude from belligerence to grudging acceptance with a brittle edge on it: "Yeah, yeah, that's what they all say," she muttered.

He chuckled, and she looked her question at him; he said, "There can't have been many of 'em, I figure."

"So what am I, a charity case in the economics of romance?"

"Hey, that's almost good," he said. "A mile off the mark, but it makes a feller think."

"If it got *you* thinking, it must've been a stunner," she said. Then, "Just an unpublished scribbler's repartee, Hardin. But what made you think I was a demivirgin?"

"I wasn't thinking in those terms. It's just that you make yourself so unapproachable, a guy needs earplugs and a titanium overcoat to get near. My grampa would've said dealing with you is like," he thrust his lower jaw forward and pursed his lips for a classic, economical Texas plains drawl, "tryin' to ram a prickly p'ar up a wahlcat's ass with a hot poker."

"Your grandparents were from Mexico," she objected.

"My mother's folks, not the Hardin clan; Gawd a'mighty, ma'am, spoke like a social leopard," he said with an eye roll, then lapsed back into his normal accent. "Took nearly seven years for my Hardin grampa to come to terms with my dad marrying a 'meskin gal.' "

He seemed to have her friendly attention now as she asked, "Do they really say things like 'social leopard'?"

"Grampa did. He bought and sold livestock around Sweetwater, up to Lubbock. He wrote a decent letter and he knew the citified ways to say things, all right, he just wanted an edge."

"I don't get it," she complained.

"Buying and selling. He used to say, 'If the city boy thinks you're three brain cells duller'n a dandelion, you got your minnow halfway in the bucket.' He just helped 'em think what they already wanted to think. It worked for him."

"Your grandpa sounds like a shrewd businessman," she said, smiling.

"Oh, yeah. A bigot, God help him, but," and he jutted his jaw forward again, "he c'd sell june bugs to a Sunday-school teacher."

She shook her head, pursuing a morsel of beef, and sighed. "You've lost me again, Hardin."

"Oh. Well, a june bug's a big flying beetle, and an enterprising kid can grab a dozen of 'em on a summer Sunday morning, if his folks don't check his pockets too well. An old sport at home; a pocketful of june bugs turned loose can liven up a Sunday-school lesson something wonderful. You'd be surprised," he said over her laughter. "But I guess you had to be there."

"Thank God I wasn't," she replied, still smiling, rising with a grunt. "The Rogue rats, I mean my brothers, would've loved it. Well, back to—" she put her hand out, palm down, head cocked to one side in a way he found utterly appealing. "What's that?"

And when he listened, he heard it too; and then both of them were shouting, waving, at the vast shadow that flitted over the lake, attended by the humming whisper of shrouded propeller blades.

Wes knew that only two Nemesis craft in existence lacked Coast Guard insignia, and he was sitting on one of them. Lazing at forty knots, the great gossamer spookship seemed to travel even slower. Only one person was inside the canopy, head turned in their direction, waving back.

"It's Jarhead," he shouted, and stood up.

After its second pass, the Nemesis dropped its nose in a shallow, formal bow above the open greensward that Colleen had discovered. "Don't try it," Colleen screamed as Cutter gained altitude for his turn.

"Relax, his gear's up," Wes called. Again Cutter passed near them, head turned in their direction, and they could see his right arm elevated, punching a forefinger forward in an exaggerated gesture toward the grassy area. That was when Colleen set off at a dead run, splashing through shallows, toward the end of the lake.

Again Cutter ducked the nose of his Nemesis over the greensward, and now Wes could see that he had the canopy partly open. The Nemesis had not been designed with this in mind; if you didn't want the canopy, you jettisoned it before punching out. If you wanted it, you didn't open it in flight. But the maneuver could be done if you pushed it partly open and kept the bird loafing slowly enough. If you loafed it one knot too slowly, you needed a hundred feet or more of altitude to recover. And Jared Cutter had less than half that much air under him. "Hold the controls with your knees," Wes said to no one nearby. "You've got a weight advantage, so you can go slower and keep the canopy wind loads down."

Evidently Cutter did not need to be told. The Nemesis bobbled in midair while less than a wingspan above the grass, and then a body was falling into the grass, and an instant later Wes realized that it was not a body at all but a brown cloth bag the size of one. By this time, Colleen Morrison had slowed her headlong sprint but continued to trot doggedly toward her goal.

Wes held up his good arm, thumb and forefinger an "OK" circle, and kept it that way to be certain Cutter would see it on his next pass. That next pass, however, began over the drop zone with a second body that became a dark green bag, and then Cutter's bird wheeled on one wingtip, the canopy in place again, and Wes saw a faint smoky trail from the engine cowl that said, even before its muted drone reached him, that Cutter had begun powering up his rotary engine for a fast climb. And as Jared Cutter passed fifty yards from his downed sister ship, he was staring straight at Wes, making a repetitive gesture: forefinger to lips, then out, then back to lips again. When he ended the pantomime with a mock salute, Wes knew that Cutter was leaving. The sense of loss he felt then was like a physical impact from inside his breastbone.

Wes had seen Colleen throwing kisses into the air. He did the same thing, then nodded and grinned like a fool, and kept waving until Cutter's pencil-slender, ninety-foot wing disappeared over the northeast ridge. He saw it again five minutes later, now only a curiously assembled group of splinters in the sky, and intuition told him that Jared Cutter was using maximum gain on his video display. He did not delude himself for a moment that Cutter was watching *him*. Near the lake's end, Colleen stood peering up, a tiny waifish figure in a scaled-down flight suit, until Cutter and his Nemesis had climbed from sight.

COLLEEN USED UP an hour lugging the bags back over her shoulder, one at a time, and sat down heavily before she fell backward, arms out in a melodramatic show of exhaustion within ten yards of her companion. Wes sat on the wing with the patience of a cat in a sunny window until she managed to exclaim, "Hardin, I'll tighten your damned bootlaces."

"*Yeahhhh,*" he whooped, and eased himself down to

the wing's trailing lip before plunging to shore. "Let's haul this bird into drydock!"

But Colleen wanted to check into those sleeping bags first. They pulled the treasures out like two children under a Christmas tree, exclaiming at some of them. "Air mattresses! And would you believe thirty-six Hershey bars," she said, holding up a carton the size of a shoebox. "Shit, no almonds. Jarhead, how could you do that to me?"

"A six-pack of Lone Star, the man is an angel," Wes replied in Cutter's defense, and then he pulled out the twin of Colleen's survival kit. "There'd better be another bush knife in here," he warned, and sighed with relief when he found it.

Colleen pulled a long bundle of nylon out. When she unwrapped it she found that it was a tiny dome tent, and inside with a dismantled backpack lay a stocky little carbine wrapped in a plastic dropcloth with an envelope attached. She laid the weapon to one side without a word and opened the envelope.

Wes had trouble extracting his nylon bundle, a tent identical to Colleen's, and found taped boxes of thirty-caliber ammunition inside a backpack. He stood up and shook the sleeping bag, dumping more articles out, including—"A walkie-talkie and a fifth of Johnny Walker," he breathed. "Cutter, if you weren't so ugly I could kiss you." Then he saw Colleen reading. "Hey: What does it say?"

She cleared her throat and read: " 'Thought I'd drop by on my way home. I'm AWOL, so burn this. Hope Hardin can walk out, got my doubts from what my passengers said but maybe a swig of good booze will help. Chickenshit SOBs cite "Overriding sensitive political issue" and won't fly in for you, but hang tight, rumor claims team en route to you on foot but I figure that could take a week. *Don't count on rumor*, but don't shoot the good guys if they show. I'll send word you've got radios. Everything here, you brought in yourselves, okay? C. C. doesn't want his stuff back, you guess which, supposed to be Mexican fed piece. Bucksaw may need those extra blades if you're cutting up spars and stuff. My personal recommendation is, just go. Saturday dawn I saw cluster of lights three klicks north-northeast of you, give or take a point, but be careful. Burn this now, Colleen. Love, Jarhead.' Aww, Cutter,'' she said, her eyes brimming. "Who's C. C.?"

"Curt Christiansen,'' Wes replied, reaching for the carbine. "The guy who greased us into the airstrip. He's not the kind who'd leave us hanging out to dry. I'll give you odds this thing doesn't have a traceable serial number.''

"So there's honor among spooks," Colleen said, half to herself, and Wes began to laugh softly as he fumbled to release the Winchester's thirty-round magazine. "Don't laugh, Hardin, I figured them for a pretty cold lot.''

He shook his head and sighed. "Colleen, maybe it never occurred to you, but—you've got more honor than good sense. That's not a guess. That's a fact. Well, ever since you signed on for this little caper, you've been a contract employee of—guess who?''

She caught her breath, her eyes widening. "Oh, bullshit. That's different, I'm, uh—''

"You can say it: You're CIA, Colleen. Guys like Christiansen call 'em the customer sometimes, because Curt's a temporary subcontractor. Just like I am. Just like *you* are. Sure we're deniable, our paper trail would lead to a naked airstrip that's practically unimproved open range in Central Oregon. But yes'm, there's honor among some spooks. Yes, *ma'am*,'' he finished. "Now gimme a Hershey and I'll talk you through loading a thirty-round magazine.''

"You ex-military types,'' she snorted. "I couldn't shoot anybody.''

She hates to back down from any position she takes, so don't argue. Give her a different reason, a small insight whispered to him. "Okay, let's say somebody starts shooting at *you*. Mean to say you wouldn't bust a few caps off over his head, just to keep him honest?''

She shook her head, but passed him a chocolate bar, and then began to study the carbine. "Just big boys with dangerous toys," she scoffed. "I even have to give you a piece of candy. You watch: We'll never use this thing."

"Umm," he replied with a faceful of chocolate. *I sure hope you're right, lady,* he thought, showing her what he remembered of the once-ubiquitous little military carbine. With automatic fire and an effective range of over three hundred yards, it hurled a slug that carried enough mass to penetrate brush without too much deflection. Better still, its recoil was acceptable to a preteen, or to a ninety-pound heller in a flight suit. No matter that she intended never to use it, Wes knew that the little weapon was now among her options.

And after another hour, with his efforts added to Colleen's against that rough oak pole, Wes Hardin saw the trailing edge of their Nemesis wing creep to the shoreline. He sweated harder than she did because of the pain, but denied it when she asked. "One more foot and our antennas will start to clear the waterline," he panted.

She nodded and grinned, until she saw his face. "You always bite your lip when you work? Don't answer; I hate it when people lie to me. Now go on board and perch your butt on the windscreen."

"Just one more foot," he said.

"Your weight will drop the bird's nose, Hardin, you doofus. And I can stick these ponderosa branches under its tail feathers to keep the antennas clear. . . . Well, don't just stand there, what's wrong?"

"Nothing. I was just thinking about an engineering education—and why I thought I had one," he said sheepishly.

They stopped for lunch when their shadows began to lengthen again, but by then they knew their dilemma. The torn skin of their Nemesis could have been patched at any service garage in the Western Hemisphere, but here they lacked the simple drills, pliers, and soft iron wire to make those primitive repairs. They chewed the problem over until they agreed that the tools they had on board would not make those repairs. Wes, wiggling his naked toes while his boots dried—like jungle boots, their fabric tops dried quickly—set his dish aside and took a final swig of instant coffee. "So I guess the next thing is for you to help me with dry socks."

"Just stay barefoot awhile," she suggested. "I'm going to."

"Yeah, but you're not going down the mountain to find the tools we need," he said.

"But you can't. I mean you're hurt."

"Feller doesn't walk on his collarbone, Colleen. I can swing a machete if I do it easy."

"And leave me alone?"

"Nope; I'll go look for Señor Goodwrench, and you'll stay here with Señor Winchester. Stay on board and try the comm set again, if you want to."

She helped him with his socks and boots, repeating over and over that she thought his foray risky, finally turning over the Beretta to him, shoving a half-dozen chocolate bars into one of his thigh pockets with the survival kit compass and money. They tried the little radios before he crammed one of them inside his suit near his left armpit. "I should be back before dark," he said as he headed for the northeast edge of the lake.

"And I still don't understand why," she said. "You could buy the right clothes and hitch a ride out."

"I dunno. Call me irresponsible. Honor among spooks, maybe. You said so yourself." He turned and moved off without waving.

FIFTY-ONE

Sunday, May 28

WHEN MIKE CONTRERAS assured his superiors that he could control Harry Rex Brown, he thought it was true. "Harry knows where we're going and for him, covert ops are SOP. Believe me, insertion teams are a way of life for this guy; he's one of us and doesn't know it." But that had been on Saturday, before Contreras discovered just how much Harry lived in his own hermetically sealed universe.

On Sunday, Mike had used timetables, maps, and logic diagrams to show why their expedition could not possibly fail, and then asked Harry to show him how it could. It turned out that Harry had not been listening closely. Instead he had been sulking because he had not been introduced, with proper fanfare, to "his" other men.

So Mike got them all together on Sunday night, perfectly aware that the old Company hands would dismiss Harry as a kook within five minutes. Mike had enough time with the Company deniables beforehand to tell them the essentials about Harry, summarizing it with: "It's a two-act play. Act One: You abide by his rules on the way in, and don't go showing him how your packs fieldstrip unless we come under fire. Act Two: We recover our assets and exfiltrate into Guatemala at double-time, no matter what he says.''

Bogosian, lank and laconic with a thousand-yard squint, provoked murmurs from the others as he said, ''Wonderful. You're telling us our guide is a flake.''

''The man is dandruff city,'' Mike nodded, ''but he keeps getting in and out of the area without casualties. If he has to play leadership games, I propose to let him until we reach our objective. If you can't handle that, tell me right now.''

They grumbled, but they went along with the idea. One of them, who was half Sioux and looked it, said he found nothing wrong with a man who saw beyond ordinary reality into his own visions. As for himself, Mike Contreras had taken orders from flakes who *didn't* know where they were going, and he was perfectly content to let Harry operate as their leader unless and until they met hostiles. Mike had sat around maintaining his State Department cover in Veracruz and awaiting a taste of action for so long he would have followed Little Red Riding Hood. And if they never met the wolf, Harry Rex Brown would never need to know that his team carried more clout than one Enfield revolver. Mike thought it would play.

The choice of team members and the travel setup belonged, as Mike said, to the guy paying the bills. As a result, Harry took Mike's word that the eight tough, hard-eyed men he met were accomplished backpackers. Furthermore, he loved Mike's travel arrangements because they were both unscheduled and first class, beginning with that chartered Grumman Gulfstream jet. It covered the 2400 miles from Salt Lake City to Belize City, on the Gulf of Honduras, in just over four hours, and deposited them shortly after noon on Monday. As Mike had promised, the Belize authorities were primed to ignore them.

Harry seemed impressed that, from Utah to Belize, no

one showed enough interest in them to run their bags through a scanner. He watched as the others picked up their luggage. Mike had already shown Harry what lay inside the B-4 bags and shapeless newer kinds of baggage: identical backpacks of very modern design, in subdued green nylon with hefty steel rails. Harry shouldered his old canvas pack and asked, "Where do we pick up our connecting flight?"

"Should be waiting in the hangar," Mike told him, nodding without a word toward a sunburnt member of the group almost Harry's height, then pointing some distance away from the terminal so that Harry could stride out in the lead. Two of the men picked up their gear, prepared to accompany Mike. When Harry paused, noting that six of their number were rapidly disappearing in different directions. Mike patted his shoulder. "It's okay, Harry, remember? They'll be along. We don't want to look like an army, do we?"

"I wouldn't want any of my people to get lost," Harry muttered, resuming his pace.

"This is where we split up," Mike said. "A couple with us, the others in two more aircraft a half-hour apart. We'll leave first in the stoll."

"I thought we were supposed to take a big Cessna."

"Not a big one, Harry, but for a little tail-dragger it's Arnold Schwarzenegger. I told you, a Cessna two-oh-six is a stoll, S-T-O-L, as in short takeoff and land. It'll be loaded with the pilot and four of us with our packs, and they tell me there's not much of a runway at Quingua."

"I know it well," Harry replied with a sage nod. "Near Chacula ruin at the Mexican border. So I'll have to wait an hour for the rest of my men. Is that the way we do it?"

Mike tried to make his sigh inaudible. "Yes, Harry, that's the way we do it." *Christ, I briefed him on all this, what was he thinking about? Oh yeah, right; he was sulking.* Mike checked his watch, which he had already set ahead an hour for the change in time zone. "By sixteen-hundred hours we should all be assembled again."

The little Cessna with its huge flaps and its English-speaking pilot was waiting, and the man wasted no time asking questions before he hauled his four passengers into the humid afternoon above the nearby swamp, turning southwest for the two-hour trip from Belize into Guatemala.

Mike had seen it before, those thousands of square miles of northern Guatemala known, since the time of conquistadores, as the Peten. A mile above that trackless jungle the treetops looked like a ruler-flat carpet of dark green, punctuated here and there by gleams of stagnant water and small green pimples that might be natural features. Or they might be manmade, overgrown for centuries as the jungle took them back from a civilization that had begun to fade before Columbus. A few ruins stood out as chalk gray piles of stone, reclaimed for the moment by archaeologists after age-long sleep beneath that green blanket.

"Yaxha," Harry called out above the engine's drone, and pointed below. Mike saw sun glints on a lake, and ruins that squatted on an island in that lake. He nodded. "Unusual layout for Maya," Harry went on.

"Good defensive position," Mike called back. "Been there?"

Harry shook his head. "It's been in here," he replied, tapping his forehead.

Gradually the jungle lowland, with its glimpses of swamp through the solid canopy of trees, gave way to foliage subtly different as they flew westward; fewer broad-leafed palm fans, more stands of conifers as the land tilted up, the soil deepening, encouraging taproots. Now they were flying from lands that had been defeated by the Spaniard's armored fist and into Maya highlands, a region that had never entirely surrendered to Spanish conquest, the old ways resurgent because Highland Maya had never really given them up. *They might not understand the dialect I learned,* Contreras reflected, staring uneasily down on forested slopes distinctly more bluish than the lowlands. *Okay, so Harry's a flake. I'm glad he's with me.*

Now they passed over deep creases in the earth where watercourses ran swift and white from the fastness of volcanic peaks more than ten thousand feet above sea level. The Cessna no longer maintained a mile of altitude above the highland ridges, and Contreras spotted groups of tan rectangles on lower valley slopes: thatched roofs. Nearby lay irregular patches of brown, cultivated land with crops too recently planted to be identifiable. Once he spotted a stark white skeleton of stone, a church with a bell tower in the Spanish style, its bell missing, its roof long since crumbled. *At least the Yucatan Maya in the lowlands still maintain most of their Catholicism,* Contreras thought. *These people have gone back to something a whole lot older.* Though not much of a Catholic himself, Mike Contreras found these thoughts unsettling as the Cessna's engine lazed back to a purr.

Their pilot had been well briefed, and Mike Contreras did not have to tell him to land without any more noise than necessary. In their descent they circled well beyond the village—it had to be Quingua—before returning to the simple airstrip, the Cessna's big flaps buffeting softly with cupped air, keeping the aircraft afloat at a speed low enough to land them safely. Contreras scrambled out first, helping the others dismount from this flimsy craft, making certain they had left nothing behind but the bags that had disguised their packs. The pilot said nothing at all, merely checking his watch, before he secured the passenger door and gunned his engine. *This guy has inserted teams before,* Contreras decided, walking with his pack toward tree shadows. "We've got an hour," he said, reaching into his breast pocket. "Smoke, if you've got 'em."

"No smoking," said Harry Rex Brown. One man merely shrugged and popped a lemon drop from his shirt pocket. Bogosian was already feeding a shorty Camel one-handed from a rumpled pack, and seemed not to have heard the prohibition. He lit up from an ancient Zippo and inhaled deeply, stretching kinks from his back. Mike watched as Harry ambled over to the impassive Bogosian. *No, not already,* he begged in silence.

Bogosian sat down and fired twin streams of smoke from his nostrils, and smiled at Harry without speaking. Harry did not make the mistake of looming over Bogosian, but squatted next to him and pushed his scruffy old snap-brim hat back. "You're Aram Bogosian, aren't you?"

"You remembered," said Bogosian, taking another drag.

Harry smiled. "Aram, how long since you packed sixty pounds up a cliff at eight-thousand-foot altitude?"

"A while," Bogosian admitted, with a smoky exhalation that Harry had to wave aside. "Don't worry about it."

"Okay, I won't. And if you were smoking Mexican cigarettes, we'd be okay. They smell very different, Aram. A Maya lives as part of the countryside, and he pays attention to odors. I have a friend named Yaxpoc, you'll meet him in a day or two; and Yaxpoc can smell a cigarette through a hundred yards of palmetto thicket. If it's some Mexican penny-dreadful brand he might just warn me there's someone else very near. But a Winston or a Camel will tell him it's somebody who can afford very expensive smoke, which may mean federales or foreigners." Again that smile. "You with me, Aram?"

"Getting there," said Bogosian, sighing. He studied the tip of his Camel. "You're claiming these people are like Montagnards, back in the Nam; they can use their noses better'n most."

"Much better, Aram. In your lungs, American cigarettes will kill you slowly like any other kind. In the bosque, they can get you killed a lot faster."

Because Bogosian had not yet told his guide to fuck off, Mike began to breathe again. Now Bogosian appeared more curious than pissed. "Boskey?"

"Bosque. The stuff we're getting into; a rain forest in the high country. The air's humid and often very still, and a penetrating odor may hang around for quite a while." Harry's grin, when he finally used it, tended to be infectious. "Have I made my point, Aram?"

Bogosian grinned back and held up the Camel. "This'll be the last one. Your point is made."

Harry nodded and stood up. "Thanks, Aram," he said.

All this time, Mike realized, the nearest of the other men had been standing well out of the way, as though their sidekick Bogosian were a boil that might rupture at any moment. Harry's back was turned before Bogosian said, "Hey," very softly.

Here it comes, Mike thought.

Harry turned, and Bogosian spoke. "You're okay, Harry. I guess this is your Nam, huh?"

"I suppose," Harry replied, "except that we don't shoot people here."

"Whatever you say, Harry," Bogosian said, chuckling. Then he turned to the others and shrugged as if to explain his mild behavior. "When he's right, he's right," Bogosian said.

The nearest man merely lifted an eyebrow and nodded as he sucked his lemon drop. *I think*, Mike told himself, *Harry's leadership qualities may surprise us.*

SHORTLY AFTER FOUR in the afternoon, Harry Rex Brown swept his arm forward in a gesture Mike had seen many times on reruns of *Wagon Train*. Mike, moving off toward the northwest at the back of the ten-man file, found himself approving of Harry Rex Brown more as Harry proved himself. The trails in this region were rocky but dry, the footing treacherous on the slopes. Harry set a moderate pace, a sensible tactic for the first day, and gave them short breaks every half-hour. Some of the men smoothed wrinkles from socks; others used the five-minute pauses to locate items in their packs that, despite careful packing, tended to make a clink or a clatter on the trail.

The sun lay an hour above peaks on their horizon when Harry passed the word that they were now in Chiapas, on Mexican soil. They descended into a valley and avoided a tiny settlement only to find the ribbon of blacktop their maps promised. While they paralleled it inside the treeline in search of a half-mile of unimpeded view, a Volkswagen bus farted past, festive with painted decoration and so crammed with crouched human bodies that Mike could not see the opposite windows.

The burly medic just ahead of Mike chuckled as their eyes met. "Like sophomores in a phone booth," he said.

"It's a co-op bus line," Mike explained. "Beats a burro. By tomorrow we'll wish we had one."

Crossing the flat of the valley they made good time, and Harry did not call another break until they had put three more miles behind them. "That ruin a mile to your left," he told them, "is Chinkultic. Sometimes a guard camps there and I'd just as soon not have him wondering about us, but from here on north you can see we won't have a flat spot."

Mike, to avoid a sunset lecture: "What do you want of us, Harry?"

"We should stop here tonight. Only one small fire, the locals sometimes do that, or none at all."

In the same way that some men will go out of their way to demonstrate a capacity for consuming hamburgers or swimming under water, these men all waited for someone else to speak up in favor of a fire, and that night they made a cold camp.

FIFTY-TWO

Monday, May 29

WES LEANED AGAINST the slickbark trunk of a madrone tree, the two-way radio in his good hand. "After I climbed the first ridge it's all been downhill, Colleen. I'm following this little peekaboo creek down a dry wash, it keeps petering out and petering back in; probably an underground runoff from our lake, over." Though the shoulder throbbed from a mile or so of walking, Hardin felt relatively fresh, only his shins feeling fatigue on the downhill slope.

Her reply was clear in the tiny speaker: "Can you see the town yet, over?"

"Yep, if you can call it that. A dozen grass shacks; actually adobe walls with some kind of thatching on top. If Cutter saw lights, I bet they weren't electric. No power lines that I can see and no sign of a road, either. I make it another klick north-northeast and five hundred feet lower, over."

"Okay, I'm marking that on the chart. Just remember it's all uphill on the way back, so get your butt in gear. It gets dark fast here, remember, over."

"I'll be fine. Where the creekbed's dry, it makes a dandy trail. Oh, by the way, I wouldn't want my pocket to start bitching at me while I'm talking with the locals, so don't call me, I'll call you. Out." He fumbled the radio into his right breast pocket and checked his wrist for the time.

The tiny solar cells on that wristwatch provided astonishingly little power to its storage battery, but it was enough to operate the watch and all of its calculator functions. He started to calculate in his head the ratio of wattage between his wristwatch solar array and the huge panels crowded onto the upper surface of a Nemesis, then rejected the mental exercise to concentrate fully on the task at hand.

In another ten minutes or so he would walk into a Maya village, unless someone refused to let him. He could feel the Beretta inside his left breast pocket, his left forearm pressing against it, the hand slung inside the suit fabric. "Better keep both hands visible," he muttered aloud, wincing as he drew his left hand out, hooking his thumb at the zipper. In the unlikely event that he needed the sidearm, he would draw it with his right hand anyway.

Colleen's survival kit booklet had tried to say a little about everything in Central America and squandered a full page on the Maya. Pre-Columbian language with many dialects; small, tireless people whose worship of the old gods lay half-hidden beneath a veneer of Catholicism; self-sufficient, conservative, living in poverty; each village led by a council of elders. Most spoke Spanish, and would be only too happy to show a stranger the quickest way out of their neighborhood. *Problem is, Morrison doesn't want out until she flies out, and that little lake is probably their water reservoir. Well, if it comes to a complaint, I'll just have to rent their lake with pesos.*

Grasping a bush with his good hand, he negotiated a knee-deep step down the dry limestone bed of the creek, stumbled, and grunted as his shoulder reminded him it was still there. He sat down on that stone outcrop, wondering whether it had been weathered into its graceful lip more by water or by bare feet, and sighed. And looked to his left, and into the platter-eyed gaze of a child no more than ten yards away. The little face did not register so much as a flicker of movement, eyes wide and bright, framed between high coppery cheekbones and a haircut that chopped straight black forelocks off across the forehead. After an instant of shock, Wes Hardin smiled. *"Buenas tardes, niño, como se va."*

The child might have been five or six, its gender impossible for him to determine, with no trousers that Hardin could see but wearing a coarse white cotton blouse that dropped to the knees. The blouse was bordered with bands of maroon and orange, clinched at the waist by a broad sash with tracings of the same colors. Continuing in Spanish, Hardin said, "Tell your papa an injured gringo is coming to visit," and then he stood up, and the child leaped away like an antelope, bounding off with only a rustle of madrone leaves, to disappear among the trees.

Misconception number one: They aren't barefooted, he thought. The child's sockless feet had been shod in little sandals with platform soles and a high-rise ankle guard like the cantle of a saddle. Hardin did the only thing he could think of to announce himself as he neared the village: He began to sing "El Rancho Grande" as he made his way slowly down.

In the tiny settlement below he could see hatless figures sitting in the afternoon sun, each of them clad in an ankle-length garment banded with reds and orange, hands busy with some communal task that involved filling bowls. The clearing had been overgrazed for its grass but abounded with stony rubble and bits of bark, and surrounding most of the village was an obvious living fence of maguey. This huge, gray blue cactus with its succulent broad leaves and thorny edges could splay its arms twenty feet, and rise over ten. They lent a homey touch for Hardin, who had known them in central Texas. Some varieties provided hemp fiber, others yielded mescal and other primitive booze, and with thorns like those any one of them would teach a lesson to a charging rhino. Across the clearing, a small figure leaned on a staff and stood watch over a few goats. A rooster strutted in moronic splendor between the huts. Then, as Hardin paused between stanzas, he saw a tiny bundle of energy in a familiar bordered blouse flicker among the huts, legs flashing in haste, arms waving in excitement. Too far away to hear, he began to sing again as he watched the villagers melt away, children urging goats toward a corral of sticks at the edge of the clearing.

He debated making a show of his pains for sympathy, or a show of good health for self-confidence, and chose neither. As the watercourse turned, he left it and moved to the edge of a cleared plot on the irregular slope, which bore thumb-sized green spears. They might have been grass or cane, but Wes Hardin had helped his father grow corn, and knew the stuff when he saw it at any stage. He detoured around it, his footfalls and the rooster's stuttering caw now the only sounds invading the stillness. Level with the tops of thatching and twenty yards from the level bare earth of the village, he sat down again to rest, and to wait. He no longer felt much like singing.

After five minutes he stood up again and took a step forward. He would never know how long those men might have waited for him to take that step. Abruptly they were just *there*, a pair of sturdy men in roof shadow, wearing short white trousers visible beneath maroon-bordered serapes with thick leather belts, both men peering at him from beneath broad-brimmed hats of straw. Their ages might have been thirty or fifty. Over their shoulders they carried carven staffs of some dark wood, slung from a leather thong near one end, a cord-wrapped grip near the opposite end.

As Hardin put his right hand up in greeting, both men unslung their staffs. Those wooden implements could have served as baseball bats, and the men who carried them were dressed in almost identical clothing. *Uniforms! These are the local cops,* Hardin decided.

When neither man spoke or advanced, Hardin said in Spanish, "I seem to be lost. Can you help me?"

No change of expression, but one turned to the other with a brief burst of something like speech, full of "sh" and curious hesitations almost like glottal stops. The other continued to look at this creature from another world, and finally made some kind of reply.

Hardin tried again, smiling. The booklet had claimed most Maya spoke Spanish. "I have an injury here," he said, patting his left shoulder carefully with his right hand.

More murmurings from the talkative one, ending when he crossed himself. Wes Hardin understood not a word, but thought his gesture might have been misinterpreted. Still, the Latin half of his family were Catholic and Hardin nodded as he crossed himself properly.

The silent one did not seem impressed, and Hardin thought that his next tentative step forward might provoke this sturdy official to use that cudgel of his. *I don't want to pull rank with the Beretta, but I can't afford a whack on my shoulder. Maybe they need more time,* he thought, and sat down cross-legged. "I hope somebody here speaks Spanish," he said wistfully.

That seemed to set both men talking, and Hardin looked away. He spotted a face peering at him from inside one of the huts, but otherwise the village might have been deserted. In the distance, a goat exclaimed "bah." "You said it," Hardin muttered.

After a long interchange, the less talkative cop looked up toward Hardin and said something unintelligible. The man's face still gave no hint of emotion, but his broad ushering wave could not be mistaken. Hardin stood up, a bit unsteadily, and walked toward them rubbing his shoulder, and only then realized that he stood half a head taller than either of them. He let his right hand slide inside his flight suit as the men stepped aside so that he must walk between them.

Hardin readied himself for jostling. A little rough handling just to prove their status might be acceptable, but he had sustained a fracture three days before, and now the Beretta lay at his fingertips. *Christ, I hope they know what a pistol is. I'd hate to have to use it, even as a warning shot.*

The men spoke short phrases now, falling in step, not touching him at all until he had walked past the first hut. Then they guided him with subtle touches of their staves toward a hut clearly different from the others in one respect. In size and material it was much the same, but its roof was a four-sided pyramid, topped with a special vertical rise of thatching to form a tunnel. Wisps of smoke from that tunneled cap said it was a central smokehole, but something else tugged at Hardin's memory. Suddenly he had it: The shape was almost an exact copy of the huge stone pyramids erected by long-dead forebears of these people, even to the rectangular temple on top. Its location was central, and from the crumbled corners revealing sticks criss-crossed inside hardened brown mud, Hardin judged that the walls were not true adobe and might be very old, many times older than the roof. He stopped when he reached the edge of the roof thatch, which brushed the top of his head, and then felt two sticks prodding him forward through the rough doorway and into a single room without windows.

At the center of the room, two small logs smoldered in a depression of earth at knee height, this primitive raised hearth contained by several courses of adobe brick. Hardin would have sat on one of the low three-legged stools but one of the staves tapped the hard-packed earthen floor, and he accepted this small insult without comment.

By now he had given them names for the subtly differing maroon decorations on their sleeves: Wideband for the relatively silent one, Slimbands for the more excitable one. Slimbands trotted off on urgent business. Wideband walked outside, turned, and squatted at the edge of the thatch, facing Hardin, the staff across his knees. Hardin tried one more pleasant sally, but Wideband only waved an idle hand before his own face as though shooing flies. The implication was clear. He was to sit tight, and quietly at that, because his only way out was full of squatting cop.

In the next half-hour, Hardin had nothing to do but study his surroundings and note the gradual revival of the village. From the sounds of it, the place boasted several children. The smells of this ceremonial jail tickled his nose, combining in an odor that was musky, slightly sour, and, at first, as alien to Wes Hardin as the breezes of another planet. Then he did identify scents of woodsmoke and cornshucks, in part because the place had live coals and, hung in the gloom across naked ceiling poles, peculiar bundles of cornshuck that proved to be icons, dolls of some sort. In a far corner lay a set of decorated pottery bowls, not stacked but separate, some of them with stubby integral feet. Near him lay the only thing that might have provided any comfort: a short-legged cot, its mattress made of cornshuck bundles wrapped and bound by twine.

These folks live on corn, make saints of corn, sleep on it, probably make beer from it. There's self-reliance, he thought. Then as shadows lengthened across the clearing, he saw the five men approaching, four of them following a truly tiny old fellow at a respectful pace behind. The man had a sparse beard and mustache, his cheeks furrowed with wrinkles, and wore a belted serape of black wool. His trousers reached to the shin and carried embroidery in maroon and orange. He moved slowly with a staff, evidently on joints brittle with age, and Hardin saw that his staff had a silver head burnished by much use. The old fellow stopped and one of the others spoke, and Wideband stood up and waved his prisoner outside.

Hardin walked out slowly, ducking again at the thatch, not letting himself wince at the twinge in his shoulder. Wideband put his staff at Hardin's breastbone, not touching him, and waited until the group had filed into the hut. Then he stood back and waved Hardin in.

The old fellow sat on the exact center of his cornshuck cot, the silver-headed staff leaning between his cheek and shoulder, and the others occupied stools at his flanks. Hardin gave up on naming them because all, except their leader, dressed much the same and wore some variation on the red sleeve decoration. Hardin stood before them and waited. The old man waited too. Then Hardin cleared his throat and said in Spanish, "I guess I'm your prisoner."

"That is possible. Or perhaps our guest," said the old fellow in the same tongue, after the faintest of hesitations.

"Thank God," Hardin said, and started to squat, and saw something indefinable pass across the old man's face. "Please excuse me, I do not know your customs," Hardin went on in Spanish as formal as he could make it.

Now the first hint of any emotion from the faces of any of these people: a faint, almost shy smile creasing the old boy's wrinkles. "You are in pain, but you maintain respect," he said, and followed it with something else in Maya. Slimbands left his stool and slipped outside as the leader went on: "This is good. If you please, red man, speak slowly to me; I seldom speak your tongue these days."

Red man? These guys are redder than anybody I ever met. Whatthehell, so I'm a red man. . . . "Is it Maya you speak, sir?"

"All Mayob," said the old fellow, letting his chin do the pointing at the others. "You may call me Holpop. Among the Mayob, courtesy would have required you to say your name first. There is no problem," he said as Hardin's mouth opened, and again he smiled. "I shall tell you when you make an important mistake."

At this point, Slimbands returned with a stool, placing it deferentially behind Hardin, and the old man indicated that he might sit. Hardin did, gratefully. "Sit nearer. I must hold your hand," said Holpop, and waited until Hardin moved near.

When the old man reached out with fingers like soft horn, he did not take Hardin's hand in the modern way. Instead, he curled his fingers over the heel of Hardin's right hand, the little finger partly circling his wrist.

Hardin decided to ignore the strangeness of this soft-spoken little oldster. "My name is Wes."

Holpop turned to the others and, to each, repeated some formula with the word *Wes* in it. Each repeated it, then placed a hand on his forehead and said something else. If they were names, Hardin missed them. Holpop then said something that, for an instant, confused Hardin. "When I am not wearing this," he said, fingering the thick black wool of his serape, "I am called Ixhuel. But now I am Holpop."

A secret name? Or maybe it's a title. "Holpop," Hardin said, and the old man actually chuckled, and then the others did too.

"Not so far wrong, but not so close either," said the old man, and repeated his pronunciation, and Hardin tried it until Holpop was satisfied with the right amount of plosive "pop." "Because we are few, I am also batab so long as I carry my staff. I always carry my staff," he added with what might have been subtle humor.

The old man then placed his free hand on Hardin's injured shoulder, the gentlest of touches, and continued to touch around the injury, also fingering the fabric straps of the figure-eight splint. Holpop's eyes, virtual slits between the wrinkles of twenty thousand sunsets, became bright. "Wes, did you fall?"

"No sir. Well, actually I did, but that was several days ago. I broke a bone in my shoulder."

Holpop's gaze turned inward for a moment. Then, "Yes, you fell. It would be an important mistake, an impudence, an—insult," Holpop finally found the word he sought, "to say a thing to Holpop that is not true. Therefore, consider each thing you say before you say it. There is time," he added gently.

I've got half a mind to try a lie. But he told me I was in pain—but I said I was hurt to that kid, didn't I? Right; a kid who doesn't even speak Spanish. And then again, his Latin kin had told him some skin-prickling things about the Indios, things bordering the occult. Which was all patently bullshit, but right now did not seem the time to test this old guy. As if to test Wes Hardin's credulity, Holpop said, "The stones foretell red men from the north, Chachacmacob, who once were here and will return to aid the Mayob."

"Yes, sir, I am from the north, and I would like to help the Maya, but I need help myself. I do not know if I am as red as you."

Evidently Holpop did not often laugh aloud, because when he did, he startled the others. "There is wisdom in that. Those who desire help may best find it on the ends of their arms. And how can we help the red man?"

Hardin drew a deep breath, and thought about the man holding his hand, and tried to phrase everything in ways fathomable to a man who talked with stones, and then began his story.

He told of a thing with wings, powered by the sun, which had flown him and one brave woman to their region. Holpop stopped him and spoke for some moments to the others, evidently translating. The men stirred, and one crossed himself.

Hardin took his time now. The slope of the mountainside had already put the village in evening shadow and it became increasingly likely that he would spend this night where he was; unless, of course, they drove him out. Now he told of men from the far south, evil men who had moved near and now offered beguiling poisons that enslaved and often killed. These evil people had come to live in the jungle not far away, perhaps seven days' march.

Subdued mirth met Holpop's translation. *I guess seven days away from here is a hell of a long way for these folks,* Hardin thought.

Holpop, in Spanish so rusty that it sometimes had him groping for the right word, then told Hardin that the Maya knew about the evil ones in the third tier of the sky who worked hellish ways on earth. Hardin wanted clarification here, and got it: The ultimate evil lay under the earth in hell where Kisin, god of the trembling earth, ruled. *Kisin*

*is ol' Nick, and brings quakes; but he's not really con-
nected with evil spirits above. These poor buggers get
zapped from above as well as below.* That made an awful
kind of sense, Hardin realized, because the dullest Maya
could see that bad weather came from above while earth-
quakes came from below.

Hardin next recounted that he had fallen during a battle
against the evil ones, and that a companion had brought
him as far as the great sunbird could take them. Now the
sunbird, too, was wounded. Hardin needed special things
to make it well again, and had hoped to find them in the
village.

After his translation, Holpop asked what medicines were
needed. Hardin got himself into a mass of confusion then,
trying to continue in metaphorical terms. He finally put it
more bluntly: They needed something to drill small
smooth holes in hard stuff, something of metal that gripped
like a leopard's jaws, and something that would glue almost anything to anything. It would help, he added, if they
had any old metal cans lying around, and something to
cut them with. And with that, he pulled his hand away and
fished out the entire wad of pesos, placing them all in the
old man's hands.

Murmurs arose from the other men; evidently they all
knew what money looked like. At this point Holpop spoke
to Slimbands again, and the man slipped away in silence.
"We understand that the Ladinos who think they own our
land want such paper," Holpop said, not bothering to
count it. "Two days away lies a city where twenty twenties
of our people live. A wide trail reaches them with noisy
carts that pull themselves. I have seen this myself, they
wear clothes as strange as yours and they trade this paper
for goods." He thought on it or a minute or so. "And it
may be true that we will need it, one day, if you say so.
We shall keep it in trust until that day comes." With that,
he handed the money over to a fellow with half as many
wrinkles, and spoke to him briefly. "Now we ask you to

share our food, Wes. This house is yours tonight, but please do not leave it for anything until tomorrow.''

Hardin agreed, though he needed to relieve himself and thought it best to say so now. He was escorted by Wideband to a midden heap beyond the magueys and found a pile of last year's cornstalks near the mound. Wideband pantomimed wiping with shucks and hunkered down, watching with some interest, as Hardin unzipped the crotch opening of his flight suit. A man had to watch where he stepped in this place; the citizenry did not put much stock in digging holes for such business.

Smoke tendrils arose from near most of the dwellings as Wes returned; meals seemed to be prepared outside the huts in roofless kitchens. Only Holpop remained inside the ceremonial structure when Wideband left him there, and Hardin soon found that the old man intended to show him how to enjoy a meal.

They ate with fingers and knives that were works of art, by the light of a refurbished fire and a pottery lamp with a wick that drew from rendered animal oil. They improved the atole corn gruel with pinches of coarse salt, slurping it from wooden bowls. He did not recognize the stringy meat until he tasted it: mutton, with a flavor that was almost barbecue and a toughness that defied swallowing unless it came in small enough pieces. Holpop watched Hardin's one-handed efforts and then took his own obsidian-edged knife to the meat. *The Spaniards claimed that flint pierced breastplates of Toledo steel,* Hardin thought, watching the old man. *Now I can believe it.*

The old fellow drank from a slender-necked gourd and offered it to Hardin, who politely declined. What he ate had been well cooked. Sometimes, he admitted to Holpop, red men grew sick from drinking other people's liquids.

Later they talked again; Holpop on his cot, Hardin on a stool—a canche, in Holpop's language—and again the old man held Hardin's hand. He gave as much information as he sought, telling of the unseasonably dry weather that threatened their crop and warning Hardin of forest spirits, asking if the red men could intercede with Great Chaac for rain.

Wes said he thought not. Then, thinking about that lake and its now dry watercourse, he asked whether Holpop's little group had ever thought to dig a channel to release the lake water only an hour or so away in the heights. "Your stream is dry but it comes from there," he added.

Holpop remained silent so long Hardin grew uneasy. Then: "Is the sunbird there?"

"Yes. We had no other place for it to land," Hardin apologized. "We want to fly it away again as soon as possible."

Holpop replied that he did not think it possible. Many generations ago, according to oral tradition even before the Ladinos came, Kisin had made the lake on a day when their great stone temple was near completion. Their carved stones shook and men were killed, and Holpop's ancestors had abandoned their temple. The lake's name? They would not give it a name, said Holpop. They used its water when good spirits brought it down, and once or twice a year a properly purified man would climb up to look at the place, but no one had ever seen a fish jump there and sometimes in dry seasons the lake simply disappeared, becoming a shallow grassy depression. But the devil himself had made that lake; of course nothing could live in it but frogs. And some of those frogs exuded deadly poison on their skins. Was it any wonder Holpop's little tribe stayed away?

When Wes mentioned again that his companion at the lake was female, Holpop questioned him closely and did not seem pleased with the answers. Did he know her well enough to vouch that she was truly human? Assured that Colleen Morrison was all too human, Holpop relaxed a bit. Had the two of them tried to make babies since their arrival? Not ever? Well then, was she so ugly or so old? Ah, then if she was both young and fetching, perhaps Wes was keeping himself pure for his own ceremonies. The old man seemed to sense Hardin's discomfort with this line of questioning, and soon broke it off. But, he warned, at such times even a red man might be vulnerable to the deadly allure of the Xtabai.

Wes had heard of that legend somewhere but had thought it was a South American invention about love. If so, it had traveled much and had taken on a more sinister cast. The Maya Xtabai, evidently, could draw any unwary man from his wife or his field. Those who pursued this ravishing creature into the forest depths were never seen again. Never. In fact, if the sunbird woman was young and beautiful it was just as well that Wes had come alone. If the village men had not driven her away with averted eyes, the women might have done it with more deadly aim.

Finally, promising to bring the village's collected implements the next morning for Hardin's scrutiny, the old fellow prepared to leave.

"I am sleepy too," Wes said.

"I will not sleep yet," said Holpop. "I must talk to the night spirits with our tunkul. If the great god Sun interrupts our pleas to the lesser rain gods, perhaps the night spirits will permit the entreaty while Sun is asleep. It is important that no outsider watch our ceremony, and I must ask you to avoid that, on your honor." Wes agreed, and now the old man sighed as tired old men have always sighed. "And I must prepare with much pohsh," he said, "and my head will be clear tonight and very muddy tomorrow."

Wes asked about that and repeated the word, which rhymed with "post." You have to drink a lot of this pohsh stuff? Can't you pretend to?"

Old Holpop gave him a pitying look. "One cannot fool spirits, any more than a red man can fool a shaman. You have not tried to make babies with that woman, but you want to. You must not, for the next three days."

"The possibility is too remote to think about," Wes replied, shading the truth a little.

"That may be." The old fellow stumped to the doorway and looked back. "But for you she may be Xtabai."

When he had gone, Wes tugged the radio out and tried to contact Colleen, off and on, until the chanting began. And then the louder chanting. And then the tunkul, which sent dust raining down from the roof thatch and tempted Hardin to sneak a peek. Instead, he tried to sleep and managed it, finally, after the tunkul stopped. By that time he had a mental picture of the tunkul: a bass drum the size of a blimp hangar, beaten by the man who tuned J. Arthur Rank's gong.

FIFTY-THREE

Tuesday, May 30

MIKE CONTRERAS WOULD have enjoyed his rearguard position more on Tuesday if he had questioned Harry Rex Brown less. He had to do it by hand-held radio because Harry sometimes moved out a hundred yards ahead of the second man in the file, and that put Mike and Harry as much as a quarter of a mile apart.

Shortly after their noon break and dry rations washed down with water, Mike radioed another question: "We're fresh enough to take the steeper slopes. Why not cut across the next valley instead of circling it?"

"Locals follow the valley between villages," Harry radioed back. "Our footprints would be hard to mask if we crossed there."

Mike thought about that. "How d'you know about the prints we'd leave?"

"See the stand of cane down there? It means soft, damp footing. Let's do it my way, Mike."

Mike nodded to himself and switched off. One of the men, twenty paces ahead of Mike, had been listening on his own unit. Now he turned toward Mike, his thumb and forefinger a circle, and grinned, and Mike nodded again. *Nobody's kept those first-day jitters. Looks like they're comfortable with Indy, and that's saying a lot. Gotta hand it to the guy,* he admitted. But that was before Harry Rex Brown struck off toward the east.

Because he did not want anyone monitoring them, Mike waited until a break. As they lounged together in the shadow of a stone outcrop, Mike caught Harry's eye and moved off as he motioned, taking out his compass. Harry followed a moment later.

"For the past hour we've been moving a few points north of due east," Mike said. "Mind telling me why we're not bearing more north, Harry?"

"Not at all. We're going to Eden."

Pause. "I'm sure we all will, eventually; Eden, heaven, whatever Mormons call it. But Harry, I'm not going today. Put that out of your head," Mike said firmly.

"No religious connection," Harry said, amused. "Eden is a little village a couple of hours east of here. After that, we won't have to worry about the locals."

"Now that, I like. Why won't we?"

Harry looked at Mike Contreras as if sizing him up for the first time, pursed his lips, then said, "Friend of mine, fellow named Yaxpoc; used to be the salt, button, and dyes trader in these parts. Retired now. He has a nice place outside Eden, and we need him."

Mike, with abused patience: "We have salt tabs, and I'm not in the market for buttons or—"

"I thought this might happen, so I didn't mention it. Yaxpoc has taken me where no other whites have ever gone. He knows these highlands and every batab in them," Harry interrupted, using the Maya word for *chief.* "Where we're going, some of the settlements aren't necessarily settled, if you get my drift. Yaxpoc will know exactly how to get us to any place within fifty miles of here, including that lake, with minimum fuss, and could even round up porters if I needed them. That's what we want, isn't it?"

"I'll carry my own pack, thanks," said Mike drily.

"No, not the porters. But I may as well tell you, north-west of Eden I need a guide myself."

Mike passed a hand through his hair. "Why didn't you tell us earlier that you need a guide?"

"Because I'm not an idiot," said Harry, with that infectious grin. "You'd have gone off without me, expecting Yaxpoc to help."

"You're really something, Harry," said Mike, pocketing his compass.

"Besides, he wouldn't take you without me along. He knows I like minimum fuss. He wouldn't be too sure about you," Harry went on with a wink. "All your packs look alike, your jungle boots too. To Yaxpoc that would look like government. He doesn't trust governments."

"But he's learned to trust you."

"Right. And what's more important right now, I trust *him*. Now, if you're ready," Harry said, striding back to shoulder that big canvas pack of his.

Mike sat down and gave an affable nod to Bogosian as the jungle veteran walked past, third in line. *I guess if an old Maya grave-robber trusts the guy, the rest of us may as well.*

THEY CIRCLED AROUND the little valley in midafternoon, staying just below the ridgeline out of sight. Harry insisted that he must go alone to Yaxpoc's place, which stood half a mile from the cluster of dwellings that defined Eden. Unlike the village's thatched roofs, the place Harry pointed out as Yaxpoc's was somewhat larger, roofed in reddish tile with small palm trees nearby.

"That tile roof is his pride and joy," Harry said, shucking his pack for the short, precipitous journey down a nearby ravine. "And it weighs a couple of tons. It took me two burro trains to get it all packed in here from Rio Blanco," he chuckled.

Mike Contreras, intrigued: "You gave him his roof?"

"Years ago. And never regretted it," Harry replied, standing up, brushing pine needles from his trousers.

I guess not, thought Contreras as he watched his guide traverse the ravine, snap-brim hat pulled securely down. *You're a jewel, Harry, even if you are cracked down the center,* he thought.

MIKE HAD WAITED long enough to become suspicious, his stubby little ten-by-fifty monocular trained on the place with the tile roof and the palm trees, before Harry appeared in the afternoon sun. Mike saw him raise his hand to his head.

Mike's speaker clicked twice and he replied immediately. "Go for it, Harry."

"Took a little bartering," Harry said, "but it's a go. Yaxpoc thinks it would be best if you gave Eden a wide berth and crossed the valley in a rocky dry wash a mile east of his place. Not much rain lately, and you can avoid the boggy spots. If you make camp on the other side of the ridge to my north, you can make small fires. We'll meet you there at seven A.M., okay?"

"You'll leave your men alone tonight, Harry?"

An unfeigned laugh. "I'm leaving them with you, Mike. Any problem with that?"

"No-o, but you might tell me why," said Mike.

"Yaxpoc wants to check with a couple of people in Eden, to check the best routes. They do it all the time."

"You don't want to go broadcasting this," Mike cautioned.

"These people have been my porters," Harry said, sounding very positive. "And who'd milk Yaxpoc's cow if he didn't arrange it? These things take planning, Mike."

God damn this guy, he's going to do what he wants to anyhow. If this is how he gets around this godawful country year after year without getting caught, we may as well accept it, Mike fumed silently. ''See you at oh-seven-hundred then,'' he said. Then he turned to the team medic, who was pretending to read a paperback he should not have brought. ''Okay, you heard the man; we'll have hot coffee tonight.'' In one minute they had erased all traces of their resting place; in two, Mike Contreras was in the lead toward the next ridge.

FIFTY-FOUR

Tuesday, May 30

No QUESTION ABOUT it, old Holpop was badly hung over when he finally entered the ceremonial hut on Tuesday morning. Wes Hardin made a mental note to avoid pohsh as he sat in early sunlight with the old man, eating bananas and salted atole. Children herded goats, women ground corn on scooped-out stones, and all of them seemed willing to ignore the stranger in their midst.

Then Wes saw the waist-high log of hardwood that lay on its side, eight feet in length, with two heavy round staves leaning against it. Evidently hollow, it bore a lengthwise slit near its top, wide as a man's hand and four feet long. From the faint dents in the surface patina of that log, he judged that someone used a lot of energy in beating the bejeezus out of the log with those wooden bats. "Is it permitted to ask if that thing is your tunkul?" he asked.

"It is permitted," Holpop replied. "Our tunkul is older than my father. Its voice can be heard far into the sky, and we use it to reach gods of the upper levels."

"I am sure they heard it last night," Wes said with fervor.

"We will see. It is used only at night in our village," said the old man. "I was but a boy when we last used it during Sun's hours."

"Oh: to speak to the sun god?"

"No; because the village batab had not time to wait for darkness. The danger was immediate, evil men who came to rob us. My father thought they had come for our wives and daughters." The old man sighed and put his head in his hands for a moment, perhaps wishing his pohsh had not been so potent.

Wes wiped his mouth and put down his bowl. "Did they?"

"No, they killed our batab and took my father and three others as guides, perhaps as slaves. None of them ever returned," he said.

"No wonder you feel that the Maya need help," Wes said, watching a man approach with a bag of woven cloth slung over one shoulder. It turned out to be Wideband and he, too, looked much the worse for the previous night.

When Wideband squatted before the old man and untied the bag's flap, Holpop spoke in Maya. Wideband replied, with a jerk of his chin toward Hardin. Holpop sighed. "These are our machines, the things we have found or traded for. I often think we should bury them all," the old fellow muttered, and began to extract them.

Wes's hopes dropped a notch as he saw the old man display the treasures. A rattail file with a broken tip, and a leather punch; most of an ancient revolver, both its grip and its cylinder missing; a necklace made of many strands of tiny coral beads, strung on rusted wire; the metal parts of a horse bridle; and large steel needles in a flat-sided tin can so old that its original contents would remain a mystery.

Wes tried not to show his dejection and held up one of the needles, half of its eye snapped off. "I suppose I could make a drill of this," he said to the uncomprehending

Holpop. Then he took the needle by its point and pressed its broken eye against his bowl, twisting back and forth. Then Wideband burst into sudden and fluent Maya, jumped up, and trotted off. "Did I say something wrong?"

"No. He believes you want to put a hole in the wood," said Holpop.

"He is correct. Not this bowl, but others things on our sunbird." Wes checked his wrist: nearly nine in the morning. Colleen would be furious at his long silence but hell, he had tried!

"We collected only those things that are foreign. We have machines of our own, and those we can always replace. All of it is yours," the old man said shyly.

Who knows, maybe we can use some of it. The tin can is ductile steel. This rusty old six-gun is so old it has a pivoting rod under the barrel to tamp black powder loads and slugs into the missing cylinder. By God, it's tempered steel; it might work as pliers! "I am very grateful," Wes said, then looked up and winced. His next glimpse of Wideband made him think the man intended to shoot him.

Wideband carried the little bow and arrow proudly, showing it off for Hardin. But the arrow's sharp end passed through a hole in the center of the bow, and the bowstring was wrapped around the arrow shaft several times. As soon as Wideband placed a smooth socketed stone against the butt of the arrow; Wes recognized the device as one that used the bow and gut bowstring to make the bit spin merrily. "Hell's bells, a Comanche drill," he exclaimed in English.

Using drill bits of cactus needle or hardwood set with chips of flint, Amerinds had drilled through shell, bone, and stone for their jewelry. In Spanish, then, he explained his delight, thanked them, and said that he must soon be on the way back to his sunbird.

"I dreamed of your sunbird last night," said the old man. "Its breast was the blue of morning, its back the blue of night, and its tail feathers were very long. You sat inside its head."

Wes, startled, said nothing for a moment. *How the hell? This old boy is pretty spooky.* "Did the dream say whether it will fly again?"

"If it did, I do not remember." Holpop's hangover must have been a wowser. "But it is you who must interpret the omens that speak to you."

Wes stood up and ran his thumb along the straps of his splint. "I wish I could, Holpop. The stones may speak to you, but my sort has forgotten how."

"No? Then what of the bracelet you wear? I think it speaks to you," said the old fellow.

"I had not thought of it that way," Wes admitted with a glance at his wristwatch, and then a small idea burst in his head. He removed the expansion band from his left wrist carefully and handed it to Holpop. "This does not speak to me in words, but with marks that constantly change. Please take it," he said.

"I cannot read the red man's marks," said Holpop.

"If you will look every day at the same time, you will see that its marks change the same way. And," Wes played his trump, "it is powered by the sun."

In awe, the old man stared down at the watch. "This is true?"

"I swear it; just as the sunbird is. But you must not keep it in a dark place. Someday it will die, but it will live longer if it sees the sun every day," Wes cautioned, placing his rusted booty in the woven bag again.

"We will keep it here for you," said Holpop, unsmiling, then turned toward Wideband with another burst of Maya, and Wideband hurried away. To Hardin he said, "Before you go, we will share a ceremony I learned in the big town far away."

I can't afford to waste any more time, Wes thought.

"It is a small thing, and takes little time," Holpop added as if he had heard that thought. Together, Holpop with his stick, Hardin still bound by that splint, they became walking wounded as they moved toward the drywash leading up the ravine.

Wideband caught them as they stood at the edge of the village. Between cupped hands, he carried a small white cylinder, and when he offered it to Holpop, Wes saw a glow at one end.

"Men in the big town do this when friend meets friend," said Holpop, and took a deep drag.

Wes had smiled as he recognized the thing as a lit cigarette. He waited as the two Maya conversed, and Wideband seemed to take pride in his inclusion. Then the staunch little cop passed the butt to Hardin, who took a long drag on it.

Then he looked closely at the thing, a ready-made of all things here in a primitive Maya village, and nearly dropped it. His smile became broad as he passed what remained of the Alas cigarette back. "I must go," he said. "Thank you for the ceremony of friends."

He did not understand the words of the two men as they called their good-byes, but he knew one thing very clearly. The old man had told him he must interpret his own omens. Alas was the Spanish word for *wings*. On the butt of that tacky little Alas cigarette he had seen its logo, faintly outlined in a blue the color of a Nemesis belly: a stylized wing.

FIFTY-FIVE

Tuesday, May 30

Ocosil, who lived in the household of an older brother, was happy enough to quit his work in the field and his brother was happier to let him. Yaxpoc, the entrepreneur from down the valley, had brought Señor Harry into Eden; perhaps, said Ocosil's brother, Ocosil would find work now with Yaxpoc.

Ocosil, grown temperamental of late because of a recently acquired habit, did not mourn when he learned that the tall yanqui did not want porters this time, though he made a show of disappointment for the sake of politeness. What Ocosil really wanted was to visit the foreigners who tended seedling plants, ten kilometers west by cart track and another kilometer into the bosque. Ocosil had borrowed his brother's horse twice that week, ostensibly to seek work in the town of San Pedro. Instead, he had cemented his friendship with the pair of senderistas who had begun to supply him with something stronger than coca leaf.

Now, standing around the little cantina table with three

other young men who knew Señor Harry, Ocosil wiped
his runny nose and accepted a glass of aguardiente. "No,
I have never walked more than one sleep in that direction," he said, studying the paper with its squiggles and
curly lines. He knew that the blue lines were water, and
blue blots were lakes. And he knew, because Señor Harry
had just told them all, that one group of brown curly lines
very near each other represented the miles-long limestone
cliff known as Nohoch Alux, the great trickster.

Ocosil had never tried to climb that treacherous mass of
rock. He saw that the spot of interest to Señor Harry lay
just to the left of a line from Eden to Nohoch Alux, but
three times farther than the cliffs. "I have heard that the
people there are very backward, very ignorant," he added,
licking mucus from his upper lip.

"But," said Yaxpoc, pausing to stress the importance
of what he was about to say, "have you heard that they
are still hostile in the old way?"

Murmurs of denial from all four younger men.

"As always, I do not wish to give offense to anyone,"
said Señor Harry. Ocosil knew what that meant: As always, Señor Harry wanted to avoid meeting anyone at all.

One of the other men sipped his drink, thinking on it,
and then suggested, "If you climbed straight up the Great
Trickster, Señor Harry, you would certainly meet no one
on that day."

When the yanqui replied that he would meet Kisin instead, they knew he was joking. But for all his easy ways
among the Mayob, perhaps Señor Harry did not know that
it was in bad taste to joke about meeting the devil.

One of the others had worked for a Mexican survey
team a year before, some days to the east. He had heard
of rumbles from the Lacandones there, complaints about
whites defiling the old ruins. But to the north he had heard
nothing good, nothing bad. If no rich and curious whites
drew him there, he said, how would he know? "You surely
know about conditions to the west, Ocosil," he went on.
"You use the trail often enough."

Ocosil shrugged and said nothing. Neither Yaxpoc nor Señor Harry paid much attention to that because their interest lay northward. Presently, with the sun peeking in under the cantina thatch, Señor Harry bought another round. For a tip, he brought out a fresh tube of some unguent that the proprietor accepted with deepest thanks. The cantina was also the general store, drugstore, and trading post, and Señor Harry pointed out that the unguent should be rubbed into the hands and arms of old women whose weaving caused them pain. Ocosil did not know any modern word for arthritis, but he knew how the finest weavers in Chiapas—women, naturally—often retired when they could no longer stand the pain. He also knew that Señor Harry had given the proprietor a gift that would double the man's modern pharmaceuticals, and ensure his friendship for yet another few years.

Ocosil watched Yaxpoc and Señor Harry disappear down the footpath, sniffled, and then took the back way to his brother's pasture. He unwrapped the slender coils of sash from his waist as he went and formed a loop at each end. The mare knew the tone of his soft whistle, and Ocosil knew the kind of succulent grasses to pick for her reward, and she allowed him to slip the larger loop over her head without complaint. Five minutes later, Ocosil had the mare in a trot, riding bareback through a curtain of pines until he was over the nearest ridge. Then he grasped the smaller loop tightly and dug his heels in.

Near the village of San Pedro the cart trail forked, and soon afterward Ocosil turned off to urge the mare up a rocky defile. Because her footing was slippery, the mare clattered and stumbled, snorting as she climbed the sort of incline that no horse should have to climb. Ocosil hung on, using her mane at times, whispering to her in the Tojolabal dialect. Once again she made it to the deer trail leading over the ridge.

Though he carried a tune indifferently and did not know what the words meant, Ocosil began to sing a phrase over and over, a Peruvian dirty ditty the two senderistas had taught him. Normally they spoke Spanish to Ocosil. He knew the tune amused them, and more important it announced him from afar to Sturdy and Slim, the only names they answered to.

It was Slim, in his usual military green trousers and mottled shirt, who met him beyond the ridge, mouth set in a way that said perhaps Ocosil was visiting more often than his hosts liked. "Is this to be a daily trip, then?"

"You said that you would be grateful for news of outsiders," Ocosil replied, his legs moving as the mare's flanks heaved.

"So soon, then," said Slim. "Get down. If it is worth killing this fine old mare, perhaps it will be worth a packet of powder."

Ocosil slid from the mare and led her by his sash, following Slim to the senderistas' little shed. The shelter was not roofed with thatch, which would turn yellowish gray and could be seen at a distance, but with something green and slick and impervious to rain; and over it lay fresh green boughs of fir. The man with the thick forearms whom he called Sturdy rolled out of a hammock and stepped from the shelter as Slim strode to him, looking no more pleased than his companion. The two men spoke in low tones for a moment, and Sturdy shrugged and Slim made a gesture with his thumb and forefinger to his nostrils as Ocosil dropped his sash over a madrone limb. Then they called him in.

Ocosil, sniffling now and then, stammered out his news with the quickness of a man who wanted instant gratification. *They are playing with me,* he decided, as they told him to go over his story again, Sturdy turning once to his modern backpack to retrieve a few pinches of off-white powder in a tiny transparent packet. Because Sturdy did not offer the packet yet, Ocosil settled down and tried to remember every detail of his encounter with Señor Harry.

Yes, he had carried loads for the yanqui before. No, he had not seen any others, but evidently they were near; perhaps as many as Ocosil's fingers and toes, but no one had told him exactly. According to Yaxpoc they were not the kind of men who wold care to have others carry their goods. The word Yaxpoc had used was *macho*. At this, Slim and Sturdy exchanged a hooded glance.

To be sure, Señor Harry had shown him a white man's map. Ocosil thought he could place his finger on the exact spot the yanqui sought, if he had that map before him.

A moment later, they produced one; not the same by any mean, and Ocosil's mouth trembled with his frustration until Slim showed him the hamlet of Eden, then the cliffs of the Great Trickster. Then Ocosil turned the map around, and it began to make sense. He broke off a twig and marked it with his thumbnail, laying it on the map. When he had measured as carefully as he knew how, he put his finger on the map. "There," he said.

Was he sure, they asked. "These numbers here," said Sturdy, "tell us it is nearly two thousand meters high. Lakes do not form on the very tops of dry ridges."

If not the ridge, Ocosil replied, then very near it. He had never been there, and knew only that Señor Harry's eye took on the glint of an eagle when he boasted of his intention to rescue a beautiful yanqui girl—oh yes, and a pilot who had crashed there.

And how long, Slim asked, had those yanquis been waiting by that little lake?

"Only a few nights since the crash," Ocosil replied, adding that they believed the pilot was badly injured.

At this, Slim and Sturdy became more lively than Ocosil had ever seen them, almost as if they had been sniffing the powder themselves. They pressed the packet into his hands and Sturdy began to remove the wrappings from a machine of some sort.

Now Ocosil made his pitch. If they intended an expedition of their own to claim whatever reward might be offered for these downed yanquis, he said, he would gladly help. After all, Slim and Sturdy could pay him in ways no one else could, and Ocosil was an experienced porter, and, and . . .

They had no intention of running into a bunch of macho yanquis, said Slim, shooing Ocosil away. In fact, Slim went on, they did not believe a word of it. All the same, Ocosil had been prompt in reporting and they had paid him for his good intentions. And now, in the name of Chairman Mao, would he go before they flogged him away?

Ocosil was feeling clear of head and light of limb as he retraced the trail. Before dark he had reached the valley fork again, and did not care much that the mare seemed to be going lame.

FIFTY-SIX

Tuesday, May 30

WHEN WES FINALLY reached Colleen by radio, she said she couldn't care less whether he came back or not, a predictable reaction for his failure to reach her earlier. But he noticed that when at last he cleared the ridge at noon Tuesday with dragging feet, Colleen Morrison just happened to be standing at the trailhead, nearly a half-mile from her Nemesis. "If I carry that stuff it'll be quicker," she had said, taking the woven bag from him, leading him along the trail they had cleared with bush knives.

En route he asked her to stop so that he could rest again. He leaned against an oak, flexing his bad arm, rubbing it with his right hand. "You might've tried harder to reach me," she grouched.

"I was in jail, more or less. Didn't want 'em to get too curious about the radio," he said to avoid a long explanation, and began to plod onward. They reached the Nemesis without further conversation.

Colleen microwaved their lunches and then, protesting

every minute, helped him relax the straps of his splint. "Four days isn't enough," she told him.

She's almost friendly when I'm trussed up but when I get healthy again, guess what hits the fan. She loves me, she loves me not, he thought wildly, and chuckled to himself.

"What's so funny," she asked sharply.

Inventing a motive, because the truth would have been lethal: "An old guy I met down there," he said. "He had to get smashed for a ceremony last night. I don't think he wanted to, it was just something he had to do."

"Maybe he was Irish," she said.

"His Gaelic was mighty rusty," Hardin replied.

Suddenly she put down her plastic spoon. "Last night," she said in a hushed voice, "I heard something I never heard before and I hope to God I never do again. I don't suppose it had anything to do with that ceremony."

"The drum," he said.

"You heard it."

"There were times when I thought I was *in* it."

She rubbed her arms briskly with her hands. "That slow pace, like a—a volcano's heartbeat. It made me think of every horror movie I ever saw. It didn't sound like a drum, it sounded like a giant moaning in a cavern."

"That's the tunkul, all right," he said. "They wouldn't let me watch."

"I had a weird—never mind; eat your beef tips."

"Go ahead, Colleen; in these parts, weird is in."

She grimaced and would not meet his eyes. "I couldn't raise you by radio, and I got this vision that you were about to be some cannibal's dinner."

With his face perfectly straight: "You're psychic. It almost happened."

She looked up, horrified. "Oh, my God, Wes."

"Then I pointed out that I was from Texas," he said, the corners of his mouth betraying him.

Her expression turned from horror to weariness in an

instant. "Right, right; I got it. They figured you'd be too tough."

"Nope. Too hard to clean," he said, and pretended surprise at her laughter.

FOR HALF AN hour, they gloomed over the pitiful array of junk he had carried up the mountain. "We've got some silicone lube," she said at length, operating the squeaky remains of that black-powder revolver. "Yeah, it might work as pliers. But what in hell," she demanded as he showed her the bow drill, "do you expect to do with that rig?"

He placed the drill tip against the plastic dish he had eaten from, used his left hand to position the stone socket, and told her to thrust down on the flat wooden bow. She did, and saw the flint tip spin briefly. Once the mechanism operated she saw that its flywheel, a stone doughnut encircling the drill, had begun to rewind the bowstring. She quickly took the device away from Hardin and rewound it, adjusting her pressure on the socket and bow. In two minutes she had drilled a conical hole through the dish. "Doesn't take much pressure, does it?"

"Very little. I might be able to do it myself," he agreed, and presently they began to plan their repairs in detail. Basically the job would involve drilling a pattern of holes and then lacing the ripped skin back together as if roughsewn. Their control cables, of course, could not be removed entirely; but the cables were made of twisted filament bundles, and pound for pound those filaments were stronger than steel. Because the cables had been overdesigned in the interests of reliability, they decided it should be possible to steal a few strands from several cables without seriously weakening any one of them. Then they would braid those stolen filaments into a new and much thinner cable, capable of being threaded through one of their needles.

The needle need not be tempered, a lucky break because Colleen had to curve it like a sail needle and heating it for that bend would remove much of its stiffness. While Colleen stoked her little fireplace near the lake's edge, Wes set about removing nylon screws to gain access to the cables in their rudder booms.

He stood on dry ground, using his left arm sparingly, and called her over for a consultation when he had finished. Their heads almost touching, Wes probing at the cable with another of his needles, he let her move past him and inhaled through her short tangle of hair. *Lord, lord; not a hint of perfume and she still smells good to me,* he reflected; and then vowed to avoid this line of thought in the future.

When they had agreed on the amount of filament to take, she helped him unwind it from the taut cable, coiling the stiff wiry stuff as they went. By the time Wes had the other rudder boom ready, Colleen had impaled a hardwood stick with the eye of her needle and heated half its length before forcing the bend into it between stones. It was a pair of angles, not a smooth curve, but it would do.

They sat and admired their new equipment briefly, Colleen judging that they might be finished with the skin repair in another two days. It was their catapult, he responded, that would take a lot more time.

She selected a trio of gossamer filament bundles, anchoring them in the crevice of a stick, moving away with the other ends in her hands. The process of braiding twenty-five-foot threads was not to be a quick one. "If you have a quicker way to build a catapult or a runway," she said, "I wish you'd tell me. When that search and rescue party gets here, they won't want to wait."

"They might take weeks," he said.

"No they won't," she said. "I, uh, I was too pissed off to tell you earlier, but when conditions are right I can use the Nemesis comm set again. Satellite uplinks, maybe."

He brightened until he saw her sober glance. "That's

great! We can call for epoxy, tools, prefab aluminum rails—''

"I tried to. The goddamn government has made its decision, and they're not interested in slim chances. There's a team already in Chiapas with our exact coordinates and they're headed this way on foot.''

"We'll just have to convince 'em to help us," he said.

"That's what I'm hoping, but it didn't sound likely. Those guys have orders to tear my Nemesis apart and sink the pieces, and bring us back dead or alive. Short of tying them up, I don't know how to stop them.''

"Then we'll just have to fly the sucker out before they get here," Hardin said grimly. "Which way are they coming from, and how long will they take to get here?''

"In from Guatemala, from the south," she said, and he saw that she was trying to braid faster. "They'll be here in less than a week.''

FIFTY-SEVEN

Wednesday, May 31

"Four days southeast from Base Ana, five at the most," said Bermudez, the senderista leader, after breakfast on Wednesday morning. He held a chart flat against a humid breeze that entered from broken windows. He looked up at Simon Torres, who stood at his side with folded arms. "What was I to do, Torres? How could I have kept the news from spreading? My squads speak Quechua when they radio in. I learned the news from the radioman; I would have had to kill him to keep him from spreading his damned wonderful news. And for all I know, that downed aircraft may have had nothing to do with the disaster here. What was I to do," he said again.

Torres shook his head. "It was out of your hands, Bermudez. How many are going on that revenge mission?"

"A dozen, all riding double on those motorcycles as far as the roads and trails will let them." Alvaro Bermudez threw up his hands. "Too much discipline now and I could have another kind of explosion here. It was all I could do to prevent them from taking all ten of the remaining machines. They may have left already; the squad leader is a fellow named Cesar Machado, college trained, speaks Maya. They all wanted to go and Machado is as good a man as we have—and,'' Bermudez added with faint satisfaction, ''Machado's was the smallest group. I figured, the smallest number who leave, the more will be left to defend Base Ana.'' His voice fell a notch. ''I am commanding a powder keg here, Torres,'' he said with the reluctance of a man admitting heresy to his favorite priest.

Torres nodded and began to peel an orange, recognizing that Bermudez spoke the truth, unwilling to say it aloud. Frantic radio messages from Catemaco had told him what the Mexican media would not: The destruction of three crucial isthmus railroad bridges, eighteen highway bridges, and the breaching of Chicoasen dam had provoked exactly the opposite effect from what the cartel had hoped for.

Radio news claimed that an accident in the national power grid had caused the brownouts across southern Mexico. From the railways, no news, but that might be expected: The railways were nationalized. To Torres, it was obvious that the Mexicans knew exactly what was happening and had chosen to keep this insurrection quiet. And if they could do that, the cartel's body blow had carried no more impact than a light slap to the belly. Mexico's counterpunch was still coming, but already they had felt its muscles flex.

As Vega had radioed at dawn two hours before, Catemaco no longer drew power from the state. Young Gaitan, driving home in the early hours from some tryst in San Andrés Tuxtla, had turned away from a roadblock and narrowly escaped an interview with the federales that, Gaitan assumed, was intended for his sort. Vega, normally a man of breeding, had cursed aloud when Torres admitted he had holed two compartments in an amphibious float during his landing. If the cartelistas could neither fly out of Catemaco nor drive out, then they must walk out or prepare for a siege. At the moment, Torres gathered, his cartel leaders were trying to decide whether to retreat to

Base Ana, a guerilla stronghold without an intact window and a mass grave that still lay open with over two hundred corpses in it, or to flee separately as private citizens.

And what should a leader expect when he attacks someone with many times his gross product? This makes two countries that have forced us out; three, if one counts the Peruvians. Torres knew that his frustration would be less if he had something to do; preferably something in a fast machine. He could have tried a run for the Yucatan in his Mangusta but he could no longer bluster his way through a roadblock, and the car could not outrun bullets. Besides, he would be running while his very tendons cried out for revenge. *I can still fly from here to San Pedro Sula and reclaim my T-Bird,* Torres mused, *but even if I carry ammunition for its guns, I am not an armorer.* The plain fact was that, though the plane's ammunition lay safely in the garage beneath his feet at this moment, where David Elath had stored it, Torres himself did not know how to charge those fifty-caliber Brownings, and could not trust a Honduran to keep his mouth shut. As for Elath, the Mexican had driven off in a van loaded with scrambler bikes and senderistas toward Chicoasen dam. None of them had been heard from since.

His only hope of action lay in the Pilatus, which sat refueled in plain sight below. He looked up at Bermudez now, suddenly aware that the man had been talking to him. "What did you say?"

"Air force," Bermudez repeated. "We should have bought a real air force."

"We still have one," Torres said, galvanized by the prospect of action. "If that Machado fellow has not left, send for him. I can fly a surveillance mission and pinpoint that lake he seeks. As it stands, he will have to comb fifty square kilometers of high country." *And I will not be available to try something stupid like landing a float plane on a road near Catemaco.* He felt certain that they would think of that eventually, and it had proven all too easy for them to demand the impossible.

Bermudez left at a waddling run, calling for a runner of his own. It was a sign of panic when a commander's communication lines were so badly damaged that he could not simply pick up a telephone or a radio and make his demands.

Five minutes later, one of their surviving scrambler bikes roared up the incline to the savaged lodge from the senderista encampment, now a shanty-town of tents and lean-tos. Torres recognized the guerrilla in the beret: one who seemed a bit cross-eyed but had looked him in the eye nonetheless, and who never seemed very far from his companion, a really hulking specimen. Torres wiped orange pulp from his fingertips with the edge of the damask tablecloth and strode outside through the door, though he could have walked through the frame of what had been a picture window.

Cesar Machado did not even shut off his engine at first. "We are behind schedule already," he said, eyes bright. "If an enemy team is really en route to that lake, we must get there first."

"And when you get where you are going, it may take you days to find those bastards or the lake," Torres said. "It is difficult country."

"We know that better than you," said Machado, an insolence unthinkable only a week before.

"I can make it simple," said Torres.

"Why are you not trying to save your skin," asked Machado in honest curiosity, and shut off his engine.

"I am a fighter," said Torres. "My weapons are simply different." It occurred to Torres only now that he had spoken from his guts. He might run sooner or later, but not while he still had weapons with real clout. *If only Elath were with me,* he thought; but Elath was probably dead. And Simon Torres was still a Colombian. "This was my base, too. We must take revenge for all, Machado."

"They say you will find my coordinates."

"If I can reach you by radio, I will try. You must give me a unit that reaches your frequencies; my jet is not here, and I must fly that puddle-jumper below,'' Torres explained. Machado kick-started the bike. "Wait," said Torres, and swung a leg over the vehicle's rear wheel. "I am as anxious as you to get started.''

Machado nodded and said nothing, but his glance carried new respect. Together, they careened down the grassy slope and into the guerrilla camp. While Machado explained his needs there, Torres tried to pretend that he did not notice the hard looks in his direction. Those who did not yet understand his mission seemed ready to confront him. *At least none of you is cowardly,* Torres thought, keeping his face impassive.

Presently the big fellow they called Teniente emerged from a tent with a cumbersome radio set, giving it to Machado, who placed it in the hands of the pilot. "The Condor will lead us to the ones who attacked us,'' he announced, not waiting to acknowledge the ragged cheer as he kicked the bike to life.

The taxiway, by now, had been cleared and the craters were clearly visible by daylight. Torres dismounted, spent half a minute learning which direction the guerrillas would take on their bikes, and replied that he would first use the floatplane to check the roads to the south and east for roadblocks. Machado's men might save a day or two if he radioed to tell them which routes lay open.

While Torres untied the ropes that held the Pilatus safe from vagrant winds, Machado sat astride his little vehicle, not moving or speaking. Then Torres glanced his way again and saw that the Peruvian was trying to say something—or not to, perhaps. "Problem, Machado?''

"With myself. I am finding it hard to thank you.''

"Thank me with bullets, Machado, but aim them at our enemies,'' Torres said.

Machado said, "I can do that much,'' and roared off as Torres entered the Pilatus.

The amphibian floats, he knew, were not very heavy, but they changed several things about the Pilatus. The two wheels per float gave the craft a different attitude, and the aerodynamic drag slowed it considerably. He would have much preferred to discard the damned floats, now that they were only an impediment, but Elath was the man who knew how to do that. Moreover, the normal landing gear for the Pilatus was now a jumble of wreckage 300 meters away in the ruins of his hangar. The more he thought about it, the more Simon Torres ached to locate that yanqui airplane.

Torres cleared the taxiway the way a stoll is supposed to, flaps down and nose at a dizzy angle, and happened to glance toward the guerrilla roadblock as he banked away. No sight could possibly have been more encouraging. Approaching the roadblock was a dark brown van, its windshield shattered, mud drying on its sides. It was the only stretched Ford van they had collected, and he had last seen it heading for Chicoasen dam with David Elath at the wheel.

FIFTY-EIGHT

Wednesday, May 31

"THOSE CLIFFS EXTEND for miles," said Harry Rex Brown's voice Wednesday at midmorning. Harry's voice came from the speaker at the ear of Mike Contreras. "Yaxpoc tells me we could make it, but it's porous limestone and every year, he says, some of it comes tumbling down. And we'd be awfully obvious up on that wall, Mike, like flies on a wedding cake. Every Maya within miles would know."

"Okay, so it's a half-day farther around, so we go around. Lead on, Harry." Mike put away his radio and, rear guard once again, glanced wistfully up at those greenery-encrusted cliffs. Harry Rex Brown was probably right about taking it slow and steady, instead of punching straight up into the high country. In a way, Mike thought, it was ironic: Harry's decision seemed the more professional one, but it was really because Harry was the amateur. Instead of getting in and out again on the double—the wham, bam, thank-you-ma'am of the hardened pro—Harry obviously enjoyed himself up here and took his good time. The pro, in any vocation, did what he did for a living; the amateur did it for the sheer fun of it. Sometimes the amateur's way paid off. Mike wondered if he had ever met a man who enjoyed his work more than Harry Rex Brown.

Mike could see the gradual submergence of the cliffs into a gray green hump of forest early in the afternoon when, without warning, an aircraft arrowed out over the valley as if fired from above the cliffs. The team melted away under deep cover, each man peering up at the intruder, most with more curiosity than dread.

"Hell, that's an ol' Pilatus Porter," said one of the men on his radio unit. "Long way from Laos, ain't he?"

"Turbo-Porter," another corrected him. "Must be Air America."

Mike clicked his unit several times rapidly, and the silence on that channel became abrupt. "It's got Mexican numbers on it. The Company isn't giving us any close air cover! Pass it on," Mike called ahead. He trained his monocular on the float plane, a Turbo-Porter, judging from its huge exhaust manifold and the characteristic hoarse buzz of its turbine. *Too damn' bad. If the Company would only risk it, a Pilatus on floats could do the job in ten minutes. No, it couldn't mulch that fuckin' ruined airplane, could it?*

The aircraft banked around their valley and passed from sight, the commotion of its engine silenced as suddenly as it had emerged. Sometimes when the wind was right, you could hear an air surveillance patrol in plenty of time. Other times, it burst into your world with the suddenness of gunfire and, as now, might leave the same way. "Maintain radio silence, pass it on," Mike called, the call passing from voice to voice until Mike could hear it no longer.

Mike began to worry then; not because his team might have been seen—that was highly unlikely—but because a civilian float plane might have no trouble landing on that little lake. Its pilot would almost certainly radio the Mexican authorities if he saw evidence of a recent air crash, and by the time Harry Rex Brown skipped onto the scene the whole operation could be blown higher than those cliffs to the east of them. On the other hand, many an airplane had crashed in such terrain without anyone ever seeing it again. Mike put his worry on the back burner and kept putting one foot in front of the other.

When the Pilatus did not return after an hour, Mike decided its overflight had been coincidence. After two hours they had reached the point where the terrain began to swallow the cliffs, and after three hours they had begun to trudge back above the cliffs. They had also gained another thousand feet of elevation, according to Mike's altimeter. From here, momentarily, they could see the Pacific coastal range of peaks. That was when Mike called a halt.

Though it was possible to use a satellite as a link back to Langley, a real-time link with immediate replies posed special problems. The simple fix for those problems, Mike had been told, was a real-time link flying eleven miles high over the Pacific, beyond Mexican boundaries. They'd told him only that they were using a Coast Guard vehicle, and that the aircraft would remain on-station as long as the rescue party needed it. Mike supposed that they had some kind of robot-controlled U-2 out there, because he knew of nothing that could hang out on the fringes of the atmosphere for weeks carrying a pilot. The comm set they gave him for that contact was very different from his walkie-talkie, a squat unit with a ladderlike antenna that must be aimed toward the southwest horizon. Someone had called the thing a dipole narrowcaster. Mike Contreras did not care if they called it an asshole newscaster, so long as it worked.

After giving his coordinates, Mike noted aloud that Control seemed to fade in and out regularly.

"This linkup has its drawbacks," Control admitted. "I've only got sporadic contact with the pilot at your destination."

"You wouldn't have a Pilatus Turbo in the area, would you," Mike asked. "Blue, big floats, Mexican registration. Made one pass near us three hours ago but I'm convinced he didn't see us.''

"Stand by one," said Control. After too long, he spoke again. "Not ours. The opposition has an aircraft fitting that description flying out of Catemaco now and then. They have some assets tending coca in your region though. Just stay out of sight. I'll try to raise our downed pilot again to keep her on the lookout. Any other problems on your end?''

"Nobody's gone bamboo yet," Mike said, using an old phrase for jungle psychosis. "Our man Harry is working out, I'd say.''

"Sounds good. Control out.''

"Alpha, mike foxtrot," said Contreras, not to identify himself but to sign off the old way, A-M-F for "Adios, motherfucker." If Control didn't know that one, some older hand would soon clue him in.

FIFTY-NINE

Wednesday, May 31

IF COLLEEN HAD drowned that little fire instead of letting it send its tendril of smoke skyward, the Pilatus might never have scored. They did not hear its first and highest pass because Hardin's primitive drill, through the Nemesis skin, resonated like claws on a cardboard crate. When he stopped drilling long enough to wipe a hole clear of powder, they heard it instantly.

Colleen saw it first. Calling, pointing: "They're here already. Oh *damn* it, Hardin!"

His gaze followed her finger in time to see the craft disappear over the high southern ridge. "Seems they are," he said, and put down the drill. "Now listen to me, Colleen: I couldn't make out the type but I'd say it's either a modified Helio Courier or a Pilatus, both popular with spooks, and on floats they could make it in here. Either one could haul us both out at the same—"

"I'm not going, they can't—"

"Please shut up, for Christ's sake! They may land on the next pass." He was collecting his necessaries as fast as he could, not forgetting the drill apparatus, talking as he went. "I'm going to disappear for a while. Tell 'em I'm off bartering for epoxy—any damn' thing. You don't expect me back for a few days. Meanwhile, try to argue them out of cutting up our bird."

"*My* bird. And I'm coming with you," she shot back, running to one of the survival kits.

He spoke with utter finality. "If you do, and there's nobody here for them to talk to, they may start breaking your bird up here and now."

He was backing away into the trees, tall pines with their carapace of vines and moss, sweeping the ridgelines with his gaze. When he was far enough into the bosque that his flight suit became dappled with motes of filtered afternoon light, he stopped. "Just keep working," he called. "And quit looking toward me."

Her face did not twist into any dramatic grimace but, he saw, she had begun to cry. "I'm not going with them, goddammit. I'll talk, but I won't go. I can claim I won't leave an injured friend—no, my lover! That'll work. You can jilt me later," she called. To Wes Hardin she sounded a bit manic.

"It might play to them, if none of 'em know us," he said. "And Colleen?"

She had to work to make it come out level, but she managed. "Yeah?"

"If they drag you off anyhow, give 'em some reason not to graunch the bird. It may take me a while, but my shoulder's better. I'll get your alter ego out of here somehow."

She simply stopped, shaking her head, and then she was running toward him. She must have remembered his injury just in time, slowing, wiping her nose with the back of a grimy little hand. "Shut your eyes," she demanded.

He did, and she kissed him, not exactly a Parisian special but soundly and long and with the warm yielding enthusiasm of an ingenue. "No fair," she said, touching his cheek as she came down from tiptoe. "You peeked."

"And you're blushing. Looks good to me."

"It would." She backed away, hearing the buzz of the airplane again. "I don't know if I've really misjudged you, Wes, but that was just in case."

"Will you get back to the damn' airplane, Colleen?" He watched her run back, admiring those fine lines, certain that she would regret that friendly overture once she had thought about it. *Good thing I didn't flip out and kiss her back the way I wanted to—and what the living hell has got into me? The woman is an ambulatory four-basket case of aggressions.*

"And dynamite, pure and simple," he muttered softly, moving further into shadow as he caught a glimpse of a blue floatplane that cruised down the length of the lake, flaps extended. It did not flare out to land, but pulled up enough to clear the smaller northern ridge and then the silence returned.

Wes did not return to the Nemesis for another fifteen minutes. Colleen would not meet his gaze, her attention seemingly focused on braiding those filaments. The job was going more quickly now, the gossamer cord shorter because of the braiding process. He took up the bow drill again and, without a word, resumed his work.

Presently: "I've thought of how we can make those lacing holes airtight," she said. He stopped drilling and let his bad arm rest as she continued, "Those nylon tent cords will burn, and the molten stuff will drip. We just drip it into the holes after we've sewn this braided filament tight."

She wants to forget that kiss. Or maybe she just wants me to. Whatthehell, I can play along. "Might work," he admitted, rubbing his shoulder gently.

"It had better. If it doesn't, and that repair comes loose, we won't have enough thrust to fly a pissant," she said.

"I've been thinking about that, Colleen. The only reason we're still here is that bringing your bird back is worth your risking your life for."

"So?" Quick and challenging.

"So rigging a catapult with some kind of delay with

both of us in the bird is an added chance for failure. Plus, my extra weight might make the difference. Plus, I can hang out here and wait for the rescue team, or walk out on my own.''

"Or I could,'' she said.

"Wait, yes. Walk out alone, no. You may be Attila in pantyhose, but you don't speak the language and the locals might treat you as an evil spirit. You're the one who should fly this thing out alone, while I work the catapult.''

She resumed braiding. "We go together, Hardin. Some people got killed once, doing something on my account. And pantyhose aren't my style.''

He began to laugh. "I reckon not,'' he said, taking up the drill again. "We're going to need about six feet of braid. How're you doing there?''

"Another half-hour; I figure on doubling the braid for more tensile strength. I just hope that plane doesn't come back for us,'' she said fervently. "You know damned well he couldn't have missed spotting the Nemesis, but the way it's backed up to shore he may have just been some rich Mexican checking out the funny-looking amphibian.''

"I hope you're right, Colleen.''

"I could crank up the comm set again and find out, but I'm not going to. These people don't want to do what I want, and the hell with them!''

SIXTY

Thursday, June 1

THURSDAY, YOUNG GAITAN Palacios showed up tear-streaked at Base Ana driving a Volkswagen beetle with its front fenders missing, his Lamborghini trashed after it low-centered on a back road. "I was lucky to get past the senderista roadblock," he said, shaking visibly as he stared out through the windowless vista.

Torres: "And the others?"

Gaitan's reply came slowly. "I saw Vega taken from his car at gunpoint. They shot his driver. Solano may have made it."

"Your father: safe?"

Slower still: "In the Lambo. I told him to wear his seat belt, but—" now more in anger than grief, interpreting Torres's expression: "It was not my fault!" Subsiding, he looked around him. "And where are the servants?"

"Perhaps you were not so lucky," said David Elath, fingering the fresh scab across his nose. "This place may be under siege by tomorrow."

Torres saw the lifted eyebrow that the younger Palacios

turned on Elath, a social inferior who was presuming to speak to Palacios with such familiarity. "Gaitan, I am not sure you realize our position," said Torres. "No more servants; they disappeared after that air strike. We now depend on my friend Elath here, and on the absolute suicidal bravery of those Peruvians who surround this valley. I cannot imagine why you chose to come here."

"It was the only one of our protected places the damned Mexicans have not blocked off," Palacios snarled, filling a brandy snifter.

"I am Mexican myself," Elath murmured; the gentlest of warnings.

"You are different. But thanks to what you did at Chicoasen dam, we have lost everything."

Torres saw Elath's smile and shrug, and chose to reply himself. "He was the hand that obeyed cartel orders, Gaitan. Thanks to *you*, he had the vehicles. If the guerrillas had not known you helped in that, they might have shot you at the roadblock."

"Then why are we here?" Palacios exploded, sloshing his drink.

"I am here because he is," Elath replied, nodding at Torres.

"And I am here because it is the only airbase that protects me while I fly military missions," Torres put in. "We lack materials to repair the runways for my jet, but so long as we have fuel drums I can still fly the Pilatus daily, and direct that group climbing into the highlands."

"Not to fly me out," Palacios accused.

"I have told you why," Torres said with a warning glance. "Bermudez is planning a back-road retreat, and I suggest you follow his excellent example."

"Then you will not fly me out?"

Simon Torres heard the note of pleading from this spoiled son of vast wealth, and like any one-time street urchin, he enjoyed hearing it. To press home the folly of treating Elath as a servant, he put a look of doubt on his face. "David, you know our cargo weights better than I.

Could you adjust it so that you might save young Palacios here?'' A sham, but Palacios could not know that.

After a long, steady look full of judgment toward the young man, Elath said, ''Not today. Probably not tomorrow. I could make room for you the next day, when we fly to Honduras to arm the jet.''

Torres almost smiled at this. Elath knew that their timetable had considerable flexibility, and that progress of the revenge team under Cesar Machado would decide the moment when Torres flew to San Pedro Sula. Several days would pass before they flew there, by which time Gaitan Palacios might be pissing himself with anxiety. Torres said, ''What you must do, Gaitan, is pray that the senderista team comes within striking distance of their prey very quickly. Until then, I fly only surveillance missions here and over that team moving southward. They are on foot now.''

Palacios hurled the snifter through a window frame in frustration and stalked away toward the kitchen. ''He is still a child in some ways,'' Torres observed.

''He is a piece of shit,'' said Elath softly. ''Nothing would suit me better than to see him leave here in his fenderless Volkswagen, but I know your loyalties by now. I say I know them; I do not say I understand them. Don't you take a chance every time you overfly that lake and its amphibian?''

They walked outside toward the garage and its supplies as Torres said, ''I don't know. What I saw yesterday hardly looks like an airplane at all. I am not even certain it *is* amphibious, but it looks as though it might be as fast as our Pilatus and I could see no obvious damage. Perhaps it is waiting to be fueled by those yanquis who are supposed to be en route; perhaps not. If it took part in the raid here, it is surely armed. No doubt I surprised them yesterday, but I could not count on surprise again.''

Elath tapped a fuel drum; rolled it to the open doors of his gutted Ford van. Together, they tipped it into the van. As Elath strapped it down next to the hand-cranked pump, he said, "And the Pilatus is not armed. If that thing takes off after you, can you outrun it?"

Torres slammed the van doors and swung into the forward passenger seat, letting Elath drive. "How can I know that? But if you could wire a few rocket launchers on the Pilatus—"

"And have the backflash peel the skin from your wings? Simon, stay away from that thing until you have no choice," said Elath with fervor. He had not said please and he no longer said señor to anyone; yes, perilous times forced many changes. . . .

They jounced downhill toward the Pilatus, their fuel drum thumping in the back of the van. As they pulled up beside the aircraft, Torres cocked his head and regarded Elath soberly. "And why are you staying here, when you could leave anytime you liked?"

"Curiosity," Elath replied with a grin. "I really want to see how this turns out. And," he added, "because the bonus you promised is not yet in my hands."

Torres's laugh echoed through the van. "No, it is in the *Banco Nacional de Honduras*," he said. "Did you think I would leave my T-Bird in any country where I am not known as a friend to the bankers?"

Elath began to unstrap the fuel drum. "Very thoughtful, Simon. I hope you think of me when we arrive at San Pedro Sula."

"Say it, my friend. You want to see your money then."

Even in the dimness, Elath's eyes were bright as he looked into the face of Torres. "Yes, I do. I think, by flying that jet in as air cover to strafe an aircraft you know nothing about, you may be leaping in with the faith and the blindness of an Arab."

"And this could be my six-day war?"

"Six days—or six minutes," Elath replied. "Could you run the fuel hose in for me?"

Torres did it, both men working silently. *Elath is right, I have no business tempting fate in this Pilatus. But when my T-Bird is armed, I will be ready for battle.* Torres said to himself, thrusting the rubber hose into his fuel filler opening. ''David?''

''Ready?''

''Yes, but something more interesting to you, I'm sure: I will pay you when you have armed my air force. I had thought you placed more confidence in me.''

''I have great confidence in you,'' said Elath, turning the crank. ''But I am beginning to worry about your tomorrows.''

SIXTY-ONE

Friday, June 2

THE PREVIOUS DAY'S repair work, as Wes Hardin remarked, passed like a dose of salts through a fasting guru. Perhaps that was because everything, every blessed detail, worked to perfection. Colleen Morrison drew the filament braid through each drilled hole expertly; not because women liked to sew, she pointed out, but because she had grown up helping build airplanes, and the fabric skin of many homebuilt aircraft was secured by skilled mechanics with curved sail needles. Hardin practiced for hours before he learned how to drip the debris of a blazing nylon cord with precision, flattening the bubbly stuff as it cooled, using a knife blade as a spatula. Even the torn edges between stitching accepted that molten nylon as an adhesive. Thursday night, Wes and Colleen had slept outdoors near the embers of the fire, their heads three feet apart.

On Friday, they tested the Nemesis power plant; first using only the electric mode, then engaging the rotary engine as well. Wes, standing where he could watch that skin repair, finally signaled Colleen to cut power. The repair seemed flawless, but at high thrust the Nemesis seemed in danger of pulling their nylon anchor cords loose.

"There ought to be some way we could float my bird," Colleen said later, "so that the waterline doesn't rise up to the propeller blades."

Wes shook his head. "I've cracked my skull trying to figure that one out. Ben Ullmer once said he gave up on water landings because a Nemesis puts her head up to rise, and that would drop the tail booms into the water. Ain't no way you can rotate to climb when it's already sitting in water." They both knew what would happen if that whirling propeller ever took the slightest dip into water: The blades would shear off instantly.

Colleen proved, on paper at least, how they could build a cradle that would slide down a slight incline along stripped poles of pine. The rails of their glass jock would support the full weight of a Nemesis, just barely, and the dimensions of the couch made it a near-perfect padded cradle for the underside of the fuselage. Wes helped strip all unnecessary weight from the craft including their couch, the TV, and even their tape cassettes, leaving only their frozen food and microwave unit. Friday by sundown, they had virtually gutted her bird and thought they might tow it, afloat, to that long grassy area the next day. They slept outside again, Wes ignoring the couch to lie near Colleen.

On Saturday, Colleen removed that figure-eight splint entirely, complaining that she did it under protest.

"We need these straps to bind the couch and jock rails together," Wes reminded her. "And we can tie the tow rope to my waist. No sweat."

But he did sweat, knee-deep in muck and water, and after an hour of fruitless tugging they sat down at the lake's edge, leaning back to back, sopping wet. Colleen was first to admit it through her wheezes: "This—isn't going to—get us there."

And that rescue team is due here any day now, he thought. *Why have I got myself into this? Why, because*

I'm a damn' fool, he told himself. *What's wrong with me, anyhow?* He already suspected the answer, and did not want to pursue it at the moment. "Listen," he said between deep breaths, "we strap air mattresses. Together. I crawl out. Sit on nose for ballast. You strap mattresses. Under trailing edge."

She failed to envision the idea for a count of three. "And use the engine?"

"Right. Then I get off. Flotation might keep the prop clear."

It was worth a try, she said, and they worked until noon on the idea. They shared the last Lone Star from his hoarded sixpack to wash down microwaved meals. Then he climbed out as far as he dared on the sloping nose and clung there, grim as a cat on waxed linoleum, while she worked those air mattresses under the trailing edge.

"This will have to do," he said, when they surveyed the job. "Most likely you'll get some rudder force to steer, and you can probably run your bird clear up into the grass. Go as far as you can, it might save us the trouble of hauling it up the slope."

"I'll try to pick my spot," she assured him.

"You've got a few inches of clearance on the prop right now but when you get underway, it'll want to rotate on you."

"I know that," she said irritably, sodden and cranky after her labors.

"But you've seen how a moving boat can trail a trough in the water, and you might even be able to rotate safely." He was smiling now. "How do you know, absolutely, that you couldn't get up enough speed to take off?"

"Oh," she said in a small voice, her eyes widening. "I don't. Oh, Wes, do you think maybe?"

"It's barely possible. If you can, you'll know it by the time you've reached that grassy area. Remember, you'll be dragging a pair of air mattresses along and that could be worse than not getting up at all. I can't advise you on that, Colleen, you understand the physics as well as I do.

Or maybe the bird can climb out with 'em. They'll be a bitch.''

"Not after I get to altitude," she said, eyes shining.

"No?"

"They'll burst when the outside pressure drops to practically nothing," she said, and grinned as he slapped his forehead.

"Smart little shit," he said with mock gravity, and then continued. "From shore, I'll be able to see back there where you can't, so watch my hand signals; if it looks like water is coming up to the shroud, I'll want you to shut 'er down right—*now*," he insisted. "Fair enough?"

"I'll be leaving you here." She swallowed, face clouding, and when he smiled and put his arms out she walked into them, and the hug became another kiss, nothing held back this time.

If Wes Hardin had ever been more thoroughly, searchingly kissed, he could not recall it. When their mouths parted, they were still holding one another: "That makes this whole trip worth it," he murmured, tugging a strand of grass from her hair.

"It's stupid to say I love you," she said, as if to herself. "But I don't have anyone else left to love, Wes."

He sighed. "I'd say this bloody airplane comes pretty close."

She turned her head, sunlight dappling her face as she gazed at the great machine nodding to itself on the water, then turned back, her eyes searching his face for understanding. "No, that's just—it stands for something I have to do. The day I turn it over to Ben Ullmer, he can cut it up for scrap. I didn't realize it until now but believe me when I tell you, I don't want to buy a plot knowing there's no one alive that I love. I hope that makes sense."

"Doesn't have to," he said, his right hand rubbing her shoulder. "It makes sense to you."

"I don't even mind much that you don't love me back," she went on, pulling away to look into his eyes. "I mean, I might augur in on this one and, and never mind the details but I built myself a Wes Hardin that I could dismiss, and it wasn't the real one, I guess." Now in a voice that was almost tiny, hesitant, trembling: "I've felt this coming, and I'm sorry to burden you with it. But no one could have been a better partner, and you're elected. I love you, Wes. Do you mind?"

He could feel her grip, those little hands still wet, now clutching at him in a terrible uncertainty. "I don't reckon it ever occurred to you," he said, lips buried in her hair, "that I might already have a case on you."

"But," and now she giggled; "you never even tried to jump my bones."

"I'm old-fashioned. First you learn about each other, and *then* you check out the bones. Besides, you would've had my balls for earrings," he said, chuckling.

"Yeah, I would have," she said into his throat. "But people change, you know. And if you need a broader hint than that—"

"All I need," he interrupted, "is some help in getting out of this flight suit." He put his good arm around her waist and started toward the couch.

Smiling now and then, with no sense of hurry, they helped each other remove wet clothing. Her motions gradually became more sensual; his hands more inquisitive; their mutual delight in discovering, in being discovered, heightened by delay. When at last they had removed the last garments, Wes began to caress those perfect breasts with his tongue, his breath shaking though the breeze remained warm. He had thought her body well proportioned, but found himself unprepared for the ripe perfection of a gymnast who had kept herself in trim. From her languid gazes, that sly smile, and the tongue teasingly held between her teeth, he decided that she, too, liked what she saw, and what she caressed.

"Just one thing, my love," she said, and pressed him back on the couch with gentle insistence, "if ancient memory serves. Remember that shoulder; you must be my pony, and let me ride."

She knows how good she looks, he thought, nodding as he smiled up at her, letting his eyes roam; hands as well. She gloried in his attention, now the complete wanton as she took him in, watching him watching her, and only by closing his eyes did he avert a climax with hers.

Then he whispered to her, his suspicions about the varied uses that couch might provide, and she agreed, pleased that he was not yet spent, pretending not to be, yet making that pretense transparent. And for a time, he was the rider, and she the ridden.

When finally they lay quietly spoon-cupped on the couch, his right hand thrown over her, she slept; and he held her that way for a long while.

THE BOSQUE'S SHADOW canopy was reaching across the lake when Colleen finished dressing herself, with many a shudder in those cold clothes. "You sure you want to go now? We've uh, kinda screwed up the afternoon," Wes reminded her, already dressed.

"The rescue party could be here any time now," she said. "That nap was a life-saver."

"Hold that last thought," he said, and kissed her gently before she waded out to the silent Nemesis, now unleashed for its dash. "We've got some unfinished business when this is over. You know that, don't you?"

"Let's hope we never entirely finish it," she called back, and he left it that way, glad to find her in such spirits. In the next few minutes she was going to need all her self-confidence.

He walked to the promontory they had agreed on, only a slight rise but positioned so that he could watch the motion of water near the propeller shroud. She warmed up the engine in both modes, echoes clamoring across the lake, the bird moving sluggishly forward, wavelets moving away from the fuselage. Though one wingtip touched the water, it lifted clear within seconds after she waved and brought the power up, a wake beginning to form behind the trailing edge, and in moments she had the Nemesis skimming.

They had not known how much resistance those air mattresses would present to the water, but clearly they were starting a trampoline effect as Colleen firewalled the engine. "She's porpoising," he said aloud, a test pilot's term for a progressively worsening up and down motion of the aircraft's nose. But now the wings of the Nemesis were gaining lift, forming a shallow upward bow at each tip, and for a moment he thought that lift might be enough to bring the fuselage clear because she had almost enough velocity and almost enough height . . .

. . . And it was not going to be enough, he saw. "Ohh, *JESUS*," he shouted, as the Nemesis porpoised one last time, its nose slapping the lake's surface hard enough to hurl water like a speedboat, and then he saw the canards flex. The Nemesis rebounded, nose high, and then the canards brought it down, settling gradually as Colleen forced a path through the grassy shallows, the engine at full thrust.

In silent fascination, one hand clasped over his skull, Wes saw that she was not going to get the craft aloft. At that point he began to run around the lake verge, hoping to reach her in time to help.

The air mattresses folded and bucked, tearing loose as they encountered some snag, the aircraft slithering on under full power. When one wingtip touched down, Colleen's Nemesis began to skid to that side, still riding higher up the gentle grassy incline, and by the time that wingtip caught firmly she was ready, cutting power in that same instant. When Wes reached the far side of the lake she had the canopy open and was sitting on its rail, her face a study in calculation.

He managed to reach the side of the Nemesis before he slid down, exhausted, against its fuselage. "Are you okay?"

"Sure. And the bird's fine, too. You know," she said,

"if we had wetted down this whole area beforehand, I think I could've reached the treeline."

He began to laugh then, unable to get his breath to do it justice but doing the best he could. Finally he lay on his back, looking up at her, and shook his head helplessly. "I thought you'd killed yourself," he said.

Colleen looked down between her feet at Wes and smiled back. "I hate to tell you this, Tex, but there's no percentage in looking up a flight suit," she said with calm impudence. "Remind me to wear a dress for you sometime."

"Will you kindly shut the fuck up and come down here?"

She was already preparing to climb down as she said, "I've already spun her a one-eighty to face the lake again. What more do you want from me?"

"Another hug might help, Colleen. Before the bottom falls plumb out of your luck bucket."

SIXTY-TWO

Saturday, June 3

HARRY REX BROWN had targeted that steep hummock in the saddleback between ridges Saturday evening, almost the instant he saw it. Fifty yards wide at its base, a small and overburdened volcanic cone to most eyes, it lay on flat ground so completely carpeted with layer on layer of rank foliage that few traces of underlying gray could be seen. Even the flatness of its sides was in some degree disguised by the humps, the ancient snags, and the jutting masses of verdure on its flanks. Its steep upslopes on all sides, however, told Harry that this was probably not a natural feature. Harry and Yaxpoc discussed it for twenty minutes as they moved down into the saddleback and into deep shadow at the head of their little rescue column. The fellow behind Harry did not speak Maya, so he was not likely to pass this discovery on to Mike Contreras.

They made camp at one end of that saddleback between towering ridges, a half-mile from that curious feature and 5700 feet above sea level by Mike's altimeter. They could not be more than one or two ridges away from their goal now, said Harry, but darkness approached quickly here. By now, none of the team doubted that any newcomer to these parts who tried to move cross-country in the dark was about six rounds shy of a full clip. Only because he could walk in lockstep with Yaxpoc, said Harry, was he willing to do a bit of recon on foot. Harry left the implication that he would seek an overlook at the next ridge.

Mike Contreras, busy setting up his peculiar little microwave radio with a mini-Maglite held in his teeth, gruffly said he'd be surprised if he ever saw either of them again. And if the two of them weren't back by dawn, Mike added, they'd find a cold trail leading northeast.

That is how Harry and Yaxpoc managed to inspect that pyramid without hindrance. Their roundabout route left them in near-darkness by the time they reached the first of the roots, thick as a man's thigh, that anchored trees into limestone blocks dragged there by people who did not use wheels or mortar, a thousand years before. Harry ignored the fallen monoliths that stood sentry beneath strangler vines; he knew what he was looking for, and knew that the lost Nephites of Israel would have hidden the best for his coming. God would have insisted.

Their flashlights provoked subtle stirrings and once, an angry chittering, from creatures that lived in this tangle of growths. Not until Harry hacked his way between hardwood branches near the top, standing with the stars in view and a breeze to cool his sweat, did he feel cold stone beneath his palms: the sloping peak of the roof. That was when Harry began to suspect he had a major find. Many pyramids in Central America had large flat tops where ceremonies had been carried out in public view. But some, often those with ornate peaked roofs of stone, had been built with interior rooms. And in a very, very few of those, priests or acolytes had built secret stairways back down inside the great piles of stone and rubble. Unfortunately, the one of these Harry had found previously had already been visited by a Spanish tomb-robber centuries earlier. This time, insofar as Harry could tell, no one had climbed to the top of those slopes since before Columbus. And deep within its living carapace, through openings so choked that a man could not have passed his hand through, Harry's flashbeam speared pictures on its interior walls; wonderful pictures in black and white, in carmine and blue, and in the yellow of the sun. While Yaxpoc stood beside him, machete in hand, Harry Rex Brown wept with delight.

WHEN HARRY RETURNED, he asked why no one had built a fire, and Mike was quick to tell him. "We've got company somewhere to the north, with air cover. The aircraft could have infrared sensors; no point in making it easy for 'em."

Harry mulled this over for a time before asking, "What kind of company are we talking about here?"

"I'm not sure you want to know, Harry. In fact, I'm not even sure you want to go any farther. You've got us this far; we're bound to hit the lake by noon tomorrow."

A two-beat silence from Harry before: "What kind of company?"

"Bad guys, Harry. You must know by now, we have assets that can monitor radio transmissions, interpret IR emissions, stuff like that."

"Mike? Exactly what kind of company?" Harry figured, if he kept asking the same damned question all night, sooner or later he would get a passable answer.

"Guerrillas. The kind of guys who chased your ass clear to Guatemala some time back. While we've been diddling around up here, there's been some major hell raised in Chiapas and Tabasco. You know Chicoasen dam? Somebody hit it, big-time. Rail bridges, highways, the works. And Mexican feds are moving in on the main guerrilla base."

"I think that's wonderful," said Harry, fluffing out his sleeping bag, then stopped to think about it. "So the guerrillas are retreating this way?"

"Not exactly," Mike said wryly. "That float plane we saw the other day? It's based at the guerrilla center. Voice-prints tell us its pilot is the same guy who was involved in one of the biggest drug-money scams ever; and he's supposed to have a Lockheed T-33 somewhere in these parts. He's good, and he's out for blood, and every day he's been talking with some bunch of ground-pounders who are heading this way and speak with Peruvian accents. *Now*, Harry, does that tell you exactly what kind of company?"

Harry rigged his bug net and considered the angles he knew in silence, and that took ten minutes. Somehow he knew that Mike Contreras would not be asleep. "If we're not armed, Mike, we can't afford to meet those people. What happens to the beautiful girl we're after?"

"We get there first, that's what happens. I'm tired, Harry. Got a long day ahead. You can bug off if you want to. That would be my advice."

"There's something you're not telling me, Mike. You have some help we can call for, in emergency. Something nearby. Am I right?"

"Something like that, Harry; maybe nearer than you think. Go to sleep."

SUNDAY MORNING, HARRY took his place behind the taci-turn Yaxpoc at dawn. The man behind Harry noticed that they were hacking their way through virgin growth as usual. "I figured you two had cut our trail last night," said the man during their first break.

"This is a more direct route," Harry shrugged, not wanting to tell more lies than he could comfortably justify. He found out just how truthful he had been when, an hour later, Yaxpoc led them over the ridge and moved out on a rocky outcrop for a better view of the valley far below.

Yaxpoc motioned Harry forward. "Is that an airplane, Señor Harry?"

Following an outstretched hand with his gaze, Harry

studied the little lake with its brown shallows shading to blue near its center. Then he saw movement: a slender ponderosa pine, vertical when he first scanned past it, now falling toward a grassy area that bordered a portion of the lake. And in that grassy area, something that glistened a metallic prussian blue, an exquisitely slender thing that might almost have been the trunks of trees felled in accordance with some precise mathematical formula. "What on earth is that?"

"Not an airplane, then," Yaxpoc said.

"I don't—yes, I think perhaps it is," said Harry, and called for Mike Contreras.

Two minutes later, Mike was fumbling hurriedly for that directional microwave unit in his pack because, he said, reception was better on that ridgeline, and he had to report sighting their objective. Harry thought it might take them another hour to get there.

SIXTY-THREE

Saturday, June 3

WHEN TORRES RETURNED from his sortie over Machado's team on Saturday, he realized a chilling fact about the guerrillas at Base Ana: Anyone who failed to see that those Peruvians were looking for scapegoats had to be blind and bone-stupid. Alvaro Bermudez, no fool, had left in the night with fifty men, heading for the southern border. With a Base Ana radioman monitoring their two-way transmissions, Torres felt that he was still a man to be valued.

The way he got out with Elath was to announce another support mission shortly before noon. He let everyone see the big aircraft ammunition cans, the size of suitcases and full of fifty-caliber rounds, and he told young Palacios the facts of life: If Palacios did not personally wrestle one of those heavy containers into the transfer van and then into the Pilatus so that the senderistas could see him do it, Torres could no longer vouch for his safety.

They emptied another fuel drum for the flight, Torres warming the engine with David Elath beside him, and Palacios drove the van only fifty meters away before returning toward the aircraft at a dead run. Torres never saw the source of gunfire, but Palacios evidently knew he was the target. Torres watched sparking puffs of concrete as a small-arms burst stitched its way to the running, then suddenly sprawling body of Gaitan Palacios. But as the Pilatus lifted from that taxiway, more than anything else Torres regretted that he had no way to save his black Mangusta, still squatting in its garage beneath the ruined lodge.

Five thousand feet above the jungle, Torres flew east toward Honduras. If the handful of Mexican F-5 jets were lurking near, he could drop down to treetop height. If some angry guerrilla on the picket line let go at him, he was high enough to avoid most of the things they could shoot. The only action they spotted en route to Honduras, however, was the ambush of a ragtag convoy of small vehicles west of the village of Amatan. "So much for Bermudez," Elath called over the engine's drone. Torres knew then that Base Ana itself would soon come under attack. *I could not return there anyway*, he told himself. *My war is elsewhere, with my choice of weapons.*

Once in Guatemalan airspace they had relaxed for two hours, Elath tugging duffel bags over those silvery ammo magazines to fool the casual eye later. Torres knew better than to try bluffing his way past customs at the San Pedro Sula airport with two huge magazines of what was obviously large-caliber military ammunition. Instead, he chose the fishing resort of Puerto Cortes some miles from the city. Puerto Cortes had decent moorage for float planes, and David Elath had taped those gaping holes in the float well enough for one water landing, though a subsequent takeoff would have been out of the question. His tactic, running aground on an unpopulated beach nearby, would seem reasonable to officials under the circumstances, and unless one of them earned a hernia in the effort they could lug that fifty-caliber ammo to a cache and retrieve it later.

In practice, the floats dug into sand so fast that the Pilatus pitched over almost on its nose, ruining its propeller and perhaps overstressing the entire vehicle. Torres abandoned the thing where it was, and took charge of the duffel bags while Elath, carrying the senderista two-way radio, went in search of a rental car. If anyone was looking for them, David Elath was by far the least likely to excite interest.

When at last Torres drove the rented Chevy into San Pedro Sula, his first act was to call a banker. Though Honduran bankers rarely do much work on Saturday afternoons, they are usually accessible by persons richer than they are. By late afternoon Torres had cleaned out one of his two accounts; only a fool would have alerted that banker by emptying both. He drove to the air terminal, chuckling as Elath cursed a problem he had never worried about before: how to keep five hundred thousand dollars' worth of Honduran money on him without looking like the Michelin man.

Torres's final fear, the condition of his T-33, proved groundless. He delayed his evening meal until he had seen that it squatted intact in a maintenance hangar, fueled and refurbished. "I suppose I could pay you another five thousand to arm it for me," he said, securing that senderista comm unit in a snap pocket of the cockpit.

"Tell me that was a joke, Simon," Elath muttered, not smiling.

They walked outside toward the Chevy. "Well, you have been paid. I thought—"

"You thought I might disappear now. You were wrong. We will come back later tonight and pay a mordida to the watchman, and then you can help me lift those damned heavy magazines into the nose of your toy." The husky Mexican folded his arms and faced Torres squarely. "I no longer know what a friend should do; arm your aircraft or take a sledgehammer to it. You will be fighting for nothing now."

"For revenge, David. To me, that is enough."

"And to me it is a risk you need not take. Ah, well," he said, with an explosive sigh. "For the moment, let us find a good restaurant."

"Where I will treat you to the most expensive meal you can order," said Torres, opening the driver's side door.

"Where I will treat you," Elath retorted, "and try to argue you out of tomorrow's insanity."

THE ARGUMENT HAD not been pleasant, but at least the arming had gone well. Simon Torres parted from his friend with a mighty abrazo, secured a duffel bag in the rear cockpit with his own cash inside, and took a room near the airport, requesting an early wakeup.

Two hours after that wakeup on Sunday morning, Torres watched his tachometer climb and signaled a Honduran mechanic to disconnect the auxiliary power cart from his aircraft. In less than an hour, roughly midmorning, he would announce himself over Machado's team and then take a bit of target practice against that yanqui amphibian. With his tip tanks he could cruise for several hours; might even refuel in Guatemala, or try for Cayo Mestizo in the gulf. The Cubans, he knew, would be glad to host any thorn in the side of Americans.

Wearing his old helmet and, incongruously, the casual suede outfit of a boulevardier on a morning walk, Torres performed the traditional postmaintenance test maneuvers while rocketing across Guatemala. He reset a trim tab slightly; tapped a dial or two; then settled back with a chart over one knee.

The landmarks of southern Chiapas began to unfold below him like a familiar painting, but Torres, lacking military radar, kept an eye aloft for Mexican contrails. Seeing none, he dropped down within a few hundred feet of the terrain before breaking radio silence; if he kept below the ridges around that lake until the last moment, the yanquis might not hear or see him until he triggered the twin Brownings.

Machado's big lieutenant answered on his second pass: "Go ahead, Condor, this is Bushmaster Two."

"I can't see you, Bushmaster. Have you sighted the quarry?"

"No, Condor. We passed through a group of huts half

an hour ago. We are now climbing higher, two kilometers south of it.''

"Let me see the sun on your machetes," Torres demanded, banking for another pass, now seeing a tiny settlement below. His T-33 needed miles for a complete circle at that speed, and Torres used up perhaps two minutes before he sizzled over the huts, scanning the heights above them. Then he saw glints of sunlight on metal, and used the comm set again. "Bushmaster, your quarry should be immediately over the ridge you are climbing. I intend to soften them up for you."

"Then you know they are still there?"

"I will know in a few moments, Bushmaster, and they will know they are under fire. Condor signing off." Torres kept the comm unit in its canvas pocket against the right wall of his cockpit and watched his tachometer needle rise, climbing behind the ridge for his turn. He wondered if that big Peruvian radioman was holding his comm unit against his chest, because Torres had heard, beneath the transmissions of Bushmaster Two, what might have been a magnified heartbeat if any heart could beat so slowly.

That yanqui aircraft had been floating at the northwest side of the slender lake, and he was approaching the high southern ridge. He throttled back, not forgetting that yanqui team supposedly en route, hoping to spot them if they were within strafing distance. By now he had lost enough speed to virtually float over the ridge, flaps partly extended, and as the lake came into view he had a moment of confusion: The amphibian was gone!

Then, in a half-roll that revealed everything below him, he saw that the yanqui aircraft had moved near the treeline on the opposite side of the lake. He also saw a dozen figures standing near it, some of them diving for cover as he thundered over. Evidently the aircraft was flyable, and by lining up incorrectly for his initial strafing pass, he had lost the element of surprise. Simon Torres cursed, rolled back level, and began a steep bank for another pass.

SIXTY-FOUR

Sunday, June 4

Machado heeded the call of his big lieutenant immediately, moving back past his men until he could hear both sides of the brief conversation with El Condor. As always, he let Teniente Gonzalo do the talking to that Colombian elitist. When Machado gave the order, his men brandished their machetes as bright reflective signals.

Then, when the silver jet had roared past, Machado glared back downhill toward the collection of huts and the rhythmic, almost subterranean basso now beating down there, filling the valley like the heartbeat of earth itself. "I do not like that," he said, as the others continued to climb.

"You should not have hit the old man," said Teniente. "He knew nothing of use."

The two were now out of earshot of the others and began to climb slowly, maintaining their distance. "Yes he did, my dear," said Machado. "I am the one who speaks his damned Maya, but they did not know that. Two of the younger ones were talking openly about a red man from the north. The old man knew, all right. Aagh," he said, and spat. "Primitives!"

Now Teniente placed a big hand on the shoulder of Cesar Machado. "Look at me, Cesar."

Now what, thought Machado, but he did it.

Teniente sighed. "You are tiring more quickly today. I can see it by your eyes. Should I carry your Kalashnikov?"

"And how would that look? See to yourself. You are already shaming the others with that load you carry." *A lover can be an infernal nuisance at times,* he noted silently. Nonetheless, his vision was becoming fuzzy by midday every day. He began to push himself faster, as if to outdistance the beat of that monstrous device behind them.

To make it worse, Teniente kept pace without evident effort, speaking in that same husky tenor as if they were both lolling about in hammocks. "Cesar, have I ever asked you to slow your pace before?"

"A very good thing that you have not," he puffed.

But Teniente would not relent. "Beat me if you like, but I must say it: If you love me, do not lead this attack."

"Shut your mouth, Huanca. The others may hear." Teniente's given Quechuan name, rarely employed, bore special power. *Another one of those ignorant Indio premonitions,* Machado told himself. "Am I to be faced with primitives in my own squad? If it is that damned drum that worries you, tell me. I will shoot them all when we return."

"Not the drum." Silence for a dozen footsteps. "Let me lead this time, Cesar. I can make my way to the head of the column in—"

"I will certainly beat you if this continues. Now," his voice rising, "shut up and soldier!"

At that moment, the Colombian's silvery jet winked into existence overhead as it cleared the near ridge, completing a half-roll as it began to climb, its passage falling on the ear like the ripping of some great canvas. It became a distant speck before it glinted, looping over and down, and again Teniente's radio set spoke in a Colombian accent. "Bushmaster, I have a dozen targets or more. If you hurry I may leave you a few."

Ten paces above, one of the men gave a low exclamation. Cesar Machado saw the phenomenon too: Tiny dots of yellow-white light emitted from the nose of the jet in a stream so rapid that, at a given instant, several of the tiny fireballs could be seen streaking toward the ridgeline. Machado had seen them before, pouring down toward him from Peruvian government aircraft. "Incendiary bullets," he called to the others, and struggled to recapture his place at the head of the column. It would be exactly like the Colombian pilot to scatter their quarry so badly in his thirst for glory that Machado would have no remaining targets.

SIXTY-FIVE

Sunday, June 4

"HELP YOU *WHAT*? Lady, we've got a few hours at most," snapped Contreras, who seemed to be the leader of the team that had trotted out of the bosque minutes before. He pointed toward the Nemesis and the pine poles that Wes and Colleen had been stripping. "We've gotta cut that thing up and get the fuck out of here!"

I was afraid of this, Wes said to himself.

"Language, Mike," said the rangy, raffish civilian in the snap-brim hat who called himself Harry Rex Brown. "Think of the lady."

"The lady," Colleen told him, holding a pine branch in one hand and her bush knife in the other, "will cold-cock the first sonofabitch who touches my goddamn bird." The civilian's eyes widened as though Colleen had slapped him. He turned away, muttering.

Wes Hardin put up one hand for silence. "Hold it."

Contreras's men had been pillaging their packs, hauling out collapsible Swedish bucksaws and taking stubby rectangular devices from their pack rails. Now they paused, look-

ing around, glancing at Contreras, and one of them split his
stubby rectangle apart. Wes saw the thing become a folding
Ares submachine gun as if by magic, thirty-two round clip
and all. The man cocked his head at the heavy resonance
that now seemed to be coming from the very forest itself and
said, "Jesus H. Christ, what's that; field artillery?"

"I don't think we have hours anymore," Wes said.
"That's a drum in a Maya village below the north ridge,
and in daylight that has to mean they've got trouble."

"A drum," the man repeated. "What do they beat it
with: telephone poles?"

"Listen, ma'am," Mike Contreras said quickly, "I really
don't have time to argue, and I'm bigger than you are."

Wes, his eyes boring into those of Contreras, stepped
squarely in his path. "But you're just about my big, peb-
bejon." Contreras towered over him, but whatthehell.
"Let's see if anything's coming up that ridge, and maybe
we can buy time to get this aircraft out in one piece. It's
flyable, I'm telling you."

"And I'm telling you, I know fuckin' well what's coming: a team of senderista guerrillas," Contreras burst out.
"We've got our orders to slice and dice this wacky contraption. Happens it's a Company asset."

"Belongs to a firm called Agrimap," Wes said.

"Right; what do you want from me, a signed affidavit
from its president?"

"I *am* its president, Contreras."

Contreras threw his hands up. "I don't effin' believe
this! Buncha murdering guerrillas on their way in here and
I'm—no, I'm not," he said, recovering his poise with lu-
natic swiftness. "I'm gonna do what I came to do. And if
we have to kneecap you, mister, we will. We expected to
carry you out of here anyway, you can't—"

Wes would never know what Contreras intended to say
next. Someone shouted a warning, and almost simultaneously the air was filled with the sound of whistling thunder
as an aircraft flew across the lake. Diving toward Colleen,

Wes got one good glimpse of the thing that hurtled from sight. "It's a T-33," he shouted.

"Yeah, the guerrillas have one," Contreras called, readying his own Ares weapon. "Now how am I going to disappear that goddamn' airplane of yours?"

"I'll tell you how: You towline it up like a kite," Colleen exclaimed. "We've lightened it a lot and if all of you can pull it at a running pace downhill, I can take off." Expressing her hope as a fact, she began to run toward the Nemesis as if the issue had already been decided.

"Good God, she's right! Grab her," Wes called. One of the men snagged Colleen, who threw him flat. Another tackled her and found himself with a double armload of spitting, cursing lynx. Turning to Contreras: "It might work, but that's a military jet up there, and I'm combat-trained. You'll never have time to demolish this plane now, but you can tow it up in two minutes and I'll be outa here. Solves your problem. How about it, Contreras?"

"Wes, you bastard," Colleen sobbed.

He shook his head in her direction. "It's one thing to let you try to kill yourself, honey. But I'm not going to let somebody else do it to you."

"I don't know what you two want," Contreras said, his eyes searching wildly. "This is crazy, man!"

"She'll show you, she's an engineer. The plane's light as goosedown. First I need your guys to lift the nose up so I can lower the nose gear," Wes said, and called out, "I saw a climbing rope on somebody's pack."

"Take cover," one of the men screamed, pointing toward the sky.

Wes looked up and saw the old Lockheed jet, only a glitter but growing fast, and then realized those blinks from its nose meant gunfire. He covered the ten yards to Colleen in a few bounds and let his good right shoulder bowl her and her captor over, kneeling above her.

Multiple impacts, oddly muffled in the soft earth, walked across the greensward fifty feet from them. They did not hear the hammering of the guns until an instant later, and by the time the jet pulled up Wes was already on his feet. "Colleen, hand me that walkie-talkie and take the other one. They'll never let you go but they might let me," he said, helping her up. Into her silently accusing glare he added, "It's your idea, goddammit, now stay and make it work!" She handed him her little radio unit without a word. He kissed her on the forehead and ran to the Nemesis.

In one corner of his mind, Wes was figuring the time it took for a strafing T-33 to return; two or three minutes, perhaps, with a pilot who seemed more passionate than calculating. Now Contreras approached on the run with a bound hank of climbing rope. *Stretchy nylon, not a bad choice for a towrope,* he decided. Favoring his left shoulder, he climbed into the cockpit and tossed Colleen's little two-way radio into the copilot's seat. "Everybody stand clear of the engine," he called, "while I get it warmed. In fact, everybody lift on the nose! It's got to come up a few feet."

Now Colleen seemed to have accepted the change of plan, and as Wes started the cold engine she urged all of the rescue team to assemble around the nose of her bird while she grabbed that hank of nylon, its loops half her height. The Nemesis came up as if on springs, in the cradling arms of men who must have expected more weight. "Clear nose gear," Wes shouted.

"Clear," Colleen shouted back. Instantly the little nose wheel, no larger than a volleyball and much more slender, popped out and the down-and-locked indicator glowed. When the men released their burden the craft sat nose elevated, the wheel pressing into soft turf.

"Ground's too soft for a rolling tow on all wheels," Colleen called, and hurled most of the rope under the fuselage while holding one end, running backward now. "Stretch it all out, half of you on each side," she shouted to the men who now stood indecisive.

"Do it," Contreras snapped, and ran toward her.

Wes scanned his gauges, knowing the engine was not fully warmed, knowing also that he could not wait. Colleen's helmet lay in the seat beside him with the little radio, and though the helmet was virtually a crush fit, he managed to force his head into it, preferring a cauliflower ear to a skull fracture in the event of a crash. He adjusted her harness to fit him as she called orders, the men running forward now until the rope formed a deep V with its apex beneath him. The whole idea was absurdly simple: If they could run fast enough to get him airborne, the engine would let him surge forward so that the rope would go slack, to slide backward from the nose strut. But a simple thing is not always an easy thing. The Nemesis was facing water, and they must first pull hard enough to skid the fuselage through an arc of rotation.

Canopy down and locked, Wes shoved his throttle to its detent and, with his other hand, pointed forward. Colleen saw him. Whatever she shouted, it must have been the right thing; he saw the rope go taut and felt an almost rubbery surge on his backside.

The Nemesis turned gently, rocking, then began to slide forward. Clods of earth spewed from the feet of straining men, now moving at a fast walk, now still faster, most of them not even looking back, and when one of them did he stumbled, releasing the rope as he half-fell and scrambled up again. They had only another hundred yards of firm ground ahead of them and Wes kept the presence of mind to hold the controls neutral, and he realized that the T-33 was making another strafing run only because he saw and heard the single impact of a fifty-caliber round through his left wing and saw a series of tiny turf eruptions march harmlessly down the clearing, the jet flashing by a moment later to miss the ridgeline by scant yards.

Not a man faltered, nor Colleen either, now struggling into a fast trot, at a pace that had the wingtips bowing upward. The resilience of that climbing rope absorbed the shock when his nose wheel encountered some small obstruction, and now they were running hard, and then he saw Colleen splash into the shallows and knew that they had done all that could be done, but it was not going to be enough if he did not flex those canards and the wings—*now*.

The instant his horizon dropped he felt, almost as if the Nemesis were his own body, the faint added surge of acceleration that came from absence of friction against the grass. He saw Colleen turn, shouting something; saw the men fling that rope away, watched two men dive facedown as his wingtips flickered above them.

And then he was aloft.

One little bobble or downdraft now, with his nose wheel protruding inches above the shallows, and he was a dead man. He flicked the toggle to cycle that nose wheel, watching the airspeed indicator because he had to gain enough altitude in the next 300 yards to bank around over the lake or slam into the mountainside, but when he spotted his shadow on the water he knew instantly why his nose gear "up and locked" indicator was not working: he was still trailing that tow rope.

"Goddamn shimmy damper," he raged, envisioning the little mechanism on the wheel strut that, oh yes, would surely snag a rope if he wasn't lucky. And he had already abused his luck. With thirty-five knots indicated, he kept his gaze riveted on his left wingtip as it knifed toward the water, the great wings straining in a gentle bank, the tow rope almost certainly flicking across the lake's surface trying to drag him down. He made the turn so broad that it ended with his high wingtip skimming trees, then straightened and bought himself another fifty feet of altitude at the expense of speed. *Just keep doin' it and doin' it 'til you get it right*, he repeated the old schoolmarm joke, and as he passed over those shallows again he could see Colleen blowing kisses.

"Hot damn," he exulted, and cycled the nose gear again. On the third try, as he was banking 200 feet over the lake, he saw the indicator flash and knew that either the rope had slipped away or the nose gear door had finally cut it in two. And when he put the nose of the Nemesis up and climbed over that lower northern ridge, he saw tiny blazing fireballs flash past his canopy.

At fifty knots, Wes knew that he might almost be motionless compared to the flight speed of a T-33. With one exception: Given a little altitude, he could dart in any direction like a rabbit evading a faster but less maneuverable greyhound. He dropped the Nemesis into a sideslip that put him beyond the ridgeline and saw the jet overtake him to hurtle away in a fierce climb. "You just keep on using ammo, Jasper," he said aloud, realizing what he had known subliminally for some time: If the jet used up all of its ammunition fruitlessly chasing him, there would be none left to strafe Colleen Morrison. But *fruitless* was the operative word. He might sustain a few holes through wing panels without much damage, but a single round of API, armor-piercing incendiary, in a vital spot and all their efforts would have gone for nothing.

It was clear that the Lockheed's pilot considered the Nemesis his primary target. Therefore, Wes decided, he must stay away from Colleen's immediate vicinity. He set the wing skin controls for maximum speed and sliced down that slope toward the village, and two hundred yards below the ridge he saw the startled, uplifted gaze of a man, no, several men, climbing that slope with slung weapons.

He was out of their range in seconds, his airspeed momentarily up to 100 knots now, but in minutes those guerrillas would be looking down on the lake. And the Nemesis carried no weapon of any kind. *Yes, by God, of one kind,* he thought, and began to climb around the nearby slopes well away from the senderistas. He grabbed the little walkie-talkie. "Colleen, it's Wes; do you read? Colleen!"

Nothing. He recalled now that he carried her radio; he had left his unit at the treeline after felling a pine an hour before. *No telling whether she'll remember where I put it.* Without any assurance that he could communicate, he swept above the ridge and back along the lake shore, keeping watch for that T-33, shaking the walkie-talkie above his head in hopes that someone would understand. To his astonishment, he saw not a soul in the open. He crammed the little radio into the big right-hand breast pocket of his flight suit to prevent its becoming a loose object caroming through the cockpit. Then, from the tiny speaker: "Wes, tell me you made it. Wes, please come in; ohh, Wes," she said in what might have been dismay or relief. "I see you, sweetheart. Now get the hell out."

"Column of hostiles about five minutes from the north ridge," he replied. "I've got enough fuel on board to dump some, and it's going right—here," he finished, toggling the fuel release as the Nemesis swung its nose along the ridge near the trailhead. Fully fueled, a Nemesis carried enough high-octane avgas to run that rotary engine for sixteen hours. His instrument readout claimed he had enough for ten. And when the fuel jettison pump began to whine, he could see the gauge visibly counting down as fuel gushed from below the fuselage.

"Colleen, I'll make a second pass here. Tell those guys with you: If they can manage a ricochet here at the trailhead, this place is going to be wall-to-wall flame." Swinging around, virtually hanging on a wingtip fifty yards above the treetops, he made his second pass and dropped even lower, the rush of avgas blanketing the treeline and swamp grass indiscriminately. He had two hours of fuel left as he began to climb again, keeping his gaze on the trailhead.

"Wes! He's coming over the lake," the speaker called, and when Wes looked he could see the bastard approach, flaps down, now smarter and slower and more dangerous than before, not wasting ammo either. Wes made the only maneuver that might save him, wingskin flexing, canards as well, and the Nemesis put her nose up and traded every bit of excess speed for 200 feet more altitude.

He leveled off almost in the path of the onrushing jet, then saw it flash by without firing only to begin a tightly controlled turn. "Thanks for the warning," he said to Colleen, continuing on to circle the lake again, now with a definite purpose in mind.

"Contreras has his monocular on the ridge, one man in view now," Colleen said, her voice breathless and soft. "We have a casualty from getting out of your way, he's not too happy with you."

"Pedalin' as fast as I can, let me know when Contreras sees more of those guys," he said, keeping the T-33 in view as it continued to bank a mile away. He came down a wingspan above the water's edge at sixty knots, making the Nemesis wallow as if damaged, trying to time his circle precisely so that he would present a tempting target on his own terms.

"Contreras has more sightings," Colleen reported. After a brief silence she added, "Several. They're aiming at you, Wes! For God's sake—"

He bled off velocity in a near-stall, regained some of it with the engine, slipping gently sidelong nearer the water as he saw the Lockheed swoop low, lining up on him. *He'll expect me to jink up again,* Wes thought as he passed 400 yards from men who were now emptying their weapons in his direction. Both of the guerrilla slugs that pierced the fuselage seemed to have no effect that he could tell, and now he saw the tiny blazes from the nose of the T-33, and instead of jinking up he forced the Nemesis down to within inches of the water.

He never saw the incendiaries flicker overhead, but when they hammered into the treeline near those guerrillas everyone on that lake saw the result. The huge fireball began near one edge of the area he had saturated with avgas, proceeding like a napalm burst until it covered a swath 200 feet in length. Wes could hear Colleen's report but had no concentration left for a reply as he firewalled his engine, wafting across the lake to build up speed again as the jet roared so near overhead that he felt his wings buffeting. When he soared up beyond the far ridgeline, the jet was not in sight. He started a broad climbing circle then, orbiting the lake while he gained altitude. At the trailhead, dry grass burned furiously and flames licked among pines near the waterline.

"My God, I could see men on fire, running into the lake," she said presently. That Contreras guy," said Colleen presently, "told me to stay here while they mop up anybody left. From what he said, they may be only a burial detail."

"They left you alone?"

"This Harry Brown guy and his guide are with me. He tells me, and I quote, he carries his Enfield for my protection. What do you carry for yours?"

"Don't ask," Wes chuckled. "Tell me if you spot the guy in the jet, you know damn' well he's around here somewhere." Then he remembered the rounds he had taken from two different kinds of weapon. "Oh, and I might be carrying a Browning fifty and a couple of smaller calibers," he said, making light of it. "No problem."

"You look wonderful up there," she said, breathing harder. "God, how my bird does climb."

"I'm getting some good air," he admitted. "I'll keep the channel open. Keep me posted, okay?"

"I hate you, Hardin, for taking my bird. But I love you too, and don't ask me why. I'll sing out if I see that asshole in the jet. Standing by," she said, and then he concentrated on an optimum climb, orbiting around that little lake as his altimeter needle revolved. A few trees continued to burn below, but now the area was marked chiefly by smoke. Evidently the bosque with its creepers and moss did not burn in the manner of a dry lowland forest.

Wes belatedly warmed up the Nemesis radar, and learned that his pursuer had no intention of breaking off the chase. When the Lockheed jet closed in again, Wes was forewarned; it approached from below and behind, exactly where a crafty pilot would position himself for overtaking a much slower aircraft. Now at over twenty thousand feet, the Nemesis barreled along at over two hundred knots, wingskins thinner, a faint whistling from tiny punctures in the fuselage as the cabin pressurization turbine compensated. Wes waited until the trailing aircraft surged upward and forward toward him, roughly a thousand yards behind, lining up for a classic sucker shot in a climbing pass.

Wes knew that when his radar display showed a sudden rise in VC, velocity of closure, the attack was beginning. Having flown the naval version of a T-33, he also knew that an experienced pilot would not begin to fire until he was within 1500 feet. When the T-33 closed near that distance Wes abruptly pulled up in an inside loop, the Lockheed arrowing past helplessly, unable to maneuver with a Nemesis at such a slow pace.

"That might work on a first-timer," Wes said aloud. "Hey Colleen, he tried to jump me again. Keep your eyes peeled for me, okay?" Static, but no reply. "Colleen? You reading me, over?"

"Five and five," said a masculine voice from the little speaker. "So there truly is a woman down there."

"Well, I'm damned. Ahoy the T-Bird, is that you?"

"It seems our portable radios are compatible," said the voice.

Latino, and sure as hell that's the guy who thinks he owns this region, all right, Wes decided, craning his neck in an attempt to locate his opponent, though his radar gave him an approximate fix. "You were supposed to be in Vegas, pal. Looks like you should've stayed there."

Now the voice faded, bits of the words unclear. "We will see who should have stayed away."

Why am I sticking around here when I'm out of radio range from Colleen? I should hightail it for the gulf and let that bozo burn the rest of his fuel. With that, Wes took a moment to open the protected channel on his Nemesis comm set, contacting the base at NAS Kingsville. They wanted more particulars, and he gave them. Their problem was that no one could help him until he reached international waters. Wes could see on his scope that the T-33 was climbing higher for a commanding height advantage so he, too, sought his best climb rate while arrowing away to the north.

The performance envelope of a Nemesis gave him much higher speed as he climbed into thinner air. At very high altitudes a Nemesis would not cruise at less than 200 knots, and he was beginning to enter that flight regime now. He considered the performance envelope of a T-33: what he recalled that it could do, and what it must not do. And then he grinned, watching his scope. The pilot of the T-33 was approaching from the side now. "If you bag me on a ninety-degree deflection shot, pal,'' he said, ''You're one helluva marksman.'' And he turned toward his opponent, presenting a flatter silhouette.

The jet broke off his approach, circling again and still higher than the Nemesis. Wes saw speed-brake panels flick open momentarily beneath the Lockheed's wing. ''I think you're out of ammo, buddy. That makes us even.''

''You would like me to think you do not have a Browning and two smaller guns,'' was the reply, near and clear.

Browning? Jesus, he heard me talking to Colleen and thinks I could bag him. Well, maybe I can. ''It was worth a try. You screw up once with me on your tail and I'll be on you like an overcoat, and you'll be a grape ripe for plucking.'' By now Wes had 40,000 feet under him, streaking toward the gulf.

''It occurs to me that you would be making slower maneuvers if you could,'' said the Latino pilot. ''You have lost that advantage. You have a very light aircraft there, yanqui.''

''Guilty as charged, wetback,'' Wes replied, noting on his scope that the Lockheed had climbed very near its ceiling now. And there, he knew, lay what pilots call the coffin corner of its performance envelope. At its ceiling, the T-33 must maintain high speed or it will stall, and at some point that speed grew so high that its wings began to flutter. *How fast? Mach point-eight or so, and he's nearly there now. I might just outrun the bastard. I don't think I will.* He continued his own climb, now almost to the level of his enemy.

''You know where we are,'' Wes taunted. ''Nearly over open ocean. Come and get me, hotshot.''

The T-33 now lay perhaps a mile behind him, and as they continued to climb toward 50,000 feet Wes throttled back slightly. ''My intention exactly,'' the Latino said. ''I have a very sturdy machine here.''

The sonofabitch is going to clip my tail booms with his wing, Wes thought. *If he can. And I'm at mach point eight, and he's closing a little. He's in his coffin corner.* ''Gotcha. You're a grape,'' Wes announced.

"I? Check your six, yanqui." It was an old phrase, announcing danger from behind. "What you can do, I can do."

But Wes thought that voice sounded a bit shaky, the kind of resonance a man develops when wing flutter vibrates his entire aircraft. "I know where you are, asshole. Allow me to introduce you to Comrade Pougachev."

A Soviet pilot had first managed the maneuver called Pougachev's Cobra, so named because the aircraft stands on its tail while still flying forward. The pilot first forces his interceptor into what would be a stall for most aircraft. Given enough power or a suitably advanced aircraft, however, the aircraft will balance for a moment on its tail, bleeding off speed at a tremendous rate before dropping its nose to the horizontal again.

Ideally, the aircraft makes little or no change in altitude in the process. The Nemesis did its best, but failed to manage the full cobra maneuver and gained hundreds of feet in altitude before mushing back to the horizontal. The T-33 pilot flicked his speed brakes as he found himself closing, unable to maneuver quickly in the thin air, and then must have realized his mistake.

Wes saw the jet flicker past below him as the Nemesis recovered. Those speed brakes had been a serious error, instantly robbing so much speed from the jet that it decelerated below stall speed. And near its flight ceiling, a stalled T-33 plummets into a rocketing dive that can rip its wings apart.

"Spasibo, Comrade Pougachev," Wes muttered.

"For that I will ram you," his opponent snarled, still with a trick left in his bag. He kicked his rudder to drop the jet's right wing and entered a spin. The only advantage to a spin was that it would slow his descent rate until the pilot might recover control. The chief danger was that some aircraft tend to regress into a flat spin from which there is seldom any recovery. The Lockheed T-33 had always been one of those.

"You'll punch out is what you'll do," Wes replied. "You never spin a T-Bird more than one or two rotations, remember?'' He reset the Nemesis wingskins to their thinnest, following the Lockheed down in a tight spiral. Its nose began to come up, but the spin continued. Wes realized that the G forces inside that Lockheed would be flinging the pilot sideways, harder and harder. "Okay, punch out,'' he said aloud.

The Lockheed's canopy flew off as the pilot deliberately jettisoned it. "No ejection cartridge—for years,'' the pilot managed to say.

Wes, watching his own G meter, began to slow his descent, unwilling to keep pace with the plummeting jet. Suddenly he found himself overtaken with the empathy of one pilot for another. *Poor bastard knew he couldn't eject, and he figured I could gun him down.* "Bail out, goddammit,'' he shouted. "You'll augur in!''

"Mayday, mayday,'' he heard, the words ripped from the throat of a man in near-panic, pulling savage G loads.

"Can't help you,'' Wes replied, leveling off. In that moment, for Wes Hardin, the man was no longer an enemy but a fellow pilot in a fatal spin, and he would know it all the way down to impact. Wes had seen the aftermath of air crashes; you sometimes filled the body bag by shaking the surrounding trees. "Fight for it, damn you! Get out of there!''

The pilot was shouting guttural Spanish now, something about the unfairness of it all, in the utter despair of a man who saw death rising up to meet him. When he began to weep, Wes fumbled into his breast pocket and shut the radio off, wiping his eyes as he watched his scope. The T-33 blip and the numbers displayed near it continued to plummet, now below five thousand feet, now below two, into jungle lowlands near the coast. Because Wes was banking as he studied the jungle, he saw the fiery impact as a blossom of orange, miles below.

SIXTY-SIX

Sunday, June 4

HARRY REX BROWN heard the pops and stutters of distant gunfire, and feared the worst for twenty minutes. He found, somewhat to his surprise, that with a pretty girl in his care he was actually ready to empty his revolver against those guerrillas when he heard men approaching. It turned out to be Contreras and the medic, carrying a man terribly burned from his abdomen downward. The medic went to his pack immediately for medical supplies.

The girl knelt next to the casualty. "Not one of ours?"

"Didn't lose a man," Contreras said with satisfaction. "We found six who were still moving, and five still had some fight left in 'em. Couldn't have that, could we?"

Harry studied the casualty, whose eyes were closed, his breathing fast and shallow. To avoid gagging, Harry turned his gaze to Contreras and said, "What happens to this poor devil?"

"He might be useful to the Mexicans, for interrogation. If we meet up with federales on our way out, this guy might prove our good intentions. We expected to bring a casualty out anyhow.''

"Don't count on this one making it," the medic muttered as he knelt beside the girl with his kit. "He's taken a lot of hot stuff into his lungs."

"What are the other guys doing," Harry asked.

"You don't want to know, Harry. Call it a cleanup detail, we mustn't leave any more evidence of this than we have to."

"Poor man," said the girl, standing up with a grimace. "The fire didn't seem to reach his upper body much."

"Funny thing, we found this one partly hidden under a big strapping six-footer who was carrying their radio, and this is one for the books: The big guy was a woman." Contreras shook his head and sighed. "All her clothes burned off and all; no doubt about it."

Harry flashed on the remote possibility that some local herb remedy might be of help. He turned to Yaxpoc, who stood apart in silence, and asked in Maya: "What do your people do when a man has been burned like this?"

"Bury him," Yaxpoc replied.

During this exchange, the burned man's eyelids fluttered open, and Harry saw with an almost physical shock that the man's eyes were crossed. His words, breathless and halting, were a stronger shock: They were Maya, directed toward Yaxpoc. "Bury me with Huanca," he said. "She did her best for me."

Harry went down on his haunches beside the man. "The woman with you?"

"She knew. Primitives always know," the man replied cryptically.

"What were you to her?"

"Tell him he shouldn't be talking," the medic snapped in English.

"Her maximum leader," said the man, and coughed.

But the phrase he had used, *nohoch halach uinic*, flooded through Harry like a sexual spasm. The man spoke such perfect Maya that he must be one of them, Harry decided; his eyes crossed in the fashion of ancient legendary perfection in these parts; and he claimed to be a great ruler. Even Yaxpoc seemed a bit in awe of that man now. Harry knew in that moment that the man would die soon. He had to, because God had given him to Harry Rex Brown.

Colleen Morrison watched the medic work for a time before she said, "I have to keep reminding myself that he intended to kill us all. Is he in a lot of pain?"

"A bit less now," the medic replied. "Less still pretty soon. He wouldn't make it even in a burn ward. But you never know," he added.

Harry knew. The burned man breathed his last as other team members returned by twos and threes, and Harry waited until Mike Contreras announced that they had another burial to attend to. "The most important thing now," Harry said, "is to get this young lady out of here. Mike, I'm appointing you my deputy to do that."

"That's, ah—that's decent of you, Harry," Contreras said.

"Well, you deserve it," Harry shrugged, "even though you brought weapons in here against my orders. Now then: Our trail is fresh and well cleared. I want you and my men to escort Miss Morrison out. Yaxpoc and I will take this fellow off into the bosque and give him a proper burial."

For a long moment, Contreras seemed to be fighting for control of his expression, the other men busying themselves at their packs, and then Contreras stuck out his hand. "Harry, it's a pleasure to take orders from a man like you. I'm sure Miss Morrison will appreciate your sending all your men with me. You'll catch up with us later, of course."

"Of course," Harry said. *In a month or two,* he added silently.

As the team filed off toward the other side of the lake to remove all traces of her little encampment, Colleen Morrison faced Harry with a smile. "You would have faced a guerrilla team for me, with just a revolver," she said.

"Uhh," said Harry, and knew he was blushing.

Now she was gazing up into his eyes, the smile almost too broad, but her kiss on his cheek seemed wonderfully genuine. "In some important ways, Harry, you are a genuine hero. Anybody ever doubts it, refer them to Colleen Morrison. Okay?"

He took the hand she offered; swept his hat off; kissed the hand. Then she took her place in line and walked off into Harry's memories.

Using a litter of pine boughs, Harry and Yaxpoc transported the body over the ridgeline and reached their goal before sundown. They needed two days to cut their way through branches down into that pyramid, and by that time the corpse was none too fragrant, but Harry did not mind. What he had in mind was not for immediate personal gain, but for vindication of scripture someday in the distant future when Harry himself had been forgotten.

Once they lugged the body down inside, Harry dismissed Yaxpoc. Harry had studied Maya pictographs for so long he could grind the colors and formulate paints himself, rendering the fats from small game to yield lamp oil and paint base without help.

Besides, if Yaxpoc did not see Harry drawing those pictures, God would be his only witness. And that is how it happened that the Great True Man of the Highland Maya came to rest in a pyramidal temple in Chiapas, awaiting discovery in the sweet by and by, surrounded by pictographs with prominent Stars of David.

EPILOGUE

Wednesday, June 14

"**D**AMN RIGHT IT'S unreal," Colleen admitted to the NSA's Bill Sheppard, straightening up from her inspection of a fuselage mold. "Two days ago I was walking into Guatemala, and yesterday Ben Ullmer hugged me. Today I'm facing the guy who called himself 'Control,' if I'm not mistaken. Talk about unreal," she said with an eyeroll. "So what brings you back to Aerosystems?"

Wes, who had escorted the NSA official through the Aerosystems plant, grinned. "An F-14—which Ben should be riding about now. That was the deal."

"I asked *him*," Colleen said, with a warning glance at Wes.

"Will you two relax? Let's take a walk outside," Sheppard replied quickly, and fell into step with her.

The June breeze tickling through her hair, Colleen perched on an access ladder than put her eyes on a level with Sheppard's. "If you people want another Nemesis mission, count me out," she said immediately.

"No need," Sheppard said, leaning against the ladder.

"But your debriefings posed a few additional questions, and I needed a day off. An FBI inspector named Payson had to go through channels to bring an F-14 near enough for Ullmer to take a hop in it, so I hitched a ride. Little by little, I got drawn so far into the whole business that I'm as good a person as any to ask you, I suppose. You mind if I'm taping this?"

Colleen and Wes exchanged glances, and she read him nicely. "Go ahead, Dr. Sheppard."

She answered each question with care and precision, correcting Wes when he needed it, putting him in his place when he tried to correct her. In answer to Sheppard's last question Wes said, "I can't say for certain, no; but I don't see how anyone could've climbed out of that T-Bird in a flat spin. And I saw it go in before I hightailed back to Kingsville."

"You had a piece of good luck there," Sheppard remarked with his shy smile.

He had a piece of damned fine flying, is what he had, Colleen thought, but she felt that Wes didn't need to hear that. "He had a good airplane," was what she said.

"No, I mean he had a friend he didn't know about," Sheppard went on. "Our operation began with a message in Veracruz passed from a man in the cartel camp. Turns out that this fellow Torres only had a pair of guns in that T-33."

"They were enough," Wes said laconically. "He seemed to be firing the usual stuff, every fifth round an API."

"To show the pilot where his shots are going," Sheppard nodded. "I know. But all those other rounds he couldn't see? They were duds."

Wes stared. "Say again?"

"Somebody didn't want him to nail you, evidently," Sheppard explained. "He left the incendiary rounds intact so that the pilot would suspect nothing, but he removed enough propellant from the other ammunition so that four-fifths of what was fired at you fell far short, even though his guns continued to fire. They tell me you took one round through your spookship. Well, you might've taken a lot more.''

"I wish you hadn't told me that," Wes said, subdued. "How'd you find out?"

"Our tipster passed it along to us last week in Tegucigalpa, Honduras, along with a rumor that Pablo Escobar has run home to Colombia to surrender. But for your ears only, I gather that whoever our tipster is, he's almost certainly the same man who armed Torres's guns. He has a code name. No matter. He's our asset, building up Brownie points with us, and one day he'll want sanctuary, and we'll probably take him. He might get a jockstrap medal, but it'll stay at Langley. With yours and Cutter's," he added. "Congratulations to both of you."

"Cutter deserves it; he's a nice kid," Colleen beamed. "Can I see mine now?"

"Ah—sorry, no. They're kept at Langley," said Sheppard.

"No shit! Why can't I wear it?" Colleen asked.

"It'd have to be on your skivvies," Sheppard warned.

"That's out; she doesn't wear any," Wes drawled.

"That's a lie and you know it! I mean—damn you, Hardin," she said hotly. *Tonight I'm going to bite his ear off for that.*

"I have no idea what you two are talking about," Sheppard said, and shut off his recorder. "By the way: This fellow Harry Rex Brown? He still hasn't turned up. If you ever hear from him again, let us know."

Colleen smiled in reminiscence. "If you want my opinion, Dr. Sheppard, I don't think he was CIA material."

"Oh yes," Sheppard sighed, "I think he is. He's a loose cannon rolling around in Chiapas. Just the sort they'd love to have on retainer. Well, I'll drop by Ullmer's office and wait for him," he said. "You can go back to building better aircraft."

"You mean Spook 5? Half complete," said Wes.

"He means Spook 6," Colleen insisted, and grinned.

WHEN LAURIE IRVINE presented her husband with tickets for a cruise to Acapulco in June, Cam did not complain. As he often admitted to friends, "Laurie can find bargains nobody else ever heard of."

After their return from that cruise in July, Irvine Glass Anchor began to make a little profit. Laurie, ever the canny manager of money, praised him. And had the Chevy overhauled, better than new.

In August she bought four new outfits for herself and seven pairs of heels, and two suits for Cam because all of his old ones had gone threadbare. "You won't believe the prices I got," she said, which was a tremendous understatement from a woman clad entirely in Gucci suede. Cam still made no complaint when the new furniture arrived, but the Karastan carpet may have been a bit much, and she definitely overstepped with the Martin Logan Monolith speakers.

"Take 'em back," Cam agonized. "My God, Laurie, do you know how much those things *cost*?"

Laurie set her jaw. "Do you?"

"Six, maybe seven grand! Christ, I'm not making that kind of money yet."

She might have suspected he would know the cost of such high-tech stuff, dammit. So she took the speakers back, and had to wait a month before Cam's business began to look really good, Cam hugging her more and shouting at her less, and before she got those Monolith speakers back she got the IBM computer to manage their money, claiming it was a floor model and practically a giveaway.

And because business only got better and better after that, Laurie never had to spend the rest of Simon Torres's seventy thousand dollars in cash, all in hundreds, which had fallen into her arms the day she stepped into the restroom of that old Bristol Britannia and opened its first aid kit.